WALK THE PATH

DAWN BLAIR

MORNING SKY STUDIOS

ALSO BY DAWN BLAIR:

Onesong

Tangled Magic

Sacred Knight

Quest for the Three Books

Manifest the Magic

To Birth a Destiny

History of a Dead Man (companion novella)

Prince of the Ruined Land

The Unicorn and the Secret (companion novella)

The Loki Adventures

1-800-Mischief

For Sale, Call Loki

For A Good Time, Call Loki

For More Information, Call Loki

For More Mischief, Call Loki

1-800-CallLoki (Omnibus of novellas 1-5)

1-800-IceBaby

Help Wanted, Call Loki

Children's Picture Books

Eggs at Play

CHAPTER 1

*R*ivic lay awake staring at the stone ceiling of the castle's basement dormitory. Magic slunk along the cold rock, oozing in and out of dark crevices. Outside, he'd seen the clouds gathering earlier in the evening and now felt the oppressive stifle of the electrical storm in the air. He couldn't hear any thunder, but he felt it. Tonight would be the night.

As if appearing by Rivic's inner knowing, two Necroathelings appeared in the basement sleeping quarters, the scent of magic carried on the air like smoke. Rivic heard several of the other Domini snoring and wondered how much of it was fake, in hopes that the Necroathelings would think the person too deep in sleep. Rivic felt that made them more of a target.

Of course, all those who had remained to train in Gohaldinest were always quarry for the Necroathelings looking for a little amusement.

Almost a month ago, the weather had warmed enough for those wishing to leave to depart the mountain city if they wished.

Rivic had nearly been one of them.

The Necroathelings made a show of walking down the aisles between the beds, the heavy cloth of their deep purple cloaks rustling, but Rivic suspected that they already had their selections in mind. A nearby Dominus shivered as a Necroatheling reached out and touched his foot. The boy disappeared.

"Fodder tonight, that one is. He won't make it," the Necroathelings snickered.

"Grab the Knight Captain and let's be going," the other said.

Kicking the coarse gray blanket off him, Rivic swung his legs from the bed and stood up. "I'm ready."

"'Tis not any fun when they don't fight." The Necroatheling pointed toward the stairs. "Guess we'll let you walk. Maybe your anxiety will increase with each step."

Rivic climbed the staircase before them but let the Necroathelings take the lead at the top. They began the trek through the winding hallways and staircases of Gohaldinest to The Playground. Keeping pace with them, watching the subtle shifts in their raised hoods as they glanced back to make sure he wasn't falling behind, did indeed increase the foreboding tension in his chest. He lifted his head a little higher, refusing to let them think that they were getting under his skin.

Ancient magicks ran over the gray stone walls as if it were salamanders skittering after him. He dared to reach out to touch one of the swiveling enchantments and wondered if the Necroathelings would be so bold to the same. After all, they didn't seem to sense the spells on the walls quite like he did.

They reached the doorway with the lion head. Sensing powerful magic coming down the stairs behind them, Rivic looked up expecting to see another Necroatheling. Rather,

Lord Cirvel stepped from the shadows, a dark figure cloaked in black robes.

The Necroathelings bowed to Cirvel, apparently not expecting him. Obviously, the Lord of Gohaldinest hadn't been back for very long. Rivic attempted to keep the emotions off his face, knowing it was better to not reveal that he had even known of Cirvel's recent travels out of the city. Tension raced up Rivic's back, but he still managed to salute the Lord of Gohaldinest.

Cirvel dropped his hand on Rivic's shoulder. "This one has other plans tonight."

"Very well, my lord," one of the Necroatheling said, then he finished the spell and both dark maeges disappeared through the portal doorway.

Cirvel smiled down at Rivic as he let his hand fall from Rivic's shoulder. He proceeded up the steps. "Come. There is something I wish to show you."

Rivic followed.

Cirvel didn't say a word as he led Rivic through a maze of the castle's hallways and doors, including some which had been concealed in the walls. Rivic wondered if he'd ever been led so deeply into Gohaldinest before.

They passed by staircases and rooms that left Rivic wondering why anyone would need this much space. There were additional libraries, dining halls, sitting rooms, and latrines everywhere. Grandiose columns of marble rose hide to the ceilings. Staircases branched off. Mirrors lined walls. Curtains hung. There were tapestries and statues, vases, pedestals with teacups, and long tables as if regular banquets were held there. Cirvel seemed right at home walking through all these places while Rivic followed in silence, waiting to discover what fate had in store for him tonight. He almost wished he'd been battling in The Playground. At least there, he knew he had a chance of survival. With Cirvel, he couldn't be so certain.

They went down a series of staircases and then entered a complex system of underground tunnels. Rivic stared at several smooth surfaces, which looked as if the rock had been melted together in places. Cirvel cast spells as they went, providing light within the inconceivably black depths ahead. The tunnel branched off in several directions and Rivic noticed even more shafts extending from those corridors. With so many passageways running beneath the castle, it seemed unbelievable that the buildings didn't collapse.

But in moments when Rivic forgot his tension and allowed himself to wonder at the structure around him, he understood why he felt the heavy compression of magic.

The longstanding spells bonding the land together were very old. The elder magicks flowing through the castle suddenly seemed to make sense. What history had this place seen? How had it come to be? Had someone been here before or had Cirvel begun all this? Was he as ageless as these passageways? All these questions left Rivic in awe.

Cirvel broke the silence. "Rivic, my gargaxes were dealt a hard blow toward the end of the last harvest season. Were they not?"

Rivic tried not to flinch, but he did swallow a hard lump in his throat. He had destroyed several of Cirvel's flying demons while living at Krithstand's tribe, where his twin sister, Nyree, now resided.

Before Rivic answered, Cirvel continued, "A certain young, naïve acolyte was a little overzealous last cycle."

"Aye, he was." Rivic gulped.

They came to a cave and Cirvel removed a torch from the wall to carry with him. "I cannot yield these incidents without some sort of penance."

"I understand, my lord."

Cirvel turned to look at Rivic, who bowed his head reverently. "I am glad to see that you are accepting of your place. Since you as a Dominus still have your soul, we shall make use of it. 'Tis time I show you how the gargaxes come to life."

Rivic stumbled deeper into the cave after Cirvel, his thoughts bearing more stress than his feet were capable of carrying. What the Necroathelings had wanted him to endure in walking to The Playground, he now experienced under the weight of Cirvel's words. What exactly had Cirvel meant? Did gargaxes use souls in order to gain their own lives?

Adding to the mounting tension building in Rivic's emotions, magical enchantments snarled around him. A few rose like snakes off the floor and hissed, opening their mouths wide to him, but they dared not approach. Some of the disturbed energies swayed as though they would attack, but all they did was threaten for the moment. He knew if they found any weakness in him, they would lay waste to him without hesitation.

These hazards focused Rivic in a way he wouldn't have discovered on his own. Paying close attention to them as they prepared to strike, he raised his own magical defenses and prepared to retaliate if necessary. He revealed no frailty, but he broached no confrontation either.

As the power moved through him, he realized that he was so much stronger than these enchantments sneaking around him. He need not be afraid of them, as they were but young servants of older invocations.

He noticed Cirvel's fingers occasionally flicking and wondered what other enchantments Cirvel dispelled.

There were so many questions Rivic wanted to ask, but he had no idea how to start any conversation that would lead to him getting answers. After several moments, he had one idea, but he didn't know how clever it was. "My lord, as your

Knight Captain, I must lodge a protest and I hope you will indulge me."

"Must be serious." Cirvel grinned back over his shoulder at Rivic. "You sound like me. You know what they say about imitation and flattery."

Actually, Rivic had no clue, but he pressed on. "I am but one person and the Knight Captain of your Domini, however, if we were swarmed by Necroathelings seeking to overthrow you, I fear we could be overwhelmed in here. Even with as powerful as you are."

"None of my other Necroathelings have been down here to see this, for obvious reasons."

"For obvious reasons, my lord?"

"Necroathelings have no souls. They would do me little good." Cirvel paused, turning slightly as he let Rivic catch up. "Besides, what would make you believe a Necroatheling, or even a group of them, would dare to attack me?"

"It doesn't have to be a Necroatheling. Could be anyone? Someone from a tribe who has been angered, perhaps. Or an upset acolyte. An assault could come from many possibilities."

"They would have had to spend quite a bit of time in the tunnels, and I am not one for bringing along company. Generally when I come here, I travel alone. Should I have to take a Shant'olin to the surface, I fully enlighten my victim as to what is about to happen to them and I leave them to wait for my return. Mind you, this alone is a very effective punishment."

"I can imagine, my lord." Rivic had to admit that not knowing but being forced to follow in the direction of an unknown fate was equally terrorizing. What was this beast Cirvel spoke of? Rivic tried not to hold his breath too much. "Might I ask, why I am getting the special treatment?"

"Because you are a Dominari."

Rivic shook his head. Maybe this was a special title for the Knight Captain. "I'm sorry, my lord. I don't understand."

"You are a Dominari. I am down several gargaxes. Your power will supply me sufficiently. If I do this two times per cycle, imagine what a force I can create." Cirvel shook his head, but let the grin broaden on his lips. "I have always wondered what it would be like to have a Dominari under my watch."

Traveling down another set of rock stairs, Rivic followed Cirvel until their progress ended in the doorway. Cirvel unlocked it with a spell and they entered a little room with a large plate glass window reinforced with shielding enchantments. Through the window, Rivic saw four pillars holding a large earthen jar plugged with a red cap. Beneath, an iron pipe ran from the ground into the bottom of the container.

Cirvel stepped up to the window and pointed toward the other room. "'Tis the birthplace of the Shant'olin. They come up directly from the planet's core through that pipe. 'Tis time to see the founding of three more Shant'olin. 'Twill be your soul that they feed on."

"What are these Shant'olin? I thought we were coming down here for gargaxes."

Rivic blenched under the chilly glare Cirvel gave him.

While Rivic fought to raise his ashamed gaze from the floor, Cirvel began to speak slowly. "I sometimes forget that I have lived with these creatures for what most would consider an eternity. I must remember that there was a time when I didn't know what they were. It still took nearly a life-time for me to understand them and their gift to the world."

Cirvel placed his hand upon the glass window and stared out toward the jar in the other room. "To answer your question in the simplest manner, the Shant'olin are precursors to the gargaxes. They are born from within the deep roots of magic at the core of this planet. They will grow, and one day they will transform into gargaxes."

Rivic tried to keep all the emotion rolling through him from playing across his face. He wasn't certain he really wanted to help bring more of the beasts into the world. "What do I need to do, my lord?"

"'Tis simple. Merely go into the room, lift the cap until three Shant'olin come out, then close the lid. After that, they will begin."

Begin what? Rivic couldn't voice the words.

Instead, he nodded. Yet he didn't see a way to get into the room from here as there was no other door. "Talcor dun," he muttered, teleporting himself to the other side of the glass. As he crossed to the jar, he glanced back over his shoulder.

Cirvel watched him from behind the window, dark eyes unyielding.

Three, Rivic reminded himself. How bad could that be? Yet he also remembered lashing out at those first gargaxes shortly after he'd arrived at the tribe. What if his magic acted uncontrollably, like it had then? What if he destroyed the Shant'olin before they were done? At least Cirvel would know that Rivic had completed the requested task.

He lifted the cap. Three wisps which looked like frayed gossamer fabric came quickly flying out. He slammed the cap down, but not before he saw several more inside rushed toward the jar's neck. Straining to escape, they pressed against the lid, bumping it, and nearly knocking it from his grip. He slapped his hands over the top to keep the cap on.

Then, pain tore through him like hot, stinging needles.

Rivic twisted, trying to see if Cirvel had plunged a scorching stiletto into his side. No one stood beside him, yet he saw the trailing end of one of the Shant'olin burrowing into him.

Another one struck, this one going through his back. He

tried not to scream. With the worst pain he'd ever imagined, he almost lost control of his bowels.

The third Shant'olin drilled into his leg. Rivic released the cap, hoping it would stay on. If it didn't, more Shant'olin would escape. He didn't know if he could even take the three that he faced right now.

Dragging the leg now splitting with pain around, Rivic pivoted as if he could make an escape. He saw the first Shant'olin beginning to emerge from his torso. Short-lived hope that it was over died as the wisp rounded on him again.

Rivic dropped to his knees as the Shant'olin pierced him. Time and time again, he felt every ounce of magic within him draining away. He tried to crawl. His lips whispered spells that failed. Would he be able to recover from this? Was it Cirvel's intent to draw all his magic out?

Raising his gaze toward the window, he saw Cirvel seated on a chair looking rather unamused. Yet while seeming concerned, Cirvel's avid curiosity wasn't hidden either.

Gaining speed in their aggressive feeding, the Shant'olin tore through him. Rivic arched his back. He screamed again, the sound gouging from his raw throat. He had to get away. Lying here kept him as their defenseless victim.

Rivic rolled onto his stomach, waving an arm in a feeble fashion at the Shant'olin swarming around him. An instinctive action, he knew in some part of his logical mind, but a poor resistance.

One of the ghostly creatures disappeared into the floor before him. Fearing it might come up beneath him, Rivic squirmed, thwarted by the efforts of the other two Shant'olin trying to keep him in place. He scooted backwards as far as he could, hampered by the pipe which connected to the bottom of the vase.

The Shant'olin rose up before him, black gaping holes

where its eyes and mouth should be. Dark eternity of death awaited within those voids.

How much more before he sank into those depths?

Once more he floundered, not quite ready to give up.

Heaving himself around and pushing to his knees, Rivic caught Cirvel's look of heightened confusion through the window as the lord eagerly leaned forward on his seat.

This was important. Rivic didn't know why and he couldn't fathom what made Cirvel so fascinated, but some inquisitiveness held the lord's observation of this event. Rivic's mind couldn't grasp the significance. Certainly, this was some sort of answer to a question he had yet to understand.

As he tried to rise, Rivic wished for some way to mark this spot, but how could he? Cirvel would notice any spell Rivic cast, assuming that he could summon a spell powerful enough with the Shant'olin draining his magic. He hadn't even had the power to teleport out from here. But there had to be something he could do.

An answer seemed to dance to him, yet like a thin ribbon swirling through the air, it remained elusive to his grasp. With a mental grab, he felt himself pin it.

The Shant'olin whirled around, then attacked from the side. Rivic collapsed, powerless to bear this torture any longer.

He rolled onto his back to stare at the ceiling and watched the ghostly wisps hungrily circling above him. One dove, certainly aiming for his heart, but at the last second it veered away and began to drift. He heard a thud and the sound of a pebble rolling across the floor. Rivic turned his head and saw a stone the size of his palm near him. The other Shant'olin floated down, also morphing into rocks.

Rivic panted, completely drained of magic and tired like he'd never felt before.

Sensing magic, Rivic lifted his head enough to see the hem of Cirvel's black robes coming toward him. Rivic knew he should get up off the floor, a proper respect, especially as Cirvel stared down his nose at Rivic, but he just couldn't find the strength.

Cirvel moved off to collect the stones and placed them in a bag beneath his robes. "You have done a fantastic job. You are now absolved of your previous crimes."

At Cirvel's urging, Rivic forced himself to get to his feet. He wobbled, nowhere near steady enough to walk.

"You should know that no one has ever been able to feed the Shant'olin with one feeding. It will be curious to see how these gargaxes turn out considering that they had such a strong life force to feast upon."

"Life force?"

"While gargaxes eat magic and tear holes into a person's magical aura in order to weaken them, Shant'olin take their power right from your soul."

"How did you discover these Shant'olin?"

"Well, that's a bit of a story. It was more like Azote acquired them for me."

Rivic stumbled against the wall and let it hold him up for a moment. "Acquired?"

"I went to Plenelia to negotiate a peace treaty. Things didn't go well. Doubly so for the Plenelians."

"Why would you need to negotiate a peace treaty with them?" Rivic knew they had no magic. A number of Necroathelings could decimate the country in short order. The Plenelians would never have a chance.

"This was a very long time ago when they sent gaxlors to attack Gohaldinest. I had to do something and, at the time, I thought a peace treaty might be the answer."

"But it wasn't?"

"Not after I found out what they had."

"The Shant'olin?"

With a hand on Rivic's shoulder, Cirvel teleported them to the other side of the wall. "Nay, 'twas a little bit more than that. They were up to some terrible things, things that should never be. So I forced renegotiations with their allies, and the Shant'olin became a tribute to me."

"What did you have to give them in return?"

"The life of their leader. Negotiation became very simple when I alleviated the problem." Cirvel gave a shrewd smile along with a slight cock to his eyebrows, as if his words explained everything and he'd say no more.

"You said the Shant'olin were a gift to the world." Rivic looked through the window toward the vase coming out of the pipe and wondered how the creatures inside could ever benefit anyone. "What did you mean by that?"

"Your loyalty to me has been proven and rectified. Let us leave it at that for tonight and return to Gohaldinest. The hour grows late, and you have training early tomorrow."

Rivic bowed his head. "I am happy to serve you, my lord." While Cirvel didn't wish to speak of the Shant'olin anymore, Rivic knew it would be a long time before he forgot the creatures and the pain they wrought.

CHAPTER 2

*R*ivic paced the narrow hallway. Each step felt like he trod his path a little deeper. Reaching out with his senses, he searched for a magical presence near him, trying specifically to find Alityka. All the acolytes remained in their classes. Any moment now they would be rising and flooding into the corridors.

He returned once more to the intersection, rounded the corner, walked a few paces, then stood waiting. He wanted it to seem as if nothing was out of the ordinary and he just happened to be approaching the classrooms when the acolytes spewed out.

Except that he really intended to see Alityka. Was she still angry at him? She hadn't sought him out since he'd decided to remain in Gohaldinest. He'd hoped that he wouldn't have to apologize, but it seemed high time to do that as she wasn't approaching him.

Why was it that he'd rather face the Shant'olin again rather than to confront her?

Archaic enchantments reached filaments toward him from the stone walls as if hoping to lick some of his magic away for their own purposes. His mood was of such to not entertain them today.

A door creaked and Rivic hesitated in his forward step.

The magic coils reaching off the stone toward him paused and shrunk back. It seemed as if they turned their heads to look for easier targets.

A moment later, the clamor of students leaving class filled the corridor. The flood of people pressed Rivic back against the wall, which he used as a brace to stretch up on his toes to look for Alityka.

Rivic watched the acolytes as they passed. So many faces he recognized, yet they now held a new fear in their eyes because of his station as a Dominus. He was no longer one of them.

He knew they whispered about him behind his back, said that he possessed a darkness in his soul that made him just as power-hungry as the Lord of Gohaldinest. As much as he wanted to deny them, there were several things that made him wonder if they were right.

First, he had his win down in The Playground. Then there had been the challenge where he'd skinned Kalt as he took the stone; he still hoped that was a dream, and not one of the weird dimensional shifts that Lord Cirvel could do so easily. He feared that the manipulation of his thoughts might have made that more than a hallucination.

Lastly, he had the murder of Melodin to contend with. Rarely did a night pass where he hadn't dreamed of the sword moving on its own and plunging into the boy. Even recalling it now still sent chills running down his spine.

He spotted Alityka walking by, touching a couple other acolytes on the shoulder. They nodded back to her. Then she streamed passed Rivic. If she noticed him there, she didn't give any acknowledgement.

Rivic moved into the current to follow, glimpses of her

golden red hair the only way he kept sight of her in the crowd.

She moved off into a room with the acolytes she'd summoned, and the door closed behind her.

Rivic's chest tightened around heavy breaths while he curled his fists at his side. Nothing good could come from her leading covert meetings like this. They might gain attention and invoke Lord Cirvel's wrath.

Another acolyte broke through the torrent of leaving students and she shoved passed Rivic as if he were a stone in a river. The girl entered the room and quietly shut the door behind her.

Rivic felt no magic bar the door. Were others expected too?

The current of people moving around Rivic slowed to a trickle. He moved back against the wall and decided to watch for a moment, nerves growing in his stomach, to see if more acolytes would show up.

The ancient magic clinging to the stone was glad to have him there. He kept having to brush it away.

His decision to use his status as Knight Captain to barge in and check on what she was doing deepened. Still, he weighed the action against the cost of evoking her anger over the intrusion.

When all had quieted, he used a count of three before he pushed away from the wall and headed into the room.

Whatever conversation they had been engaged in stopped the moment Alityka looked up and saw him. They turned, each one of the acolytes slowly facing him. He felt magic gathering in a couple of their hands.

"I would hope that you would not be so senseless," Rivic warned.

Alityka stepped forward. "You're not wanted here, Knight

Captain Rivic. You have made your alliances very evident. I suggest you leave."

"Have I? I daresay that I have been nothing but faithful to our friendship while you are the one that seems to swing on a pendulum."

"You would insult me?" The sharp look in her eyes softened as Alityka looked at the other acolytes, who seem to have lost a little bit of faith in her. He could tell that he'd just instilled her worst fear and wished he could take back his words, for none of that was what he had meant.

"Return to your guard, Knight Captain. We are merely arranging a study group, and nothing more. 'Tis --"

"Nothing more," echoed one of the acolytes with her.

Rivic stepped closer to Alityka. "This isn't the first clandestine meeting I've seen you having. If I've noticed, who else has? Cirvel?"

She raised tightened fists up to her stomach, then released her tense grip to cross her arms before her. "I don't know why you decided to stay and I don't really care. 'Twould have been easier if you'd returned to the tribe. You've betrayed me and as it stands, I need you to leave."

"What can I do?" He wanted to say more, but the acolytes stepped in closer to him, putting themselves between him and Alityka. She had their loyalty and he had no desire to hurt any of them. He retreated toward the door. "All right. I shall let you get back to your study group."

Rivic stepped outside to the hallway, but remain there for a little bit longer, hoping to overhear a small snatch of conversation that would indicate what Alityka was up to. He knew she was preparing the acolytes for something, but what. If only she would let him in on her plans. She had no idea what the Necroathelings were capable of. There was no way that a group of acolytes dedicated Alityka's cause could stand against a few, let alone all, of Cirvel's Necroathelings.

Rivic heard nothing, not even a harsh whisper before he heard the footsteps of the acolytes leaving the room. He stepped across the hallway and leaned with his back against the wall and crossed his arms over his chest. Alityka came out and saw him waiting, but she just shook her head and hurried off to her next class.

He stood there for several more moments wondering if he should report this to Lord Cirvel, as he knew he should. Maybe if he did, maybe if he let Lord Cirvel question her, she would confess what she was up to.

This made him feel just as guilty as Lord Cirvel in fostering no challenges against him. He would just have to let Alityka go and keep their conversations in private. Maybe if he could talk to her a little further, he could convince her to share her plans and include him for the greater good of all.

Knowing that was really the only course of action he had, he returned to his duty of guarding Gohaldinest castle.

Yet, his thoughts strayed to the reason he wanted to speak to Alityka: the Shant'olin. He knew he couldn't tell her as much as he wished about them, but if he could ask her questions, maybe she could fill in some of his missing knowledge. Did she, or maybe Lihn, know more about the Shant'olin, or were they unaware of the existence of these creatures?

They were an effective punishment, Rivic recalled Cirvel telling him. What if Lihn angered Cirvel to the point he decided to feed her to the Shant'olin rather than putting her in the glass prison? Dragzel had mentioned that sometimes Cirvel kept her in there for far too long. What if the Lord of Gohaldinest decided to try a more immediately painful torture?

The thought of Lihn facing the Shant'olin brought sickness to him so swiftly he thought he might retch right there.

With a slow, deep breath, he straightened his shoulders and resumed his pace through the halls. Even though he could force away the thought of Lihn against the Shant'olin, his own experience didn't diminish from his mind.

A new idea went through Rivic, giving him hope to get through this. Could this be a way of bringing Cirvel down? His mind wrapped onto that concept fiercely.

How many would it take to force Cirvel to his knees? He needed more information: how many Shant'olin were in the vase, was there another way to contain them, would they do to Cirvel what they did to him? Did the Shant'olin go so easily through Rivic because he lacked his shell as a novihomidrak? Would Cirvel have his own protections to counter against the Shant'olin? Remembering how Rivic had felt his magic drain away while he'd been attacked, would Cirvel's magic react the same way?

Rivic had to keep being subservient to Cirvel in order to gain further answers; maybe subtle questions and inquires could be made, and research in the vast library done.

Now more than ever, Rivic knew he needed to make amends with Alityka.

CHAPTER 3

"*F*ind her!"

Lord Cirvel's words echoed in Rivic's head as he stood in the black and white tiled hallway outside of the antechamber. Through the diamond-shaped lattice windows, he watched the blizzard -- the weather's last, frigid effort to not give way to the raining season, fall outside while his body shook with the adrenaline of being wakened and summoned.

An acolyte had left the castle and Rivic was to fetch her back.

He stepped closer to the window and put his hand to the glass. "Why did you leave, Alityka?" he whispered as if the answer would come in a snowflake.

With the slush deepening at the base of the castle, the city would be slick and hard to traverse. If Alityka had gone beyond the walls of Gohaldinest, the mountain path would be covered over, making travel through the forest and away from the city dangerous and cold.

Pushing the thought away, he felt for Alityka's magic within the castle. He put his back to the wall so he could close his eyes and concentrate harder, trying once again to follow the magic.

Alityka wasn't in the castle.

Was it possible that a Necroatheling had grabbed her and taken her to The Playground?

Lord Cirvel would have been aware of that and wouldn't have found it necessary to send Rivic out searching for her.

A ripple of magic touched his heightened awareness. A teleportation spell from further out in the city. She had fled the castle. But where had she gone after that? He searched further, stretching out toward the forest, and found her beyond the gates of Gohaldinest. Why had she gone so far out?

Catching a flash of silver and blue, Rivic saw a little beast slink its way toward him. The cahaster jumped up on a nearby table and sat back on its haunches, turning blue-green eyes toward Rivic. In the near darkness, the intensity of Dragzel's eyes gave them a luminescent glow. "Don't let her do it."

"Do what?" Rivic asked.

Dragzel crossed its front legs over its chest and snorted, little sparks shooting from its mouth. "Milady Lihn didn't say. She just told me that you would be sent out after Alityka and I was to deliver that message to you. I've now delivered it."

Rivic reached out and caught the cahaster as it tried to dart off the table and away. He held Dragzel out at arm's length. "What is Alityka going to do?"

Dragzel squirmed, trying to dig his little claws into the fleshy parts of Rivic's palm so he could squeeze away. "I don't know. Milady Lihn didn't say." He grunted. "She just begs that you make sure Alityka doesn't do it."

Rivic turned Dragzel and set him down on the floor. "I'll do my best."

As the cahaster dashed away, Rivic continued tracking Alityka's magic. She'd come down from the dormitory, crossed the courtyard, then took to the little cove where he'd once hidden and waited for Cirvel to leave Lihn's tower.

There, her magic had whisked her away outside of Gohaldinest.

He followed now, letting the light remnants of her magic sweep him toward her.

Led by her magic, Rivic landed near the road just beyond the walls. Cold assaulted him as he stood knee-deep in a snow drift surrounded by trees. He searched for indications of Alityka's trail moving through here, but he didn't see tracks.

Maybe he'd been wrong about her being outside of Gohaldinest.

He could still feel the ripple of her magic. She'd been here.

With another swift glance around for evidence of the direction she'd gone, Rivic then levitated up until he was above the forest trees. From the higher vantage and being able to see the other mountain peaks, he could see the snow-line didn't go too much further down from his current position. He thought of the flutterbirds he'd seen from Cirvel's balcony and wondered if they'd been able to get far enough away before this storm hit. The tiny birds had returned prematurely to their mountain home and he hoped it hadn't cost them their lives.

He still didn't see any signs of Alityka.

Panic gripped tightly in his chest as he lowered himself back to the ground. What if she'd decided to skip out on classes now? She'd been putting herself at risk more and more often, since before he'd become the Knight Captain of the Domini. He couldn't let her do that, yet she refused to listen to him. She'd called him a traitor.

The fact he'd decided to remain in Gohaldinest hadn't calmed her anger. Returning to the tribe instead of staying and continuing his magical training would have been rash, like the flutterbirds migrating too soon.

Gohaldinest sat in the short distance behind him. The city's outer wall resembled a thick dark line contrasted against several windows of houses in the upper city, which were filled with candlelight against the pale dusk of the cloudy evening sky.

Rivic knew why he'd been chosen to go out after Alityka. Cirvel wished to discover who Rivic was loyal to: the Lord of Gohaldinest or Alityka?

Rivic trudged to the mountain trail and started walking down it. The snow only came up to a little over his ankles here, but it quickly melted and soaked into his pants. The wind stirred the snow, pushing it in white swirling tendrils toward the trees where it gathered in sloping mounds.

He looked for Alityka's trail and still found none, yet he could feel her magic in the air. She had to be nearby. "Alityka?" he called out.

No response. He walked down the trail and searched the forest trees. "Alityka!"

The wet hems chafed his legs as they rubbed back and forth with his plodding steps. His arms hastily became numb.

He'd expected to find her quickly, long before he grew this cold. He abraded his hands over his arms trying to warm them. "Alityka," he called out again.

A shrieking cry tore through the sky and made him look up. A gargax with its long tail whipping behind it turned in its flight and zoned in on him. He felt it coming. It dove, but Rivic kept walking as though the gargax were nothing but a minor nuisance.

"Dominus," it spoke, "what iz the meaningz of your being out of Gohaldinest?"

Certainly, Lord Cirvel was giving him time to return with Alityka before releasing the gargaxes to find her. Why was this one here? A patrol maybe.

"I'm the Knight Captain and I am not leaving Gohaldinest," he answered, not wanting to let the demon know that someone else was also out here in the woods. Had it been Alityka's plan all along to let a gargax come and fetch her? "Lord Cirvel sent me out here."

Rivic found himself growing tired. He knew the dangers of being out in the cold, especially with the gargax nearby, but part of him wanted to lie down at the base of a tree and not wake up. His eyelids drooped.

"Unlikelyz! Youz are tryingz to leave now."

Much too sleepy, he knew he had to remain focused on his task and not let this gargax annoy him. "Go ask Lord Cirvel yourself. He knows I'm out here." With a flippant wave, Rivic turned and started to walk away.

The gargax pounced on his back and knocked Rivic to the ground. They tussled and went sliding down a rocky slope.

"Get off me, beast," Rivic yelled, shoving the gargax's head into the snow.

The gargax's muzzle snapped near Rivic's arm. Rivic kicked it, then scrambled up the hill. Claws dug into his leg and dragged him back down. Rivic flipped onto his back, intending to strike the beast with his other foot, but the gargax landed a bite into Rivic's thigh. As the pain flowed, Rivic felt his magic draining fast out of him.

He kicked at the gargax again, his blow glancing off the gargax's tough hide. It brought more flaring pain through his leg, which the gargax still held in his mouth.

"Sleepz now, little maege," the gargax cooed while sucking on the wound.

There were worse ways to go, Rivic decided as he leaned back against a rock and closed his eyes.

"Yourz magic iz so strong," the gargax sighed as Rivic groaned. The gargax gnawing on his leg didn't hurt so much from the blood draining out, but rather from the magic being feasted upon. "I've neverz haz the likez of it before. Ahh."

"And you shouldn't have tasted it this time," Alityka's voice raged behind the gargax.

The creature tilted its head to look up, a sensation Rivic felt down through his calf. Then it gave a shriek and tore away, its wings fluttering as it tried to scramble back.

Rivic felt himself impaled through the chest. He opened his eyes to see the white mane of a unicorn before his face, its horn piercing between his ribs.

As the unicorn drew away from him, Rivic observed Alityka spearing the gargax to the ground on her sword. The beast melted away into a muddy gray pool of liquid, which slipped under the snow.

The unicorn looked at him with dark brown eyes.

Rivic knew he had to get up. More gargaxes were on their way. He could feel them. He tried to stand, but Alityka shoved him back down. She used a dagger to rip open the material of his leggings above his knee and expose the place where the gargax had bitten. At her gasp, he looked down.

She rubbed his uninjured leg, her hand cold and wet from brushing away the snow that had been covering him. "There's hardly any blood," she snapped in an accusing tone. "I can feel the tear in your magical aura, but the gargax itself barely did any damage to you. Only a couple small breaks in your skin? How is that possible?"

Rivic met her blue eyes. "There are things about me that you don't know and I can't explain."

"Fine. Then why don't you run on home and tuck yourself into bed before the Necroathelings come for you next?" She rose and stomped through the snow to the unicorn.

"I can't do that."

"Why are you here?"

"Cirvel sent me to bring you back."

Her eyes narrowed. "So, you're hoping to return with me and get the prize from Cirvel for being a good lap dog? Do not think I will make this easy for you."

"I'm not here for Cirvel or to do his bidding, other than I wanted to find you and keep you safe. You know what he's capable of," Rivic said as he got up out of the snowbank.

"When did I become your concern?"

"When I found out you were Ellonia's sister. She stood against the whole tribe to convince your father to allow me and Nyree to stay when they would have thrown us back out into the world. The least I can do is keep you from getting hurt now."

"Would you let me care about that?"

"Ali," he said trailing behind her.

She whipped around. "Don't! You don't get to call me that. You lost the right of familiarity when you decided to leave Gohaldinest."

"I'm sorry for what happened between us, and for you feeling betrayed. I'm sorry. At the time I felt it was the right thing to do. But as I walked toward the gates, it didn't. Nyree convinced me to stay."

Alityka glanced off into the woods, but Rivic couldn't tell what she was looking at. "Fine. Look, I forgive you. Now go back to Gohaldinest and cover for me. Please do this much."

"He's released the gargaxes. He knows you are outside of Gohaldinest. If he senses I've returned without you – and Cirvel will know you are still beyond the walls -- he will make it worse. He might send more gargaxes."

"Or Azote," Alityka whispered softly, her gaze drifting aside with thought. Then she glanced back at the unicorn. "Can you purify him, maybe heal the magical aura?"

The unicorn ran its horn through his chest a second time.

He saw it coming and attempted to maneuver away by turning aside. The animal moved faster than he did. Rivic expected to feel a stabbing pain, but there was nothing. He looked down at his impaled chest, expecting blood. Nothing. He noticed he could even move some. It was like the horn wasn't really inside him, at least not in the way that two physical objects occupied the same space after being merged together.

As the unicorn backed up again, Alityka moved beside the animal and placed her hand on its neck.

"Who is this Azote?" Rivic briefly remembered hearing the name somewhere but couldn't place it.

"A large gaxlor Cirvel has bound to him with magic." The words were spoken in a quick, almost dismissive fashion. "All right, fine, don't go back to Gohaldinest. But don't follow me any longer. Walk around and pretend you are searching for me. I will find you shortly and we will return together." Her gaze slid off to the forest.

"Why? What are you doing?"

Again, she glanced toward the trees. "Something I don't know I can trust you with."

Rivic stepped around Alityka and scanned in the direction she kept surveying. "What's out there?"

She grabbed his arm. "Nothing! Now please leave."

"Ali-tyka," he said, finishing her name at the sharp warning that flared in her eyes, "would you please quit risking yourself?"

"Can I trust you? Really trust you?"

"Aye!"

She stared at the unicorn for a moment. The animal gave a snort as if resigned to a decision. She returned with a nod as if a silent communication had gone on between her and the unicorn.

"We need to be going," Alityka said, now looking toward the treetops. "More gargaxes are coming."

Rivic set his weight tentatively onto his injured leg. He had hoped that the unicorn had healed him, but it obviously hadn't. "Why did the unicorn run its horn through my chest? Why aren't I dead?"

"My task first, then I'll explain." Alityka turned to the unicorn. "Will you submit to carrying him?"

The unicorn bowed over one extended front leg.

"Thank you," Alityka said, then she whistled.

A clump of snow fell from the branches of a tree nearby, the splatter creating a deep hole with the force of its dropping weight. The splashing sound made Rivic jump.

"Come here and get on," Alityka instructed, redirecting his attention.

Rivic approached the large animal and wondered how he was supposed to get on its back. The unicorn huffed near him and stared with those big brown eyes. He glanced down at his chest again, still amazed that he wasn't bleeding, He reached over to touch her horn, verifying that it was solid and real.

The unicorn lifted her head and nudged her nose against him.

"Get on the unicorn," Alityka said.

"Just climb up on her back?"

"Aye, and do it quickly."

"Does she have a name, something she'd like me to call her," Rivic muttered, feeling it wrong to use the creature without so much as the nicety of calling her by her name.

"If she wishes to, she will give it to you," Alityka said. "'Tis urgent that we be moving now."

He awkwardly tried to jump, but he didn't get nearly high enough. Alityka laughed at him. "Come here." She leaned over and laced her fingers together. "Put the foot of your uninjured leg in here and I'll boost you up."

He still wasn't certain what he was supposed to do, and it felt strange stepping onto her hands which dipped under his weight. He seized the unicorn's mane and pulled, trying to haul himself onto its back. The animal sidestepped, turning in protest, and knocked its leg against Alityka. She hoisted Rivic onto the unicorn's back and helped him to straighten. He clenched the unicorn's mane tighter.

"Loosen up a bit or you'll make Twinkles nervous. She might bolt if you unnerve her too much."

"Twinkles?"

As if in response, Twinkles backed up and Rivic felt like he might slide off. Alityka placed her hand on the unicorn's neck to calm it. "Seriously, loosen up," she chided.

Rivic forced his fingers to release the unicorn's long white strands. He put his hands on each side of her neck, wishing he had a better handhold.

"Clasp onto her gently with your legs," Alityka said. "Just move with her. You'll be fine if you flow with the rhythm."

"Easy for you to say. You have both feet on the ground."

"Come now. Sitting as you are, you look as if you could be a Dominari," she said with a smile.

"What's a Dominari?"

"A champion chosen by the unicorns to save the world." She raised her head just a little. "Someone pure of heart and brave."

Rivic glanced down at the strands of unicorn hair wrapped around his hands. In the fading blue light of the evening, the color of the sky reflected in the mane and reminded him of the blue webbing that twice swathed him. "That's not me," he muttered.

"Nay, I suppose not."

Was she thinking of the dark secret about destroying two

villages he had shared with her? If so, he couldn't tell as she had turned to face the woods.

"Look, I know you don't want me to care about you, but there are things you should know. Cirvel has something under the castle. He took me –"

His words stopped as she started walking between the trees and he saw a dark shadow move across the ground ahead.

Another unicorn emerged from the forest. Alityka swung up on its back as if it were the most natural thing in the world. Once she got settled, she waved to Rivic. "Let's go. Tempest says the gargaxes are nearly here and the unicorns have a circle ready for us."

Many questions piled through Rivic's mind, but it seemed a better use of energy in figuring out how to get Twinkles to follow Alityka. Fortunately, the unicorn knew what to do better than he did, and they started forward. The loping steps rocked Rivic back and forth more than he expected and he tightened his grip on the animal's mane.

"Do you know the plan?" he asked the unicorn. "I hope you know what's going on."

CHAPTER 4

*R*ivic shivered as the chill in the forest air moved right through the tunic covering him. He briefly wondered why Alityka didn't feel the cold and realized that she'd bulked up her own tunic with fur. Picking up the thin material in his fingers, he did the same. He might as well make it dry while he was at it. If Alityka seemed to notice his magic, she didn't show it.

Alityka and her unicorn, Tempest, moved forward through the trees ahead. They'd been traveling for longer than Rivic had foreseen. How much further would they go? Would Cirvel notice his disappearance as well? What if they were gone all night? With panic in his chest, he wondered what else Cirvel could do. He knew he needed to convince Alityka to go back before Cirvel's anger intensified, putting her on the receiving end of some horrid punishment, like the Shant'olin. He wished he knew how to get his mount to catch up to her.

"Come," Alityka urged, turning partially around to look back at him. "What the unicorns need to do will be quick. We can make it back to Gohaldinest, even after my explanations, if you hurry. Now, where was it that Cirvel took you?"

But Rivic didn't know how to make Twinkles move any faster, so he continued at the unicorn's pace. "'Twasn't so much where he took me, but rather what we did. There were all these underground tunnels; 'tis like a maze and I don't know how he made his way through. When we got to this place where a window separated it into two rooms, he showed me these creatures called Shant'olin locked away in a huge vase. He took me there because I had destroyed so many of his gargaxes while I was with the tribe." He wondered if Cirvel would make Alityka pay for the gargax she had just destroyed.

"I don't understand how the two are related."

He had missed that part of the tale. "They eat souls and eventually become gargaxes. Have you heard anything about Shant'olin before?"

"Only in whispers and rumors."

"They are not rumor and what they do to a person is terribly painful."

"What do they do to you?"

"I don't know," Rivic answered, frustration edging into his voice from his lack of understanding about what had happened to him. "They went right through my body and it felt like they were tearing me to pieces."

"Interesting," she said before falling silent.

After a little way, he began to get use to the unicorn's sway and sat up a little higher.

"You do realize that you're going to have to visit Cirvel to heal that bite?" she asked.

"If I don't?"

"Your aura is draining magic out of the rips in it. Gargaxes, typically, don't only break the skin with their teeth, but tear the person's magical aura because they eat magic, not flesh. Only Cirvel can heal that wound. If you don't get it fixed, all your magic will slowly seep out of you. Worse, the longer the wound is unhealed, the more you are feeding the gargaxes with your power. You could make them very strong."

He sensed there was something else she was trying to tell him. Rivic wondered if all women had the ability of double speak. First Nyree, then Ellonia, and now Alityka. Why did he feel that they were always trying to communicate more to him than what their simple words were saying? Why couldn't they just speak what was on their minds? Why did he have to guess?

"You better come up with a story to tell Cirvel about why you tangled with a gargax," she continued. "But at least you won't have to worry about the gargaxes controlling your thoughts. You should be glad that Twinkles and I heard you calling and came back for you. Why did you follow me anyway?"

He realized that Alityka didn't know Cirvel had sent Rivic after her; she thought he'd come of his own volition. Perhaps if he'd been a better friend, he would have. "I felt your magic outside of Gohaldinest and figured you were trying to make Cirvel mad at you. Trust me, 'tis not a good idea. Why did you leave the city anyway?"

"I have a task to complete."

She had mentioned an errand twice now, but she'd never gone into any further details, which Rivic took to mean that she didn't want to share. He remained silent in case she did.

Then he realized how deeply she led him into the woods. "Where are we going?" He knew he could be out of the forest in a flash with a teleportation spell, but he just felt like he shouldn't. Secretly inside him, he had a little voice telling him to feel the magic and go with the flow, that all was well. Sontre' had always told him to trust his gut. He relaxed and listened to the sounds of the forest. The scent of pine in the air reminded him of his time with Ellonia. He couldn't wait to be back with her.

A deep longing stirred inside him. This life might only be temporary, but for the moment this realm was his. He had two choices: either stand by as the world withered or make the space that he occupied with in it as blissful as he could. He got to choose what he filled it with and to share it with those he wanted to.

Twinkles slowed, breaking Rivic from his thoughts as the hypnotic sway ended. He looked up. Several unicorns had moved in a huddle around them. They flanked through the trees, first just a few, then tens, and then what seemed to be hundreds of the animals.

Encircled by the unicorns, Rivic felt a wall of magic as they passed through an invisible barrier and he found the air warmer here. The unicorns closed in behind them.

Alityka dismounted, taking the center of the ring. Twinkles stopped, and Rivic wondered if he should dismount. Afraid he'd never make it back onto the unicorn if he got off, he stayed where he was.

Mist swirled around Alityka and when it dissipated, she stood before the unicorns in buckled plates of golden armor over her acolyte's dress and a winged gold helm on her head. Looking around at the gathering of unicorns, she raised her arms up as if in triumph.

Rivic realized the truth of her magic. "You're the Dominari."

Rivic glanced around at the sea of white unicorns surrounding them through the forest trees. So many had gathered for Alityka. He couldn't believe he hadn't realized who she was when she had been speaking with Twinkles and Tempest. "You are the champion of the unicorns." Worse, he suddenly realized that he'd been baited here into the middle of the forest. The dragon had told him there was another champion on this world that would need guidance and tempering.

Alityka's golden armor flashed in the moonlight as she stalked toward him. Her eyes grew fierce. "Tell me, Rivic, what are you?"

He clenched his jaw, bringing his mouth in tightly around his tongue to hold it in place. He felt magic ripple through him, physically trying to force him to speak while he swayed on the unicorn. Releasing her mane, he slapped both his hands over his mouth. He thought he might retch.

She pointed at him. "Tell me what you are!"

He grabbed onto Twinkles' neck as he fell forward. "I'm a novihomidrak." Relief and horror formed a terrible poison in his stomach. How was it that she could make him speak those words so forcefully and without thought to cloak them in another term to hide the truth?

Yet she looked puzzled by his admission. She glanced around at the unicorns, then back to him. "Very interesting. That explains a lot."

"Does it?" he asked with a choke, still not certain that he wouldn't vomit. "Like what?"

"Your high level of magical ability, a level which matches Cirvel, even if you are afraid of it."

Rivic had to let the jibe roll off him. Alityka was here for her own reasons, not because of him. Yet, longing to discover her purpose, he asked, "Why are you out here?"

The words seemed difficult for Alityka to say, and she struggled with her admission almost as much as he had. "I find myself in quite the predicament. My magic has been tied to a spell within the castle and, as it is, will never catch Cirvel's attention. 'Tis a situation I must fix. I have gained Cirvel's trust, but to get closer to his secrets, I need more magical ability. He's got to notice me."

"How do you plan on doing that?"

"The unicorns are going to take over fueling the spell I am currently maintaining. 'Twill allow me to have my full magic back."

He sensed more to her plan. "Do you think that will be enough?"

Her nose gave a displeased wrinkle. "'Twon't be." Now her lips tightened as well. "But I don't think you want to hear the rest of it."

"Try me."

Alityka turned and walked a couple steps away. The unicorns moved around her and she reached out to pet some of them closest to her. She glanced back. "'Tis terrible, Rivic."

She knew what he'd done. "Worse than destroying your family and the tribes where they'd lived?" he asked, hoping that reminding her would make her loosen up.

"Aye!" She hugged the unicorn nearest her and buried her face against the beast's neck. Tears filled her eyes when she rolled her face away. "I must do the unthinkable."

He didn't even know what her plan was, but fear rippled through him. It must be awful indeed. How else could he account for her being so distraught? "Must you? What could you possibly do that would be so dreadful?"

Alityka pulled away and stepped out of the circle of unicorns. "I want to have them break their bond with me."

"You don't want to be a Dominari anymore?"

"Oh, Rivic, how can you not understand?"

He remembered Ellonia telling him that he would have a hard time adjusting to life in the tribe because he'd been raised in the woods. It had made him feel like he'd never fit in anywhere. Now, Alityka's comment returned that feeling to him. "I don't. What do you mean?"

"If they break our connection, I will become extremely powerful."

"At what cost?"

She growled, tightening her fists at her side as she stomped. "Why do you have to ask me that? Take back your question."

He now knew what Lihn had been afraid Alityka would do and why she'd sent Dragzel to beg Rivic to stop her. "Nay! What does this cost you?"

"I will do whatever it takes to defeat Cirvel. I'll approach the task with near mindless obsession."

He felt the vagueness of her answer and knew that the layers went so much deeper. He pushed back. "Which means you will make your attempts at him very obvious, and the moment he suspects you are up to something, he will decimate you."

The look on her face told him that her own thoughts echoed his. "I've tried the long way," she raged, "but I just can't have patience any longer. 'Tis taking too long."

"Lihn doesn't want you to do this."

"'Tis not her choice."

"Well, 'tis a bad idea and I think you know it. What 'twill it take for me to talk you out of it?"

Her eyes sharpened. "Give me formidable allies. Promise me that you will help me find a way to defeat Cirvel for the good of all the tribes. With your power, we have a chance of standing against him."

"I can't. I've just barely gotten control over it. Aye, what Cirvel is doing to the tribes, keeping them scattered and at minimal levels of magic is horrible, but 'tis not diabolical."

"Now you would rate his crimes on a scale?"

"Maybe he has a reason for his actions. Cirvel is not a man who does anything without thinking it through; he's very methodical. I'm just saying that we haven't asked him what his motivations are." He could see he wasn't convincing her. "Ali, we need to go back. We've been out here too long."

With a disgruntled noise, Alityka rolled her eyes and glanced away. Tempest nudged Alityka with its long nose. "All right," she muttered. "I need to transfer this spell, then we can be on our way back to Gohaldinest."

"What is this spell?"

A look of distrust passed through her eyes. She drew her shoulders back, straightening up, and squared her jaw. "I am hiding the true identity of someone within the castle."

"Who?"

"Her name is Tarylihn. You know her as Lihn." Alityka faced Tempest, then ran her hand along the unicorn's nose. "She is in a greater danger than you. If Cirvel finds out you are really a novihomidrak, he will kill you without a second thought. If he discovers the truth about Lihn, his tortures upon her would be worse than death. The entire world would feel the consequences. You know first-hand that Cirvel has no mercy."

Rivic wanted to leave. He scoffed and ran a hand over his face. "'Tis probably not much about Lihn that Cirvel doesn't know about," he spat. "She's sleeping with him." The words felt dirty in his mouth and he hoped it shocked her into thinking that maybe Lihn wasn't the person Alityka thought she was.

"I know." Alityka cast her gaze downward. "Some wars," she said, shaking her head, "demand unimaginable sacrifices."

"You know that she beds him willingly?" he uttered, the surprise he'd sent out rebounding onto him.

Alityka shrugged. "She made that choice so I didn't have to."

Rivic thought he might choke.

"Look, 'tis a reason there aren't many female Necroathelings, let alone acolytes who rise in the ranks. He doesn't believe women can be powerful and he actually wants to protect them. For as evil as Cirvel is, he has a large streak of chivalry. We knew that flaw was how we'd be able to get close to him." She spread her arms out again. "Because of what I am, he would know my magic and want to possess it. Tarylihn didn't want his darkness to touch my soul. She chose to be a wall between me and him, and she let herself be the one to get intimate with Cirvel."

The anguish behind her statement seemed to weigh her down. "I have to fight for her, to help her get back where she belongs."

"But she doesn't want you to do that by throwing away what you are." It struck Rivic suddenly that he was doing just as his novimather had once instructed him: tempering the champion of this world.

"Why don't you worry about your own concerns?" She pointed to his leg where the gargax had bitten him. "As soon as Cirvel discovers the hole in your magical aura without much of an accompanying flesh wound, Cirvel will look deeper, as I did. As a novihomidrak, you are the only thing that threatens him, and he will destroy you. I hope you have a way of explaining that. I'm not even certain how you've kept it from him this far!"

She was right. Cirvel already suspected something about his magic, but this would force further investigation.

Alityka returned to the unicorns. "Now, let's get this transfer done so we may return to the castle."

The unicorns began to shuffle about, their shifting weight crunching on the snow and making a cracking sound that vibrated in the trees above. Wet slush dropped from the trembling branches. An odd hum arose from all the encompassing noise.

Alityka held out her arms and closed her eyes. "Pac'tael malibroem soknee alikatal."

As the enchantment surged and spread through the forest, a nervous tickle crawled along Rivic's neck and shoulders. He wondered if this anxious feeling was that of his novihomidrak abilities sensing the unicorns' energy tugging from Alityka. He fought to hold himself steady.

A snap pulsated through Alityka's magic like the musical twang of an instrument's plucked string. Opening her eyes and relaxing, she placed her hands on the nearest unicorn. "Thank you."

"Are you still you?" Rivic asked.

She gave a half smile. "Aye, the bond with the unicorns still holds. Only my spell has been transferred. They will take care of their sister now."

The draw of magic on his leg pulsed. He felt so exceptionally tired. "Why did you confess to me about Lihn?"

The unicorns all started to back away and the forest grew quiet as they retreated.

"A Dominari, by the very nature of the unicorn's magic, cannot outright lie. I can also sense lies when they are told to me, as well as force the truth from someone when I ask the right question. How do you feel?"

He realized that she was now using that magic against him. "Exhausted."

"Do you know what you're going to tell Lord Cirvel when he comes for you?"

"Nay."

"You still have some time. Now we should return. I'll do the honors." Alityka reached over and touched Rivic's arm. With her spell, everything went black as if he'd blinked. When he opened his eyes, they were back in the castle at the top of the stairs to the domini's quarters.

"I should probably inform Cirvel that you are back." Rivic took a step and stumbled, collapsing to his hands and knees.

"He sent you after me?"

Rivic realized that he hadn't told her that Cirvel had sent him. He tried to stand, but the very walls around him seem to press him down. "Aye. Now I need to go make my report."

She knelt beside him as he sat back on his heels. "You can't go anywhere but to bed. You're weak. Cirvel will know we are back."

"Ali, don't make his anger worse."

"I'll be fine, I promise. Let's get you down to bed. Your gargax bite has you too drained for anything else. By morning, Cirvel will have sensed the disruption and will have traced it back to you. I suspect you'll be seeing him early."

Rivic nodded as she helped him to his feet and assisted him to the basement. She unbuckled his armor and pulled the plates off him. He collapsed into his bed, barely aware as she covered him with a blanket. He swore he was asleep before her footsteps had reached the top of the stairs.

CHAPTER 5

*R*ivic woke early the next morning to discover the previous night hadn't been some sort of bad dream. His clothes were all covered in dried blood and mud.

He quickly went upstairs to change and dropped his soiled clothes down the chute. The torn and lightly bloodied pants, he placed on the floor and burned with a cazidor spell after checking to make sure no one was around.

As he washed the wounds, he noticed the yellowed skin looked infected and oozed with thick, slimy pus. He felt the magic seeping out of him from the injury. Alityka was right; he'd need to see Cirvel for healing, but he'd wait to see if the Lord of Gohaldinest sought him out first. Rivic then hurried down for morning meal.

His leg continued to sting as he headed to the room where the domini and a few advanced acolytes had class. Taking his seat and being silently glad that today wasn't one where he started out with sword training, he scratched the itching wound while hoping that Cirvel would seek him out swiftly.

During the lecture portion of the lesson, every time he

rubbed his thigh, he looked around to see if anyone else could sense the magic pouring through him. He felt it, but did anyone else? He didn't think so, though it was hard to tell if the Necroatheling instructor, Bredic-na, did or not.

Halfway through class, Lord Cirvel entered. He exchanged a look with Bredic-na, who nodded before stepping aside for Cirvel to have the podium.

Cirvel's dark eyes surveyed the class before he spoke. "I have been told that a pupil was out of Gohaldinest last night and was attacked by a gargax, but my gargax never returned to report to me."

Rivic wondered if he should pretend to be curious as he noticed the others glancing around, but Cirvel had sent him out after Alityka. They both knew that. Why was Cirvel pretending that it was more than that, unless there was someone else who had been outside of Gohaldinest too? Or perhaps this was a test to see if Rivic would lie and try to hide his whereabouts.

After a moment, Cirvel smiled. He left the podium and started walking down the aisle. "But since it seems all my trainees are present," Cirvel said, "I'd say the accusations are false. I have come personally to issue a warning: a student wandering outside of Gohaldinest without permission is not permitted. I certainly hope we do not need a demonstration."

Cirvel continued to stride between the tables, occasionally stopping to inspect someone's notes. "I came on other business anyway. Bredic-na, I will be removing one of your students from class today. Please make sure to catch him up tomorrow."

"Aye, sir," 'Bredic-na said with a bow.

Rivic gave a sigh of relief as Cirvel stopped beside the table where Rivic sat. "Come with me," Cirvel said, looking down at Rivic.

Rivic slid from his seat. "Aye, sir."

Cirvel walked in silence, two Necroathelings moving ahead of them and two following. Rivic wasn't certain where they were going until a Necroatheling opened a door ahead and exposed a room with rows of bookshelves filled from floor to ceiling.

Cirvel strode into the library, shadowed by his Necroathelings, leaving Rivic to follow behind. Cirvel outspread his arms. Instantly, several of the bookshelves swung wide open revealing a magical workspace hidden behind the wall. Since the Necroathelings looked unimpressed by the sparkling magic, Rivic figured they were used to seeing this. He, on the other hand, felt his head go reeling.

"You took longer to find our little, lost acolyte than I thought it would." Cirvel spared Rivic a glance.

"The snow and the wind... there were no tracks to follow. I had to keep sensing out her magic."

"Why did you not seek me out when you returned? You should have come and told me that you'd been bitten by a gargax."

Rivic tried to look ashamed, a feat not too hard considering the chiding words. "I was embarrassed. I'd hoped 'twould heal on its own."

Cirvel nodded, but Rivic couldn't tell if his answer was acceptable or not. "What was she doing?"

At least Cirvel had turned the conversation back to Alityka. Rivic straightened. "Practicing, my lord. She wants to get stronger to impress you."

Deeper inside the workspace, Rivic saw a tight, ascending, spiral staircase. He couldn't tell if it went up into one of Gohaldinest's many towers since Cirvel didn't go that far into the room. Instead, he stopped at a workbench where a round flask burned over a tall, unnatural flame.

"Alkelker," Cirvel explained. "'Tis the stone of the

gargaxes. It must be kept over a continuous magical fire in order to keep it from hardening back to rock."

"You make the gargaxes?" Rivic asked.

"I do not," Cirvel commented with disappointment. "The primal gods designed the gargaxes."

"Primal gods? I thought the gargaxes came from the Shant'olin."

"The gaxlors. They initially created the Shant'olin as a weapon against the maeges." Cirvel opened a cupboard and began gathering items from within. He tipped his head toward Rivic. "As you know, the Shant'olin go through the metamorphosis to become the gargaxes. But the gaxlors are the original beings of earth and stone fashioned by the creator of this planet. There were here long before us and they will remain when we are all dust."

"I very much doubt that you ever plan on becoming dust."

"As true as I wish that to be, all things die. I do plan on a good, long span though." Cirvel snorted his amusement. "Enough of gargaxes though. Let us return to your previous comment. Why would Alityka wish to impress me?"

Rivic thought on his answer for a moment, wishing he didn't have to speak it. Finally, he settled on, "Because she wants to become a dominus."

Cirvel picked up the flask of liquid Alkelker and poured a little into a pestle. "Strange, don't you think, that she would choose now to begin to impress me. Are you sure that it is me and not yourself she wishes to excite?"

"M-m-me?" The word shuddered from Rivic with heavy implications.

"Why, of course. A deep friendship has stirred between the two of you. I would dare to say that she wishes to keep up with you in order to have more time at your side."

Rivic slapped his mouth closed, afraid more incoherent

and stumbling words would fall from his lips. In order to hide Ellonia, it might be best to let Cirvel hold this belief.

"Do you know why the gargax bites don't heal on their own?" Cirvel asked, casting a sideways glance at Rivic as the Lord of Gohaldinest began to stir the potion before him.

Rivic wondered why Cirvel bothered with the mundane tasks of pouring and mixing when his magic could easily carry out those duties. But nearly as quickly as the thought came to him, Rivic realized that Cirvel worked the ingredients manually because he enjoyed the work of blending the compounds. The combining of raw components to see how they interacted was what drove Cirvel.

He knew Cirvel waited for an answer. "Because the gargaxes eat magic. A wound that is continuously being chewed on wouldn't heal."

Cirvel looked pleased. "Very good. Did you know that I never had any intention of healing their bite?" He pulled a brown jar off a nearby shelf and took the cork out. He dumped some in his palm, then added a pinch to the pestle. The rest he tossed onto the fire before recorking the bottle and returning it to the shelf. "I figured that if someone got bitten, then they were conspiring against me and I should let them die."

"What changed your mind?" The question felt brave as Rivic asked it.

"Lihn. She challenges me to be more benevolent." From another jar, this one blue, he weighed out some of the contents which he then added to his concoction. "She even came up with the cure for me. Do you know what really activates the healing?"

Rivic shook his head. "Nay, my lord."

Cirvel stopped stirring and picked up a black bottle from the shelf before walking over to Rivic. "Hold out your hand."

Rivic held his breath as he lifted his palm out toward

Cirvel. An image of spiders running from the bottle all over his arm came to mind, and he fought the urge to jerk back. They were, after all, just spiders, and more importantly, only a fear presently created in his imagination.

Cirvel popped the cork out. Tipping the bottle, he tapped the sides gently. His manicured nail clicked against the glass.

A sparkling white powder sifted down over Rivic's hand.

"'Tis ground unicorn horn."

Rivic flinched, scattering the dust to the floor.

Cirvel turned back and added a few sprinkles to the mixture. "The unicorns have a great power to heal all sorts of magical wounds. They can purify mind and body. Unicorn hair can be an amazing suture." He held up the bottle. "But ground unicorn horn, that is the concentrated center of their magic. You remove a unicorn horn from the head and you kill the unicorn. One such creature has given its life in exchange for the individual who needs this remedy. Do you believe that person is worthy?"

"I would certainly hope so," Rivic answered.

Cirvel measured and added a few extra herbs into the pestle then used a mortar to mash it all together. "We'll need to apply this remedy fairly quickly once 'tis ready."

Cirvel smirked as he pointed to a chair, watching with a triumphant gaze as Rivic settled down into the seat. Rivic forced himself to look comfortable, though he was so uneasy that he felt stiff enough to come right off the chair.

"Do you not consider yourself worthy?" Cirvel asked. "You received the bite, but did you also destroy the beast?"

"Nay. 'Twas Alityka's doing."

Cirvel looked even more humored by this. "A dominus saved by an acolyte. That must wound your pride a bit."

Rivic had to know if Cirvel had sensed the unicorn magic or not. "'Tis plenty sore. But why send me and the gargax out to find her?"

"Because she broke the rules. A far worse punishment should befall her."

Rivic shivered, glad that Cirvel had turned back to stir his potion before seeing Rivic's response. "Why hasn't it?" Rivic asked, knowing that by speaking these words, he dared putting Alityka on the line.

Cirvel pivoted around, his eyebrow raised with curiosity. "Do you wish an honest answer?"

"Aye."

"Because I wanted to know if you were going to return or if you would use the chance to escape. I am still not sure why you decided to remain and send your sister home."

Rivic felt his heart quicken. He knew he stood on the precipice he'd been approaching for several months. Sontre' and the Guardian wanted him here. Alityka and Lihn had urged him forward. Nyree had told him to make the leap. "I want to be a Necroatheling."

"Really?" Cirvel's gaze darted to Rivic's leg.

"Aye."

Folding one arm over his chest, Cirvel placed the other on it so he could rub his chin. He looked uncertain of how to phrase his next inquiry. "Then be a good lad and answer my question. What has given you such power that you obviously have strength, but not the training to go with it, and, dare I say, a fear about it?"

"I am a Dominari, or I was until I came here to study from you." Rivic lifted his chin, surprised that the lie came so easily to him. He didn't know why he had said it either. Alityka had told him to come up with a story to tell Lord Cirvel and he hadn't been able to concoct any tale at all. But now that it was out, he found it might help draw Cirvel's attention away from Alityka for a bit. "I have no wish to be a champion. There is nothing to be gained in that path. You have made me see the truth."

Cirvel paused in his movements, but he couldn't withdraw the smirk from his lips. "I see."

Rivic held his breath, wondering if Cirvel would condemn the words as a lie. He didn't, but rather went back to work on the compound. After a moment, Cirvel tamped the stirring spoon against the bowl and set it down onto the counter. Then he adjusted the flame beneath the bowl.

"'Twill take a moment longer to simmer everything together," Cirvel said, walking over to Rivic. He clamped his fingers down on Rivic's shoulder. "Let's take a little trip, shall we? Talcor dun."

They appeared in the forest outside of Gohaldinest. Rivic half expected a small shove as Cirvel liberated him, but instead Cirvel merely lifted his hand. A thick cloak of fur rested over Cirvel's shoulders. Though Rivic's dominus tunic had long sleeves, the cold breeze whisked through the thin material.

"Summon a unicorn," Cirvel said. "Prove to me that you are a Dominari and call your unicorn to you."

Rivic had no idea how he was to prompt the unicorns out of the forest. Was he supposed to invite it -- here unicorn, here unicorn -- or maybe scream? Tinkles! What if it was far away and couldn't hear him? What even made him think that one would come to him? Why had he evoked such a lie? Did it have something to do with the ground unicorn horn that Cirvel had dumped in his hand?

A bird's song came through the trees and gave Rivic an idea. He whistled.

Moments passed. He whistled again. His heart set a thundering gallop in his chest as he realized that Cirvel's irritation grew. The panic in Rivic's ribcage was the only thing getting closer.

"You are no Dominari," Cirvel said. "Why would you choose to tell untruths to me?"

"I am not being false. If you understand the powers of the Dominari, then you know I cannot lie." At least he felt brave in this statement, even as he did not know why the words came from him. If only his courage would keep him warm. He shivered.

"Then where is your unicorn?"

"Do your Necroathelings always stay within hearing range of you?" Rivic knew he couldn't back down now. "'Tis possible her tribe is out of range, or 'tis too difficult for her to get through the snow. Maybe she just needs time."

Cirvel did not look pleased. "Your arguments are good, but you cannot prove yourself."

Rivic wondered what punishment that might bring. Maybe Cirvel meant to leave him out here magicless to freeze. "Then perhaps you should find another way to test me."

"The appearance of a unicorn is the only reliable way to tell if one is a Dominari."

Rivic saw a flash of white through the trees and he raised his hand to point. "Then 'tis a good thing she has arrived."

Cirvel turned, his mouth dropping open as he saw the unicorn walking toward them. He moved toward it, but the unicorn skittered around him and went to Rivic. She remained just outside of Cirvel's reach, even as he stretched out again to touch her. In her nervousness, Rivic took a light hold of her mane and kept her from bolting while he stroked his hand down her long neck. With the warmth of horseflesh beneath his palm, the chill leaving his fingers made the rest of him feel even colder.

"That's enough," Cirvel snarled. "Release her and let's return to Gohaldinest."

Rivic let go of the unicorn's mane and gave her a couple pats before he stepped back. "Shall I?" Rivic asked. He took a hold of Lord Cirvel's fur robes and said, "Talcor dun."

His moment of triumph didn't last long under the rage now lit in Cirvel's dark gaze as they appeared in the castle.

Cirvel, with his lips tight and his eyes narrow, pointed toward the chair where Rivic had been sitting before their little adventure into the forest.

Rivic followed the gesture and sat down quickly, afraid that if Cirvel spoke a word of command to him, it wouldn't be a good one. He thought of Lihn in the glass prison. At least Cirvel wanted something from her; Rivic might not be lucky enough to be released before suffocating.

"Pass'eay," Cirvel said and the portion of the leggings around Rivic's wound split in two. Cirvel smeared some of the Alkelker mixture on Rivic's leg. The heat burned Rivic's skin, but not a deep searing pain like he'd expected.

"'Twould seem he only got one good bite on you and not even deep enough to do more than merely break the skin. What happened to my gargax?" Cirvel asked.

"He was impaled to the ground and melted away."

"Impaled to the ground?" It seemed like something Cirvel had never thought of. "The gargax melted away, you say? Is this how you dispatched so many of my other gargaxes previously?"

"Aye. Some." Rivic wondered if Cirvel was unaware of the gargaxes' weaknesses and decided to keep secret the other ways of magically dispatching the demons.

"Hmmm, 'twould seem the center of our planet is even more capable of absorbing a gargax's energy than I had previously thought. Interesting." Cirvel held his hand above Rivic's thigh. "Aidol'kiw."

The bite marks healed and faded almost in an instant.

"There," Cirvel said, standing up and returning the bowl to the workbench. "Now you won't be bleeding out magic and leaving a fine trail behind you." He leaned against the wood, not turning back.

When Cirvel said nothing more, Rivic wondered if he was being released. He cautiously slid from the chair. "Thank you for healing the bite."

Cirvel's stance stiffened and his movements seemed to jerk as he restored items to their rightful spot. "Do you know why I allowed you to stay in Gohaldinest after you requested so strongly to leave?"

"Nay, my lord."

"Because you will make a wonderful Necroatheling."

Not sure if it were fear or defiance, Rivic responded, "Why do you believe that?"

Cirvel swung around, facing Rivic. "I watched you after the ceremony where you became not only a dominus, but my Knight Captain. You shook for a little while, aye; a sign that your body was throwing off the trauma of what you'd been through. But then you ate your meal."

Cirvel let silence hang in the air as he adjusted the flame beneath the Alkelker, his eyes occasionally flickering to look at Rivic as if judging the right length of time before speaking again. "'Twould be typical for most people who had murdered someone to remain with a sickened feeling for quite some time, maybe days." He straightened and stepped away from the worktable, his fingertips lingering on the polished wood as he moved. "But you repressed those emotions quickly, returning to your normal state more rapidly than most. You are a killer at heart."

Realizing the truth in Cirvel's words, Rivic wondered how he could deny the accusations. He had eaten. He'd sat there right across from Cirvel, shared conversation even, as Cirvel had offered him more food. He hadn't comprehended the motivations behind Cirvel's behaviors that night, but the seemingly ordinary activities had been a test.

Cirvel leaned his hip against the wood and folded his

arms across his chest. "Do you know what happens to a Dominari when the bond with the unicorn breaks?"

"Aye."

"Now, why would I not want that creature to become one of my Necroathelings? Tell me the thought of possessing that kind of power doesn't thrill you."

At first, Rivic thought he might successfully evade the question, but the words bubbled from his chest as if they had a life of their own. "I cannot." The more he lingered on Cirvel's idea, the more Rivic felt his own fingers tingling as the magic excitedly latched onto him.

"But the Dominari is not quite ready to break the bond." Cirvel's voice once again filled with irritation. "I am sure that we shall speak more of this, but for now, leave my sight and return to your studies."

Rivic fled the room, discovering quickly that he didn't know what part of the castle he was in. He maneuvered through the hallways until the maze became familiar to him, but he didn't feel safe until the other domini surrounded him. Even then, he felt like a traitor in their midst.

CHAPTER 6

The search for Alityka led him to the library. In the middle of the rows of books was a section of four support columns and glass walls. A couple of acolytes currently practiced magic within the area. Alityka sat at one of the study tables off to the side. He came to stand beside her.

"Rivic, I'm glad you're here," she said, glancing up over her shoulder at him with a soft smile. "Did he heal the gargax bites?" She whispered so quietly that he doubted a normal human could have heard her.

"I'm fine. They are healed." He glared at an acolyte who watched them and tried to listen into the conversation. "Has all been right with you today?"

"As you can see, Dominus, I am here."

That wasn't a direct answer to his question, so he prodded, "And safe?"

She hesitated with a brief pause. "I am unharmed."

He tried to decipher exactly what she meant by that, but she set the book she was reading aside and brought another closer.

"Look what I found," she said, rolling back several pages. "I've been trying to research about the gargaxes and I came across a watcher of worlds reference. 'Tis something Cirvel or someone like Cirvel wrote a very long time ago. Perhaps they have forgotten about it. Do you think 'tis possible? Here, read." She pushed the text in his direction.

His arms felt stiff and his armor heavy, but he leaned forward to read the passage Alityka pointed at.

Like the Drifter, this boy we found could move through dimensions and time. He seemed completely unaffected by the years. Claiming that he was a kind of caretaker, he said he observed worlds through portals and stepped into situations when they needed his help. As such, he said that his duty was to be a watcher of worlds.

Rivic shook his head.

"Don't you see? This is what we need," she spoke exasperatedly. When Rivic shrugged, she continued, "We require a watcher of worlds. If we can find some way to trap Cirvel, even temporarily, a watcher can move Cirvel from this world to another dimension where he would be harmless and unable to get back here."

Sontre' had mentioned to Rivic about a hierarchy of champions, but his memories of this were faint. "What is the difference?"

Alityka scanned the book a little further along in the passage. "It says that Drifters can only place objects in a single dimension off from themselves. Watchers use windows and doorways to go through multiple dimensions and see the objects they seek across the cosmos."

Rivic sat down beside her. "How are we going to find a watcher? How are we going to trap Cirvel? Have you noticed how powerful he is, how well his moves are plotted, and how sensitive he is to everything which goes on around him? I doubt that he is oblivious to this very conversation we are having now."

"What would you do then to stop him?"

"I don't know. I just think we have to keep serving him until we find out what motivates him."

"Motivates?" She scoffed. "When are you going to quit being scared?" Her voice was sharp as her angry eyes narrowed on him.

"I'm not scared," Rivic protested, but it sounded weak even to him.

"You are totally afraid." She dragged the book back toward her and slammed it shut. "You have always feared your magic and you let that dread possess you. Everyone senses it."

"Nay, they don't."

"Fine. Shall we talk about what happened in the forest? You are the first person I've seen who had been bitten by the gargaxes and the pain alone didn't damn near kill you! That's not even considering the magic that was draining from you. I saw it, Rivic, and try as I might to overlook it, I can't forget what I saw: you hoped the gargax would exhaust you. 'Tis like you don't even want your magic."

"I don't," Rivic admitted. "I've never liked the magic. I shouldn't even have it."

"Well, you do. So, accept it and use it."

Rivic shook his head. He didn't know that he'd ever be able to savor it, not with so much pain behind his power.

"When are you going to quit being afraid? When another of your loved ones gets put into jeopardy again? Who will it be this time? You've got to leave the last of your fear behind."

He knew what she was saying was true, even though he wanted to refute it. He remained silent.

"Miex'calidori. Badimazulien."

A bubble surrounded them. With her angry face set

tightly, Alityka turned to face him. Rivic sat back in his chair, glad that the curve of the magic shield made him bow his head so he wouldn't have to look at her.

Alityka drew a deep breath of the enchanted air around them. "No one outside can hear us, so do tell me: what did you do that makes you so afraid?"

Rivic hated her mocking, and even more the force she put behind her demand for him to answer the question. "I destroyed two villages before I had any control of my magic! Remember?"

Her face momentarily softened before her eyes narrowed on him once more. "'Tis that it? Only two? What makes them so special?"

"My parents and my aunt and uncle were in those villages."

"Never hurt a living thing since then?" she asked sarcastically.

"Wrong!" he spat back. "I killed Melodin when I became a dominus."

"Do you understand anything about our mission, or what we need to do here? I do! And as a champion of the unicorns, I have a responsibility to keep this world from dying and shriveling up within the universe. I will do whatever it takes, even letting a clansman die. Are you, as a novihomidrak, willing to do the same or not?"

He felt the pull of the unicorns' magic on him and fought the urge to say he was willing.

"Don't try to convince me that you stayed to help us," Alityka snapped.

Rivic grabbed her arm, but when she fiercely glared down, he released his holding fingers. "I stayed for me. I have learned so much here. Is what he's doing here really so evil?"

"Not this argument again! He's killing people!"

Rivic nearly bit his tongue in snapping his mouth closed so fast. She had a point. "But why is he doing it? Why?"

"Because the people of the tribes get too powerful and he fears them overthrowing him."

"But why?"

"He's hungry for power."

"Nay, he's not. A man who has his fill is not hungry. He has rulership of Gohaldinest, the people are subjugated, and he is more powerful than an entire tribe. There is nothing for him to fear. Nor does he worry about imaginary outcomes. He plans how he wants things to be."

Alityka's mouth kept moving as she went to interrupt each sentence, but in realizing he was right, she stopped each time.

"Have you ever seen him not be confident?" Rivic asked. "He may have Necroathelings around him to guard him, but is there anything that would make you think that he needs them? Is he less magical or incapable?"

"Nay," she answered weakly.

"So, what makes you think there is anything you can do, right now, to defeat him?"

Tears gathered in her eyes. "What am I to do? He's tearing my world apart."

"Is he, Ali? Is he really? Or are you just telling yourself that so that you can empathize with all those around you whose lives he has injured?"

"How can you of all people ask me that? Your sister--"

"Is a victim. What I realized is that I can't fix or guard Nyree. She has to accept responsibility for herself. She kept trying to tell me this, but I felt as if I had to heal her. Instead, she wounded me to keep me away. Do you not see that Cirvel is doing the same thing?"

"Nay, I don't see it."

"You're asking yourself the wrong question. You need to

be asking why he does what he does. If he is more powerful than a tribe himself, why does he attack the tribes? Why does he have an army of Necroathelings? Why does he want more? Why does he train people to use their magic only to keep the levels of the tribes down? What is driving him? What would make him go to these lengths? We both know he's not insane. He's too clever and calculating."

"Stop!" Alityka wiped the tears from her face. "I can't listen to this."

He dropped his hand on her arm as she moved to get up and move away. "Aye, you can. You need to hear this. Because if he's protecting something on this world that we don't know about, how do we endanger that if we try to overthrow Cirvel? We have to know what we're doing."

"What exactly does that mean?"

"It means we can't put ourselves against Cirvel. The only way we find out his motives are if we prove we want to fight with him. Lihn once told me that it didn't matter how we win, only that we succeed."

A spike of silence came down between them. He remained steadfast in his decision to not do something that wasn't his own natural inclination. Then she snorted and flung her hand in the air. At her dismissive, twirling wave, the magic bubble around them collapsed. Alityka's gaze shot daggers at him before she turned and walked away.

He slammed his hand flat down on the table as he collapsed into the chair where Alityka had been sitting and put a fist against his mouth, wishing he could scream. For a moment, he glared around the room, taking in the other acolytes entrenched in their studies and a dominus hunting through the rows of books. He watched someone drop their books on a refiling cart and leave. A small story took up in his mind that the acolyte was pursuing Alityka. Maybe in believing what he should be doing, his mind invented scenarios from innocent happenings.

As the rage seeped away and his emotions leveled, Rivic reached for the book Alityka had been reading. Curiosity took over and he opened it up. It took him a few pages before he realized that it was about the truths and myths of the gaxlors. He closed it and looked at the spine, then opened it again, listening as the bindings cracked. Not only was this a book that only Necroathelings should have access to, but no one had spent much time reading it. He wished he knew how far into it that Alityka had been.

One thing for certain, Alityka now had perilous knowledge, and she was desperate enough to use it.

CHAPTER 7

*T*he next few days felt awkward and unsettled as the rainy season refused to give up its grasp. The sun tried to come out from behind thick gray clouds, but found itself continuously rehidden behind dark rainstorms, punctuated by jagged flashes of light and deep rumbling that rolled in threatening waves right over the castle.

The thunderstorm made the evenings turn to night early. After dinner, raindrops fell as Rivic practiced with the other domini on the training grounds. The weapons master lit torches around the arena, but the rain-doused flames combined with the light coming from the castle windows did little to light the area where they battled. Only when lightning spun out from the clouds did the area brighten enough to see, and only for a moment.

The padding beneath Rivic's armor quickly dampened in the storm and started to chafe. The pressing of boots into the slick grass brought mud to the surface, mixing the ground to a slushy brew. The churned earth splattered against them. Rivic kept cleaning slimy clumps from his face and armor.

He swore Weapons Master Glayth kept them out here longer to temper and test their endurance.

Returning to the castle tired, wet, and muddy, Rivic noticed a Necroatheling waiting at the door. Their eyes locked and Rivic quickly glanced away as if pretending not to notice the dark shadow of the man standing his purple cloak. He tried to hurry by with the other domini.

No such luck.

The Necroatheling placed his hand on Rivic's shoulder. "Knight Captain, you are requested to fetch the acolyte, Alityka, and tell her to attend Cirvel presently."

Rivic's tunic itched and the moist padding didn't help. He thought about refusing the Necroatheling, saying that he needed to change first, but if he only needed to get Alityka then changing could wait for a little while longer. Better wet than to protest against a Necroatheling.

The Necroatheling's grip didn't loosen. It held and caught Rivic's attention so firmly that he turned and glanced up at the face beneath the hood. A hard, serious look preceded the remainder of the Necroatheling's instructions. "Then you are to escort the remainder of the acolytes in her dormitory to the amphitheater."

"'Tis night. Why drag them out so late?" Rivic asked. "Besides, I'm wet. I shall go after I've dried from the storm."

Magic sizzled through him and it took a moment for Rivic to realize that he was now dry. "Lord Cirvel's present mood is not one to be questioned or tested. His humor is short. He does dislike taking retribution."

"Who is being punished? Is it Alityka?"

The Necroatheling's head jerked up. He gave a quick look around, then gazed back down at Rivic. "I suggest you be quick." Then he vanished in a swirl of purple.

Rivic bolted for the tower. Only once he reached the

stairs did he stop to calm his breathing and his emotions. He couldn't go in there all flustered.

He opened the door to the dormitory and strode in as if he belonged there. A short while ago, he had. It felt natural to return here now.

He hoped Alityka was here.

Rivic saw her braiding her hair by candlelight as she prepared for bed. She didn't look up, but the other acolytes did, some even lifting their heads off their pillows to follow his movement through the dormitory. Ignoring the awkward stares, Rivic strode across the dormitory while refusing to peer at the location of his former bed. He really didn't want to know if Cirvel had already filled it or not.

"I'm tired and I just want to get some sleep," she said, her fingers still working at her braid as she stared at his reflection in the mirror.

"I don't desire to fight with you. I never meant to get into an argument," Rivic said.

"Aw, lover's spat," said an acolyte nearby.

Rivic's glare forced the boy to look quickly away, then to hide under his covers. Rivic knelt beside Alityka's chair, his hand on the wood for support. He opened his mouth to start to tell her that Cirvel was angry and wanted to see her, but a series of bells began to ring out.

Alityka's fingers dropped from her hair, the braid unraveling, as she listened. Her eyes widened. "You're here because of that, aren't you?"

Several of the acolytes cowered under their blankets. Those who remained unhidden stared with wide, blank eyes as if fear had whisked their spirits away to mental refuge.

"I was sent to tell you that Cirvel requested your presence. Don't let him punish you --"

The wooden chair creaked under her adjusting weight. "Shh!" Alityka stood, rising right beside Rivic. A panicked ripple of heat came off her as he heard her quickening heart-beat. She gulped a supply of air. "Everyone settle," Alityka shouted. She quickly began to count all those present.

Bells continued to chime.

Alityka's hands shook as she looked back down at Rivic. "Me? Cirvel sent for me?"

Rivic nodded. "And I am to take the rest of the acolytes down to the amphitheater."

"Not surprising," she mustered. "Do you know anything else about why we are being gathered?"

"Nay, though the Necroatheling who sent me spoke of retribution."

"Are they coming for you?" one girl asked. Rivic recognized her as the person who had handed him the cool cloth after his shameful battle with Kalt-na.

"Nay," Alityka said, but Rivic could tell she forced bravery into her voice. He also realized that she hadn't told a lie: they, presumably the Necroathelings, weren't coming to get her; she had been told to go to Cirvel. "'Tis none of us. Everyone stand up, dress quickly."

"Alityka, what's going on?" he asked.

She responded by pushing him aside. "I'm pretty sure the Knight Captain should be getting his charges ready to go."

Once again, she subtly reminded him that he had no idea of what really happened in Gohaldinest.

Though the acolytes remained where they were standing, they all looked around nervously. Only Rivic kept watching Alityka, wondering what exactly was going on.

The bells started to quiet.

Alityka glanced around the room. "Kelvja," she said, stepping toward the center of the room, "I must go report to Lord Cirvel. Make sure everyone is ready to follow the Knight Captain down when the single bell chimes in a few moments."

"Ali?" a frightened voice came from the crowd.

"Please, Kelvja, do it. You can handle it." Alityka's voice sounded hesitantly frightened and Rivic noticed her trying not to curl her hands at her sides.

"I will take care of them," Rivic said to her.

She gave him a short, disbelieving glance. Realizing that everyone in the dormitory watched her, she tried to smile. "'Tis not one of us. We are all here. I am head of the dormitory and that is why I am being called." Her gaze once again sought out Rivic and he noticed the shadow of fear within them. Then, without meeting anyone's eyes, she strode to the door and vanished from the room.

It felt as if everyone now turned to Rivic, and he had no idea of what to do.

Kelvja stepped up on her bed so that she stood taller than most of the acolytes. "Get ready to head out. The night is probably cold and the ground wet from the storms. We do not know if we will be outside for a while, so be prepared."

The acolytes began to move around as directed. As everyone neared being ready to leave, Rivic wished for the single chime Alityka had mentioned to ring out so they could be on their way. Instead, it remained silent.

"Let's just take a seat and give it a moment," he said finally.

The acolytes seemed to drop where they stood, some of them landing on the floor.

It felt like they were waiting for an awfully long time. Many of the acolytes were yawning, but no one wanted to crawl into bed when they feared that they would just be getting up right away.

He wished he could ask one of them what this was all about and what was going on, but he knew that as the oldest in the room without Alityka there, and being a dominus, he had to appear more knowledgeable and ready to handle whatever was coming.

He began to fear that he had missed the chime in the noise of everyone getting ready. Certainly, with his noviho-midrak senses, he would have heard it.

Rivic wanted to pace, but he knew that he'd just be increasing the tension of the others. Instead, he started a game of magic. He would say a spell and let the others answer as to what it did. He found that he quickly had to go to intermediate magic, and soon had many of them giggling and laughing.

He tried to smile as one boy answered, "It makes a pig snot all over the place as it's snorting." The boy even included sound effects of spitfire going everywhere, which had a few of the girls groaning in disgust, but many still giggled anyway. But every time Rivic felt the grin pulling at the corner of his lips, he felt nerves coiled tighter in his stomach and he remembered why he was here with all the other acolytes.

Then the belt tolled.

Fear replaced the momentary joy at staying up late playing games. Silence overtook mirth in the room as everyone listened to the bell's receding din.

"Let's go." Rivic ushered them all toward the door.

One girl lingered behind, tears running down her cheeks. Rivic suspected she knew what was about to happen. "I'm scared," she told him. Can I hold your hand?"

Rivic knew that providing her comfort might also give him strength enough to get through this; he would have courage for both of them. He nodded and held his hand out for hers. Her fingers slid against his palm. For just a moment, it reminded him of the many times that he and Nyree had taken each other's hands for support. He quickly blinked back invading tears as he walked with the girl down the stairs and out to the courtyard.

Necroathelings directed the acolytes from the different dormitories in the direction that they were to go. They were not in the courtyard long before they were ushered inside a section of the castle which Rivic knew well. But instead of going up to Cirvel's chambers as he normally did, Rivic and the acolytes were guided downstairs. Briefly, Rivic thought the Necroathelings might be steering the flood of people to the chamber that led to The Playground, the last place he wanted to be with all the acolytes. He felt himself walk through a curtain of magic and knew he'd been teleported somewhere. It wasn't The Playground, but it was somewhere very similar.

With awareness, Rivic realized that the last time he'd been in these halls, Cirvel had brought him here with magic; he hadn't come on foot then. He'd stood in a comparable hallway as he'd waited to become a dominus, but this entrance was different. The girl at his side seemed to know the way.

Walking out onto a large platform, Rivic now had a sweeping view of the amphitheater from above. Rows of bench seats staggered along the slope downward to the arena below where Rivic had become a dominus. Feeling the presence of magic, Rivic glanced to his right and saw a balcony seat surrounded by a waist-high wall. Two Necroathelings were currently inside making preparations around a large, rather ornate chair which Rivic could easily picture Cirvel sitting in.

The line kept moving ahead of Rivic. Across the way, he noticed other domini leading in acolytes as if they had all been sent to gather their former dormitories and escort them here. Necroathelings guided the students onto the rows of seats.

Rivic looked around for Alityka, hoping to locate her. How would he pinpoint her among this mass of people?

As he was about to sit down, Rivic heard Alityka call out his name. She waved, then came racing down the stairs, forcing her way past the acolytes to get to him. Cutting into the line, she gave a quick smile to the acolyte she forced back.

Alityka sat down as Rivic did. He saw her eyes were red and swollen before she glanced away from him. She pretended to take care in adjusting her position on the bench to avoid looking at him.

"What's wrong?" he asked.

Distress overwhelmed her, making her unable to speak.

"What's happening?" he asked again, grabbing onto her wrist.

Her tear-filled eyes raised to meet his. "Cirvel said someone was caught outside, probably trying to run away. Azote is demanding a sacrifice."

"I don't understand," he whispered.

"Every cycle, Azote rounds up several children to bring here for training. He does that just to increase their magical ability."

"Fattening them up?"

Upset wrinkled her face, a tear escaping and running down her cheek. "In a manner. Cirvel…" Alityka shook her head. "…he sends the weaker ones to Azote as a sacrifice. Many of those chosen to come here by Azote fear their fate, so many times they try to run. They are always caught."

"And then…" he muttered, knowing he had to drag the words out of her even though he knew he didn't really want to hear it.

"They bring the acolyte here as a show, to demonstrate what happens to maeges who try to cross Cirvel or escape." She wiped some fresh tears from her eyes. "I've been trying to stop them for the last couple of cycles. I thought I could keep the acolytes from running this time. I was supposed to protect them. We were so close to making it through the season without any sacrifices. This is all my fault."

"Your fault?"

"Sempt did not run."

"You know him, the one they are sacrificing?"

She nodded, pain overtaking her so she temporarily couldn't speak. With an unsettled breath, she loosened her throat enough to answer. "He was part of my tribe before we had to split." Alityka leaned closer to Rivic and her voice dropped even lower, a whisper hidden in the low fearful buzz of people asking questions around them. "Azote brought him here two cycles ago."

"So, Azote had already chosen him for a sacrifice? He had to be scared."

Alityka's gaze met his, her face now filled with hardened strength. "Sempt knows what I am. He trusted me to protect him. We had proven his worth to Cirvel. He had no reason to fear."

"Then why do you believe this to be your fault?"

"'Tis my error. Cirvel chose this boy on purpose to send me a message."

Alityka's thoughts became clear to him. "You think this is your punishment for going outside of Gohaldinest?"

She said nothing, but her eyes held the confirmation, especially as she turned them away from him as if hiding in shame.

A Necroatheling appeared in the center of the arena. His hands clasped tightly on the shoulders of a sobbing teen kneeling before him. The crowd around the arena fell silent.

"Lord Cirvel," the Necroatheling shouted, "this boy has been caught trying to flee from Gohaldinest."

Rivic glanced around to see that Cirvel now sat in the boxed balcony seat, Lihn at his side. Cirvel rose and approached the surrounding wall. "Why would anyone wish to take flight from our fair city? After what wonders you have seen here, why would you wish to go? My lad, what claim do you have?"

Rivic trembled, remembering telling Cirvel that he had no wish to remain in Gohaldinest beyond the season. The echo of not leaving insinuated how much this message was for him too.

Sempt tried to utter something, but he shivered too hard to speak.

"We've got to do something. What can we do?" Rivic whispered to Alityka.

She merely shook her head. "We can't defeat Azote."

Rivic barely heard her over Cirvel's voice ringing out, "Feed him to the gaxlor."

A muffled sob sounded from nearby. Alityka glanced down the row, then reached around a boy who sat between her and the one who had cried out.

Only now did Rivic realize that the little girl he'd come down from the dormitory with had become separated from him and sat on the other side of the boy.

"Rsysci, come sit behind me," Alityka called. "Come on. Hurry. Paesun, move over. Let Rsysci in. You can come down here to her spot if you want more room."

The acolytes on the bench behind them shuffled so that the girl could sit behind Alityka. "Rsysci, don't watch. Here, braid my hair." Alityka reached up and loosened her hair from the leather tie, which she handed to the girl. "Do not look, all right? None of you should witness this," she said around to the children. "Keep your eyes on the back of the person in front of you, understand? Don't watch."

Rsysci nodded, then reached out for Alityka's red-gold hair as Alityka turned forward again.

Dread filled Rivic as a demon flew down from above and landed on the compact clay floor of the arena.

"Sempt wouldn't run," Alityka muttered as if reaffirming what she already knew in her heart and giving Rivic a side-long glance.

"You don't have to watch this either," he told her. "Put your head against my arm and don't look."

"I have to. For Sempt and his family. I have to let this make me really angry so that I remember it for a long time."

"Nay, you don't."

Azote took a bow-legged step toward Sempt.

"Aye, I do," Alityka protested. "Just as you watched your punishment as the Necroatheling defiled your sister, I must bear this. I chose to go outside the walls of Gohaldinest. This should be me facing Azote. But Cirvel rarely gives his punishments directly."

Contrary to what Alityka claimed about Sempt not being a run-away, the lanky teen in the arena stepped backwards from the approaching gaxlor. He seemed to be very afraid and wanting only to flee. Sempt cast a spell, but it didn't even touch Azote. Sempt tried another. The gaxlor laughed.

Rivic watched, feeling utterly helpless. He couldn't sit here and be idle. The hairs at the base of his neck rose and he felt his lips twitch as if responding to the teeth that wanted to appear. He made to rise.

Alityka grabbed his arm. "Don't. There's naught to do, 'tis not anything even you can do. You'll only make this worse."

"But, Ali, he should punish us if that's what this is, not the people around us."

"Be still. You'll only end up getting hurt or dead."

Everyone trembled around Rivic and he wanted to snarl at their fear. His hands curled. The claws he knew that were just beneath the surface wanted to come out and tear into someone just as easily as they had the fish in the lake. How could he sit here and do nothing when he had these abilities, when he was an instrument of destruction?

Rivic had to know. "Do you really think Cirvel would do this just because you were outside of Gohaldinest?"

"Aye," Alityka answered.

Azote reached Sempt. The gaxlor took the boy, who shrieked in terror.

"Then I can't let him do this. I have to stop it." Rivic started to rise, but Alityka fastened her grip tighter around his arm. He thought about shaking her off, but he realized someone else also had a hold of him. Pressing his face against Rivic's forearm, the boy on Rivic's other side clung to his hand.

Sempt hollered, his words – half magical, all terror – made no sense.

A crunch rent the air. Bones snapped.

Sempt howled, his face red and contorting, eyes bulging with panic.

The boy slapped his hands over his ears, forgetting that he still held onto Rivic so that the back of Rivic's hand pressed against the boy's head. Alityka rasped as tears slid down her cheeks. She pressed her fingers to her lips as she rocked back and forth, but she did not look away.

The scream stopped with the collective gasp of the audience filling the void.

Azote dropped the body to the clay floor before stepping away and spreading his wings for flight. The crumpled and bloody mass remaining behind no longer resembled a boy.

"Do you still feel," Alityka asked Rivic in a whisper, "that what Cirvel does here is not evil?"

CHAPTER 8

*R*acing through the people-flooded hallway, Rivic had his target set on the black cloak ahead of him. While Cirvel traveled leisurely through the corridor surrounded by his Necroatheling's, Rivic shoved with utter determination through the stunned crowd leaving the small arena. He pushed aside a Necroatheling, partially ducking under an arm, and came up in front of Cirvel.

Rivic gave a bow, quickly showing that he was paying reverence to Cirvel and not attacking, before the Necroathelings decided to strike. "Lord Cirvel, may I have a moment of your time?"

"Certainly, Knight Captain." Cirvel gave a dismissive wave of his Necroathelings and motioned for Rivic to enter a nearby room.

Rivic felt the magic drop around him as soon as he passed through the entrance. He suspected they were no longer on the same floor with the Necroathelings outside the door, but he couldn't confirm it before Cirvel closed the door.

"Something troubling you, my dear Knight Captain?" Cirvel strode through the room with the utmost confidence, as though he hadn't just witnessed a savage execution. Did the sight of brutal death no longer phase the Lord of Gohaldinest? "I'm certain that due to your haste, whatever you must need to tell me is of the utmost importance."

Rivic felt his lips tighten with the question he needed to ask. He had to have the answer. "Did you kill Sempt because Alityka was outside of Gohaldinest?"

Cirvel gave a slow nod before he spoke. "I am sorry that the sacrifices to Azote are so disturbing, but acolytes must know the penalties for leaving. Had the boy tried to make it down the mountain, he would have surely frozen to death before long."

"That doesn't answer my question though. Did you sacrifice Sempt to Azote as a lesson to me and Alityka?"

"You and Alityka?"

Rivic's breath caught at the mistake he'd made. "Aye. If you had trust in me, you wouldn't have sent the gargax out. Since the beast could never give you a report of what it saw, you are uncertain of what we were doing. You felt it was taking me longer than it should to return her to Gohaldinest. But did you punish that boy because of our actions?"

"Should you choose to vilify me of such a crime, how am I to deny such accusations? Words alone cannot sway what you obviously believe me capable of doing, but I suggest you not start seeing demons in every shadow. Such an action can make you too fearful to walk even in the daylight. Besides, the sacrifices are meant to be a warning, so if you and Alityka choose to take it as such, then it has served its purpose, as distressing as it may be."

While it wasn't a straight answer, it was no denial either. Yet Cirvel's face held a curious expression which Rivic couldn't decipher.

"Is that all, Knight Captain?" Cirvel asked with irritation

hitching into his voice. He placed a hand to his side and grimaced.

Rivic realized he had overstepped his bounds in questioning Lord Cirvel. He knew he needed to make amends and fast. "My deepest apologies, Lord Cirvel. As an intermediary between the acolytes and your Necroathelings, who have a tendency to be overly harsh when your mercy is not available, I wanted your reasons behind this display. How else will I adequately warn others of what they should be doing if I do not understand what is fully expected? Please know that Alityka had full knowledge of what was happening when the bells started ringing, but I did not. This is the first of the sacrifices to Azote that I have seen. I realize you take the safety of everyone here very seriously; you have our best interests at heart, but you expect no challengers. I say that only out of respect."

Cirvel's other hand came to his side and his jaw tightened as he spoke. "Along with the adequate dose of fear that I see in your eyes."

Rivic nodded, acknowledging the truth of Cirvel's words. "Reverence, Lord Cirvel. You have my devotion." As Cirvel leaned to the side, his gaze darting away, Rivic realized there was more going on here. "Are you in pain, my lord?"

"An old injury acts up tonight." He started to hobble away. "If you were quite through bowing and scraping, 'tis late and I have other matters to attend before I shall sleep tonight. I suggest you take to your bed, for the morning and your training will come far too soon."

Cirvel began working up magic in his hands, but he held onto it while he pivoted away from Rivic. "I find it interesting that I was not compelled to answer the questions you put forth to me."

Rivic realized that Cirvel was referring to the abilities of a Dominari. Had Cirvel placed a lie in his words as a further test of Rivic's claim to being a champion for the unicorns. Having no idea what to say, Rivic decided it might be best to remain silent.

Keeping his gaze dropped shamefully toward the floor lest Cirvel read the truth in his eyes, Rivic started for the door, but soon realized Cirvel had already vanished. When Rivic stepped out into the hallway, he was indeed on a different level of the castle and alone.

Rivic moved back inside, knowing that he didn't have anywhere to be and this vacant chamber would give him a moment of peace. He pulled the door mostly closed behind him and walked to the far side of the room. Moonlight streamed through the window, shining off his red and gold armor. He put his head into his hands.

What had made him remain in Gohaldinest? Why had he let Nyree talk him into staying rather than returning to the tribe? That was where he wanted to be. Not here.

The sound of a footstep in the hallway made him turn. He didn't see anyone through the space between the doorway and the frame. Surely Cirvel wouldn't have come back.

Casting a light spell, he magically pushed the door open a little wider.

Still nothing.

But Rivic could hear a faint heartbeat just a little stronger now. Someone definitely stood in the hallway.

He moved toward the door.

As his eyes adjusted to the moonlight filtering through the room and dropping into the darkness of the hallway beyond, Rivic began to make out a dark cloak.

A Necroatheling watched him.

Rivic shuddered. *Not tonight*, he thought, knowing he couldn't take a trip to The Playground now. His emotions were far too raw for that.

The Necroatheling turned to face him just a little more,

lifting his head and letting a bit more of the light beneath his dark purple hood. Rivic's heart stopped, plunged, then thundered with wrath.

Kalt.

The Necroatheling swiveled and walked away.

Had he actually seen Kalt? Rivic's chest constricted tightly around his heart and lungs. Maybe it had been a trick of the light and shadows.

He had to know.

Rivic slid out of the room and ran after the Necroatheling.

A flap of a dark plum colored cloak whipping around the corner was the only sign that the Necroatheling hadn't just disappeared. Rivic kept running, taking the stairs up two at a time. At the top, he looked both directions and only the smell of spent magic told him which way he needed to go. He headed right down the hall.

A door creaked.

Rivic barged through, slamming it completely back against the wall on its hinges. The Necroatheling stood at the window but did not turn as Rivic entered.

Rivic drew his sword. "Kalt, is that you?"

"'Tis I."

That was all Rivic needed to hear as he rushed for the Necroatheling.

Kalt raised his hand and magic went up around him. Rivic stopped, sliding on the stone to keep from hitting the magical barrier.

"What are you doing back? I thought you were trapped."

Kalt turned from the window and lowered his hood. Coils of red ran beneath his skin as if someone had branded him with searing heat. "I was. But with your sister gone, Cirvel has found another use for me."

Rivic hardened the feelings that threatened to invade his

chest. He would not feel sorry for this man who deserved every punishment he received, even though the scars on Kalt's face looked horribly painful.

Kalt didn't seem surprised that Rivic didn't respond. "Please put your weapon away. 'Twill not do you any good here, against me, not until you become a Necroatheling."

Rivic held onto the sword for a moment longer, then thrust it back into the scabbard. He barely let his gaze drop from Kalt as he did so. "What use did Cirvel have for you?"

"It doesn't matter." Kalt shook his head and dropped the magic from around him.

A moment later, a second spell encompassed both of them, but rather than a shield, this felt more like a bubble to hide their noise from outsiders. Rivic bent his knees and curled his fingers into fists preparing for Kalt's attack.

Kalt raised a hand. There were signs of the same angry red, coiling scars on his hand and wrist as well. "I mean you no harm. In fact, I owe both you and your sister and 'tis because of that debt that I am here now, why I lured you away to this room." He leaned back against the wall as if he were too tired to stand. "I've known Aliytka since she first was called as a Dominari. In fact, I was there."

"Were you part of her tribe?"

Kalt shook his head. "Our tribes traded goods. We grew crops, while they were more hunters and foragers. We got dried meats and goods from them, while we provided beans, corn, and things like that. But Alityka and I played together, along with a whole bunch of other kids, when the adults got together to do their trading. I had just found out that I was heading to Gohaldinest to train with Cirvel and pretty upset about it. She was only eight cycles and here I, a scared teenager, was crying on her shoulder."

"Don't really care about your story," Rivic said, shaking his head and putting his hand on the hilt of his sword.

"Right, but 'tis important, I promise you. She told me she had a plan for taking down Cirvel, but that she would need people in place that were close to him."

"So, you agreed?" When Kalt nodded, Rivic scoffed and added, "Following the plan of a girl eight cycles old? You're a smart one, aren't you?" Yet even as he said it, he thought that Alityka had also played him, saying that she needed people who were willing to get close to Cirvel to aid in his downfall. Did it matter that she was several cycles older now or was it still a folly?

"Fine," Rivic spat, "you're helping Alityka."

"You're the one that wanted me to keep it short. If you had witnessed what I had, you might feel differently." Kalt paused, raising his eyebrows as if emphasizing that he had no intention of telling Rivic now. The action pulled on the skin around the scars on his face and he winced as if they were still tender. "She told me that she needed help to defeat Azote. She's onto something. She can do this. With Azote gone, Cirvel loses a large part of his protections."

"Do you believe she can bring down Cirvel too?"

"Nay, not by herself. She might be capable of handling Azote. But Cirvel is too strong and I don't even want him acknowledging her. She's better remaining unseen."

Rivic wanted to tell Kalt that Cirvel had already taken notice, but thought that Kalt might not be able to take an emotional wound along with all the physical ones that currently covered him. "You've been letting Cirvel think that she is weak and not capable of advancing."

"I have to. You know what Necroathelings are capable of doing. If she progressed toward that, the unicorns would have no choice but to break their bonding with her. That alone would make her into a monster, but if she were a Necroatheling at that moment, she would be capable of horrible destruction. Do you really want any of that for her? Do you want to drive her to either of those extremes?"

"Nay." Seeing the situation in the way that Kalt framed it, Rivic knew he'd been right to stop that night with the unicorns. What would have happened if he hadn't gotten to her in time? Was that why Cirvel had sent him? Did the Lord of Gohaldinest also not want her to break the bonding until a moment of his choosing?

"You understand." Kalt nodded. "Then your duty is the same as mine: safeguard Alityka's status at all costs."

When the Necroatheling said nothing further, Rivic pointed toward Kalt's head and asked, "What happened to you?"

Kalt raised his arm up slightly as if reaching for his face before realizing what he was doing and stopped. He flipped his hood up while turning away, hiding the scars beneath the material. "You neither care, nor does it help what has been done to your sister, so it matters not. If you want to help Alityka, make sure she doesn't do anything foolish. I can't watch her and keep her out of Cirvel's sights like I once did."

Rivic noticed the cloaked meaning beneath Kalt's words; the Necroatheling had been responsible for keeping Alityka from advancing. He figured that Alityka wouldn't thank Kalt for it, not considering how frustrated she'd been with her situation.

Kalt glanced briefly at Rivic, then began walking with his shoulders slumped forward. Something had happened to the Necroatheling. Rivic wanted to say something more, but he really didn't know what. The last thing he wanted was to offer comfort to Kalt.

Stopping at the doorway and placing a lingering hand on the jamb, Kalt said back over his shoulder, "If you don't stop her, Ali will do something foolish." Then he continued on.

When Rivic felt like following, he found the hallway

empty except for a trace of magic. He paced the corridors of the castle, trying to process the information Kalt had given him and how exactly he would deal with it. There was always the possibility that Kalt had lied to him.

But Kalt had also given him a warning.

Alityka. She was going to do something dangerous.

CHAPTER 9

"Good job, Dragzel," Lihn said down at the cahaster as she opened the door further for Rivic and Alityka to enter.

The cahaster smiled up at Lihn as he sauntered by her, rubbing against her leg like an enthusiastic cat. Then he darted into the room and leapt gracefully into a chair sitting at an angle to the table. Several books sat open as if Lihn had been busy studying and abandoned everything to receive her guests.

Alityka and Rivic waited while Lihn locked the door behind them. Rivic used the moment to study where he was. He already didn't remember most of the trip here. After Dragzel had caught up to Rivic and ordered him to follow, they ventured into a part of the castle Rivic hadn't explored. The crevices and cracks in the gray stone wall oozed with an abundance of residual magic. Like he'd experienced so often before, the tendrils reached for him, but these were different, thicker, stronger, arcane. Fighting to ignore them made his head spin until he was so woozy he thought he might pass out.

They had caught up to Alityka along the way. When she had finally knocked on the wooden door, the sound reflected the door's thick, but time-dried nature.

Now, they stood in a hexagonal-shaped library where the multiple wall sconces did little to chase away the darkness. It felt like a water well. Magic pooled in the surrounding stone walls, locked in by the books, shelves, and cupboards, until the oppressive stagnation filled the hollow room like a hand inside a glove.

Smiling briefly at Rivic, Lihn started to lead the way back to the table. "I'm glad Dragzel caught up to you."

Rivic tried to utter some sort of acknowledgement, but the syrupy feel of this ancient library reminded him way too much of being locked in the room with the Shant'olin. If they appeared here now, it wouldn't have surprised him. Maybe he was being overly sensitive.

Alityka joined Lihn at the table, but Rivic found himself unable to sit so easily. Instead, he roamed this new surrounding and hoped he could solve why he felt so unsettled. Three nights had passed since the encounter with Kalt, and in that time not a single Necroatheling had chosen him to go to The Playground. He'd found himself with way too much time to reflect. While his mind had gone over so many things, he had yet to determine how he'd inform Alityka and Lihn about his encounter with the Shant'olin. For now, it was far easier to explore this library, even if lingering ghosts of magic loomed over his shoulder.

Most of the books on the shelves were covered with a thick layer of dust, but some had recently been pulled off and cleaned for use. Along with the bookshelves, there were also two small cabinets hanging on the wall. Between them drooped a gloomy painting of a city weathering a terrible storm. Looking at the lopsided artwork brought a depressed feeling to Rivic. This room already had a dark gray feel to it as if it were shrouded in smoke, and the painting enhanced that mood as if the repressive sentiment came right from the composition itself.

"I thought it might be a little safer to meet here," Lihn said.

Feeling drawn to investigate deeper than merely the surface of the room, Rivic opened a cabinet and found several empty bowls and flasks inside. "What makes this place safer?"

"This is where I get to work. I am allowed to practice all sorts of magicks here, though Cirvel is often with me."

"He comes here with you?"

"Aye. I am rarely ever alone in here without him, but I often wonder how much he pays attention to me. He is usually reading. He's gone through every book several times."

"How?" Rivic asked, looking once again at the dust coating the books. "They're all filthy. They don't look like they've been handled in cycles."

"Cirvel has only to touch the spine of a book to read its contents."

"But I've seen him reading books, carrying them open in one hand and flipping the pages while he walks," Rivic protested.

"He reads both ways. It depends on how quickly he wants to take in the information," Lihn responded with a knowing smile.

As Rivic re-examined the shelves, he saw that several books had a fingerprint on the spine. "So, he is reading them with magic?"

"Aye."

"Is there anything in particular that he seems to reread?"

"Nay," Lihn said. ""I have not noted what he is reading. Every now and then he comments on an interesting fact he's come across. I've tried reading some of the books here, sometimes because our classes call for certain passages and Cirvel tells me the best place to look, or I've seen it in other books during my reading, but there doesn't seem to be any reason for this library. The texts aren't special and contain no powerful magicks. Nothing dangerous or even spells warranting being segregated from the other library. In fact, Cirvel has told me that most of these books are duplicates of ones he has in his personal collection, so why he's reading them here is also beyond me."

"Because he's here to monitor you," Rivic said. Was it possible that Cirvel examined them in much the same way they studied him? Cirvel was not one to be ignorant of a situation and he always wanted the upper hand. "Why does Cirvel not know about us and our plots against him?"

"He probably does, but we hope he doesn't realize the truth about what we're doing. It puts our lives in jeopardy, but as long as he thinks we are furthering his plans, we are safe. 'Tis a slender tightrope that we must tread carefully."

"I don't understand. He doesn't like people challenging him. Why does he let us?"

Alityka broke her silence. "We three in this room have more magic than most. We're special. Considering that his own powers are choked, he might not be able to get through our natural shielding like he can others with lesser power."

"Choked?"

Lihn answered, "Cirvel's dragon mother spun this world off from the Wells of the Onesong."

"Dragon mother? You mean Cirvel is a novihomidrak?"

"You didn't know?"

Rivic shook his head. Up until now, it had only been a guess Rivic had surmised from Cirvel's power and arrogance. Sontre' had said that only one novihomidrak could injure another but had never verified that Cirvel was one. Now he had the confirmation.

"Was a novihomidrak," Alityka corrected. "He has gone evil. He is a Necronosti now."

"Necronosti?" Rivic asked.

"A novihomidrak that taps into the darkest magicks of chaos."

Lihn didn't look pleased at Alityka's answer. "He's still a novihomidrak," Lihn amended Alityka's words. "But aye, he has done something terrible to allow chaos to access his soul. I had always hoped that I could find some way to contain him, like a genie in a lamp."

Now he understood why Sontre' hadn't confirmed that Cirvel was a novihomidrak; he'd become something even more dangerous. "That's why you said we had to confine his magic. Is it even possible to defeat him?" Rivic thought of his time spent trapped within the painting and couldn't imagine a worse fate. Yet wasn't that exactly what Cirvel deserved.

Lihn answered, "Until you confessed to Alityka about being a novihomidrak in the forest, I didn't think it was probable. Now it is achievable."

But where Lihn saw a glimmer of hope, he saw a steep cliff of risk that he wasn't certain he wanted to walk off.

Lihn noticed his hesitation and continued, "His magic is powerful and different from any other I've experienced. There is human and dragon magic, but 'tis something else as well."

"Something else?" both Rivic and Alityka asked in near synchronicity.

"Like unicorn magic," she said. "Except 'tis not. I'm hoping 'tis a weakness we can exploit. Novihomidraks are supposed to be human. If he's got another type of magic naturally flowing through him, it's got to come from some- where. If we can figure it out --"

"I can't," Rivic burst, bringing Lihn to silence. "That

mysterious portion of his magic makes him too powerful for us."

"Are you going to do this again?" Alityka shouted, slamming her hand on the table. "This world is dying and people are being killed. Will you stand by and do nothing?"

"I don't see what else we can do!"

Lihn raised her hand toward Alityka as if requesting calmness. "We have some advantages. Everyone born on this planet has access to the Humline and a trickle from the Onesong. Not being native to this planet, Cirvel's connection to the Humline is not nearly as strong, and the knowing he should receive from the Onesong is gone. He is, for all intense purposes, blind.

"Wait! Cirvel isn't even from this world?"

"Relax, Rivic. 'Tis hard enough to explain this without your energy scattering in confusion." Lihn paused as if refocusing her thoughts. "Nay, Cirvel originally came through the Wells of the Onesong to help this world."

Rivic felt a chill come over him as instinct kicked in and allowed him to sense the purpose of novihomidraks. "He came here to help? What was his mission?"

Lihn shook her head. "I don't know. He won't talk about it, but I get the sense that he's still trying to succeed; it's like as long as he doesn't give up, he hasn't failed at it."

"Then there must be some clue as to what he's doing."

Lihn started a denial, but Alityka's face shifted as if unable to restrain her words to mere thoughts. Restless energy carried Alityka as she stood and went to a bookshelf. She seemed determined not to speak.

Finally, Lihn broke, "Cirvel is trying to control all magic in the world."

Rivic exhaled a long breath. "Why?"

"He believes those without magic are contemptable and those with scant ability as inconsequential."

The pain of watching Kalt-na hold Nyree against the wall renewed itself in Rivic's chest as if it were happening all over again. Cirvel had seen Nyree as worthless, as something he could damage and throw away for the purpose of punishing Rivic. He looked to Alityka. "Do you get this same feeling or something more? You have always been adamant about bringing Cirvel down. Do you know more of his plan?"

Rivic felt Lihn's hand touch his arm.

Alityka shrugged, never looking away from the spines of the books she currently stared at. Her noncommitment made Rivic return to Lihn with a questioning look.

Lihn gave him an awkward pat. "Alityka is in a strange position. As a bonded Dominari, she always wants to look for the best in people. She is completely veiled to his true purposes and has only his actions to judge him by. 'Tis why we both accepted the roles we had to here and why her fury gets so intense with him when he lets others carry out his orders, like Azote killing Sempt. She knows that Cirvel ordered it and she wants to hate him, but she is completely incapable of feeling that. 'Tis herself that she is frustrated with rather than him."

"'Tis also why I've been so angry with your refusal to step into your power and heal your connection to the Onesong. I feel as if you want to remain ignorant of his plans," Alityka said softly.

Suddenly feeling like a pawn that everyone wanted to exploit, he asked, "So because only a novihomidrak will be able to defeat him, I'm merely here because I'm the one capable of kil... hurting Cirvel. Has the Onesong developed this whole elaborate plan just to destroy this one man?"

"As long as he carries on with his current intentions, Lord Cirvel is an enemy to this world and to the Onesong itself."

"But how can we say that? We don't know what he's doing. He doesn't do anything without thinking it through."

Alityka snorted at his adamant words. "You sound like a Dominari."

"Maybe novihomidraks have the same flaw of only seeing the best in people," Rivic retorted, twisting in the chair toward Alityka. "Maybe that's what makes a champion, having compassion and seeing the gray where others only see black or white."

"Nothing good can be in the heart of a man who keeps others subjugated with terror and death," Alityka screamed back, her face red with irritation.

Lihn was calmer than the other two when she spoke. "Enough. We must work together. Rivic, 'tis my hope that once your connection to the Humline is restored, you will have the knowing we need."

Rivic wondered over Cirvel's severed connection to the Onesong. Did the Lord of Gohaldinest endure a detrimental struggle over the loss of that awareness? Could Cirvel's battle entail a stronger sense of bereavement which led to his cruelness? Understanding these answers might be the key Rivic needed to keep his heart from going wicked as it sometimes demanded, even as Cirvel seemed hungry to draw that malicious darkness from him. Was this a side-effect from the demise of a lost connection?

"Can you do anything to help him?" Rivic asked Lihn, while Alityka issued a growling scoff nearby.

"I cannot. Not with this world being spun off from the Onesong like a leaf broken from a tree on a twisted stem."

"But you said you could restore my connection."

"Your situation is different, and you are unique among novihomidraks."

"How so?"

Lihn adjusted her position on the chair, now leaning slightly across the table. "You remember about your life before the dragon took you. Alityka told me that you remember how destructive your magic was and about the tribes."

"I don't understand what that has to do with this."

A momentary flash of frustration moved over Lihn's face. "Novihomidraks do not remember their lives before they were taken by a dragon, and those that do often go insane. That is the first deviation you possess from other novihomidraks. The second is that the dragon took your connection to this world's Humline in hopes of hiding you until you grew into your power."

Rivic recalled the yellow thread being cut from him. "But Sontre' gave it to Nyree."

"True. Some of it. But all is not lost. What we have might be enough."

"Could it be that I recall my childhood because that thread was taken from me before I emerged from the pearl?"

"Could be. We don't understand enough about this. It was an experiment."

Alityka entered the conversation now, "There's also a good chance that if this world is ever restored to the Onesong, you will go crazy."

"Then why should I reinstate my connection? What makes you think I would even want to help while knowing that could be my fate?"

"Why did you have to say that?" Lihn snapped at Alityka. Turning back, she continued, "Rivic, 'tis unprecedented territory and there is not any evidence that such would happen. Rejoining this world to the Onesong might very well be impossible."

"But novihomidraks are champions of the Onesong, so we have to try, right?" Rivic got to his feet and pushed the chair to the table. Calmly, he let his hands slide along the top bar to rest at the span of the chair's back and he leaned with light pressure into it. "I have to assume that Cirvel plans to return this world to the Onesong. I might be better off to stick with my own kind on this."

As he started to walk out of the room, Dragzel raced around him and sat back on his haunches in front of the door.

"Out of the way, Dragzel," Rivic warned.

The cahaster slowly lowered his front feet to the ground and hissed. The scales along his back seemed to bristle. The sight of it was enough to stop Rivic. "If you walk out this door without even asking what Cirvel has done to his own novimather, then you betray every trust I have ever put into you."

Rivic turned to question Lihn, but she spoke before he did. "He keeps her chained in a cavern beneath Gohaldinest. The only times he releases her is when he needs her power, whether to give a show of strength, present a grand ceremony, or to eat a Necroatheling."

Rivic could scarcely imagine the thought. "Do the Necroathelings follow Cirvel so obediently that they would sacrifice themselves to fulfill his mission?"

Alityka started to answer, but Lihn held up her hand. "Motivations are always tricky, but when someone holds your reins, you will go where they wish. If you balk and refuse, a couple painful slaps will pretty much do the trick to overcome resistance or fear."

For all the double-speak others around him said, this one was the loudest and most clear: if he'd submitted before, he could have kept his sister from harm and off the dark path she currently walked. If he took the opportunity now, he might be able to save someone else from such a fate.

"But how do you know that his plan to help this world 'tis a bad one? Maybe he wants to reestablish his awareness of the Onesong to get a sense of the outcomes to guide his decisions."

"Have you not been paying attention to anything since you got to Gohaldinest?" Dragzel muttered as he slinked around Rivic back toward Lihn.

Lihn's mouth tightened as she started to shake her head. "The Humline tells me there are negative influences and it might not go as Cirvel intends, that we are better off to stop him entirely."

A larger picture was coming into view for Rivic. "But you're only getting a trickle of the whole flow yourself. Can you say that what you are perceiving is accurate?"

"Aye."

Everything inside Rivic said her answered carried the heavy bias of hope with it rather than the confidence of knowing. "Why does he keep you cloistered away, especially if you still aren't giving him the secrets of the Onesong?"

Lihn looked down at a foot she dragged along the floor. When she raised her gaze, she first looked to Alityka, then to him. She reached out to catch Dragzel as the cahaster jumped up to her lap.

Rivic started to understand. "This has to do with the spell that Alityka met with the unicorns about, 'tis what you sent Dragzel to tell me to stop her from doing."

Another glance shifted between Alityka and Lihn, ending with Alityka's eyes growing wide with fright. Lihn reached over and placed her hand on top of Alityka's. "I have to. 'Tis time he knew."

"But—"

"You didn't tell him directly in the forest, but you should have. Obviously, his connections to the Humline are still stronger than we thought." Lihn turned toward Rivic. "I am a unicorn."

Icy cold knowledge landed in Rivic along with the feeling that Lihn had been right; he should have known. He should have figured it out at least. Alityka had said she was fueling a spell on Lihn. She had said that Lihn's true name was Tarylihn and that the unicorns would take care of their sister by backing the enchantment from that moment on.

Rivic turned away, needing a moment in his own thoughts. Or at least the one that kept screaming at him: if Cirvel found out Lihn was a unicorn, her life would be in peril. He knew it wouldn't be good for Cirvel to discover the truth about any of them, but suddenly Lihn seemed to have the most to lose, though he wasn't quite certain why or how he knew this. That wasn't quite true; it was the connection that Lihn spoke about.

"So, the reason we have impunity is because he can't sense us through the Onesong and you believe that because he doesn't realize that you're a unicorn, that I am safe?"

"There's more than that. A lot is going into suppressing my magic. We knew that for me to intrigue him, he'd have to sense something special about my magic, but we couldn't have him being threatened by it."

"Or discovering the truth about what Lihn is," Alityka added. "You realize what danger that would put her in, don't you?"

Rivic nodded but added nothing else. It let them fall into silence which seemed to end their conversation with a mute agreement that Lihn's secret would be kept.

"Don't end there," Dragzel said. When Rivic looked back, he expected to see the cahaster talking to him, but Dragzel had spoken to Lihn. "'Tis time everything is out. I stopped him from walking out the door, but now you need to make him understand."

The room became so quiet that Rivic could hear his own agitated breathing. Lihn and Alityka remained silent. Rivic glanced down to see Dragzel staring at him, the ridge above one of the cahaster's eye slightly higher than the other. Rivic wanted to ask why the cahaster inspected him thusly, but he realized that it didn't matter.

"Why do I have this link if the Humline was cut out from me?" Rivic asked. Lihn had said she could restore his link. Was he ready? Did he dare to hope that it might work? Would it be the edge he needed to quit following Cirvel's dominating footsteps?

"When we decided to try cutting the Humline from you, we didn't know how it works or what exactly would happen," Lihn confessed. "We only knew that we had to take a chance and we wouldn't know the result until you returned to me to repair it."

"We?" Rivic really doubted that Lihn was talking about her and Alityka. He suddenly had the feeling that there was someone else. "How do you even know all this about novihomidraks?"

"Because when the dragon took you, I was on my way to you." Now it was Lihn's turn to spare Alityka a quick glance. "Well, I didn't know it was you, per say, until you told Alityka you were a novihomidrak. Back then, I was going to take the source of the energy I was feeling somewhere safe and make you a Dominari when you were older, but I was too late. I encountered your novimather just after she had taken you. This is when I learned of Salvarae's plan. I delayed mine to ensure that this world had two champions to take on Cirvel together."

"Salvarae?"

"The Guardian of Gohaldinest."

"The Guardian is your mother?" Alityka asked.

"Aye, she is my novimather," Rivic said with a nod.

Alityka roared with laughter. "So, you and Dragzel are half-brothers!"

Dragzel jumped to his feet with a spitting hiss. He glared

at Rivic before he jumped down out of Lihn's lap and went to curl up on a pillow under the table, his back turned to them.

"And brothers with Cirvel too," Lihn put in gently.

Rivic didn't quite know what to say or do. He hadn't given much thought to who Cirvel's novimather was when they'd first started this conversation, but now... Everything seemed to have changed. Not only was Cirvel a novihomidrak and someone that Rivic was to defeat, but now it seemed that Cirvel was akin to an older brother. They were family. Him, Cirvel, and Nyree. Suddenly, more than anything, Rivic wanted Cirvel to know this and to find out if Cirvel had any remorse over his actions.

After a long moment of silence, he continued, "So you and my dragon mother have been planning this for a long time?"

Lihn seemed relieved that he'd finished his thoughtful pause. "For days on end, there have been forces working to stop Cirvel. Salvarae has tried many things, but even she doesn't know why she was brought here by Cirvel, only that she was made his prisoner.

"She spent a long time determining how best to screen Cirvel in order to sneak someone in for an attack. She has blinded him as best as she can. She knew she would have to do the same to whoever she selected to be her new novihomidrak," Lihn continued. "When she encountered me in the forest after she'd taken you, we devised a plan to take and return your Humline connection as best as we could. We had to be sure that Cirvel didn't sense you first, or we might've been discovered. We wouldn't restore your connection now if we believed it would put you in danger."

"My mother, your mother," Dragzel sneered, "gave me the task of delivering messages between her and Lihn. We all have risked our very lives to make sure you came to Gohaldinest safely and intrigued Cirvel enough to keep you without wanting to kill you. Once he discovers what you are, you better make sure you can handle yourself."

Rivic thought about Dragzel's words and nodded, then focused on Lihn. "I'm ready now."

"Ready now? For what?" Lihn asked.

"To restore my connection to the Onesong."

"'Tis truly your wish?"

Rivic took in a hesitant breath. "Aye. If Cirvel is a novihomidrak, then we must have every advantage against him. The souls of many depend upon it."

"Very well. Then we should get this done." Lihn looked under the table for the cahaster. "We need it, Dragzel. Will you go fetch it?"

There was a moaning and grunting as the cahaster slinked out, then jumped on Lihn's lap before hopping up on the table. He looked at Rivic, his muzzle wrinkling in a way that Rivic wasn't sure if it was a sneer or something else. The cahaster turned in a circle on the table, his head low. Then he said to Lihn, "There's really not much left. Sontre' gave most of it to Nyree. Even mother isn't sure what it's going to do."

"Dragzel, we have to try. Please get the vial."

Still with his head low, Dragzel gave a kind of half shrug, then bounded from the room. He slipped right through the door as if it weren't even there.

"So Dragzel has a fragment of the thread that was taken from me?" Rivic asked.

"Aye, Salvarae wanted me to take it, to see if there was any way that I could nurture it. I knew it wouldn't be safe with me, that Cirvel would feel it. I had Dragzel hide it away somewhere so even I don't know where it's at. That was the safest thing to do."

"I take it this nurturing didn't work."

Lihn's eyes held a distinct sadness. "I'm not sure there was anything anyone could do. If Salvarae could have foreseen

Sontre' giving its essence to Nyree, I'm not sure Salvarae would've tried the deception. Under any other circumstances, Sontre' would have been doing what was best."

"Or if I had just let the Necroathelings take it."

"Don't think like that. What were you supposed to do, lie down and show them your belly?" Alityka asked with a snarl. "You were fighting like you had been trained to do. Don't regret that. Besides, Salvarae may very well have been testing to make sure that she had done the right thing in choosing you. The last thing she would've wanted would be a novihomidrak that gave up so easily."

CHAPTER 10

$\mathcal{D}$ragzel returned with a vial held between his teeth. He jumped up on the table and set the vial carefully down. It rolled toward Lihn. Inside was a little sliver of yellow. "I told you it wasn't much."

Lihn picked up the vial and inspected the thread inside. "It'll have to do."

Alityka rose. "I'll keep watch out and keep a magic bubble around you. Hopefully you two won't be detected."

Lihn nodded as she stood up. "Thank you."

Rivic waited, wondering what he needed to do. After a moment, he felt Alityka's magical shielding arise around them.

"'Tis so small," Lihn commented as she uncorked the bottle and dumped the thread into her palm. Her lips pursed as she pinched it between her fingers. "Tip your head back."

Rivic looked up toward the ceiling. Lihn's hands came over him with the yellow thread dangling.

"You might want to close your eyes."

He did as she advised.

"Careful," Dragzel said.

"I've got it," Lihn breathed out.

Rivic felt a tickle on his forehead. Reflexively, he started to reach up for it, but Dragzel's paw landed on his arm. More wiggling against his skin nearly made him open his eyes.

"'Tis too short. I told you," Dragzel muttered. "You can't stretch it anymore."

"Nay, but I can suture it."

"Adding your own in? My lady Lihn, you don't know what that will do."

"Nay, but I've got to try. Swear to me that you won't tell your mother about this, both of you."

Dragzel issued a low, unhappy growl.

"What's going on?" Rivic asked.

"Keep your eyes closed," Dragzel said practically against Rivic's ear.

"There, I'm done," Lihn said. Rivic felt her step back. "You can open your eyes now."

The gloomy library appeared less macabre. He blinked a couple of times, trying to get his eyes to adjust to the strange, new incandescence. "T'is it?"

"Nay, we have more. We need to see if this opens your vision and how you react. Relax and let your energy flow." Lihn moved around the table and sat down across from him.

A wave of dizziness swept over Rivic and he let his eyes drift closed. Against his closed lids, he saw the air sparkling around a meandering labyrinth in a lush garden. In the comfortable cushion growing around him, he saw the journey he had to take within the Onesong.

Rivic saw himself standing on a path. It was almost like he was watching an image of himself in a mirror through a light fog.

The cloudy haze rent in two, spewing blinding white-gold light from the tear. Rivic threw a hand up to shade his eyes against the searing light, slowly lowering it as the glow faded. The dark castle towers pushed from the brightness. Gargaxes and gaxlors circled in flight in the dusk sky over Gohaldinest.

Yet it was the strange orange light on the turrets which had Rivic's attention until he realized what was happening. Flames rose from the buildings, surging from windows and where rooftops had once been. Rivic wondered if this was not fog around him, but rather smoke. His hands tingled as if sensing the looming threat of destruction before him.

"What is happening now?" Rivic asked, knowing he was responsible for the sight before them. He placed his hand on his thighs, rubbing the palms against the material to wipe away the sweat.

"'Tis only your fears. Release them," Lihn responded. "Follow the song."

At first, Rivic didn't understand, but his magic ebbed and flowed moving in sweet lullaby, and he found himself beginning to relax.

His calamitous vision faded and a nighttime sky appeared. The three moons rose and departed quickly as if time had been sped up. In the nocturnal dome, the stars exploded, shooting bursts of light in their wake as they streamed out into the universe. His vision spun, following the newborn comets. Suns, supernovas, nebulas, clusters, and so many things that Rivic had no words for but knew instinctively what they were, flew by.

"You have a beautiful view of the Onesong," Lihn said.

He didn't even wonder how she saw his vision. "'Tis not the same for everyone?"

"There are always differences. I have rarely seen an image as pure as yours. You do like to make your world beautiful and so it is reflected into the universe."

At the edge of Rivic's vision, everything grew black and

slowly shrank in around him. In no way did it feel uncomfortable. There was nothing strange or distant about it either. A thin strip of blue, gold, and white energy existed in the gap between space and this emptiness: the edge of creation. Here, the universe breathed and hummed. This was the origin of all energy that created everything, the very beginning of existence itself.

"What is the song you hear?" Lihn asked.

Rivic listened. "Zewalli sha sha zay, zewalli sha sha shay, zewalli sha sha zay," he sang.

"Soci'tay a deima. Soona ha," she joined in, and Rivic knew that she was singing what she was hearing. Their music repeated several times, words staying the same, but harmonies changing.

Then Rivic snapped back to his body, every cell of him alive with an electrical hum of the world around him. This new awareness moved so powerfully within him that he rose from his chair.

A great roar echoed through the castle. In the quaking sound, Rivic heard a voice call to him. "My child, you have learned to hear the Humline. Praise be to the Onesong. You can claim your full novihomidrak powers now."

In the resonances of the Humline, Rivic realized the truth: if Cirvel had his way, he would eliminate humanity from the bloodwave.

As the revelation rang through him, Rivic wasn't certain if the awareness was his own, his novimather's, or the Humline's. It seemed to come from all directions around him at once, nearly sweeping him off his feet. As he strengthened his weakened legs beneath him, he caught sight of Lihn examining him.

"Your perception is heightened right now. Give it a moment while I let Alityka know that we are done." She flowed gracefully away from the table, her long hair swaying.

The animalistic movement pulled a torrent of energy through him.

The magical bubble dispelled, and cold air rushed in around Rivic. His skin sensitive and his mind abuzz with so many new sights and sounds that the collapse of the bubble doubled the vibrations, leaving him undefended.

Rivic placed his hands on the table and flexed his fingers before him. For a moment, he thought he'd start seeing the bright blue webbing that proceeded those moments where he'd release his devastating magic. Though he didn't have the sight of it, he felt the energy wrapped around him.

Maybe he'd been better blinded to the Onesong.

"How's our champ?" Alityka asked. "He looks a little peaked."

Somehow, Rivic managed to raise his head. "Cirvel seeks to cut humanity off the bloodwave. We need to figure out how to stop him."

"Wait!" Lihn said, bending forward over the table toward Rivic. "Did you say that he intended on cutting off humanity from the bloodwave?"

"Aye, 'tis Cirvel's plan."

Alityka and Lihn exchanged looks before Alityka responded, "That would kill everyone who didn't have magic."

"As well as endangering everyone else, especially those who haven't learned to properly control their magic. The bloodwave holds things steady. Without the connection, it could overload certain people with magic," Rivic added. "We have to find a way to stop him."

As he finished, the cahaster jerked, his head swiveling toward the door. He gave a low hiss before scrambling from beneath the table and hiding under Lihn's skirt. "Oh dear," he muttered in his fleeing.

The library door swung open and Cirvel entered. His

forward stride halted, and he swallowed the words he was about to utter as he saw Alityka and Rivic in the room. "I didn't realize Lihn had guests with her." He didn't retreat, but rather stood there staring at them.

Lihn slipped from her chair and went to Cirvel. "My lord, they were helping me study. You know, I've fallen behind in my classes of late."

Cirvel took two strides around her, briefly touching her fingers with his as he passed, and came to stand beside Rivic. "I would think that Knight Captain Rivic would have other duties to attend rather than to tutor a couple of acolytes with their studies."

Alityka had bowed as Cirvel entered and now she stood with her hands folded together before her. She lowered her head as she spoke, "I'm sorry, Lord Cirvel. 'Tis my fault. I had grown so accustomed to studying with Rivic that it only seemed natural that I request his help when Lihn said we needed to get extra assistance."

Rivic marveled so much at the diminished change in her energy that when he caught Cirvel looking at him, he felt a flush hit his cheeks. A wane smile pressed awkwardly on his lips.

"Let's see what you've been studying," Cirvel said, reaching out for the books scattered over the table. "The geometric magicks of enchanted items." He glanced back at them. "Perchance are you having issues with spheres?"

Lihn giggled as she dipped a little, then looked up at Cirvel from beneath thick lashes with her deep brown eyes, a sweetly seductive maneuver. Rivic noted the manipulation in the shift from the determined woman she'd been just moments ago. Having seen the transformation in both women now, Rivic wondered if he had a false self he showed to Cirvel just as readily. Did Cirvel see beyond their masks?

Lihn smiled then as her words came easily, "That is precisely it."

"What explanation were you giving them?" Cirvel's dark eyes turned to Rivic.

His throat tightened. Cirvel knew just as well as the others that Rivic had had less magical training than them. He wasn't even sure if he ever remembered any mention of geometric magic. "I was telling them that they should ask their teachers because I couldn't give them the assistance they needed. Of course, I didn't know what help they wanted until I was here, otherwise I would have said something earlier."

Cirvel's hand clamped onto Rivic's shoulder. "Maybe I should give you some additional reading." He dragged Rivic with him over to one of the bookshelves and pulled a text from among the others. Slipping it to Rivic as they turned, Cirvel said to the women, "Study hard for a little longer. When you are done, Lihn, I expect you. I shall make sure you have a complete grasp of the subject."

"Aye, my lord," she said with a curtsy.

"As for my Knight Captain, I need to take him with me now as I have some tasks for him. I doubt you'll be needing his assistance anymore."

Rivic wanted to look back at Alityka and Lihn as he was forced from the room, but he was afraid of what such a glance would tell Cirvel. Best to focus on what lay ahead and not behind.

The door closed on their heels. Cirvel's fingers clutched Rivic's tunic to heave him along. Once around the corner, Cirvel shoved Rivic against the stone wall. "Why do I suspect you were as thick as thieves in there?"

"Nay, my lord. Studying—"

"Do you understand your duty as Knight Captain?"

"Aye, my lord. I am to watch and protect against enemies of Gohaldinest."

"Do enemies only lie outside the walls?"

"Nay, my lord."

Cirvel pointed back toward the library. "Do you think the women in there could be enemies?"

The heated warning of danger brought sweat to Rivic's brow. He searched Cirvel's face for what the man expected as an answer. Rivic suddenly wished for that sense of knowing he'd had so readily when he'd been with Alityka and Lihn. "My lord, they are only acolytes. I'm certain they don't pose any threat."

"'Twasn't the question I asked. I asked if they could be."

"I would hope not, but I suppose 'tis possible." Rivic gulped down on his answer, hoping it was a good one. Why hadn't he allowed Lihn to give the Humline back to him? If it gave him an advantage in situations like this, if he'd sensed Cirvel coming before he'd entered the library, wouldn't it be worth the risks?

"Walk with me."

Rivic followed Cirvel's order without hesitation, while aware that Cirvel could just magically transfer them anywhere in the castle he wanted. Why did he waste time walking? Where was he leading Rivic? Again, other than a dangerous sense of terror, Rivic wished his awareness were expanded beyond merely this present moment. What he wouldn't give right now to receive a fuller picture? Did Lihn, in being the creature she was, have a way to give those around her a sample of what it was like to be so connected? Was that why she enthralled the Lord of Gohaldinest?

Cirvel began to speak, "You'll notice I never asked Alityka a question, yet what she answered me with was the complete truth. She did miss the times the two of you would study together, and she did suggest to Lihn that they get your assistance."

"I'm afraid I fail to see your point, my lord."

"Would you agree with me that Alityka travels a treacherous path?"

"She seeks to impress you. Maybe she feels like she's been an acolyte for too long and that she should be a Dominus now."

Cirvel's mouth straightened to a thin line as he nodded slowly. "You pretend to make assumptions about what she's thinking when I suspect that you've already had this conversation with her."

Rivic felt his heartbeat thundering in his chest. Knowing Cirvel was a novihomidrak, Rivic realized Cirvel had to hear this as well.

"I rather like having a Dominari under my watch," Cirvel said. He stopped before a wall with a tapestry hanging over it. "I rather do wish you would convince her to use her powers. She has not progressed as I would have liked. I believe her presence could be of great benefit. Do you understand?"

"Nay, my lord."

"Then let me be quite clear. I know that you lied to me about being the Dominari. Rather, I have known about her for quite some time."

Rivic didn't know what to say.

Cirvel smiled and raised his index finger to his lips. "But this will be our little secret now, right? I want the Dominari to impress me, but without coercion on my part. Your urging will be so much better. Let's see how powerful she can become."

"Why?"

"Knight Captain Rivic, do you miss the potential I see?"

"Aye, my lord. Apparently I do."

"Stay by her side, push her to grow while you are working on your own training. She will strive to match you, as is her nature."

Her nature! Cirvel had to be aware that if a Dominari couldn't succeed in their task, the unicorns would break the bond with the Dominari and create a dark creature whose only thought was of killing.

Cirvel reached forward and tapped the book which Rivic had forgotten he was holding. "I see that you followed the thought to its completion. Aye, I want to bring forth that dark, unbound energy and allow her to become a creature more brutal than any Necroatheling. When you have finished your training and she has transformed, the two of you will be spectacular and unstoppable."

"Why? What purpose would that serve?" Fear of the destructive magic rose within him. "What would you have us do?"

Cirvel's face took on a look of wry delight. "Our secret, remember? Just the vision of it tempts me beyond reason and I very nearly want to reveal all to you."

"Please, my lord, let me understand."

Once again, Cirvel put a finger to his lips to hush Rivic. "Nothing stays bottled up forever. Soon, you will learn. For now, you must make sure to keep Alityka from becoming an enemy of Gohaldinest. She must be faithful to you. In the meanwhile, I must go prepare for Lihn. Now, so long as you don't tell Lihn or Alityka about our conversation here, nothing cruel will happen to either one of them. Just fulfill your part of the bargain. Are we in agreeance, Knight Captain?"

"Aye," Rivic muttered, still not sure what he was committing to, but realizing that he really didn't have another choice.

"Good. Then we shall see each other again soon." Cirvel pivoted on his foot and continued down the hall. "Nothing stays bottled up forever."

CHAPTER 11

The deepest sleep Rivic had had in a long time broke to instant alertness. Beneath the blankets, his body tingled with awareness.

Alityka was in trouble. Not just any trouble, but the severe kind that could get her killed.

Had Cirvel decided to go after her?

Cirvel had said nothing would happen to Ali as long as Rivic remained quiet and didn't tell her about Cirvel's purpose to break her bond with the unicorns. But what would happen if she decided once again to do that on her own? Was that why he'd awaken?

Rivic tossed the blankets back as he flipped onto his back, leaving a tangle of material around his legs while he reached out to magically sense where Alityka was. "Please let her be in the dormitory," he whispered. If she remained in the tower, even if she were preparing to leave, at least he could get to her before she headed out to do whatever was on her mind.

Realizing she wasn't in the dormitory and she hadn't been

there in quite a while, his breathing deepened and he reached out further. He felt the morning close at hand. Soon he'd be expected to get to training.

Was she running from Gohaldinest? Had she overheard Cirvel's threat and it scared her into fleeing? Or had he said something to Lihn?

What would happen if he missed training because he went to drag Alityka back? What if Cirvel sent Azote after her and made her another sacrifice?

Rivic kicked his legs free and rose. Still trying to track Alityka's magic as he put on his clothes and armor, he pondered over the wisdom of his choice. His novimather had said to temper the other champion, not that he had to keep her from her own deadly stupidity. "She's rash," he whispered again, remembering the words from his dragon mother. Anxiety thrashed through him again, sending his skin prickling with alertness once more. What was she doing?

Rivic dashed up the stairs out of the Domini's basement dormitory and raced through the castle. He still didn't have a sense of Alityka's current position and hoped he'd catch it as he moved.

He came around a corner and saw a Necroatheling. Instantly he slowed his pace and tried to be casual.

"Knight Captain, what are you doing?" the Necroatheling asked.

"Patrolling," he replied. His mind raced through the many permeations that might happen if he admitted he was looking for an acolyte who might be in trouble. On the one hand, it might help him build a defense for missing training if it came to that. He might also like help in locating Alityka; her trouble was that intense. Yet, he didn't want Alityka getting into trouble if he could prevent it. This situation posed a double-edged sword he needed to walk carefully.

"Something feels wrong. Do you not sense it? I'm afraid acolytes are up to some mischief this morning."

The Necroatheling reached up and lowered his hood while he took a nervous look around. "What are you doing? Do you want to get her into trouble?" Kalt asked.

Rivic didn't know whether to feel relieved or angry. "Where is she and what is she doing?"

Kalt didn't point the direction, but the way his gaze shot to the wall might have been a direct arrow. "If she wanted your help, I'm certain she would have come to ask you."

"Instead she asks you?" Rivic took a step back and placed his hands on his hips.

Kalt rolled his eyes. "Trot along to training now, Knight Captain. I have a better advantage to assist her than you do?"

Cold terror rippled through Rivic again. "Aye, you do have an advantage standing guard here in the hall, but she needs me."

"She's fine. There's no one home."

"She's in over her head and I think you suspect it too." Rivic headed toward the wall where Kalt's gaze had drifted. "How do I get in?"

Kalt didn't appear pleased, but then Rivic had no desire to make a Necroatheling happy, especially this one. "Walk forward. 'Tis an illusion."

Rivic stared at the wall. It was a pretty good illusion. He reached his hand out wondering if he were about to walk into the wall. Instead, a breeze hit his fingers as they disappeared behind the image that wavered in front of him.

Looking back, Rivic said, "Nyree trusted you and enjoyed your company. Someday, I hope your actions tear you apart as you realize what you lost."

"You're wasting time."

Feeling braver, Rivic stepped forward, letting the magic

swallow up around his arm. He glanced back at Kalt, but the Necroatheling had once again flipped up his hood making his face undistinguishable. Turning, Rivic ventured through the wall.

The hallway that opened on the other side of the illusion didn't look different from the one he'd just been standing in, except that it felt so much colder. A draft wafted through the air, brushing against Rivic's face with icy fingers that lingered like the tendrils of deep magic within the castle.

He called out in a hushed shout, "Ali?"

A chill crawled along his spine. What had she gotten herself into?

"Ali," he bayed again as he started to traverse the corridor. He sensed that no matter how much he bellowed, she was beyond hearing him.

His feet rolled over little bits that crunched beneath his boot. Picking up his feet, he saw tiny bones crushed over the stone. Something fed on mice here.

Stepping around the other bones, Rivic hurried beyond the dank spot. At a turn in the hall, larger bones littered the area. He didn't want to know what animals had become prey here, fearing that wandering humans might be one of them, but until he saw some skulls, he'd assume they were merely larger mammals.

Shortly, Rivic saw a sword laying near the wall. Weapons, only a few propped upright, began to litter the hallway as if they had been kicked aside. Blood dried black coated several of the blades. The scent of death deepened here. Footprints in the dust near the wall and an outline revealed that Aliktya had stopped momentarily to pick up a weapon. Whatever lived down these halls, she was heading out to kill.

Azote.

The answer rippled over him.

He drew his sword and started running. Alityka had already found the beast. Rivic could practically feel her raising her ill-gotten weapon against the gaxlor.

"Talcor dun." Rivic began flashing himself through the corridors to get to Alityka faster. Spell after spell he cast, zipping along with a speed much faster than running.

Rivic appeared in a cavernous room where Alityka stood just inside the doorway.

Alityka tightened her grip around the handle of a large axe. The weight of its head was too heavy for her and she could barely keep it from tipping out of her hands.

Rash and reckless.

He slammed into her, knocking the ax from her hold. The metal weapon clattered to the floor and skid away as Rivic seized onto her to keep her from falling.

"What are you doing?" she screamed.

A fluttering in the rafters alerted Rivic to the fact that Azote stretched out his wings somewhere in the darkness above them. Certainly, the gaxlor had seen both of them.

"I caught you, my dear," Rivic said, praying that Azote wouldn't know Alityka's true intention of coming here to kill the beast. "I told you I would."

"What?"

Rivic slapped his hand over Alityka's mouth as he leaned in close. "What do you think you're doing? Talcor dun."

He flashed them as far down the hallway as he could. When they came out of the spell, he felt her resisting. "Talcor dun matahass'n," he shouted as she called out, "Talcor dun ro'da'hassay." The force of the two spells colliding shattered Rivic and Alityka apart, thrusting them backwards into the air and slamming against opposing walls. They dropped to the floor at the same time.

Aliytka landed in a crouch. She raised her hand, ready to fire a spell. "What are you doing?"

Rivic's tailbone hurt from landing against the floor. He tried to get his knees up while his back hollered in pain, but he knew he had to push to his feet before she shot magic at him. "Stopping you from making a mistake."

"I nearly had him."

"Did you?" Rivic screamed back. The echo of his own voice in the hallway made him realize they really needed to stop shouting at each other.

"Let me deal with this."

An axe whirled through the hallway, cutting the air between them. It collided with a wall and clattered to the floor. Rivic knew Azote would be next.

Alityka ran for the fallen axe. Rivic chased, catching her around the waist just before she picked it up. "Talcor dun!"

Alityka swung at Rivic. He evaded and caught her next punch too. "Talcor dun!"

Further down the hallway, she dropped her weight, breaking free. Her leg swept out for his. Off balance, he fell, but he twisted to hold onto her. "Talcor dun."

She tried to counter with another spell, but the sound clipped as they vanished.

Rivic came up from behind, seizing her once more around her waist. He lifted her off the ground.

"Shi'baten to'a helcord," she hollered.

Rivic felt his feet lift. "Talcor dun."

They came out of the spell rolling. Rivic landed against Kalt's legs. A short distance off, he heard Alityka whimper in pain.

"Azote is coming," Kalt said as he reached down and attempted to help Rivic to his feet, but Rivic yanked away and glared at the Necroatheling.

"I don't care," Alityka raged. "Let him come. 'Tis three of us now that he will have to deal with... if you are fighting with me." She looked pointedly at Rivic.

"This is insane, Ali, and you know it. Why would you even think of taking Azote on?"

Tears were in her eyes. "He killed Sempt. I can't let that go unpunished."

"If you hurry away, I will make excuses with Azote. It might calm his wrath," Kalt informed them as he looked at the illusionary wall.

Rivic put his hands on Alityka's arms, but spoke to Kalt. "You can't take him on like this."

"If nothing else, he can rip me apart as you said. You two need to go now."

Alityka's anger-filled face seemed too close to Rivic's. "This is my fight. How did you even know I was here? Why did you come?"

"The Onesong told me to come get you, that you were in danger." His grip tightened on her. "Can't you see that I can't do this mission without you?"

"That's not possible."

"You two really need to leave!" Kalt shouted.

Rivic looked up and saw the Necroatheling standing with his feet apart and his hands raised as if he were holding up a shield against a powerful force shoving him backwards.

"Don't you dare," Alityka warned shaking her index finger at Rivic. "I won't leave Kalt and I won't let you deny me this battle."

"Get her out of here!" Kalt hollered.

Rivic reached out and grabbed onto Kalt's purple robes and yanked both the Necroatheling and Alityka. "Talcor dun proximitious."

They appeared in another section of the castle where Rivic released his hold on Kalt, but he flashed two more times with Alityka until they were standing outside in the courtyard. Acolytes rushed around the grassy area as they headed either to breakfast or to class.

"What were you doing?" Rivic asked. He wanted to shake her, to yell at her, but he somehow managed to keep his voice to a thick whisper. Though he felt safer in the public place, he still didn't want anyone overhearing.

"Nothing. I'm doing nothing now." Alityka broke away from his hold.

"I meant with Azote. What were you doing going after him?" When she still refused to give him an answer, he added, "Please tell me what you were thinking."

She seemed to acquiesce as her face softened. "Azote is my problem. You are the one who has to defeat Cirvel. I'm not even sure how I can help. But Azote... I can make that monster mine to deal with."

"Now? Without a plan?"

"I wasn't going to attack him!" she shouted back. Then she remembered where they were and lowered her voice. "I was actually going to study him. I wanted a look at his lair."

"While he was there?"

"He wasn't supposed to be."

"Well, he was, and he thought you were hunting him." How Rivic knew this was beyond him, but he felt it with certainty. "Whatever made you think 'twas a good idea to go out after Azote?"

"Kalt told me Azote was gone."

"Kalt? And you trusted him? He's a Necroatheling!"

"You don't know him like I do." Alityka's eyes widened and she slapped her hands over her mouth. "I'm sorry."

Rivic released her and stepped back. "You can't trust him, Ali. Why didn't you come to me? If you want to take down Azote, I'm behind you. We have to, because as long as Azote is free, he'll defend Cirvel. But don't do this alone."

She nodded while keeping her gaze downcast as if she were ashamed. "Aye, all right. But we need more information on him."

Rivic gave a smile to show he wasn't upset with her as he nudged her shoulder. "We need more information on everything we're doing."

"Get to class, Rivic. I'm sure you're already late." She turned and started to walk off, her head down and her shoulders sagged as she headed in the direction of the doorway that would take her to the tower dormitory.

Watching her go, Rivic wondered if there was anything that he could have said to make her feel better about her failed mission. He doubted it.

But at least he'd kept her alive.

A chill made Rivic realize someone had moved up beside him. It was Kalt. Rivic moved to face Kalt while positioning himself at a distance safe enough to watch for an attack.

The Necroatheling had his hood raised over his tipped head. "Very good."

"You sound like that was a test," Rivic commented.

Kalt pulled out a scroll he had strapped to his side beneath his cloak. "I need you to get this to Alityka."

Rivic stepped forward, but he remained a good arm's length away from the Necroatheling. He stretched, leaning in to accept the curled paper. "What is this?"

"Something she needs."

Rivic unrolled the refined parchment. It had a different texture than that used by the acolytes in their lessons. Comparatively, this was like silk to stone. He looked to see if Kalt cared that he was looking at it, but the Necroatheling's attention remained on the area around them.

Rivic took a moment to study the fancy golden swirls written on the scroll while Kalt kept watch. Rivic couldn't read the magic beyond recognizing that it was a strong spell. When he released the bottom edge, the parchment coiled back up tightly. "Why are you giving this to Alityka?"

"I told you: she needs it."

"It looks dangerous."

"Cirvel will be traveling deep into the caves beneath Gohaldinest tomorrow. That would be an optimal time to use that unnoticed. You've passed the test. Protect her." Then, Kalt disappeared in a plume of purple smoke.

CHAPTER 12

*A*lityka pointed at the scroll Rivic held. "Well, let's open it up and take a look."

As Rivic unrolled the scroll on the table, Lihn and Alityka moved in closer. He wished they'd stay back for another moment, but knew they had to be as curious about the golden magical writing as he was. Dots of multicolored pastel light danced over the page as the curlicue pen strokes sparkled in the flickering candlelight.

"'Tis a locator spell," Alityka said, her voice hushed by awe.

"Let's not be in too much of a rush with this," Rivic said, thinking of Cirvel's warning to him in the hallway. He had no idea how long Cirvel would be gone, especially since the Lord of Gohaldinest had merely gone in the tunnels beneath the castle. Rivic wanted to wait until Cirvel gave them a longer opportunity.

"What are we supposed to find with it?" Lihn asked gazing to Alityka.

"Something that will help us defeat Cirvel. Going between dimensions 'tis an excellent way to identify what we need." Alityka pulled the scroll toward her, picking it up off the table. "Let's find out. Grandehest almed sokatay –"

"Now?" Rivic yelled at her.

"You did say Kalt told us to use the spell while Cirvel was gone," Lihn reminded him.

Alityka glared but kept reading, "Fornesta oosida."

A fire erupted around her feet. Rivic reached to yank her out of the magical flames. The Necroatheling had tricked them.

Instead of heat, Rivic felt the tug of an enchantment, then Alityka fell against him and they both tumbled to a gray stone floor. At first, Rivic thought they might be in another part of Gohaldinest castle, but he didn't recognize the hallways.

Alityka picked herself up and brushed her red hair out of her face with her fingers. "Why did you do that?" she shouted angrily. "Don't you know how dangerous it is to break into a teleportation spell, especially a dimensional one?"

"I thought you were in trouble," he retaliated.

Alityka searched the floor around her. "The only trouble is how we will get back. The scroll is gone."

A sense of knowing rippled through Rivic. "We will be called back when 'tis time for us to leave. We are stuck here until the spell reactivates on its own."

At the sound of footsteps coming toward them, Rivic pushed her behind him and said, "Vochey." His sword, Honor, came to his hand.

A voice called out, the words sounding familiar yet unknown. A young man in white robes turned the corner. He carried a lantern, obviously prepared to swing it, but had no visible weapons.

Rivic noticed the man's eyes were red and his cheeks stained with tears. Alityka reached out to grab Rivic and stop him from attacking, as if he would after seeing the man's distressed state.

Again, the man spoke, but Rivic didn't understand what he was saying.

Rivic attempted communication. "'Tis Dominari Alityka, and I am Dominus Rivic," he said, nudging her aside.

The man gasped, looking between them as confusion filled his eyes, and then he dropped to his knees. "Lady Alityka. Lord Rivic!" He carefully set the lantern on the floor, raised his hands, and bowed forward to put his head to the ground. "My father would be honored to have your presence here." His annunciation of the words was a little foreign, as if he could speak their language, but wasn't well practiced at it. After a moment, he sat back on his heels.

"I'm sorry," the man said, tears coming to his eyes. "'Tis been several emotional days for me. And now the very person whose lineage mark was on my father's palm for all the days of his life stands before me, as well as…" He choked. "…the woman in white I've heard so many stories about." A special shine came to his eyes as he glanced Alityka over.

"Lineage mark?" she asked.

"May I?" He reached up, took Rivic's hand, and searched the palm. "'Tis too soon then? Lady Alityka has not placed it yet?"

"We are neither Lady nor Lord," Alityka said. "Why do you call us so?"

"Because you are individuals held in reverence by my family."

Reverence? Alityka mouthed to Rivic.

Rivic ignored her and helped the man to his feet. "What is your name?"

"Galault. Galault Taburath."

Alityka's eyes widened in surprise came to Rivic and he realized she must have had the same thought he had: Cirvel had called him Rivic Taburath. Was it possible there was some relation?

Alityka charged forward with her question. "The name of your father?"

"Do you not know it?" Galault asked. His forehead wrinkled in confusion.

"Humor me, boy!" she snapped and Rivic felt a second press of her unicorn magic surge onward.

He raised his eyebrow at her use of the word, *boy*, for they were so close in age. As it stood, Rivic felt certain that she was actually younger than Galault.

Galault gave the smile of one being humored as he answered, "Steigan Taburath, king of New Lilinar."

Questions plainly filled Alityka's eyes. The only word familiar to either of them that Galault had spoken was the surname *Taburath*.

Galault's face furrowed as if distrusting the claim of her identity. It seemed like this Galault was familiar with her, but not the other way around. Rivic wished he had a moment to pull Alityka aside and explain this to her, but she charged ahead. "We should like to see him," Alityka interrupted.

"Milady, I would have figured that you would already know." The words were spoken slowly. Galault's eyes had filled with tears once more, but suddenly brightened as he looked up at them. A dance of grief and gladness played across his face. "Ah, nay, I suppose you wouldn't, not if this is the first time. I know why you are here. I should have figured that today would be the day you'd come. You are seeking the one to help you to defeat the Destroyer of Civilizations. I can provide you with that answer."

Alityka glanced at Rivic, sending him an excited smile. "You can?"

He went to an archway in the hallway and waved his hand. "Vaca chi ca'dada." Magic rippled over the opening and shroud it with a mist so dark blue that it nearly seemed black. Images of many different locations rose to the surface like the reflection of clouds on a lake.

Alityka followed Galault. "Dimensional magic in a doorway. Are you a watcher of worlds?"

"Wait," Rivic muttered, holding Alityka back. "Let's slow down."

"Do you not see?" she snapped at Rivic. "He can open up another world. We can go get help, bring other novihomidraks here."

"There is not a way to access the Wells, milady. They remain closed off. You will not find novihomidraks to aid your cause in any world or dimension that is still connected to this planet," he answered. "I can only give you time, which is what you need, and point you toward the person who can assist you."

"Very well." Alityka took a deep breath. "I am ready. Show me who can help us."

"Wait," Rivic insisted a little louder.

Galault flipped through the images until he found the one he sought. He tapped it. The picture expanded on the column of magic. Rivic could make out a stone room with a wall of murky glass. The dark form of something moved in a space just beyond the obstruction. This was the person Alityka would meet. How dangerous would that person be?

Galault lifted his hand toward Alityka. "Here you go. Let us be quick. I will cross this threshold with you and stay in the intermediate dimension so I can drop you through to the other side. I will pull you back when I think you are done and will return here with you."

"I'll go with her," Rivic said.

"You cannot. Every time Alityka made a journey, she was alone." Galault grabbed Rivic's arm. "Alityka's first trip is to visit someone she does not know, but who knows her. She will be safe."

"I'll be fine," she reiterated with a gentle touch to Rivic's arm.

Then she and Galault blinked away.

Rivic watched as Alityka appeared alone in the image before him. She stood in the small chamber, her white acolyte's dress crisp in its brilliance against the drab gray stone. An older man stepped toward her through a doorway in the dark glass wall. He appeared to be a warrior, though age had taken its toll. His smile seemed genuine, as if he were delighted to see her. Though Rivic couldn't hear what was being said, keeping Alityka in his sights was better than not knowing at all.

Alityka and the gray-haired gentleman continued to speak. The man smiled often, an action that erased cycles away from his age and made him seem much younger. He handed a book to Alityka, holding onto it for a moment nearly too long before releasing it to her.

Then Alityka disappeared from the image before Rivic and a younger man entered the view, stepping up beside the elder warrior. They spoke for a moment, then moved on.

An instant later, Galault and Alityka returned to Rivic. Galault looked tired. But Alityka seemed vibrant as she studied the pages of a book she'd been given and smiled happily. "He spoke in odd riddles, almost like he was laughing at me." Alityka flipped through the pages. "'Tis some sort of spellbook and 'tis written in my own hand. How could it be that he would have it?"

"Start counting now, Lady Alityka," Galault said. "Every encounter you have now will most likely have some additional action required from you. When you start to juggle time, you need to remember what pieces were where to ensure that you have them when the occasion comes."

"Like writing this book?" Alityka said, half question, half statement.

"Aye." Galault waved his hand to dismiss the magic in the doorway. "You have much to be about and will be visited soon. You need to be prepared."

"Visited?"

Galault shook his head, his eyelids giving a weary droop. "I must rest and resume my post. I have set you on the path, but now I must resume my duties."

"Your post?" Rivic asked.

"Our good king, my father, is dead. I am attending as his Honor Guard." After a moment where Alityka and Rivic just stood staring at Galault, the man turned and motioned with his hand for them to follow.

They trailed him around the corner. There stood a beautiful carved wooden tree on a door of glass and wrought iron. The walls were also made out of the same materials, though a little darker. It resembled the odd wall he'd seen in the portal image.

"Is this like the one where Alityka just came from?" Rivic asked.

"Aye, very similar," Galault answered.

Torches burned on the other side of the walls. Through the smoky glass, they could make out the silhouetted form of a person lying within the inner chamber.

Alityka reached for the door handle, but Galault stopped her. "There is oil on the floor, milady. Once the reed torches burn down, they will ignite the oil, set the room ablaze, and burn the remains," he said. Fresh tears slid down his cheeks.

"How did the king die?" Alityka asked.

"Stabbed by my eldest brother. There is no justice to be had because not a single soul saw the blade slide beneath my father's breastplate. I should have told my father." Tears rolled down his face as he looked at Alityka. "I'm sorry I didn't tell him. Guilt will forever be my penance."

"Why would you believe this could be your fault?" Rivic questioned.

Galault gave his answer to Alityka without glancing at Rivic. "Several cycles ago, I saw my father's murder in a transition picture as I practiced my dimensional magic lessons. Since these alternate realities can be so tricky and deceiving, I chose to say nothing."

"Did your father deserve to be slain?" Alityka inquired.

"*No!* I mean, nay. My father was a hero, a champion who fought to rule his kingdom again."

Tears sprang once more into Galault's eyes. His face appeared young, but those eyes were weary and had seen much over a short number of cycles. "You have come from another era to seek my father. Yet the timing is strange. His mission has ended; yours is just beginning, 'tis it not?"

"We could have used your father on our side. 'Tis too bad we are here late."

Galault smiled ruefully. "Who do you think you just met?"

"That old man you took me to see, that was your father?"

"Aye, in another lifetime."

Alityka looked confused. "Another lifetime? Is that a riddle, or should I understand your meaning?"

"My father's life was complicated and vast. Rest assured, you will come to understand."

"Galault, as a watcher of world, why didn't you just deal with your brother?"

"Lady Ali, the course of time runs for everyone. Were we not so early on in your journey, you would know this most of all. 'Tis the same reason I cannot interfere with the Destroyer on your behalf, though you will surely ask. Chaos lies in the crossings of such interventions. Karma results where chaos escapes. I choose to let my brother not taint me with the chaos he attracts into his own life. His karma will be what he deserves. As will Cirvel's when the time comes."

"Tell me of your father. What stories will be sung about him?"

"He was amazing, you'll see. He was a Dominari until you returned. 'Tis said that he travelled through time to defeat his foes."

Alityka's forehead wrinkled with concern. "Who were his enemies? Who would stand against a king who is a Dominari?"

"He wasn't always a king," Galault said, finally able to return Alityka's smile. "He came from much humbler beginnings. Yet, 'tis a story I cannot tell you."

Alityka broke away, irritation clear on her face as she seized Rivic's arm. "His father is the means to which we defeat Cirvel?"

"Aye, my father is part of what you need."

"Part?"

A fire lit around Alityka's and Rivic's feet.

"The locator spell is pulling us back," Rivic announced as he felt the magic tug at him.

"Nay, not yet." Alityka moved her feet as if she were trying to step from the fire. When she realized she couldn't, she reached out for Galault and tried to take a hold of him.

Galault stepped back out of her reach. "My work here is not yet done."

The spell tugged on them. "He's a watcher. We need him. We can't go without him. Nay!"

Her voice faded, then the scream returned. It changed to a cry of rage as she collapsed to the floor emptyhanded. They had returned without Galault.

CHAPTER 13

*R*ivic walked through the empty, darkened hallways the following day. The meeting with Galault played over and over in Rivic's mind so much during training that he wasn't certain he remembered what he'd been learning. The thoughts didn't stop as he patrolled the corridors outside of Cirvel's chambers, even though the Lord of Gohaldinest still hadn't returned.

As he paced, he searched for magic and listened to the ancient tendrils which sought after him and called his magic to them. A breeze wafted through the hall and teased at the lower corner of one of the newer tapestries. He thought there might be something behind it, but when he reached out to lift it slightly, the door at the opposite end of the hallway opened with a bang, slamming so hard against the stone that the latticework windows behind Rivic shook.

Rivic pivoted, putting his hand to his sword and preparing to draw.

Two Necroathelings entered first, followed by the angry swirl of Lord Cirvel in his black robes. "Another failed attempt," Cirvel snarled.

A third Necroatheling behind Cirvel held a bundle the size of a toddler wrapped in blankets. They all seem to stop, giving momentary hesitation as they saw the Knight Captain there. Rivic released his hand from his sword, letting it slide the short distance back into his scabbard as he saluted. A part of him wished that Cirvel's departure had lasted longer.

"Hail, Lord Cirvel!" Rivic said.

Cirvel shoved his way through the two Necroathelings before turning to face them all. "Dispose of the body. Knight Captain, you're with me."

Rivic didn't want to be with Cirvel in this mood. But Rivic had been here on duty and now Lord Cirvel requested him. He couldn't turn away from his responsibility.

As the Necroathelings went to leave, Rivic thought he saw a small foot wearing a moccasin fall from beneath the blanket. Rivic spun around and followed Lord Cirvel while shoving the image from his mind. Contemplating a dead child scared Rivic too much.

Cirvel sat at the long table with his head in his hands. Rivic couldn't say that he'd ever seen such a defeated look on the Lord of Gohaldinest. What were these plans that were so important to anger him at their failure? An even more, why had they failed? Why had a child died?

"You require my service?" Rivic asked.

"It has been a long day and my magic is drained. I would like some tea."

That was all, Cirvel merely wanted Rivic to bring him a drink? The simple task done well might bring Cirvel to open up and provide Rivic with information. Had Rivic really seen what he believed he saw? What was Cirvel trying to do? Where had Cirvel gone this time?

"Aye, my lord." Rivic bowed before he cast the spell to take him down to the kitchens. Once there, Rivic told the cooks what he needed, received the requested drink, and teleported back. He hoped he hadn't left Cirvel waiting too long. Now, the parlor was empty, but the library door was open. Rivic entered and saw Cirvel sitting in a chair with a book in his hand.

Rivic placed the tea on the stand beside Lord Cirvel then moved to stand in a guard position at the door. He tried to garner some sympathy for Cirvel, who weakly picked up the cup and took a sip. "I take it that your trip was not a success. I am very sorry to hear that."

Cirvel rested the cup back on the wood and gave an apathetic twirl of his hand. "It was not the trip that was unsuccessful. It was the endeavor that I sought to remedy that failed."

"Is there any assistance that I might provide that would be of help, my lord?"

Cirvel's cold, dark eyes softened just a little. "I am in need of the sapere and am having difficulties finding an adequate person to take the position."

Rivic remembered the old man reeking of unnatural magicks who had promoted him to a Dominus. The memory of it brought a shudder. He wasn't certain he could wish that fate upon anyone. He certainly didn't want that outcome for himself, but as Alityka kept reminding him, they had to do whatever it took to get close enough to Cirvel for him to reveal his secrets. It was the only way to find a way to defeat him. "What do you require in that person?"

"A child blessed of dragon magic."

Rivic thought of the lifeless toddler being carried by the Necroatheling and understood; the child had failed whatever test needed to be performed. Deep in his stomach, the rolling sensation of this realization sickened him. He fought back the ill feeling.

Then he saw Cirvel's gaze on him.

"A child is not required. The person could be older. The

ceremony is, however, more brutal then." Cirvel glanced away. "I would prefer a baby, someone a couple months old who could be trained early and have the longest life possible. And someone who would remain by my side." He reached once more for his cup.

The barbs of Cirvel's words were not lost on him, yet Rivic didn't know what else to say or do. At a complete loss for action, he bowed. "Do you require anything else? Shall I resume my guard?"

Cirvel held the rim of the teacup against his lower lip, but he did not drink while he seemed lost in contemplation over Rivic's question.

"My lord?" Rivic added after a considerable length, one where he was starting to feel uncomfortable.

Cirvel stared at the window across the room. "Do you know what it's like when you have long range plans that no one understands or can even begin to comprehend?"

Rivic wasn't certain how to respond, but knew the question might be rhetorical or merely Cirvel thinking aloud. "I imagine it gets very lonely not having someone to converse with or share ideas," he said, wondering if he could evoke more.

Cirvel began to nod slowly. "Several thousand cycles I've had these plans. Treshauna was the last one to understand."

"Treshauna?"

Cirvel issued a dismissive wave as he shook his head. "Someone from long ago."

"So you don't share what's going on with the Necroathelings?" Rivic knew he pushed perhaps a little too hard. He didn't want to make Cirvel wonder why Rivic pried, but considering the lord's tired state, this might be the only opportunity.

"Nay." His gaze broke from the window. Lowering the cup back to the table, Cirvel smiled and twisted his hand. A small blue stone which seemed to flash in the candlelight appeared in his fingers. "I'm sorry. I seem to have gotten lost in thought for a moment. Your words have spurred an idea, but I need you to fetch Madame Orcee for me. This will allow you to teleport to her shop, which I do believe you know where 'tis located, and back." Cirvel reached out and dropped the stone into Rivic's hand.

Inclusions ran through the rock like the intense jagged outlines of lightning bolts. Little sparks lit at intersections where inclusions overlapped. As several bursts exploded at once, Rivic nearly dropped the stone.

Cirvel didn't seem to notice Rivic's distress. "Chances are good that she already knows you are coming and will be waiting, but if she isn't, you have my permission to bring her at sword-point. Why I keep her around is beyond me." Again, he paused a moment while absorbed in his own thoughts before he added, "Keep in mind that whoever is in the shop is Madame Orcee, whether she looks like you remember her or not."

Several months had gone by since Rivic had skipped class for an excursion into the city with his twin sister, Nyree. At Madame Orcee's Tea Shop, the eccentric woman had read their tea leaves. In the aftermath of Rivic's punishment for his truancy, he hadn't thought much more about the strange oracle in her little eatery.

But what was the meaning behind Cirvel's counsel? In recalling the strange tingling pricking at the edge of his skin while he'd been in her shop, he already knew she was more than she appeared to be.

Rivic grasped the stone in his left hand. "Talcor dun."

When he regained focus, he stood in Madame Orcee's shop, the stone now in his right hand. Dizziness undulated over him and he wobbled on his feet.

The scent of spices and teas came next, followed by a

voice. "I wondered when he might call for me next. Come, let us be done with this. I prefer to be here rather than in his company, I'm sure you understand."

A young girl with extremely dark skin, a shade brown lighter compared than the tight curls of black hair which encompassed her head, rose from a mat placed on the floor. She'd been kneeling, a cup of tea before the mat, and black leaves splattered all over the white wall.

This was not the Madame Orcee he remembered, but her words and Cirvel's counsel indicated she was.

She tilted her head and gave a smile. Her white teeth, along with the pink tint of her mouth and gums, seemed a stark difference to her complexion. "If you had your sister's gift, which should have been yours, you would see so much more clearly than you do now."

"How is it possible that you understand alternative scenarios?" he asked.

"Do you ask how the birds fly? Oh sure, there are some physics and mechanics involved, but do you ever ask yourself how they fly? Or maybe a better question of *why* they fly? Nay! You accept it. Birds fly. They do not need to know how it is they can soar in the air. Not a soul teaches them this. They merely follow instinct."

"So you are acting on instinct?"

She crossed her arms over her stomach and leaned back slightly on her feet. "In a manner of speaking." She nodded her head while grinning.

Flustered and not sure what else to do, Rivic reached out for her. "Let's go," he said, his tongue striking the words. The mention of his sister unnerved him. As far as he knew, Nyree had never met this woman standing before him. As for acting on instinct, his natural proficiency had destroyed two villages and killed all his living relatives, save for his sister, in the explosions.

Madame Orcee spun away from his grasp with a laugh. "Are you sure you don't want a reading, your own reading, first?"

"Quite," Rivic answered. "Cirvel is waiting."

"For shame. The leaves said you might be interesting in hearing what they would like to tell you." She pointed at the black marks on the white wall.

"They are wrong. Now come with me."

She shrugged before reaching out to wrap her fingers around his wrist. "I suppose you will come and see me at another time."

"I'm not sure you should wait for it. Talcor dun."

As Cirvel's antechamber came into view, the blue stone had shifted back to Rivic's left hand. Another ripple of vertigo swelled through him and he placed the stone on the table, wanting it out of his hand.

But there was something else.

Something dangerous.

It pressed against his dragon aspects and he wanted to snarl. Knowing that only Cirvel and Madame Orcee were in the room, he fought to suppress it. Yet the powerful tendency forced him to look away toward a wall. When he finally won the internal battle and returned to the conversation already going on between Cirvel and Orcee, Rivic noticed that Cirvel's face had changed, elongating slightly, and his lips growled around a mouth full of sharp teeth. Even for as scary as Cirvel had become, Orcee moved closer.

"Now a show of force is not needed. I came, my lord, I came," Orcee was saying.

"Aye, but sometimes I think you like to forget what you are dealing with, what I allow in the ways of your particular idiosyncrasies."

As Cirvel spoke back to Orcee, Rivic wondered if his own face had changed like that when he'd discovered his dragon teeth. The curious sight of it enthralled Rivic rather than repelled, yet he knew he needed to hold his position and not give himself away.

Cirvel pushed his cup along the surface of the table toward her.

She cast an astringent glance at it. "'Tis more beneficial if you are drinking it as I pull out the leaves."

"Other oracles just read the leaves settled at the bottom of the cup; they have no need to make a mess," Cirvel growled back.

Orcee pulled out a chair, taking up the cup as she settled down into the seat. "As you request, we can do without the show." She looked down toward the bottom and swirled the small amount of remaining tea around a couple of times.

"I want specifics about acquiring what I need. There is no need to embellish on anything further," Cirvel instructed.

Orcee's brown eyes sparkled with mischief as she continued to study the leaves. "But there is so much here, as always, my lord."

"Just what I need."

In Cirvel's growing anger, a sense of danger rose within Rivic again. He wanted to draw back, to let his own mouth reshape itself to the dragon teeth, and to feel the claws rising to the surface on his fingertips.

Once again, Rivic glanced away, curling his fingers into his palms and resisting the advancing urges.

He didn't understand why Madame Orcee made Lord Cirvel irritated, but these base novihomidrak reactions brought some understanding to the guarded tendencies Rivic felt when he was around the woman.

Orcee continued as if she were weary, "I await the day when you are not so boring and instead appreciate all I do for you."

"Just what I need," Cirvel repeated with heavy annunciation.

Orcee shrugged, then looked back down into the cup. A moment later, she began to grin and turned her gaze to Rivic. "Very observant."

Cirvel and Rivic exchanged a curiously confused look before Orcee continued, "Your apprentice will not make your mistakes. He wonders what you are missing by not getting everything I see and has decided to not make the same mismanagement. When he seeks me out again, he will not make the same error as you and will ask, nay, command me to tell him everything."

With a chill going through him, Rivic realized that he'd barely had that thought. It hadn't even been long enough for the decision to settle into his conscious mind. Had she read his thoughts, or did she see it in the tea leaves?

Cirvel's face darkened. "He is not my apprentice; he's a Dominus trainee."

"But your Knight Captain," Orcee interrupted quickly.

"And if the fool should want you to tell him everything and let you dig as deep as you wish into his business, that is his choice, as unwise as it might be."

"Could be that your apprentice is more innocent with so many fewer dark secrets than his mentor."

A ripple of danger tingled over Rivic's back. If Orcee didn't stop her taunting soon, he would have to make her quiet. Rivic wasn't certain why he felt this way, only that the settled decision came swiftly.

"Enough. I am not training the boy. I leave that to his teachers. What do I need to know now?"

She tipped the cup to the sides as she stared down into the bottom. After a length, she dipped her index finger into the dregs and pulled several leaves out onto her fingertip. These she dabbed against the palm of her other hand. "What you thought impossible is being delivered." She recovered from the statement with a deep breath. While Cirvel's elation grew, Orcee seemed to be defeated, as if she'd lost a battle she'd been assured to win. "Babies are on their way. You will get what you require."

Cirvel looked quite pleased and perhaps a bit relieved. "Very good. Knight Captain Rivic, please see Madame Orcee home."

Orcee wasn't done. She slapped her hand on the table and examined the leaves splattered on the wood as she drew back her hand. Then she laughed. "Too bad they all will be snatched from your grasp!"

She rose from her chair and stepped back, her gaze never leaving the leaves on the wooden table. She chuckled again. "How very proud your mother becomes at once again seeing you in defeat."

"Nay!" Cirvel said, rising from his chair.

Orcee covered her mouth with her hands as she continued to snicker. "What you need is coming, but you shall not have it. How very clever." She took one last look back down at her hand and the few leaves that still clung there.

"What do you see?"

"You, my lord, told me to reveal nothing more than what you needed to know now. I follow your command."

"Tell me!" Cirvel raged, magic beginning to twist around his moving hands.

Orcee pointed a warning finger at him. "You are locked in by your own magic. You asked and I told you what you requested. You cannot force me to do more."

She momentarily sagged on her feet as if this undeclared battle between them took an extreme tole on her energy. "What you need is coming. 'Tis not meant to be yours though. You will have to wait to see what time holds."

"If you don't confess what you know, I will find a way to make you."

Orcee moved toward Rivic, ignoring Cirvel's threat as if she'd never been touched by one of his punishments. "I'll be home now, if you'll take me."

Tiredness had seeped into her deep brown eyes, making them seem far older than Orcee currently appeared outwardly. Her fingers weakly grasped Rivic's wrist, showing that she had no more strength in her.

Rivic nodded and gave one last look to Cirvel to see if they would be stopped. When Cirvel said nothing, Rivic picked up the stone and let the magic whisk them away to the tea shop.

CHAPTER 14

*R*ivic dragged himself out of bed far too early the next morning. He felt as if he'd fallen asleep right in time to wake up and get the day started.

He skipped the morning meal to hurry out onto the training field due to his lateness. None of the other domini had arrived yet, but in the early morning chill, a warm glow coming through the open door of a stone building attached to the castle drew him in. Moist heat and strange clanking sounds greeted him as he drew closer. Spying inside, he saw the weapons master working away at hammering the reddened iron of a sword blade.

Master Glayth caught sight of him. "Glad to see the Knight Captain out first on the field today."

"What are you doing?"

"Preparing new swords. You Domini do go through them quickly."

"So, you make them?"

"Aye. Did you think they just appeared on the rack and ready for students?"

Rivic wasn't certain what he thought, especially since he

hadn't given it much attention before. He shrugged. "I guess maybe I just didn't expect you to do it."

"The best way to know your weapon is to make it yourself."

That seemed to make sense. And yet, Rivic's memory recalled something he wished he hadn't: that moment when his sword had seemed to move on its own and killed Melodin. Why wasn't he able to forget? He felt a surge of energy behind the memory and a question popped out, "Is it possible to put enchantments on the weapon?"

"Aye."

That answer Rivic already knew in his heart, but it seemed like a preface. "Would you do it while you were working the metal, or afterward?"

Glayth finished hammering and plunged the metal into a pool of water. "Depends on how strong you'd like the magic to be. Ones worked in during forging are far more powerful than those placed afterwards."

"Do you do that with any of the swords you create?"

"Aye, I have. Wouldn't be interested in learning, would you?"

He almost answered with the negative, but a small tug from his gut told him to take Glayth up on the offer. "I have made one before when I was with my tribe, but it was a crude effort and I always felt it was incomplete."

"'Tis a start then, but would you like to continue, maybe learn what was missing from your earlier attempt?"

He must have given just enough of a nod for Glayth set his tools down as he said, "Good. We'll find a time to work it in with the rest of your training. Now, can you help me take out the weapons?"

Rivic helped Master Glayth carry the racks of swords out onto the training field. Ordinarily, Glayth used magic to move them out each morning, unless there was a strong, warm body to help him transport them. Rivic suspected Glayth liked the physical activity over the use of magic.

The other domini showed up and began warming up. Today they would work with swords. Rivic had no need to pick a weapon from the rack as he already had his.

Three quarters of the way through training, Lord Cirvel strolled out onto the ground, walking right through several of the armed combatants who continued their attacks while avoiding Cirvel. No one dared to hit the Lord of Gohaldinest. Rivic continued his strikes against his opponent, not caring that Cirvel was on the field. He knew that was actually what Cirvel was looking for. Determination, aggression, concentration, all necessary elements for a good Necroatheling.

Cirvel crossed over to Master Glayth, keeping his back to the Domini as he spoke to Glayth. After a moment, the weapons master raised his hand and called out, "Knight Captain Rivic, come over here please."

Rivic put the sword into his scabbard and jogged over to Cirvel and Glayth. He tried hard to control his deep breathing from the exertion he been going through, not wanting to look worn out, but he could not control the ample inhalations he needed. "Yes sir?"

Cirvel tapped him on the shoulder, then turned to walk off. After giving Master Glayth a questioning look and receiving no confirmation from the weapons master either, Rivic followed. He wondered what Lord Cirvel had in store for him now. They didn't go far before Cirvel began, "I've been hearing some interesting facts about your magic."

"Like what?" Rivic tried to stomp down the fear in his stomach. He couldn't afford for his nerves to give him away now.

They stopped before a doorway into the castle and Cirvel faced Rivic.

"That perhaps it is special. That perhaps you have been favored." Cirvel put his hand beneath Rivic's jaw and tilted Rivic's head to look them over and inspect them. Rivic gasped as he saw the yellow covering over Cirvel's eyes. In some ways it reminded him of the way his sister's eyes looked occasionally. Cirvel smiled at his reaction. It lasted only a second before Cirvel's eyebrows once again furrowed as he continued to inspect Rivic. "Give me your hand."

Rivic offered his hand to Lord Cirvel. Cirvel pulled the blade out from beneath his robes and made a quick cut along the outside edge of Rivic's palm.

Rivic hissed with pain and tried to snatch back his arm. Cirvel held onto it, staring at the growing amount of blood.

"You do bleed." Cirvel healed the wound. "Have you been favored by a dragon, boy? Are you a sapere?"

Rivic shook his head. "I don't know what you're talking about."

"Come with me." Cirvel threw open the door and entered, rushing down the castle hallways.

Rivic once again had a hard time keeping up with Cirvel's quick pace. Cirvel's long black hair swayed across his back as he hurried forward. Meanwhile, Rivic felt the sweat rolling down him and it didn't help to cool his nerves. He could practically feel the anger coming off Cirvel.

"People say that I am arrogant." Cirvel's lips curled into a sneer. "But are you so naïve that you would believe that I wouldn't know what type of magic you have? Do you think I'm so much a fool that I wouldn't realize you had dragon magic? Do you not understand that I have seen through your every deception in trying first to cover Alityka's magic by saying you were a Dominari, to your sordid attempts at hiding your own power?"

Rivic couldn't speak. Several more steps, around a couple of turns, lapsed while Rivic tried to keep up with Cirvel. It seemed as if the Lord of Gohaldinest put no effort into his stride.

"Answer me, lad!"

Rivic flinched at Cirvel's tone, the rage seeming not to only be coming from Cirvel but the very walls of Gohaldinest as well.

"I don't know," Rivic said. He still couldn't overcome his own shock. He had been silly and naïve for thinking that Cirvel wouldn't know what type of magic he had. A man of this power... of course he knew! He placed his left hand on the scabbard to keep the metal from bouncing against his leg as he ran to keep up.

"Let us be done with this, shall we?"

"Done with what?" Rivic asked, his heart thundering as a chill swept down his arms.

"Done with the lies. Let us find out the truth about you, shall we?"

Rivic tried to make a sound which he hoped Cirvel wouldn't take as a commitment to either side.

"Good." Cirvel faced a tapestry. "Satatie recor'malem hari sacodion vanache chekom ra tanasae."

The tapestry shimmered as magic overtook it. The weaving turned to a wooden doorway with thick iron plating covering the spaces between the boards. Magic frosted the air, swirling through the gateway. The round, domed bolts impaling the iron through the wood seemed like solid bars of a prison door to which the only way out from was death. Whatever was behind this door was never meant to get out.

Cirvel raised his arms. "Plon myk radenish fa vencor tora ving rith allion warch'do nee iths groben da tali'ack suda tae."

The waves of magic rolling off Cirvel forced Rivic to take a step back. He blinked his eyes as he felt momentarily dizzy. A flash of silver caught his gaze and forced him to look up.

The wood and iron no longer blocked their path, but rather it looked like a gaping hole with a gossamer veil.

Cirvel turned with a smile to Rivic. "Your sister walked by this door with me one evening and said that stone by stone this city would move. Do you feel that is a possibility?"

With as much magic as protected the doorway and the arch it stood in, Rivic didn't see how that would be possible. He shook his head while wondering what Cirvel had been doing here with Nyree. Had she been just as scared as he was now? Of course, she wouldn't have been able to feel the ancient magicks, but maybe the complete unknown was more frightening than this.

Cirvel held out his hand and a long wooden staff appeared. He clenched it tightly, thumping the end on the floor with each pace they took. On the other end was a round yellowish-orange glob of amber and a long needle extended beyond that. The needle vibrated as they moved down the halls, letting it sing out a high whistle accented by each stomp against the stone. Something about it both exhilarated Rivic and terrified him.

Before them, a great arch doorway appeared. Cirvel stepped through. There was a staircase and he went down, straight down, steeply. The way ended with a great wooden door reinforced with wrought iron work and a solid latch. Rivic fully expected the doors to be locked, but when Cirvel touched the latch, it clicked and opened at a mere press.

Cirvel shoved both doors, swinging them wide open. He stepped through the entryway and flung his arms wide as he walked forward. "Who is this boy and why is he here?" Cirvel demanded to know, his voice extraordinarily deep and growling. "Is this some plot you have against me?"

At first, Rivic wondered who Cirvel was screaming at, but then he saw the yellow eyes open. The dark blackness ahead of him seemed to shrug off sleep and ripple as it rose, and Rivic recognized the dragon.

"Guardian, I demand answers," Cirvel hollered.

"I wish you wouldn't storm in here and disturb my slumber," the dragon responded.

"You serve me." As if to prove his point, he took the staff and jabbed the needle into the dragon. Blue sparks flew from the black scales.

The Guardian didn't even look annoyed. "You should be ashamed of yourself, Cirvel. No other novihomidrak would dare to betray his dragon mother."

"I wouldn't know about that," Cirvel said. "We will not have this conversation again. You will answer my questions about the lad."

The dragon swung her head toward Rivic, and for a moment, Rivic thought she might admit to having birthed him as well. "He looks like a boy on the verge of becoming a man, perhaps showing a tendency of being a little destructive with his magic."

Cirvel slammed the end of the staff down on the ground and yellow sparks skittered over the stone floor. "I can find nothing extraordinary about the boy, but everything about him says that he is special."

"Then there you have it. He is special. Now, why disturb my slumber for that?"

"I am in need of a new sapere."

"And so, because the Wells are closed, you think to make this boy a servant of the dragons, a helper to you, because he is special?"

"I do."

"It is not that easy. To become a wise one who serves the dragons takes many years of training, of special education, to learn skills that he cannot get here under you."

"Do it anyway. He is special, you can mark him. Make him my new sapere."

"I cannot mark him."

"Why not?"

"He would serve you better as a Necroatheling, for he is similar to you."

Cirvel gave it a moment to take this in, then gasped. "He is a novihomidrak."

"Aye, but not a perfect one like you," the Guardian admitted.

Cirvel's eyes narrowed. "Are you saying that this boy could stand against me?"

"This boy could stand against you. Or he might not," the Guardian taunted. "But you know the youth cannot oppose you, since you are so powerful of a novihomidrak, so I don't know why you are bothering to worry about him. He is special, but he is also flawed."

"That is exactly what my tests have revealed about him. His markers are on the bloodwave of this world. I cut him with my dagger."

"I had to split the pearl between the twins. He will always be vulnerable," the Guardian told Cirvel plainly as if she were bored.

"Why did you create another novihomidrak?" Cirvel asked. "I need a sapere, not a novihomidrak. You have spent your time working on this child and then you refuse me what I truly need saying that it will take too much time?"

The dragon laid her head back down on the ground as if this conversation was ended and she closed her eyes.

"Call your weapons to you," Cirvel demanded to Rivic. "Let me see them."

"He has only one," the Guardian responded, not opening her eyes.

"One?" Understanding rippled through Cirvel. "Another flaw. Your magicless twin has the other. Call your weapon."

Rivic had gotten used to being quiet and didn't know if he could now find his voice. He certainly wasn't going to offer the information that he could call Nyree's weapon to him as well. "Vochey Honor," he said, his voice barely a whisper. His sword came to his hand.

"As a novihomidrak, he is flawed," the dragon repeated. "But there is another choice. He will make a strong Necroatheling for you. Will you train him, mentor him?"

Cirvel's eyes were filled with venom. Rivic realized his life hung in the balance. He dropped to kneel before the Lord of Gohaldinest. "Please, Lord Cirvel, let me serve you as a Necroatheling."

"I do not know what you and your sister are up to, but I will figure it out."

"My sister has no magical ability," Rivic said. "I came to Gohaldinest because your Necroathelings kidnapped Nyree. I only stay because you have manipulated it. If you wish to have my oath as a Necroatheling, I will give it." Especially if it kept Nyree safe.

Cirvel levelled the pointed end of the staff at Rivic. "You are dangerous."

"I swear," Rivic began, not daring to glance up at Cirvel, "I will do whatever I need to in order to prove myself. Teach me what it means to be a novihomidrak and I will make sure no other Necroatheling stands before me."

Cirvel remained quiet.

"You know a mentor couldn't be provided for him," the Guardian said.

Cirvel's black robes snapped as he turned and started for the doorway.

"Do you not see how you can use this to your advantage?" the Guardian asked.

Cirvel glowered back at the dragon. "The task was mine to complete. I must see this through myself."

"And what if you can't?" The Guardian let a silent pause hang in the air. "He might be flawed, but he could carry the mission."

Rivic felt like an interloper to an argument he shouldn't have been privy too, yet he couldn't help watching for Cirvel's reaction.

"I need a replacement for my sapere, not for me. When will you quit fighting and start helping me? Fine. You want to play it this way? I will meet your request." Cirvel's tight face pulled into a snarl as he turned severely narrowed eyes toward Rivic. "I will have your oath as a Necroatheling to me sooner rather than later."

He snatched up Rivic's hand and dragged him out of the room. With a flick of Cirvel's hand, the door slammed shut behind them and Rivic heard the heavy lock sound in the door.

Cirvel took a deep breath. "I apologize. This news has come as a great surprise to me and I seek your understanding to forgive me."

"Of course," Rivic answered, half breathless and stunned that he was still alive. Of all the ways he'd thought of Cirvel discovering the truth about him, his novimather blurting it out was not one of them. He felt quite certain that Cirvel could have killed them both over the confession.

"I must find the cahaster who is willing to accept you. Once I have done that, we shall discuss this further." Cirvel began to walk in silence through the underground tunnels slightly ahead of Rivic, who, afraid of being lost, followed closely behind.

The luminosity from the stone of Cirvel's staff emitted the only light for Rivic to see by. Everything outside the ring fell quickly into blackness and Rivic couldn't see the many turns they took until Cirvel changed directions.

"How do you know your way around in here?" Rivic asked finally, hoping that he would have a clue of how to return to the city above if Cirvel disappeared.

"Blink down your dragon lids," Cirvel ordered. "You do have those dragon aspects, do you not?"

"I do not."

"Ah, your sister's strange eyes," Cirvel said with a slow nod. "Tomorrow we should sit down and discuss what all you know about your own abilities and discover what you still need to learn."

Rivic gave his acceptance, even though he still wasn't certain that Cirvel wouldn't tear his throat out. Why that hadn't happened yet was beyond Rivic's comprehension. Not that he wouldn't be grateful for that.

"I apologize for leaving you in darkness then. I have long asked you for your loyalty and trust. Maybe now I need to extend my own sincerity back to you." Cirvel raised a hand and muttered something in an odd language. A bright, shimmering line of red began to dangle in the air. "Dragon magic. If you had dragon vision, you'd be able to see it without me having to reveal the spell. It helps leave a path so that dragons or novihomidraks can find each other."

"So this is your breadcrumb trail?"

"Of sorts. I discovered it back when I was lost."

"You were lost?"

"I did not come to this world by my own choice. I was sent here to be a champion. I made several mistakes and was captured. Not my finest hour." Cirvel nodded, then continued, "I managed to escape to these caves. The nights grew so cold and dark as I lay there listening to the water dripping off the walls that I thought I might lose my mind. I cowered in fear, waiting for my captors to come and find me. Every time the water dripped, I thought it might be them and their footsteps echoing in the distance. I took off, running blindly through the caves. I blinked down my dragon lids as I went. Of course, with the dragon vision, I had enough sight to find my way through the tunnels, but that didn't stop my terror. I came across this red line and it led me to safety."

"That means there was another novihomidrak here before?"

"Nay, 'twas not a novihomidrak who place the magic here, but a dragon."

While Rivic let the information settle in, Cirvel went on, "I have walked this trail so many times since that I no longer need my dragon lids. My power now feels the way along the trail."

Now that Cirvel had mentioned it, Rivic felt it too, the magic that seemed to call to his as if they engaged in a dance. "Who were you running from?" Rivic asked. "Who thought to capture you?"

"Fools," Cirvel said sharply. "Mortals who believed they could trap my power, but were mere children playing with fire."

"Forgive me for saying so, my lord, but obviously they had you running. They must have endangered you enough for you to fear them."

Cirvel snorted. "I feared what evils I found on this world. There is much you do not understand about novihomidraks, but we will work through that later and you will come to understand what I unveiled. Until then, I beg you not to judge me."

"What about the dragon that set this trail? Did you find him?"

"This trail is old. Look here and you can see where the magic frays."

As Rivic went to inspect where Cirvel indicated, he

noticed that Cirvel's eyes had gone yellow as Nyree's often did, except the pupil was a true slit rather than having taken the shape of a torch. Seeing the surprise splash across Rivic's face, Cirvel smiled. "Aye, if I'd been observant, I would have seen the signs sooner and known the truth. That Salvarae had to split the powers between you succeeded in keeping you hidden. But now, everything about you is so clear."

The sensation of a threat vibrated below the surface and Rivic felt the swallow in his throat as a good sign that Cirvel hadn't ripped it out yet. "My lord, I have no idea of what I am. Nyree seemed to have a greater understanding than I ever did. I am excited to learn from you. Now, you were speaking of frays in the magic?"

"Aye. You asked if I found the dragon... I did not. This trail had been placed long before I discovered it, even predating the city built atop of these caverns." Cirvel seemed to debate for a moment, but came to his decision quickly. "Gohaldinest was originally built to safeguard the two dragons who lived here."

"Against?"

"Many things. You will begin to understand as we begin your lessons. That explanation will take more time than we have, and my search for a sapere becomes twice as required now. I have other arrangements to make as well. 'Tis time we get back."

Cirvel waved his hand. Wind snapped in the air, forcing Rivic to close his eyes. When he opened them again, he was back in the Domini dormitory and alone.

CHAPTER 15

"Someone's been to see Mother," Dragzel said, covering his nose with his paws as Rivic met the cahaster in the hallway a short distance from the stairs to the Domini's basement. "You smell just like Cirvel now. That didn't take you long."

"What do you want, cahaster?" Rivic asked. "I've had a long day training and I'm looking forward to supper and a bath."

"I'm pretty sure that odor isn't washing off of you."

"Dragzel!"

"All right! Alityka wants to see you and she's in enough of a hurry that she probably doesn't care if you stink. You could probably be covered in stable manure and she wouldn't care."

There seemed to be a pressing urgency in the cahaster's tone. "Why? What's happening?" Rivic stopped to kneel by the cahaster.

"You weren't the only one to visit Mother recently."

At first, Rivic thought Dragzel might have meant Alityka, but realized that the cahaster would have said the Guardian if it had been Alityka. Besides, how would have Alityka found her way through the tunnels alone?

"All right, I can see I'm going to have to spell this out for you," Dragzel said at Rivic's continued silence. He went on in a secretive tone, "I took the spell Kalt gave Alityka to Salvarae to see if she could find a way to adjust how much time it gives before recalling the caster. Ali wants to try it again and see if the modifications worked."

"Now?"

"Aye, now."

Rivic shook his head and tsked at the thought of a champion needing temperance. Over and over, his novimather's words rang through his head as Alityka continued to prove the truth of her being. "Let us be on our way."

Dragzel herded Rivic to Lihn's library. Rivic stepped inside and found Lihn sitting at the table in the center of the room, a few books spread open in front of her. The magic she'd been practicing collapsed at the sight of him.

"Blessed day, Rivic," she said with a bright smile. "Alityka should be here soon. She said she wanted to attempt a second visit to Galault. I expected her already, but it appears she is late."

Dragzel jumped up on Lihn's lap and eyed Rivic over the table. "You should probably tell her about your visit."

Rivic's blank mind took a moment to figure out what the cahaster was referring to, but it came with a sudden rush of adrenalized fear. "Right! Cirvel knows I'm a novihomidrak."

"What? How?" Lihn asked.

Rivic went through the story about Cirvel taking him down to see the Guardian. "What am I going to do? Cirvel wants me to take the Necroatheling oath now. There's no way I'm ready to handle that kind of magic."

"He'll have to find the cahaster who is willing to take your soul first."

"I don't even know what that entails, or why."

Lihn leaned forward in her chair. "The Necroatheling store their souls in cahasters in order to keep them alive longer. It would take a significant amount of damage for the body to die. That's why no one's been able to get close to Lord Cirvel so far. His Necroatheling guards are nearly immortal."

"That doesn't sound that bad," Rivic said. "It might even out the fact that my sister and I had to split the protection of the dragon's pearl. I might be able to take Cirvel on if I'm a Necroatheling."

Dragzel placed his front paws on the table. "I'll do it."

They looked to Dragzel as if they had misheard him. "What was that?" Lihn asked.

"I'll do it." Dragzel sat back on his haunches. "The number of cahasters is getting slim. The dragon hasn't birthed any in quite some time. While he hasn't asked me directly, Cirvel has been indicating that he'd like me to take a soul. I already know what's going on and how important this is. I will house Rivic's soul."

"There's one other thing that you have to do," Lihn said. "You can't officially become a Necroatheling and gain access to that magic until you take a life."

"I've taken a life," he said, remembering the day when he'd received the title of dominus.

"That one doesn't count," Lihn said. "You have to do it in a ceremony to bind your Necroatheling powers to you."

"I'm certain that Cirvel will have a ready victim for me."

The door creaked open behind them and Alityka entered. She had clearly been in a fight, her hair mussed and tangled, half hanging in her face, but when she saw them, a delighted grin lit across her lips. She reached up to wipe a trickle of blood from her mouth before it ran down over her chin.

Rivic felt his breath steal away at the sight of her. He

froze, feeling pinned and unable to move. "Ali, what happened?"

"By the gods, Rivic, it was brilliant!" She walked forward, her hands gesturing before her. "The Necroathelings took me to The Playground."

Rivic came out of his chair and pulled a seat out for Alityka as she raked her fingers through her hair in a failing attempt to calm it. She dropped a bag on the floor and leaned toward Lihn. "That was so much fun."

"Wait, Ali," he said, slipping back down into his seat. "You shouldn't be hurt. That's not what happens. Did they actually make you fight someone?"

Alityka laughed as she sat down. "Gods, nay, Rivic. This was afterward when they were trying to get me to leave. I wanted to stay. There's a Necroatheling out there who has a really fat lip now."

"Oh, is that what I was sensing?" Lihn asked.

"Nay, that was probably the limp I gave him." She slid her hands across the table and took ahold of Lihn's fingers.

"Ali!" Rivic shouted. "You can't just go taking on Necroathelings."

"How are you going to hurt them, Rivic? Come on, have some fun. You can be as destructive as you want with a Necroatheling and they are just going to shake it off. Quit fearing your magic."

He sat back, feeling chastised and reserved while Alityka and Lihn spoke rapidly about the battles. Was Alityka right? He'd spent so long trying to control his magic, but did he do so out of fear? Did he walk a line, afraid of what would happen if he let loose? If he were truthful with himself, he'd have to admit that he was.

"Oh, look!" Alityka jumped up and pulled up the bottom edge of her acolyte dress. "I won a brand."

When Rivic first looked at it, he thought it was a bird.

Then he realized it was a circle with lines and arcs coming out of it. The figure itself couldn't be identified as a simple geometric shape, but rather several combined.

"They called me the 'flying sword.' You should have seen me. It really was incredible. I don't know why you don't like it." Her last line she said directly to Rivic. Then, as if ashamed by her comment, she pointed back to the brand. "These three lines here in this sword-like area, they represent us and how we will defeat Cirvel."

Lihn at least seemed to appreciate the humor. Rivic just felt uncomfortable with the joyous reaction to Alityka's bloodlust. He hoped that her actions toward the Necroathelings wouldn't reciprocate punishment from Cirvel. Tempering. His dragon mother had understated what he'd have to deal with in that area.

"Let's get to it, shall we?" Alityka fetched the scroll from a bag set beside her on the floor. "The Guardian might have been able to modify the spell for us."

"I'll keep guard for you," Dragzel said as he departed from Lihn's lap to a pillow beneath the table. He swirled around, curled into his normal sleeping posture, and closed his eyes.

Rivic closed the door and cast a locking enchantment.

Alityka spread the scroll on the table and looked to Rivic. "We shall be quick. I want to speak to Galault again. I knew you'd want to be there, so I also had the Guardian modify the spell so we can both safely go."

"Then let's do this." He reached out and took Alityka's hand.

Alityka recited the spell. For a moment, the blackness which swallowed Rivic felt a shade different than it had before. Then the sensation was lost. Emerging on the other side of the magic, they found themselves in the same hallway where they had first met Galault.

Alityka stumbled, eyes closed, as she shook her head as if to clear it. "That was a powerful spell."

Rivic placed his hand on the hilt to his sword. He felt every sense sharpen to full alertness. Magic rippled behind him and he spun around.

Galault stepped out from a painting on the wall. "Why have you returned?"

"We need help," Alityka said after a gasp of surprise at Galault's sudden appearance.

"I have given you all the help you need. I told you 'tis my father's assistance you must pursue."

"But how? How do I do that? Please help me understand what I must do."

Galault's eyes filled with tears as he looked to the floor and shook his head. "I was told this would be hard. I want nothing more than to please you by giving you the information you require, but I cannot."

"If you won't tell us what we're supposed to do to recruit your father, then how about telling us how events play out? Give us the start at least."

Galault reached back into the painting and pulled out a chair from somewhere off to the side of the frame. Sitting down, he leaned over his legs, resting his elbows on his knees, but keeping his hands free so he could gesture with his hands. He turned his gaze to Rivic. "So, my father first meets Alityka in the forest when he's chasing what he thought were bandits. It actually turned out to be gargaxes, but he didn't even know what those beasts were or even of their existence. Alityka said to him, 'For you to not understand who you are, what you are becoming, that would be unfortunate.' Then, she came to him later in the catacombs and told him not to be afraid of his own demons."

Rivic felt as if Alityka had told him the same statements.

"That thing about being unfortunate, that's what he said

to me. I knew he was mocking me." Alityka said thoughtfully. "Is that all I say to him? I appear and disappear?"

"Well, nay," Galault said, as if curious as to why she was asking these questions, as if he were making himself perfectly clear.

"Nay? What more do I say? Why should he even listen to me or believe me?"

"Well, he just does. You were chanting the old rites."

"Old rites?"

"Coom ra wialca do, sha belieka ne. Ha ne." Galault's voice faded out as he went along. "Oh, right, you haven't created the religion for the Goddess yet." He pointed at Rivic. "Well, you will, and it'll be great."

"The words sound like the dragon tongue," Rivic muttered his thoughts aloud. "For the Goddess in Her Love I serve. Praise her."

"Goddess, did you say?" Alityka asked. "Who is this Goddess?"

Shock filled Galault's eyes. "Why you, Lady Alityka, of course."

The mocking smile fell right off Alityka's face. "Me?" She glanced over to Rivic, who felt his cheeks flush, as if he had any answers for her questions. With her natural beauty, it wouldn't be hard to imagine Alityka as a goddess.

Fortunately for him, she let the surprise and curiosity fade quickly before she asked, "How long has it been since Rivic created this religion?"

Rivic nearly laughed out loud. Leave it to Alityka to ask a clever question which would reveal how much time would pass before Galault's father would live in this world.

Galault smiled, revealing that he also caught the intent behind Alityka's question. "Two thousand cycles."

"Two thousand!" Rivic exploded.

Heavy breaths rushed in and out of Alityka's mouth as

she grappled with the fathoms of that gap. "What makes the passing of two thousand cycles necessary before we take down Cirvel? Why aren't we able to do it now?"

"I'm afraid that my father would be much better to answer that then I," Galault answered as he rose from his chair and guided Alityka to sit in his place.

"How do we get through two thousand cycles? I mean, surely none of us actually live that long. Not a single person that we know will be alive." These thoughts all seemed to register in Alityka's mind and heart as she collapsed into the seat Galault offered.

Rivic recalled Cirvel telling him in the tunnels that he'd had several thousand cycles to make his plans. Had Cirvel already lived through at least two thousand? How many more would he live? Would Rivic, in also being a novihomidrak, have an equally long life? Long enough to span that time easily? When Rivic pulled himself from his own thoughts, he noticed Galault studying him and Rivic glanced away. How much of his own theories had Galault caught in that brief moment where their eyes had locked?

"I suppose we do have the time travel spell. We could just go there," Alityka stated.

"Nay, you don't." Galault rested a hand on Alityka's shoulder. "You must live in your time."

"But people are suffering now. If we have to wait two thousand cycles to stop Cirvel, countless others will struggle under his tyranny. If I can't stop him now, I might as well go where I can do some good. Otherwise, I won't be there and I have to see this through."

Galault eased down on his knees beside her and took her hand. Before he started to speak, he studied her hand in his as if it were a most precious valuable. "I assure you that because you continue to live in your time, you force the postponement of Cirvel's plans for the same time. 'Twill take both of you to halt what is going on in Gohaldinest. Your actions there will carry you to my father's time. Have faith that because I am here, my words are true. You will find the way."

For a long moment where he seemed on the verge of tears, Galault remained beside her, holding her hand, and staring at her face. Then realizing he'd extended the time longer than he should have, he stood up and released her gently. "Trust me."

"I do, but please tell us how we do it. I trust you and I'm not even sure why, but I don't see how your words could be true."

Galault looked warily at the frame of the painting he'd first emerged from as if he were wondering if he needed to dive back into it. "I fear telling you too much. What if I mess something up?"

"What if you don't tell us something that we need to know and it messes everything up?" Alityka said, obviously trying to use Galault's own fear against him.

But Galault had obviously thought this through too. "I'd rather take the chance of saying nothing. It might be different if I could know that everything was happening as in the stories that I know."

"Why don't you just tell us how we defeat Cirvel?" Rivic asked

"I could do that, but there are so many pieces to this puzzle that all must be placed just right. My part is slight in the end, my help needed more now than later. 'Tis truly my father that you need if you wish to win. And if I told you how it would go, choices would be made that would alter the outcome. As a watcher of worlds, I cannot do that. I cannot let you make choices of the heart that would defy what needs to happen. Victory comes from pain. You must make the choices that I know you need to. You must do things that in later retrospect you will wish you hadn't. That is what it will take to win. As a watcher of worlds, and someone who has already seen many possible outcomes, I cannot in good conscience tell you. All I will say is that the game is bigger than you even know."

Realizing that Alityka's next sharp words were going to be scathing, he stepped to push her backwards. "Nice try," he whispered, hoping it would soothe her. He doubted that it would. Then he turned back to Galault. "I'm sorry, Galault. We've been so focused on the future and what we need to do that we haven't even asked you if there's anything we can do for you."

"I'm afraid that what I need is something that you couldn't grant me." He paused before he went on to explain, "I wish I could have seen my father's greatest moments rather than hearing about them afterwards. So many people have told me about his exploits, but they all seemed unbelievable to me. I don't know how he could do all that; it doesn't seem like the same man I knew growing up."

"Come with us now," Alityka said, reaching to touch his arm. "We need your stories and the knowledge you have. 'Tis the only way for us to figure out how to stop and eventually defeat Cirvel. You wouldn't have to tell us what happens, but rather if we were going in the right direction according to the stories that you know."

"Nay, I'm sorry. I can't. And I can't make you understand my reasons. Go now." Galault turned toward the painting and made to step back into it.

As if the spell heard the command for them to leave, Rivic felt it wrapping itself up around them.

"Not without him," Alityka shrieked. She jumped toward Galault and embraced him in a tight hug.

"I can't go," Galault protested, trying to break away.

Alityka's eyes widened as she fought to keep her grip on

the young man who, though being scrawny, was larger and outweighed her. After a moment of hesitation in which Rivic debated about kidnapping versus knowing the help they needed, Rivic embraced both Galault and Alityka to hold them all together. The world dissolved around them for an instant.

The three of them collapsed in a breathless heap on the floor of Lihn's library.

Beneath the table, the cahaster opened one eye. "More for the party," Dragzel said disapprovingly. Then he curled into a tighter coil and went back to sleep.

CHAPTER 16

The oppressive darkness of Lihn's special library was the first thing that Rivic took in, quickly followed by the various body parts entwined with his as he, Galault, and Alityka tried to get up off the floor. The scent of spent magic swirled around them, amplifying Rivic's awareness and bristling against his novihomidrak senses.

"I am a watcher of worlds," Galault protested with dignity as he climbed to his feet and brushed his hands over his white robes. "You cannot do this. You cannot hold me against my will. I can easily return. 'Tis naught which can be done to imprison me."

Alityka disentangled herself from Rivic and jumped to her feet to grab onto Galault's arm. "I'm sorry. Our spell was ending and we desperately need your help. Please help us figure some things out."

Rivic caught sight of slender silver slippers and the edge of a green dress covering a woman's legs. Lihn had approached and was aiding to get everyone settled.

"The help you need is my father's. He is the hero, not me." Galault broke away from Alityka and saw Lihn. "Oh, hello!"

"Bright blessings, Watcher," Lihn said. She folded her hands together in front of her. "I am Lihn. Can I get you something to eat or drink?"

Rivic pushed himself off the floor and straightened himself up while he tried to decide how angry over Alityka's actions he should be. Discovering Lihn's ease, he wondered if she knew this would happen and had been expecting it. How irritated should he be over Alityka having the courage to bring Galault back with them if the action was exactly what needed to be.

"Um," Galault said, obviously trying to process all the information as well as the question she had issued. It seemed to overwhelm him for a moment. Then he said, "Lihn Harvestendale?"

She brightened. "Aye."

Galault's shoulders rolled forward as he threw a hand over his mouth. At first, Rivic thought Galault might be choking, but then realized that the watcher of worlds was laughing. "Oh, my stars," he managed finally. He spun around in another circle, taking in the room around him. "Where are we? Are we in Gohaldinest?"

"We are."

His rotation slowed as he went around one more time and came to a stop once again looking at Lihn.

"Is there anything wrong?" Lihn asked, tentatively placing her hand on Galault's upper arm.

Galault threw his arms around Lihn and hugged her tightly. Tears flowed down his cheeks and Lihn began to pat his back in that off-putting way one does when trying to comfort a stranger. After a moment, Galault broke away and wiped his face. "I'm sorry. 'Tis truly been a hard week. Now here I stand with Rivic, and Lihn, and Alityka." He held up his hands toward each of them as he said their names. He gasped as he bent over to look once more under the table.

"And Dragzel!" Once again, he had to take a moment to wipe away the tears that overflowed him. "And I can't even talk to my father about this."

Now his body started to heave like he might vomit. His knees threatened to give way beneath him.

Lihn seized a chair and slid it to Rivic, who had grabbed onto Galault to keep the man from falling and coaxed him to sit down. Lihn moved in to rub Galault's back while he cried into his palms.

Alityka pulled another chair up beside Galault and placed a comforting hand on his knee. She waited for several moments, lingering until the hard sobs had given way to steadying breaths, before she spoke. "Can you explain why you are so overcome with emotions at being here with us and not being able to tell your father about it?"

"I'm sorry. I must be a completely miserable sight right now." Galault took the handkerchief that Lihn offered him and dried his face and nose with it. "I've grown up with stories about all of you. Lady Ali, I've known you my whole life, yet here we are and you have no clue who I am or who my father is, which puts us at the beginning."

"How does your father help us? What role does he play? If we could bring you here, don't you think we could bring him here now"

Galault appeared overwhelmed by her questions. "My father always said that the two of you met out of order. As you know, the first time he met you in the tomb of Saint Steigan, he said that he knew you quite well, but you were not familiar with him." Galault placed his hands on the table and leaned forward, but he kept his eyes on Alityka. "Remember as well that only a novihomidrak can kill another. My father isn't a novihomidrak, but rather someone chosen in your stead, Dominari, to keep the world safe until you returned. He is not part of this timeline. The question becomes what you have intended for me now that you have pulled me into your plans."

Alityka lit up with excitement. "How would you like to watch your father become the great man you knew him to be? How would you like to help him?"

"I don't understand how that could happen."

"You have a special ability."

Sadness coiled over Galault's face. "My father always treated me like I was special. He loved all his children, but there was something different in his eyes when he looked at me. He guarded me above the others." Grief filled his young eyes. "I loved my father. I really don't know what my life is going to be like without him. I don't know how you think I can help, but if you say I will get more time to be with him, I will take it."

"You'll be his guardian and protect him in his time," Alityka promised.

"Tell me what I have to do," Galault said.

"You know his stories and you know what happens to him, what things he will need. You'll get to watch him become the man you knew him to be. We will need to know his moves. We need you to be watching him from another dimension, guiding him and us."

"Aye, guiding you. I think that should be all right." He glanced around.

"Then we just have to find the right dimension for you, somewhere that Cirvel won't discover you, but that you can watch from."

"I might be able to help with that. I found a place many cycles ago and I've been there exploring since we last spoke. I just never imagined that I'd be watching my father from there, but aye, I believe it will work. I'll make sure. If not, I'll keep looking for the right plane." Galault got up from his chair and went to the wall where the painting of the city in dark, gloomy clouds hung. He stretched up on his toes to remove the painting from the hook and brought it back to the table. Lying the painting face down, he took the canvas from the frame. The wooden stretchers behind the canvas gave way from age.

"Sorry about that," Galault said as he removed the canvas along with slabs of wood.

"'Tis all right," Lihn said. "I didn't really like the painting anyway."

"I'm not sure anyone would have," Rivic said, remembering how disheartened the artwork made him.

Once the canvas was free from the frame and the debris cleared away, Galault flipped the frame over so it faced right-side-up. He placed his hands over the opening in the center of the frame. "Vada chi acada. Return this to the wall after I am through. It will cast an image of the original picture hanging here." He started to climb up on a chair to step through the painting.

"Wait," Rivic said, trying to stop Galault, "how do Alityka and I travel through two-thousand cycles of time? What will stop Cirvel?"

Galault drew back. "You're right. I am leaving something unfinished. I believe I have something that will help."

Magic rippled across the opening beneath Galault's hand and for a moment Rivic thought it might be a mirror. But the reflective blue and black surface rippled as Galault swished the image away with a flick of his wrist. A forest appeared and Galault swiped that aside as well. A library came into view. It seemed very much like the column in the tower where Cirvel kept Lihn. Galault stuck his hand into the frame and twisted the room around, drawing a section of the library closer.

Galault reached through, bending all the way down and stretching until the frame was up around his shoulder. Then he placed his head into the opening as well. After a moment of grunting while he maneuvered his shoulders around, grasping the side of the frame with the one hand still outside, Galault shoved himself out, dragging a book out last. "Got it," he announced.

He opened the book and flipped through it. Finding the page he was searching for, he ripped the paper from the binding and presented the spell to Alityka. The book he tossed back into the library. "This will help you. 'Tis all I can give you right now, and I must be going. I do not belong here and I should not stay too long. 'Twould be devastating."

"A spell to change things to stone?" Rivic said, while Alityka examined the paper.

Galault turned and put his hand on Rivic's shoulder. "'Tis not a quick route for either one of you. Time must be allowed to pass, but that doesn't mean events cannot be influenced between now and then. Good luck." He finished climbing up on the table and stepped over the boundary of the frame to disappear inside. The ripple from within the picture frame vanished.

As promised, the image of the gloomy city returned.

With a sigh, Lihn placed the frame back on the wall.

"You played on his emotions, Alityka," Rivic chided. "I'm not sure it was fair to use the grief over his father's death to get him to do what you wanted."

"He needed a push, Rivic," she fired back as she pressed a finger against his armor. "I promised him what he needed: more time with his father. I won't regret doing what must be done."

CHAPTER 17

*R*ivic's unease started as soon as he woke. He couldn't explain why he felt it, why he had continued to feel apprehensive ever since he'd been with Lihn and Alityka. Weapons master, Glayth, even commented on Rivic's distraction.

Toward afternoon, the tension ascended from the center of his back up to his neck, giving him a near constant tingle in his nape. He felt a perpetual sneer beginning to form on his lips.

Then he realized that he wasn't the only one feeling restless.

The castle seemed to buzz with activity, but he found no source of it. Maybe Cirvel planned to make him a Necroatheling today. Determined that he needed to find out what was going on, he headed toward Cirvel's chambers.

Sunlight fell through the latticework glass across the black and white tiles, making diamonds of light on the floor.

Dragzel rushed around the corner as if he were being chased by Necroathelings. Seeing Rivic, he slid over the tiles as his short legs stopped their frantic churn. His claws extended, trying to catch himself in the cracks between tiles as he spun out of control. For a moment, he seemed to be floating over the smooth floor as he made a hysterical turn. "Rivic!" he screamed, once again picking up speed, and then nearly colliding into Rivic's boots as he skidded to a halt. "You have to do something!"

"About?"

Dragzel backed up a little bit and crouched as if indicating that he was about to jump on Rivic. Rivic held out his arms in time to catch the cahaster. Dragzel climbed up onto Rivic shoulder, going around the back of his neck so he could sit on the other shoulder and speak in Rivic's ear. "Cirvel's putting Alityka in with Azote. He's setting up the sacrifice right now."

"What? Why would he do that? Who told you this?"

"Lihn just told me. She so distraught that she's throwing up in her chambers. She's been a nervous wreck lately. I think this just kind of topped it."

"Maybe I should go speak with Cirvel and find out what this is all about." Rivic continued walking toward Cirvel's chambers.

"Didn't you hear me? He's getting it ready right now. There is no reasoning with him. He's already made up his mind."

"Why would he do this?" Rivic's stomach churned, bringing the sour taste of sickness to his throat and mouth. Alityka going up against the gaxlor. He could still hear the crunching sound of the boy's body as Azote crushed and discarded it. "Did Cirvel find out about our plots against him?"

"I don't think so. Cirvel wouldn't just put her in with Azote if he had discovered the plan. He'd do something much worse. Death doesn't continue to punish people for their betrayals; 'tis too easy"

"What do I do?" Rivic asked, not certain how he could help if he wasn't supposed to go speak with Cirvel.

"I don't know, but you have to do something to help her."

"I'll go to Cirvel and tell him that I want to stand in her place."

"It doesn't work that way. Cirvel won't let you substitute for her. But isn't there some Necroatheling magic you could give to her or something?"

"I'm not a Necroatheling yet," he reminded the cahaster.

"Novihomidrak magic then? There has to be something."

There was nothing he could think of. She needed something more, stronger magic, or an effective weapon.

That was it!

"Go back to Lihn. Tell her to stay strong. I may not have much, but I might have a way to help Alityka. Even if it just gives her a slight edge. Right now, Lihn needs you, and Alityka needs me."

Dragzel jumped down off of Rivic shoulder, but looked back as he said, "I knew you'd come up with something. I hope 'tis enough."

"Me too." With that, Rivic began to run through the hallways.

He pushed his way beyond people coming through the castle hallways, then through the courtyard to the dormitory tower. He raced up the stairs hoping that he could make it to the dormitory before she left.

A couple of the kids sat on the steps, their head in their hands, crying. He watched their eyes go from sad to fearful as he hastened by them.

One of them, the girl with the mousy blonde hair who once handed him a rag to soothe his bruised face in what felt like another lifetime, stood and turned on the stair. "Please don't take her. You were her friend. Please," she begged, "stop this."

Rivic stopped, his hand upon the door handle, and faced the girl. "'Tis because I'm her friend that I'm here." He opened the door and slipped inside.

One of the other girls had just finished tying off the end of Alityka's thick reddish-blonde braid. The girl's eyes widened with shock as she saw a reflection of Rivic in the mirror set before Alityka.

Rivic lowered his hood and stepped further into the dormitory.

Alityka turned, saw Rivic, and touched the girl's arm as she whispered something. The girl nodded and hurried from the room. Alityka rose and reached for the helm which sat on her bed. She had called her Dominari armor to her and stood there in the splendid gold plates covering her white dress. He noted that she had picked up a pair of leggings to put on beneath the skirt.

"I had hoped you would be the one to come and get me." She slipped her helm on then checked the braces around her arm.

"Actually, I'm not. Lihn just told me what's happening. I'm glad I got to you first. He knows about us." The words blurted from his mouth before he meant them to.

The look in Alityka's eyes seemed to snap. Instantly, the pain was gone from them. "What do you mean?"

Rivic pulled her a short distance away where hopefully no one would be able to overhear them. "He knows you're a Dominari and he knows that I'm a novihomidrak."

"How did that happen?"

"He's always known about you, about your connection with the unicorns. You've never been able to hide it from him."

"Which means he probably knows about Lihn too." With a deep, resolved breath, her shoulders straightened. "It changes nothing. I won't run, Rivic. I'm going to face this. I have to.

'Tis my only chance to prove to Cirvel that I am strong enough."

His lips suddenly felt dry and he licked them to moisten them as he spoke. "I understand. Let me offer you some help. 'Tis not much, but 'tis what I can do for you. It might give you a slight advantage. He untied the sword belt at his waist and handed it to her, weapon and binding.

She stared at it for a moment. "Your Dominus blade?"

"You're allowed a weapon. It doesn't say it has to be your weapon. This has an enchantment upon it to make sure that it has an extra advantage. I gained it for being Knight Captain. Please, take it."

Alityka didn't look happy as she received the sword in her hands. She held it for a moment as if deciding whether or not to hand it back. Then, she placed it around her waist. "You should leave now. Cirvel will be waiting for you. I don't want you to be here when they come to get me."

Now was his turn for indecision, but he knew he had to accept this just as much is Alityka had accepted his sword. He nodded. As he went to the door, he glanced back and said, "You're not alone, Ali. I am right there with you."

She gave a faint smile. "I know. You always are."

He hated leaving Alityka behind as he felt like he betrayed her in doing so. She smiled and nodded, indicating for him to go.

Rivic paced the halls, hoping to work off some of the nervous anxiety he felt. He had to calm down before he went face-to-face with Cirvel.

Inside the amphitheater, the amassed crowd went wild with cheers and laughter. He turned to glare at the walls as if he were staring at everyone inside. How could they be so exuberant when a young woman was about to go up against a demon? Didn't they care a life was at stake? Or was it just entertainment to remove them from their miserable lives for a bit.

He had to trust that Alityka could handle herself. Even more, Cirvel wouldn't do anything that would actually harm one of the most unique maeges in his collection. Would he?

Knowing that fact might be his only advantage, Rivic entered the amphitheater. The audience area had been darkened, leaving the mass throng of people bathed in muddy brown. From this vantage point, Rivic couldn't see the current entertainment going on in the illuminated arena. Only one small, yellow view of the compact clay field was available at the very end of this aisle, making Rivic feel as if he went through a tunnel. As expected, a Necroatheling touched Rivic's arm to get his attention and then pointed toward Cirvel's box. Rivic nodded and started moving along the darkened rows in that direction.

The posted Necroatheling opened the admittance doorway for Rivic. Cirvel's magic spilled out, assaulting Rivic's senses. Rivic entered to find Cirvel and Lihn already seated. Two Necroathelings stood guard inside, one on each side of the door. They gave Rivic a wary look but allowed him to enter and move up behind Cirvel and Lihn.

"Good," Cirvel said glancing back over his shoulder, "you're here just in time for the entertainment."

Lihn gave Rivic a worried glance. Rivic returned a steady, slow blink with a short accompanying nod as if telling her silently that he had been able to speak to Alityka and helped her as much as he could. This seemed to appease Lihn and she turned back right in her seat. Rivic remain standing behind Cirvel.

Out on the clay floor of the amphitheater, a short juggler, his face painted white with large red lips, currently worked at hula-hooping while juggling seven balls. The jingle bells on drooping ends of his floppy hat rang out every time he caught and re-tossed the ball.

The watching crowd gasped as a fat, miniature horse bolted out of one of the side gates and ran toward the juggler. Dust kicked up in the wake of the tiny horse. Rivic noticed that it had a horn tied around its little head as if it were unicorn. The juggler dropped all his balls, grabbed onto the hula hoop, and made a mad dash around the arena below.

The crowd laughed with delight as the pony gave chase sending the juggler in pretend panic around the field. At last, the juggler, his face split by the red painted lips, came to a stop and held an index finger high in the air as if he'd had an idea.

Lihn shifted in her seat, crossing one leg over the other, and layering her hands on top of her thigh. Tension bowed through her shoulders.

The horse continued to run in circles around the juggler until he tossed the hoop around the horse's neck.

The animal came to a stop. Upon its back appeared a standing girl with long raven hair which hung around her face. The silver trimming on her black robes indicated she was a representation of Lord Cirvel. At her arrival, the juggler scurried away.

The girl seized the hoop from around the pony and flipped from its back. After a moment of dancing around with the ring, she tossed the hoop into the air and it exploded in a circle of fire, eliciting awes from the onlookers.

The juggler came back, his outfit now changed. He wore a white flowing dress and a wig of red curls. He hadn't gotten it on quite straight and kept fighting to push the unruly strands out of his face as he ran for the unicorn.

Cirvel pointed out to the arena. "Look, it's our good Dominari," he laughed. He clapped his hands together and called, "Bravo."

Before the juggler reached the center where the mock Cirvel and unicorn were, the girl stepped up beside and pulled the horn off the horse. The animal dropped to its knees and rolled onto its side as if falling down dead. The girl in black raised the horn and began to laugh as the juggler cursed. The juggler rushed forward and the girl in black slid the horn between the juggler's arm and his chest. He spouted a ribbon of red as if gushing blood and collapsed down upon the unicorn.

Rivic tore his eyes away from the scene long enough to spare Lihn a glance. Her lips trembled and she had her hands folded so tightly in her lap that her knuckles were whitened. He could feel the restrained and silent agony rippling through her.

He wanted to say something, to let Cirvel know that he knew that Cirvel mocked them. He didn't dare say a word.

The girl dressed in black walked around the juggler, who disappeared along with the pony. The crowd applauded as she walked around in triumph.

She headed to the center of the arena. In a flourish of her robes and a thunderous boom, she disappeared. In that moment, the amphitheater when dark.

Applause sounded.

Flames flickered to life in the wall sconces once more bringing back the light. A Necroatheling now stood in the center of the arena where the girl had been.

Delighted, Cirvel clapped again. "Bravo!"

Between all the spent magic floating in the air and the foreshadowing scene he had just witnessed below, Rivic could hardly breathe. He really wanted to collapse into a chair, but he didn't want Cirvel to take notice of how effected he was.

It took Rivic a moment to realize that the Necroatheling's robes were wrapped tightly around someone that he held.

Rivic had seen this before and knew that the Necroatheling held Alityka.

The Necroatheling threw open his robes revealing Alityka standing tied in iron chains. She been gagged and Rivic now saw his sword in the Necroatheling's hands. Would anyone realize that it was the Knight Captain's blade? The Necroatheling reached up and pulled the helm from Alityka's head. He tossed the helm in one direction and the sword in the other. He then stepped forward toward Cirvel and bowed before disappearing.

"This isn't fair," Lihn said.

Cirvel turned his head to give Lihn a cool look with his dark eyes. "If she can't handle the chain, then she is not fit to be here."

But more than that, Rivic could feel the magical enchantments on the chains. It would not be a simple matter of merely breaking them. These would take more power and he hoped that Alityka knew the appropriate spells.

As the crowd was coming down from realizing the predicament that Alityka was in, their mood changed and grew with excitement as Azote entered the arena. He floated down from above, steady flaps of his gray wing's slowing his dissent. As he landed, he put his arms in the air and roared. Then he marched toward Cirvel and pointed back toward Alityka. "You dared to bring me a sacrifice in chains, and a mere puny human female at that. Do you fear her so much, or are you just weak?" Azote raged.

Cirvel uncrossed his legs and placed both feet flat on the floor as he laced his fingers and leaned forward toward Azote to call out, "You may find her more formidable then you believe. You will find her magic worthy. Assuming, that is, that you can capture her. You may be thankful that I gave you the head start."

Azote gave Cirvel a snorting sneer. "We'll see about that."

The winged demon stalked back toward Alityka, who struggled with the chains.

Rivic desperately searched through memories, wondering if he'd ever seen that Alityka knew something that could help get herself free from the chains before Azote reached her. Without her helm, her head and neck were left vulnerable. One slash from Azote's heavy arm could knock her unconscious or even kill her.

Alityka struggled with the cloth in her mouth, trying to use her shoulders to get it out.

Lihn covered her face with her hands. "Lord Cirvel," she sobbed.

Cirvel reached over and patted her knee.

Azote reached for Alityka, intending to choke her with one hand. Alityka ducked and managed to hook the lumbering demon's fingers into the cloth and pulled the gag out.

Lihn shuddered out a breath of relief.

Now Azote had Alityka in his hands. Rivic swore he could hear Alityka choking as Azote lifted her off the ground.

Azote cast Cirvel another look of irritation. In that instant, a blast shoved Azote back and he dropped Alityka.

She landed on her feet, barely keeping her balance in the wrap of chains.

Vines wrapped up around Azote's legs, in snarling him and keeping him from walking closer to Alityka. At first, Azote seemed angered by the vines coming from the clay earth, but he dissolved them, showing that they were nothing more than a mere annoyance. The ground turned to quicksand beneath him, and again Azote got delayed, though it didn't seem like long enough. He flapped his wings and pulled his legs from the quicksand.

"See? This is getting good," Cirvel said.

Lihn looked pale.

Alityka gave a quick look of disappointment as she realized that Azote wasn't trapped any longer. But rather than watching Azote as he took flight, she looked down once more, focusing on the chains around her.

Rivic pressed his palms flatly against the material of his leggings, hoping to stop his hands from sweating. He scarcely dared even to breathe. He certainly didn't want to watch. The sounds of the crowd alone told him that the fight was not going well. He wasn't even sure which side the audience was on. Were they rooting for Alityka or for Azote?

"Cirvel, please, give her a fighting chance." Lihn had turned toward Cirvel and placed her hand upon his arm.

Azote swooped down on Alityka, making her duck as best as she could in the chains.

For a brief second, Cirvel looked as though he considered Lihn's offer. Then he gave a small shake of his head. "You have kept things from me for far too long. Let this serve as a warning."

The second time the demon descended on Alityka, she nearly stumbled under the metal's weight.

"Please, I will do it. I will give you what you want," Lihn pleaded.

Cirvel still looked unimpressed.

Another roar from the crowd returned Cirvel's and Lihn's gaze back to the arena.

Alityka had managed to free one hand from the chains to grab onto the sword, but in doing so, she had sacrificed her balance. She had fallen over and lay helplessly prone. Azote stomped toward her, the ground shaking beneath his feet as each step grew louder and louder like thundering heartbeats. He aimed right for Alityka's head.

"I'm pregnant," Lihn announced, grabbing onto Cirvel's

arm. "The child will give you the key that you need to know. Please stop this."

Rivic couldn't help his gaze darting to Lihn at this information. She in turn cast a sorrowful look toward Rivic.

At the same time, the spell on Alityka's chains weakened. Whatever she was doing, she was slowly chipping away at it. If she could somehow keep this up for just a little bit longer, she might soon be free of the chains. If...

Rivic wished he could do something for her right now. He gathered and exhaled a long steady breath, letting his magic reach out toward her to reinforce her waning strength.

A blast knocked Azote back. As he recovered and started storming forward once more, a second one caught him, and then a third. The chains turned to parchment all around Alityka and she ripped them in two, rising to her feet with the sword as she did so. Rivic fought hard to not cheer along with the audience at Alityka's freedom.

The crowd's triumphant exhilaration wasn't enough to make Rivic look away. He had to know Cirvel's answer.

"You have lied and misled me too many times for me to believe this. Until the signs show me that 'tis true, you will be treated just the same." Cirvel's voice was colder and darker than Rivic had ever heard it, even when the Lord of Gohaldinest had been angry with him. Yet Rivic knew it was true from the look in Lihn's eyes. If all this were true, then it would be only a matter of time before Cirvel had his answer.

A fourth blast knocked Azote so far back that he slammed into the wall. Vines came out and wrapped around the demon's thick gray body. The look on his face bespoke of his realization that the tide of this battle was quickly turning.

Alityka ran over, grabbed her helm, and put it on her head. She turned with a fierce look and charged for Azote as he came free of the vines on the wall and tromped toward her. Within mere moments, they were locked in face-to-face combat.

The noise of metal striking stone filled the air, the incessant tapping sounding as if one were mining rather than Alityka fighting for her life. Rivic's sword did cut into the gaxlor, though Azote healed immediately from each blow.

At this, Alityka darted away from Azote long enough to perform her spells. She slid the sword away in the scabbard when she could, bringing it back out only when Azote drew too close to her. She just had to keep him off. The taint of magic swirled in the air. At one point when Alityka dashed away, Azote looked toward Cirvel and gave an approving nod. Rivic saw the small smile light on Cirvel's face.

"Why do you seek to gain his approval when you are obviously so much more powerful than him?" Rivic asked.

Cirvel cast Rivic a sidelong glance, his smile growing slightly. He shook his head, indicating that he would not give an answer to that question. It felt as if Cirvel mocked him and told him that some things were beyond his understanding. Maybe, in this case, that were true, but Rivic no longer believed that Azote was a primal god as Cirvel had once tried to tell them. Not when Cirvel was so much more powerful than this creature that he had given Alityka to as a sacrifice.

The gaxlor jumped toward Alityka. Alityka feigned, trying to dodge the blow that she thought Azote was bringing her with his right hand. But Azote slashed up with his other hand and caught Alityka across her chest. She screamed as part of her breastplate cut away and began hanging at an awkward tilt from her other shoulder. As blood soaked into her white acolyte dress, Alityka pulled the breastplate off her and thrust the armor to the ground. Azote gave her the time to do this without attacking, yet he looked so pleased that now he had her soft belly to rip open.

Cirvel's head flinched just a little bit has he glanced over at Rivic. "She lied to you, you know, in the worst way that a Dominari can lie."

Was this some sort of test? Did Cirvel not know that a Dominari could not lie, or was he seeing if Rivic knew about this ability? Rivic raised his chin. "How do you figure she lied to me?"

"By pretending to be more powerful than you. By trying and using your power for her own purposes. She saw herself superior to you, a Dominari superior to a novihomidrak. And she lies," Cirvel said, broken by the audience giving a ruckus cheer as Alityka screamed in pain, "by presuming that she could love a glorious creation like yourself in a way befitting of your magical heritage."

Rivic's gaze sought Alityka out in the pit below. She currently backed away from Azote, her left hand trying to staunch the flow of blood coming from her left shoulder. While she still held her sword tightly in her hand, her sword arm hung limply. Blood flowed in a thick stream down her arm and would soon make her fingers slick on gripping the hilt. Azote stormed toward her, stalking his prey.

But it was Ellonia who came to his thoughts. If Azote killed Alityka, how would Rivic be able to face Ellonia? Worse, he imagined gargaxes coming after Ellonia in a confrontation that matched what was playing out below.

Cirvel's mouth dropped open. "She's not the one."

At the sound of shock in Cirvel's voice, Rivic broke his gaze away from Alityka and looked at Cirvel. Cirvel stood and turned toward him. "Alityka is not the one. The two of you are not lovers," he snarled. "You dared to deceive me!"

"My lord," Rivic said with a bow, knowing he had but one chance to get this right for both his sake and Alityka's. "You have never asked me if Alityka and I were lovers. Your Necroathelings, however, have delivered you unreliable information. I would dare to say to you that it is their fault for the rumors that they have spread."

Cirvel looked thoroughly disgusted. He stood as he pointed at Alityka and shouted, "Azote, zat'eit ooktsa Dominari."

At Cirvel commanding Azote to finish Alityka off in the dragon language, Lihn looked to Rivic for a translation, though the fear in her eyes told him that he already knew she was aware. Her glance was just a last attempt at hope. Rivic looked back to Alityka, ignoring Lihn's soft cries as she buried her face in her hands.

Cirvel began to sit down, but Lihn stood up, slapping her thighs as she rose. "I won't let you do this," she screamed back at Cirvel. Lihn rushed to the edge the box and leaned over the wall. Rivic felt her magic gathering. But as she opened her mouth to chant the spell, Alityka rose up, her sword slashing in the air as Azote rushed in toward her. She had been feigning that the injury was worse than it truly was and sent the sword deep into the gaxlor's chest.

Azote stumbled backwards, reaching to pull the sword out. Alityka raised her left hand. "Paltradin halcarda roo'ki-tak." Azote turned to stone and froze in a position of holding onto the sword by the blade.

A look of shock passed over Alityka's face as she reached up and yanked the sword out. She tossed the weapon aside.

Rivic felt her rising magic full of hatred. A blue glow wrapped around her hands, golden sparks snapping. She screamed out in rage as she rushed for Azote.

"Halt!" Cirvel shouted. "We have a winner."

Alityka managed to stop before touching Azote, but she glared up at Cirvel in his box and lost the magic from her hands down to the ground. The earth exploded in front of her, throwing her backwards with her arms up to shield her face. Azote fell forward into the gaping hole, onto his face, making another cloud of dust rise into the air.

Cirvel rose, stepped to the edge of the box, and began to clap. "Congratulations, Dominus Alityka. You have proven yourself worthy."

The crowd roared with enthusiasm.

Cirvel turned, his eyes dangerous as he glared at Rivic. "Fetch her, Knight Captain, and make sure she is given what she needs to begin her Domini training. Get her well settled in." He looked to one of the Necroathelings and tipped his head toward Lihn. "See her safely to her tower. She is too upset tonight for the discussion which we must have. Stay with her and make sure she comes promptly to breakfast at first light. That will be soon enough."

Rivic followed Lihn and the Necroatheling out the door. She slumped against the Necroatheling as they walked down the stairs and Rivic could hear her sobs. He couldn't wait until he got to the doorway that would allow him access to the arena and he could leave the horrid sights and sounds behind.

Alityka was standing over the hole in the ground where Azote still lay as stone face down. She held the sword in one hand, her breastplate in the other. She must have heard Rivic approach because she turned toward him, a smile on her face. "I beat him. I'm alive. And I have a way to defeat him."

"You heard Lord Cirvel promote you to a Dominus?" Rivic asked, unsure of how much she might remember after the explosion.

She nodded.

"Lihn told Cirvel she is pregnant," he added.

Alityka sheathed the sword, then untied the belt from around her waist. Handing it back to him, she said, "'Tis too soon. We must hasten along our path."

Rivic caught up with her as she began to walk out ahead

of him. "'Tis a dangerous road we're on and I really don't want you and Lihn on it. Especially if she is with child. We must protect her."

"Then 'tis a good thing I was just made a Dominus. 'Twill give us more time together."

Rivic grabbed her arm and spun her around to face him. Dark bruises clutched her throat where Azote had grabbed her, and her face held matching dark spots. Anger clenched in his stomach like a fist ready to punch something. Yet, all the irritation he had planned on screaming at her faded. She had just put her life on the line. "Let's find you a bed and make sure you get a good night's sleep."

CHAPTER 18

*R*ivic patrolled the empty hallways outside of Lord Cirvel's chambers, his footsteps echoing off the hollow rooms. Dominus Johan, who had been napping when Rivic relieved him of duty, had tried to convince Rivic that patrolling while Lord Cirvel was gone was a complete waste of time.

Rivic didn't see it that way. Rather, he thought this would be an opportunity to get to know every inch of the hallway where Cirvel lived. He'd seen enough trapdoors and hidden access points throughout the castle to know that there had to be even more in this hallway than met the eye. Being Knight Captain, and with his duty to safeguard the private chambers of the Lord of Gohaldinest, he had just cause to be here. No one would question it even if Cirvel was currently away. Besides, he never knew if the other Domini or Necroathelings had orders from Lord Cirvel to test Rivic's devotion.

Tonight, it seemed as if everyone had gone to bed early. Had he missed something?

Or were magical spells dulling his senses in preparation of the Necroathelings coming for him?

They couldn't take him if he wasn't in the basement, right? Maybe. In that time, the Necroathelings might come in and choose someone else to take to The Playground. Then he could get a good night's sleep.

Dragzel came tearing around the corner before him. The cahaster stopped, one paw raised in the air while looking at Rivic with his head lowering, then Dragzel tore off again in the direction he'd been going.

"Dragzel!" Rivic called out, trying to keep his voice from a shout.

At first, he didn't think that the cahaster was coming back, but then Dragzel stuck his head around the other corner. Blue-green eyes glowed at Rivic through the darkness.

"Aye?" Dragzel said tentatively.

"What are you doing?" Rivic went and knelt down beside the cahaster.

Dragzel's head gave a couple jerks as he looked around. Then, with eyes as innocent as he could possibly make them, he answered, "Nothing."

"Why don't I believe that?"

"You're not a Dominari. You don't have anything against me."

"Only your coy words and not-so-innocent looks."

"Still can't prove anything."

"Why did you stop in front of me? You could have probably zipped on by me and I wouldn't have even noticed you?"

Dragzel did one of his little shrugs. "Thought you were someone else."

"Who?"

"Lord Cirvel."

"You acted like that would have been a surprise."

"Would have been." Dragzel cocked his head. "Lord Cirvel has left Gohaldinest."

"Why? Where did he go?"

Dragzel's head seemed to duck between his shoulders. "Don't know. Just told he was gone. Got things to do. Bye." The cahaster started to run off.

Rivic reached out and snatched his tail. Dragzel spun around with a hiss, looking just as shocked as Rivic felt. What had made him snag the cahaster? The energy pulsated through him.

Dragzel's eyes grew even wider. "Now you really feel like him. Let go of me."

"Tell me what you're doing." Rivic's voice went deep and had the edge of a growl to it.

"I'm looking for milady Lihn." The cahaster scrutinized Rivic in such a way that made Rivic feel this time was different, that Dragzel hadn't found Lihn in any of the usual places. Finally, Dragzel added, "She's missing."

"Missing?"

"Gone. Vanished. Disappeared without a word."

Rivic sensed the fears in Dragzel's teary voice. "We'll find her."

"Pft!" The cahaster disappeared while Rivic watched him go. He wished the feeling of dread would leave so easily. The cold tingle at the back of his neck suggested that he needed to look further into this. Finding Alityka might be easier. He headed to the library, knowing that she'd been spending a lot of time there recently and her energy suggested she was there now.

As he headed into the library, Alityka was leaving with several books. He held the door open for her. "A little light reading?" he said, glancing down the spines of her books. They covered a variety of magic topics. "Tell me you don't really mean to go through all of these."

"Cirvel is gone. You know that, right?" she asked, her voice dropped to a quiet level. "I don't suppose I can talk you into missing one night of sleep. Lihn and I would like to run some ideas by you, see if you can figure some things out with us."

"You've seen Lihn?"

"Aye, we spoke just yesterday."

"Did she seem all right?"

"What's with all the questions?"

"I just ran into Dragzel. He said Lihn has gone missing." He tried to rein in the trepidation he felt, but fighting the sensation only seemed to deepen it.

Alityka tapped her foot. "We should go check the glass prison."

"I suspect Dragzel already has. He was tearing through the castle pretty fast. I suppose it wouldn't hurt for us to double-check."

Alityka nodded half-heartedly. She remained silent while they walked to the room which held the glass prison, only to find it empty.

"We'll find her." It was all Rivic could think of to say.

Alityka nodded, but her spirit had faded.

Rivic felt Alityka's magic brush him aside as she stretched out with her own. After a moment where tears sprang to her eyes, she began to hurry from the castle, then broke into a dash across the courtyard. Rivic followed as she ran for the tower and took the stairs up two at a time.

Rivic reached the blue column at the top of the stairs after her, wondering why she just stood there staring at the pictures, her mouth slightly agape. "What's wrong?"

"Her room, 'tis not listed here."

"What do you mean?" He began to flip through the images in the column. She was right.

"Cirvel has her cut off from this world. He's locked her

away in her room and removed the access here. That's why I don't feel her anymore."

Rivic started to guide her down the stairs. "We might not be able to reach Lihn, but that doesn't mean that Galault won't be. He's a watcher of worlds. He'll be able to find the dimension where she's being held."

"Aye, Galault. He might have seen something or perchance he can find something out."

They went to Lihn's library where they found Dragzel curled up on the pillow beneath the table. He opened one bright blue-green eye at them but didn't bother to lift his head. "About time you two showed up."

Dragzel slunk from the shadows, his head downcast as he came toward them. Obviously he had held onto the same hope they had. When Alityka saw him, she dropped to her knees. The cahaster ran into her arms. Alityka pressed Dragzel against her face while she sobbed against him. He mewled back.

Rivic turned, not sure if he'd be able to contain his own emotions. Before he reached the door, his mind tossed out a question to him: *why did they feel as if they had already lost?*

"I didn't know you'd be waiting for us," Alityka said, petting the cahaster.

Dragzel issued a sound which Rivic couldn't tell if it was a sigh or a sob. "I want milady Lihn back."

"I know you do."

Rivic turned toward the depressing painting of the city in the rain, pondering if he should remove it off the wall and place it on the table. He wasn't certain how this was to work.

"I told you that Cirvel would do something bad to her after that news she dropped on him," Dragzel said to Alityka. "I told you we needed to get Lihn out of here."

"I know and I've had some thoughts on that," Alityka said.

Rivic looked back over his shoulder at her. "Where can we take her that Cirvel won't be able to find her?"

"Not where," Alityka answered with a grin. "When."

"When?"

"I've been thinking a lot about this. Galault said that I traveled through time to speak to his father several times."

"He also said you were always alone when you went on these visits."

Her eyes brightened. "He did. But that doesn't mean that I don't take Lihn with me and leave her in another time. I could take her somewhere as easily as I've taken you with me. 'Twould be so simple."

"All right. So, we take her to another time when she will be safe. How will we know Cirvel still won't find her?"

"We have Galault keep an eye on her." Alityka placed her hands on him. "Rivic, I have to keep her safe and I think this is the only way to do it."

"Then we have to find her first." He pivoted quickly toward the painting. "We must contact Galault now. He will be able to find her across the dimensions." He forced as much of a commanding tone into his voice as he could.

Dragzel raised his head off Alityka's arm. "Unless Cirvel is already keeping her in a genie lamp."

Rivic recalled Nyree telling him once that Cirvel had trapped Kalt inside one of the strange lamps for as long as she wished, and he thought of his own time as a prisoner to the painting. Would Galault be able to see that possibility too? What purpose did imprisoning Lihn have anyway? Cirvel risked her miscarrying the baby from the stress. Was that what he wanted? Cirvel had to have some strategy in play, but what?

Cirvel knew that Dragzel would be distressed about Lihn and that it would tear Lihn apart to worry about Dragzel. He knew the cahaster would agree to anything to see Lihn again.

"Did you ever make the offer about being the container for my soul to Cirvel?"

Dragzel took a wary step closer to Rivic. "I did. But he didn't seem so committed to it."

"He didn't?" Alityka questioned.

"He said he wasn't certain that would be necessary."

"What did he mean by that?" Rivic asked.

"I don't know. He certainly didn't explain it to me. No one ever explains things to cahasters."

Ignoring the peeved sound in Dragzel's voice, Rivic continued, "Cirvel doesn't like to trust things will work out the way he wants them to. Nay, he likes assurances that people will do exactly what he wants them to do."

"What do you think he's up to then?" Alityka climbed to her feet and brushed off her legs. "You think separating Dragzel and Lihn is how Cirvel gets leverage to make them both do what he wants them to?"

"Aye," Rivic responded. "I think Cirvel planned this separation so we would be devastated by it too. We get to see how upset Dragzel is. He's playing our emotions and knows we will naturally be worried about Lihn, especially knowing that she's pregnant. We've participated exactly as he wanted us to so far."

"So what do we do?"

"We summon Galault and we tell him everything we know about Lihn so that he can find her. Meanwhile, we have to pretend that we don't even know she's missing."

"What about Dragzel? He can't pretend that he doesn't know. Cirvel wouldn't believe it."

"Nay, but he would believe Dragzel waiting to accost Cirvel the moment he returns. Dragzel makes himself at home in Lord Cirvel's chambers."

Dragzel grinned. "A little dragon sleeping in his sheets.

Oh, he'll love discovering that!" The cahaster rubbed his front paws together.

"Exactly," Rivic said even as Alityka began to smile. "We refuse to let him position us exactly as he wants us."

"We keep it on our terms," Alityka said.

"Aye, our terms." He stepped up to the painting, a sudden feeling of knowing what to do filling him. "Vocha chia cada'-dada. Galault, please come forth. I beckon your aid."

The blank space within the frame wavered and an image came into view. Galault stepped forward into the picture and he appeared happier and younger than Rivic thought he'd ever seen the watcher of worlds. "Lord Rivic, how may I answer your call?"

CHAPTER 19

$\mathcal{T}$he clamber filling the dormitory as each Dominus readied for the day's training broke to complete silence. The candles in the wall sconces flickered as if ancient magic skittered over the stone behind them in a hurry to flee. Rivic, who was pulling his armor on, felt several of the other Domini salute before he became fully aware of what was happening around him. He turned from finalizing the buckle on his armor to see Lord Cirvel standing at the base of the staircase.

"Domini, stand tall," Rivic barked, embarrassed that he was the last one to attention and everyone knew it.

A smile flickered across Cirvel's lips. "Relax," he said, patting the air with his hand. "Knight Captain Rivic, please gather your belongings."

Rivic gulped. "I have my sword and my armor already," he responded, not sure what else Cirvel could be referring to.

"Nay," Cirvel laughed, "all of your belongings."

"Everything?" he squeaked.

Cirvel looked beyond humored. "Everything that you own that you wish to take with you."

As Rivic turned once more, he spared a glance to Alityka. She caught his look, her eyes filled with an ample amount of curiosity too. He dove for the small chest beside his bed and started clearing it out of his meager belongings.

Rivic felt Cirvel approach behind him and remove the red cape from his armor. "Dominus Hoydin, you will become the new Knight Captain." Cirvel handed the material to the other boy.

"Aye, sir," Hoydin fought beyond his confusion to salute. "Thank you, Lord Cirvel. May I bring you honor."

"Of course you will," Cirvel answered dryly as he began to walk down the aisle between the beds and give inspection to the other domini.

Rivic carried his few possessions in his hands. He approached Cirvel, wondering if he was being thrown out of Gohaldinest. Had Cirvel found out about his plans with Alityka and Lihn? Was he being banished? Could he finally go home to Ellonia?

He doubted it would be that easy. Until Cirvel was defeated, no one was safe from his tyranny.

That didn't stop Rivic's heart from thundering with apprehension. "I'm ready, Lord Cirvel."

Cirvel looked him over. "Is that all you have? Never mind. Come along."

The comment left Rivic feeling inadequate, yet he kept his mouth shut and proceeded to follow Cirvel up the stairs. He soon came to realize that Cirvel was walking back to his chambers. If Cirvel required his presence, why not just send a Necroatheling to fetch him? Why had this request justified a personal appearance?

Cirvel pointed to a new doorway not far from his chambers. Rivic had walked every inch of this hallway, looked behind every tapestry, and he knew there hadn't been a room here before. "These are your new quarters." Cirvel reached out and pushed the door open revealing a bedchamber beyond.

"Excuse me, but what do you mean by my quarters?" Rivic asked, peering inside but not daring to enter.

Cirvel glanced to the floor and looked for a moment as if he struggled with what exactly to say. "I have spent some time contemplating you. Please, let us step out of the hallway and you can put your things away."

Rivic stepped into the room which was nearly as large as Cirvel's. It smelled fresh in here as if the presently closed windows had been opened earlier. The furniture matched the same pieces from Cirvel's room, almost to the point where Rivic wondered if Cirvel had put them in here and replaced the furnishing in his room with new ones. The desk, the bed, the table, all served to remind Rivic of his days in the painting where he'd watched Cirvel. He didn't know if this was a blessing or a curse and he wasn't certain about what to say.

Fortunately, Cirvel spoke first. "I do believe the Guardian is correct. I should begin to tutor you," Cirvel said close behind him.

Rivic swallowed hard, straining to find his voice. "You do wish to teach me then?" He didn't really want to put his belongings down here, unsure of what exactly was happening, but Cirvel's waiting expression made Rivic place the few items on top of the dresser.

"That has always been my desire," Cirvel chuckled. "'Tis not uncommon for a novihomidrak to take on an apprentice. Most novihomidraks are given a guide at their birth, to help them learn about their aspects as well as gain strength."

"You want to instruct me as a novihomidrak?" Rivic recalled his novimather saying that she couldn't provide a mentor for him, regretting it. The Guardian had only told him to destroy Cirvel, made it seem like there could only be one or the other in this world. Certainly, Cirvel knew this, yet why would he make an offer to train the one who could bring his destruction?

"Aye," Cirvel laughed again. "I wish for you to be by my side. Our novimather may believe that you are flawed and only useful as a Necroatheling, but I believe having a novihomidrak at my side could be my greatest asset. I will rule, but you will bring the world to its knees before me."

Once again, Rivic's only value was in his ability to be destructive.

Cirvel stepped over to the large wardrobe and opened the door. Right now, only one thing hung inside. Cirvel pulled it out. Rivic recognized it immediately: the blue travelling cloak Ellonia had made for him.

"I do believe you arrived with this," Cirvel said. "'Tis something to your liking?"

With a jolt, Rivic stopped himself from moving forward to it. He didn't want to look overly anxious. He shrugged to keep himself from speaking lest his words betray him.

Cirvel hung it back in the wardrobe. "You have much to learn about being a novihomidrak. Were you attuned to your power, you'd know that the young lady who created that for you cared very deeply for you."

Rivic noticed Cirvel's hand never actually left the cloth, continuing to lightly grip onto the fabric.

"This confused me at first," Cirvel continued, "which is why I mistook Alityka for your lover. This cloth was woven to Alityka as well. 'Twould seem the maker is someone both you and Alityka have in common, and 'tis that fact that I missed."

Try as he might, Rivic couldn't help his thoughts from going to Ellonia.

Cirvel's mouth flickered as he exhaled an amused huff. He composed himself quickly. "Let us use that as a basis, shall we?" With a wave of his hand, the wardrobe filled with several silken blue robes. "Before you ask why I'm doing this, let me explain something to you."

Rivic waited for what Cirvel had to say.

Cirvel stepped away from the wardrobe and motioned with his index finger between them. "You and I have been drawn together from the moment of your novihomidrak birth. I felt it." He clenched his hand close to his chest. "Do you not see, not feel it between us? Nay, I know you do. We are connected. You are better than any Necroatheling could ever hope to be. I don't want you merely to serve me. I want you to stand with me."

Fear tickled along the outside edge of Rivic's arms. It reminded him of when he met Cirvel and the Lord of Gohaldinest's magic kept prodding at him trying to discover who he was. Was Cirvel testing him? Rivic didn't want to show he knew too much too soon. "To do what?"

"I want to fully be able to trust you. There is so much about being a novihomidrak that you don't understand. I want to teach you, to show you what power the Onesong can hold for those like us."

Rivic moved closer. "Then show me."

"Do you really wish to learn?"

"I do."

"I can see the truth in your words, but I must still have your oath as a Necroatheling to assure your loyalty to me."

"I said I would give it," Rivic said, ire backing his words since he'd already sworn to do this. Why did Cirvel press the issue again?

"Is something the matter?"

"Nothing, my lord," he said.

"Ah, see? There now, you have lied to me."

Rivic recovered quickly from being called out. "I just wonder what you are up to. I do not know you to do things for other people unless there is something in it for you."

"A statement for which you are not wrong." Cirvel gestured for Rivic to sit. "As I previously stated, I had much to think about. Deciding whether I really wanted a lineage brother or a powerful Necroatheling was my first question. I soon realized I could have both. But I had a problem."

Rivic slid the chair closer to the table. "What would that problem be?"

"In good time. There is much we need to do and discuss. But first, I do have something more to show you." Cirvel turned and led the way from the room.

Rivic closed the door behind him as he entered the hallway. He wanted to lock it, but it didn't feel like it was his right to do that. Not yet at least. Not until he was certain this wasn't all a test and that Cirvel wouldn't throw him back down in the domini's basement. Or worse.

Cirvel opened the door to his antechamber and swung the door open. A small, white piece of folded parchment lay on the table. That was the first thing Rivic noticed as they entered. The second was that there were no Necroathelings on guard in here, which brought Rivic swiftly the realization that there had been no Necroathelings all along since Cirvel fetched him from the dormitory. It brought an eerie ripple over Rivic.

Cirvel's long, slender fingers picked up the folded parchment from the table. "As you know, I have been out traveling. I went to visit many tribes. I had the pleasure of calling on your sister."

Rivic tried to hold his calm. "And how is Nyree?"

"I am afraid to report that she was not very happy. I asked if she would like to travel with me and maybe find a place more suited to her liking. She agreed and began her journey with me."

"She is your novihomidrak sister."

Cirvel laughed. "As I am well aware now, which is why I was not surprised when I heard she was not happy at the tribe. Staying put never suits a novihomidrak very well. I have found her a place where she will be much happier, I believe, and procured her a position which should be beneficial for both of us."

"Is she here in Gohaldinest?"

"Nay." Cirvel thrust the parchment toward Rivic. "She has prepared a letter for you. Please sit and take a moment to read it while I gather a couple of things."

Rivic held the parchment knowing that Nyree couldn't have said very much on the single sheet. The wax seal seemed to be unbroken, but that didn't mean that Cirvel hadn't been with her as she'd written it. He took a chair and slid his finger beneath the seal.

Nyree had never feared Lord Cirvel. Rather, she'd always given preference to assisting him, even after all that had happened. Maybe fate would have served them better if she'd been the twin bestowed with magic. He wasn't certain he wanted to see what she'd written, what advice she had for him now.

He unfolded the letter.

The inside was blank.

He flipped it over to make sure that he was holding it correctly. Nothing was written on either side.

Cirvel re-entered the room, a book in his hands and a woman walking behind him carrying a tray of tea. He gestured for her to place the refreshment platter on the table, then gave her a slight bow. "Thank you, Madam Orcee."

The middle-aged woman with her hair pulled back in a

bun nodded. "Always a pleasure, Lord Cirvel." She exited through the door that went into Cirvel's private reading room, but as soon as she passed through the frame, she vanished.

Cirvel spread out the tea, sugar, and cream between them and proceeded to fix his drink. "Did you finish your sister's letter?"

"I did." If Cirvel thought that Rivic would break down and get angry over the blank sheet of paper, Cirvel was wrong. "Unfortunately, it didn't say what she was doing on her travels with you, where you left her, or what she is doing."

"I am very disappointed to hear you say that. I went to a lot of trouble to care for your sister."

"What did you do? Where is she?" Rivic tried not to panic, but he felt it rising in his chest. Maybe the letter had truly been blank because Nyree didn't know what to tell him. Or maybe she'd been too fearful to write anything.

"I took her to Plenelia and found her a young man I believe she'll be quite happy with. She now has status, a loving husband, a warm house, and freedom from the events that happened to her here."

Cold shock burst over Rivic. "Married in Plenelia?"

"I am certain that you are aware that they put to death any maege that enters their land. Negotiations had to be made for my presence to be allowed." Cirvel paused while fixing Rivic with a stare. "I risked my life."

Rivic very much doubted that. The thought turned Rivic's stomach. He knew that Cirvel had never been in any danger, yet for him to claim that he had been, sickened Rivic. If anyone had been in danger, it was Nyree.

"I have proven to them that she possesses no magic," Cirvel continued. "She is quite safe and happy, as I'm certain her letter stated."

"Her letter said nothing. The parchment was blank." The words fell so softly from Rivic's lips that he barely heard them himself. If Nyree were really in Plenelia, would he ever see her again?

"Really?" Cirvel asked. "That is certainly too bad. I had hoped that she would put your mind at ease about her safety."

"Why? Why did you take her to Plenelia to be married off?"

Cirvel glanced down. "I assure you that I was only trying to do what was best for both of you. She could not stay here any longer after the incident; the memories were just too painful for her, and you were not letting go of your anger even after Nyree repeatedly asked you to. Too many people here knew what had happened and there was no way I would have been able to provide her with a husband when everyone knew of her disgrace."

Disgrace! Rivic fought to not spit the word back in Cirvel's face.

"I'm sorry, but 'tis how 'twas seen. She was not happy at the tribe. Krithstand and his men were not very trusting of her. She was constantly fighting with the council. Nyree was on the verge of leaving herself and my arrival made things better. As you know, your sister is far too frail to travel alone. Yet I had to take her where no one would ever hear the story of what happened to her here in Gohaldinest, and that meant Plenelia, where those with magic are not welcome."

"And her position? What is she doing for you?"

"Not for me. For all the peoples of the world. The Plenelians have many magical devices in their keeping. I have convinced them to let her catalogue them."

"How did the Plenelians get these things if they don't like magic, and how is Nyree making a record of them going to help the world?"

"You will glean understanding of this when we get to discussing the history of this world. Until then, rest assured that your sister, our sister, is safe."

"What about when they see her eyes? How will she be safe then?"

"Believe me when I say that not a drop of magic passes into Plenelia. For as much as they do not like maeges, those with magic fear to tread there as well. Even I dislike the sensation, even though I have held many treaty sessions within Plenelia."

Rivic wanted to believe Cirvel, but he feared this was just another game of half-truths.

"Come, let us not worry over the past any longer and rather focus on the path that presently lies before you. I had other reasons for my travels," Cirvel said. "I had to find out what would make you stay. Not only for you to dwell here in Gohaldinest, but for you to remain at my side."

"You have already convinced me that I need to be stronger and that I cannot learn what I need to know if I return to my tribe. Now, as you tell me that I have even more to learn as a novihomidrak, I realize that you are my only teacher. I do not know what more you believe you would need to keep me here."

"Every man has needs," Cirvel answered plainly. "There will come a day when you will understand that fulfilling those needs can be found anywhere. Until then, I see your heart is dedicated to someone who doesn't live within the walls of our fair city."

Rivic thought of the blue traveling cloak hanging in the wardrobe and of Cirvel's recent trip where he admitted to being in Krithstand's village. Rivic's stomach clenched.

Cirvel turned in his chair and waved his hand. The wall behind him dissolved, revealing built in shelves from floor to ceiling. In the faint blue light pouring out from the back, Rivic saw that each shelf held a multitude of genie lamps. It seemed like there were ten across and three of four rows deep. The sight of them brought chills to Rivic.

A genie lamp appeared in Cirvel's waiting palm. A shimmer of magic rippled over the wall and Rivic knew that a mirage of the lamp had appeared from wherever this one had come from, making it impossible to discover where it had originally been. "You do not fully understand how to read a world's Humline, I see. Once you are a Necroatheling, we will remedy that first." He set the lamp on the table.

Rivic wondered if he should take it. He watched Cirvel for any signs.

"You do understand that agreeing to stand by me as my lineage brother gives you a certain rise in station and with that comes definite benefits?"

"Such as?"

"Your own quarters, for one. Your studies for another. Master Glayth will continue to train you with weaponry, and I hear that you have recently expressed an interest in forging your own blades. This I see as a valuable skill. Other than that, I will be taking over the remainder of your education from here. Necroathelings may still come for you in middle of the night. 'Tis necessary training, but you will not have to attend classes." Cirvel smiled broadly. "Or fear for the safety of those you love."

"Alityka?" Rivic croaked, wondering if he could press for her well-being.

"Well now, you don't love her, do you? She is a friend, certainly, but I was thinking of someone a little closer to your heart. Someone who is otherwise unprotected without you." Cirvel reached out, brought the lamp closer to him, and rubbed it.

Smoke poured out of the lamp and from it a woman materialized. She crouched on the table as if she'd ducked when the magic consumed her. She looked up, fear and tears in her scared eyes. "Rivic?" Ellonia asked.

Rivic rushed to stand. He embraced her and swung her off the table. He kept his body between her and Cirvel. After a moment, he put one hand to the side of her face, keeping his other hand securely on her back. Tears ran down her cheeks, but he saw the relief in her eyes, and he didn't bother to wipe the moisture away. "Are you all right?"

She nodded, then leaned her head against his shoulder.

"I am glad to see that I guessed correctly." Cirvel's words were slow and full of amusement.

Rivic released Ellonia and turned back to Cirvel. "Why is she here?"

"Because she means something to you," Cirvel responded as if the answer should have been plenty evident already. "Having her here is the last piece of insuring that you will pledge yourself as my lineage brother. You no longer have to worry about her safety."

Rivic released Ellonia and took a couple steps toward Cirvel. "I don't want her here." He hoped Ellonia didn't take the statement personally; he didn't want her anywhere she could be used to manipulate Rivic's actions, like being forced to stay. "Her tribe needs her. She is their healer."

"And they will find another. Certainly, she has no more knowledge of herbs than anyone else can learn. She has no special magic or awareness. Yet she will be a tremendous help to you and could possibly benefit both of us."

Did that mean that Cirvel didn't know about her future-sight?

"She is the daughter of their leader, Chief Krithstand. He will not sit idly by while his daughter is missing."

Cirvel's eyebrows raised in amusement. "Oh, I dare say that he knows exactly who took his daughter. He will not rise up against us."

Rivic felt the magic, but didn't know what Cirvel had done. Rivic turned back for Ellonia and found her gone. The genie lamp rocked back and forth on the ground near where she had stood. Rivic dove for the lamp.

"Vochey, lamp," Cirvel said. The golden pot disappeared before Rivic's hand even got close to it.

"Let her go," Rivic insisted. Then, after a pause, he added, "Please."

"One step at a time. I've just elevated you to a status that will have others questioning who you are and why I would do this. You will have to prove your worth and you may make some enemies. You want Ellonia to be safe during this transition period, don't you?"

Cirvel was good. Rivic didn't like it and it took him a moment before he could answer, "Aye, 'tis best to keep her out of harm's way. Are you trying to tell me that I need more power to keep myself and Ellonia safe?"

"'Tis time for your first lesson which I have demonstrated here. People cannot be trusted to make their own decisions. They will never choose wisely and certainly not for the good of all, but only to benefit themselves. We, you and I as novi-homidraks, have the obligation to make sure the inhabitants of a world do what is best for everyone."

Rivic nodded, biting back the words he wished to say.

"You do not believe me?" Cirvel asked.

The answer came unrestrained from Rivic. "Tyranny serves no one."

As often happened when Rivic said something he was certain would displease Cirvel, the Lord of Gohaldinest only smiled and seemed amused. Cirvel's dark eyes seemed to sparkle. "Tyrants definitely serve only themselves." He shook his head. "Do you know what the word 'Dominus' means?"

Rivic indicated that he didn't.

"It means Lord, stemming from an origin of one who dominates. When one of the acolytes, like yourself, becomes a Dominus, it means that you move into a position of learning to rule others. Necroatheling means 'dark prince.' 'Tis a higher rank and one that must be blind to emotions in order to cut through to the truth of a situation. Removal of their soul represents that they are ready to make hard decisions and to do whatever is necessary to protect their world."

"Have you given up your soul?" Rivic asked.

Cirvel nodded slowly. He took another sip from his glass. "'Twas necessary." He continued to nod, but a little more fervently now. "This world had been lost."

"I have heard," Rivic commented with caution, "that you seek to save humanity by removing humans from the bloodwave."

"'Tis one of those hard choices that must be made."

"But everyone will die when you succeed. You will be the last man, a sole survivor alone in your castle on the hill. Is that really how you want to exist?"

Cirvel's eyes roamed Rivic with a slow flatness, the brilliant spark gone. "I hope I have not misjudged you."

Rivic dropped to bended knee beside Cirvel. "Nay, my lord. Forgive my curiosity." He hoped he hadn't revealed how much he knew of Cirvel's plan. If Cirvel had only spoken about this to Lihn, then Cirvel might begin to wonder where Rivic had gotten this information. It would only be a small leap to guess that Lihn had told Alityka and she had told Rivic.

"Return to your chambers and get settled in. We shall be having the ceremony to make you a Necroatheling soon. I have much to prepare."

Rivic stood and stepped back.

"Think on what I have said."

"Aye, my lord. I shall." Rivic left the room, trying not to flee. But once he was out in the hallway, he leaned back against the wall while his stomach rolled with sickness. One thought prevailed: Cirvel had Ellonia.

CHAPTER 20

*R*ivic couldn't sit still. He didn't even want to look at his new quarters Cirvel had provided for him, let alone get settled in as Cirvel had suggested. Instead, Rivic found himself pacing the hallways of the quiet castle. Everyone seemed to be off to their classes and instruction today, everyone except him. Even Dragzel wasn't to be found.

He wandered to Lihn's library and stared at the gloomy painting of the city, half wishing that Galault would appear and talk to him. After that, he thought about heading down to visit with Master Glayth and perhaps work at the forge for a bit, but he didn't make it there. From one of the ramparts, Rivic watched Glayth in training several acolytes below in the field, and that was as close to the forge as Rivic felt like going. His arms didn't have the strength in them to do the work, nor did his mind have the focus he needed.

As the day wore on, he made his way to the main library intending on reading about genie lamps, but he found a red, padded, wing chair in the sun by one of the tall windows and dropped down into it. From there, he stared out over the city of Gohaldinest unable to see anything but the tops of buildings. Soon, the coolness of the shadows beginning to creep over him as well as the rumblings in his stomach, which reminded him he hadn't eaten anything yet today, forced him to rise.

Heading back through the library, he saw Alityka sitting at a table with her usual scattering of books. It really had gotten later in the day than' he realized for her to be here now. Rivic had been waiting to break the news to Alityka all day. She needed to know. She'd know what to do.

He shoved the book she was reading away from her. She gave him an inquisitive stare.

"He's got Ellonia," Rivic admitted. He found himself trembling.

"What? Ellonia? Here?" Alityka asked.

"Aye. Cirvel's trip was to go fetch her."

"She's not in a dungeon or something, is she?"

"She's safe."

Alityka gave him a disbelieving look. "What does that mean?"

"He's put her into a genie lamp, and I don't know which one. He says he's going to keep her there until after I become a Necroatheling, promising me that she won't come to any harm."

"We see how well that worked out for Nyree, and Lihn, who we still haven't seen. You know Cirvel doesn't keep his promises," she sneered.

"I am more concerned about what your father will do now."

"Father will never stand for both of his daughters being within Cirvel's grasp. Is there nothing you can do to get Ellonia away?"

Rivic shook his head. He wasn't sure his heart was in it

either. The idea of Ellonia here in Gohaldinest appealed to him.

"How long do we have until Cirvel makes you go through the Necroatheling ceremony?"

"I don't know. Soon. He said he wants it done swiftly."

"Do you have any good news to pile in with all this bad that you're bringing me?" Alityka snapped.

"I have my own private quarters now. Cirvel wants to keep me close to train directly with him," Rivic said, feeling as if that wasn't going to be anywhere near the good news she was seeking. Judging by the look on her face, she certainly didn't think it was anything but more bad news. "Sorry," he added.

She reached out to gather and close the book she'd been reading. She tucked it under her arms, which she folded over on the table. "Do we have anything we can use to our advantage?"

"I don't know what," Rivic said. "I'm out maneuvered. As long as he has Ellonia, I won't go against him. The last time I did, Nyree paid for it. I won't let anything happen to Ellonia."

Alityka's posture stiffened. "Does that include helping me to defeat Cirvel? Or helping to find Lihn?"

"Aye. Maybe. I don't know." Rivic let his arms drop beside him. "I can't even think straight right now. Too much has happened too fast. I never thought he'd discover Ellonia, and he's moved my sister to Plenelia."

"What?"

Rivic realized he hadn't even taken a moment to explain that to her. He sat down in another chair at the table. "Cirvel took Nyree to Plenelia and married her off. I don't even know if I'll see her again. My only chance is through Cirvel." He hung his head. "I'm sorry."

"Does he know Ellonia is my sister?"

"If he knows you're Krithstand's daughter, then aye."

"Then he has us both trapped. He knows that Lihn is my friend and Ellonia is my sister. He entangles us with the people we love to keep us where he wants us. Even though you may feel hopeless in the position you are in, you have achieved the status I had tried to get into. You need to use it to your advantage without fear and keep getting closer to Cirvel. The more he believes you are in his confidences, the safer the people we love will be."

He nodded, knowing that she was correct. She always seemed to know more and plan better than he did, no matter that his novimather had said she needed tempering. Her wild spirit left so many more possibilities open. "What happens after I become a Necroatheling? If we find a way to trap Cirvel or defeat him, can I get my soul back?"

"Aye, 'tis known as reincarnations, which means to enter the flesh again. Kalt explained it to me once. He watched Cirvel reincarnate a Necroatheling." Her words faltered. "Cirvel then put the man to death for betraying him."

"Ali, how can I have the strength to do this? I have control of my magic, but my emotions hold so much fear."

"'Tis not that I am never afraid. I merely realize that I have to make a choice: do I stand by and watch as Cirvel destroys everything I hold dear, or not? I feel like the unicorns chose me, not because I was special – I was an eight-cycle-old girl, but because I knew how to make up my mind about what to expect in life. I will defeat Cirvel. Even if it takes two thousand cycles to do it."

"'Tis it? Make up my mind?"

"When your sister was taken by the Necroathelings, did you not make up your mind to come to Gohaldinest and get her? Did you not achieve that eventually? So you had a few mishaps along the way perhaps, but you did get her out. That all was a choice." She looked off at the library, then came back to him with her gaze hardened even more. "When I fought Azote, I made the decision to survive. I did not think about the odds against me. If I had, I would've faltered. 'Twould have cost me my life. I expected to live. I have plans beyond defeating Cirvel; I want to fall in love, have children. I keep these things in my mind as a sacred picture to remind me what I'm fighting for."

"I've never let myself dream beyond the immediate moment."

"That is your flaw. Because you live so firmly in the present, you live in fear of what lies ahead. Aye, you live in the now, but you must turn your vision toward the future you desire." Alityka made chopping movements with her hand, first downward to represent the present, then sideways to indicate the time to come. "Without dreams beyond your current conditions, you will remain terrified of the world to come and won't want to change it."

Every word she'd spoken was true. He leaned forward over the table and placed his head in his hands. "All right. Then I seek to focus on a time when Cirvel has been over-come and Ellonia and I can build our lives together."

"Are you committed to that vision?"

"Aye." A ball of trepidation curled in his stomach and it took him a moment to realize the truth of the energy behind it. "Nay. Not for the long-term, not for two thousand cycles. If 'tis going to take that long, I don't know how Ellonia can still be by my side. 'Tis hopeless."

She lay her hand over his as he drew back to sit up in the chair. "But 'tis a vision you can see and might be all you need for now. Do you think having children is the last thing I want before sliding into the grave? Or even if having children will happen? Will I be an old, withered woman completely unat-tractive in two thousand cycles? Will I even be able to hold a sword? I tell you that none of those fears will I let hold me back."

"All right. I shall keep the vision of Ellonia and I being together in the future in my mind and hold that image. Maybe the Onesong will show me how this works as we go along and I discover how to bring her to the other side of time."

"'Tis possible. Believe it."

"I shall."

At the sound of a small poof, something landed with a resounding thud on the table, giving all the books a slight jump. "Ow," Dragzel muttered, raising himself up and shaking his head. He rubbed his paw against the side of his face. "I think he knocked a tooth loose."

"Dragzel, what happened?" Alityka asked, gathering the cahaster into her arms.

Dragzel's grin widened. "I think I've annoyed our great lord. Finally, I get under his skin. He still won't tell me where milady Lihn is, but this is the third time he's sent me away. He will weaken."

"Until he drops you somewhere like the glass prison and you can't get out."

"Wrong. I placed a doorway spell on part of it before I even started. That was the second place he put me." Dragzel's shoulders shook as he waggled his head back and forth in his own self-gratification.

"He'll put you in another dimension next."

Dragzel crawled out of Alityka's arms back onto the table and slinked around to face them. "'Tis not me I'm worried about. He can do whatever he wants with me. I keep hoping he'll decide I'm too much trouble and send me to milady Lihn. That's the best I can hope for."

"And the worst?" Rivic asked.

"That he'll injure my mother. After milady Lihn, she is the most important to me. He knows this and he is already displeased with her."

"Would he dare to hurt his own novimather though?"

"Aye. Please keep her safe, Rivic. You've seen how he keeps her. 'Tis not how dragons are meant to live. I have begged her to produce him a litter of cahasters, but she says she has offered up enough of her own for his purposes. Between her refusals and milady Lihn's denials, his temper is short."

Rivic stood and gathered the cahaster up. "Let's go pay our lord a visit. If nothing else, it will get you back in his room without you returning under your own power. That should be another point of irritation."

Dragzel grinned happily.

"Rivic, be careful," Alityka said.

Holding the cahaster all the way to Cirvel's room, Rivic felt dread pressing through each of his footsteps. He swore Dragzel had gotten much larger since he'd first come to Gohaldinest. Pausing for a moment beside the door to his new room, Rivic considered for an instant about grabbing the blue traveling cloak Ellonia had made for him. But he doubted Cirvel would send him away just for coming in with Dragzel. Besides, Ellonia was here now and he didn't want to give any impression that he wanted to leave.

Rivic knocked on the door to the antechamber, where a Necroatheling promptly answered and allowed him admittance into the room.

"Sit," the Necroatheling stated, pointing to a chair at the table. Then he went and knocked on the door to the reading room.

"Stop shaking," Dragzel muttered.

The cahaster was right. He would survive this current moment. He refocused on the thought of him and Ellonia being together without any worries in their lives. He would practice what Alityka had been talking about and found that the exercise brought him a measure of calm.

Cirvel entered behind the Necroatheling. His dark eyes immediately set upon the cahaster. Rivic felt certain that Dragzel stuck his tongue out at Cirvel, but quickly pretended to be washing himself.

"I had not figured to see you again so soon," Cirvel said.

"Nor I to be here," Rivic responded as he tried to gauge how much of a mood Cirvel was in to bargain. "However, I come to you with an idea. It came to me when Dragzel landed on the table right before me."

"Oh?"

"Aye. I ask for Dragzel to be the cahaster that holds my soul."

The stone appearance of Cirvel's void face made Rivic certain the answer would be an unequivocal refusal. But then his eyes flickered, and the expression softened a margin. "I have heard such a suggestion before and discarded it. That beast's temperance is not suited to storing the soul of a Necroatheling. Why would you even seek this?"

"To further unite us. 'Tis my understanding that your mistress, Lihn, has raised Dragzel to be the only cahaster capable of speech, which makes Dragzel quite unique. The fact that this cahaster was a gift from you to Lihn binds a special position to you. By having Dragzel contain my soul, I am not only binding myself to you, but to our novimather and Lihn as well, instilling a complete foundation of loyalty among us all."

Cirvel's face darkened and he flipped his fingers dismissively. The Necroathelings bowed and exited the room via the doors they stood the closest to. As each one shut behind them, as if giving a soft acknowledgement that they no longer had to be there, Cirvel remained silent for several moments. "Bravo. How long have you been working on those words?"

"Not a shred of disrespect was meant," Rivic said, sliding

from his chair to kneel on the floor while still holding Dragzel close. "I meant every word."

"But why this cahaster? Dragzel, was this your idea? What are you scheming now?"

Dragzel squirmed from Rivic's hold and jumped up to the chair and then onto the table. "My lord, I wish only for what I have always sought: the safety of milady Lihn. While this poor boy sees it as a way of making a foundation of loyalty, I see it for what 'tis: a hope that you would wield mercy on my dear mistress. I have naught else to offer and you know it."

"Where is Lihn, my lord?" Rivic asked. "'Twould seem this discussion should involve her as well, as it is her gifted cahaster."

"I shall consider what you both have said. Leave now; I have far more pressing matters to be concerned with at present. I expect to not see either of you for the remainder of the night. Am I making myself clear, Dragzel?"

"Aye, my lord." Dragzel bounded from the table for the door with Rivic following behind. Once out in the hallway, having passed the Necroathelings standing guard, Dragzel finished with a look back at Cirvel's door, "I'll see you again this evening."

a knock at his door the next morning woke Rivic. He lumbered from the soft feather mattress, begrudging the cold stone floor beneath his feet and the chill that hung in the air even though he dragged a blanket with him. He clutched it close as he answered the summons.

Bright morning light streamed through the latticed window, glaring into his eyes and forcing Rivic to squint at the silhouette of the man before him as it took the shape of a Necroatheling. The shadow of the hood didn't cloak the Necroatheling's sneer. "Lord Cirvel requests your presence in his reading room."

"I'll be there momentarily." Rivic shut the door, then locked it for good measure, even though he knew the security wasn't much against a Necroatheling. It was more about letting the Necroatheling hear the clicking of the latch than keeping him out. But even Rivic had to ponder why the castle would even bother with locks when any of the maeges, even a fairly accomplished acolyte, could teleport right into the room.

Knowing these thoughts to be those of a refreshed brain

after his first decent night's sleep in what seemed like ages, Rivic pushed them away and went to get dressed. He paused, touching the blue traveling cloak hanging in the wardrobe. He'd been afraid to even look at it last night when he had returned here. He wouldn't have known what to do if it all had been a dream.

For a moment, Rivic stared at the domini armor and debated whether or not to put it on. His status may be elevated, but his title had not. Until then, he supposed he should wear it. He buckled it on over his wheat colored tunic and brown leggings. He still hated the red color. Once again, he looked to the blue cloak, grasping the arm near the gold and silver trim around the cuff. He released it and shut the wardrobe door.

Rivic stepped from his room, but rather than finding himself in the black and white tiled hallway, he stood in Cirvel's reading room. Cirvel sat down in his usual chair at the table.

"I heard my Necroatheling woke you this morning," Cirvel said, picking up a steaming teacup beside the book he currently perused and taking a sip.

Rivic glanced back at the door behind him and saw it closed. The light magic of a teleportation spell lingered. "I'm sorry, my lord. 'Twas the first good night's sleep I've had in a while. The accommodations are very comfortable," Rivic said, feeling the need to cloak the apology with an explanation.

"I fully understand," Cirvel said, setting the cup down. "'Twas why I let you sleep so late. But be warned that from here on out, your days will continue to start early. You know that I am an early riser, unless I am engaged in morning entertaining."

The memory of Lihn in Cirvel's bed rushed back. Rivic tried not to choke. "Aye, my lord."

"I thought we should begin today's lesson with a basic overview about what novihomidraks are and what they are not. Let's begin, shall we?"

Rivic took a seat.

Cirvel leaned back, casually crossing his legs. "As you obviously know, novihomidraks start off as humans that have been taken by dragons and incubated for about ten years or so."

"Years?"

"Aye." Cirvel nodded. "I realize that is a foreign word. I shall explain. A year is typically one circle of a planet around its sun. The people of this planet refer to years as a cycle, which is an approximation. I say approximation because this planet has a strange dual orbit due to a slight wobble on its axis. I believe 'tis the effect of the three moons and the various gravitational pulls which causes a sort of tremor on the planet's surface."

As Cirvel spoke, the top of the table turned black and white dots appeared like stars within the fathomless depths of the wood. A planet appeared in the center, surrounded by three circling moons. The image shrank back to adjust for the addition of the sun in the center and several other planet-like objects orbiting the sun.

A shiver went through Rivic. How was it possible that Cirvel knew all this? "We're here," Rivic pointed to the planet that had been in the focus a moment before, "...and all this is around us?"

"Aye."

Rivic wasn't certain what to think or feel. Cirvel had to be a god to know all this. How else did one gain such a vantage point to behold what lay on the table before him?

Cirvel mistook Rivic's overwhelm for lack of comprehension. Placing his hand on the table, Cirvel lifted the image of the galaxy from the surface into the air before them. "Maybe this perspective will be clearer."

Rivic stared at the floating model before him. He had watched the stars may times, but he'd never imagined that the stars could look back down at him. "Is this the Onesong?"

"Nay," Cirvel laughed. He waved his hand toward the levitating simulation. "'Tis only a meager part of the Onesong, like a single cobblestone in the whole of Gohaldinest. The Onesong's vastness could not be shown in such a minuscule area."

"Oh."

"Let us move on, shall we? As I was saying, this quiver caused by the moons shifts the planet a touch out of its original orbit and gives it a second, somewhat longer orbit. As the second orbit completes, the gravitation pull corrects the wobble and puts the planet back on the original trajectory. The shorter orbit takes place higher than the longer one."

In the model before Rivic, the rotation of the planet began to take on a second course around the sun and an ellipse formed like a trail to show two distinct loops.

"So sometimes the cycle is a little shorter and sometimes 'tis a little longer?" Rivic asked.

"Aye, now take this planet here which only has one orbit around the sun. One complete trip around is called a year. It finishes one and begins another. The actual days, the time it takes for a planet to rotate from sunrise to sunrise, within a year may vary between each planet. Novihomidraks considers a year against what their home world year is."

"I still don't understand why we don't call our cycles as years then."

"For this planet, we have to make a slight adaptation using an average between the two orbits since the dual orbits make the years of unequal length. I tried using an alpha-beta system for longer than I should have before I gave up and decided to continue the use of the word cycles. Just know that every cycle on this planet is not the same line as the cycle before it or the cycle after it. Most people here don't notice the difference. I'm sure you never have, but you may as the cycles continue to progress and your novihomidrak age grows. Does this make sense?"

Rivic couldn't say that it completely did, but he figured it would in time. He nodded, just tucking away all this information in the back of his head.

Cirvel continued, "Novihomidraks have no memory of their life before being claimed by the dragon."

"'Tis not true. I do have memory what I did before the dragon took me. I remember the dragon swallowing me and my sister."

"Really?" Cirvel uncrossed his legs and leaned over the table. "'Tis very interesting. "Maybe because there were two of you, the dragon could not wipe your memory. It makes you even more of a unique specimen of a novihomidrak."

"So, you have no memory of your life before the Guardian took you?" Rivic asked, feeling awkward in the question. He remembered the callous warning Alityka had given him about his own mind perhaps being weak if the world was ever to rejoin the Onesong, but he had to pretend he didn't know this.

"Nay, and there is a belief that if a novihomidrak did remember their life before, they would go crazy."

"Crazy?"

"'Tis said that the knowledge of their birth parents and their early life would be too much for them to handle and they would go insane." Cirvel paused. "That doesn't stop many novihomidraks from searching crowds on every planet they go to for a familiar face."

"Should I be worried because I still have my memories?"

If Cirvel knew about the untouchable stars overhead, maybe he knew this answer as well and Rivic had to know.

Cirvel gave another one of his short little laughs. "Nay. The difference may be because your parents are already deceased or have something to do with being incubated with your non-magical twin. You seem quite stable and thoughtful. I believe you have nothing to worry about."

Rivic knew that Cirvel might not be thinking about a time when the world was returned to the Onesong, but he appreciated the reassurance that he'd be all right anyway. Those were words he needed to hear.

"Now, do you know why novihomidraks are created?" Cirvel asked.

"To be champions of the world."

"Incorrect," Cirvel said, deflating Rivic when he thought he had the answer. "Novihomidraks are actually champions for the Onesong. Generally, novihomidraks are assigned to a problematic world, to go in and solve their problems in an effective, discrete way."

Rivic felt the muscles in his neck tighten as he knew that Cirvel was drawing him into the one question that he had to ask. "What happens if a novihomidrak fails on his mission?"

The corners of Cirvel's lips up turned, but he didn't show any teeth. "Do you wonder what happens to the world if a novihomidrak fails, or do you wonder what made *me* fail?"

Rivic lifted his chin slightly. "Both."

Cirvel leaned back in his chair once more and crossed his legs. "I failed because I was given an impossible mission. Ordinarily, if the world is too far gone, the dragons spin the world off of the Onesong and it slowly dies. There is no hope once it has been strangled from the Onesong."

"Has this world been *strangled off?*" Rivic asked, his dry mouth finding issues with saying the last two words.

"Very nearly. There is not a way for you, me, or the Guardian to make it off this world at this time."

"We will die with the planet?"

"There is a distinct possibility."

Rivic wasn't certain how to recover from an answer like that without asking Cirvel if there wasn't something they could do. Better to keep it a vague discussion about novihomidraks for now. Instead of what he wanted to ask, he queried, "So how do novihomidraks get their mission?"

"Novies, as we like to call ourselves, receive missions from the Dragon Council. The dragons guard the Wells of the Onesong, which is the interweaving of the Wells throughout the entire universe and the connections of each galaxy. Imagine a tree growing up and branching out, with little bubbles at the end of each branch, and that is a close representation of the Onesong. The Dragon Council assigns novies to missions and the novi travels the Wells to get to the planet. If the mission is thought to be long-term, the Dragon Council also sends a sapere along with them."

"What's a sapere?"

"The word has its meaning in the phrase 'wise one.' Saperes are not novihomidraks, but they have been blessed with dragon magic. The biggest difference visibly is the appearance of brandings somewhere on the sapere's body. They must submit themselves to the dragon and the dragon gives them their brand. Saperes are an unfortunate necessity for a novihomidrak stationed for a long-term on a planet. Not only are the saperes capable of healing wounds inflicted from one novihomidrak upon another, but they have special skills that aid the novihomidrak in their mission."

"Such as?"

"They assist in opening the Wells of the Onesong. Typically, once travel has been established from one world to another, the Wells stay open for a good period of time, but they do close slowly. Saperes can widen the opening."

"Why can't I as a novi do that?"

"There are some things that even I do not have an answer for and this is one of them. 'Tis a mystery of the universe to me. There might be the knowledge out there somewhere, but I have yet to learn it."

"You speak as if you can just gather information out of thin air."

"'Tis very possible," Cirvel said. He held up his hand. "But that 'tis a lesson for another day. We are starting simple, remember?"

Rivic leaned forward. "Did you bring a sapere with you to this world?"

"I did. He was a young man then. You've seen him. He's the one who made you a dominus."

Rivic decided to see if he could get a little more information out of Cirvel. "He seemed quite old and frail. What happens if he were to die?"

A look of genuine concern passed over Cirvel's face. "That is, indeed, a very real and scary possibility. But we do have hope. I hadn't wanted to speak to you about this yet, but now might be an appropriate time, seeing as how you have reminded me once again that time draws short. We have a dragon, our novimather, and she is capable of blessing another sapere for us. You only need to find an appropriate person, someone willing to become a sapere, someone was strong magicks already running through her, and with strong magical lines."

Cirvel had tipped his hand the moment that he used the pronoun her. He meant Ellonia.

Rivic tried hard not to show that he had noticed Cirvel's intent, but he debated whether Cirvel's sharp eyes missed the flicker of Rivic's awareness or not. Those dark depths were so shrewd and cunning that Rivic could never fully trust what was going on in those eyes. "Do you think the dragon will bless someone? It just seems to me that she has the choice to not do such a thing as well."

"Let me deal with the dragon."

That was the most anger Rivic had ever heard come out of Cirvel. For a moment, he thought that Cirvel might completely lose his calm. But Cirvel once again took an austere face and pretended as if his rage had never happened. Rivic wondered if the Guardian would speak to him if he were to go down and seek her out. She was, after all, his dragon mother as well.

"Tell me what novihomidrak abilities you have of which you are aware?" Cirvel said.

Rivic wondered if he should tell Cirvel all of them. Would Cirvel know that he was lying? What if not telling Cirvel about a power meant that he didn't learn what he needed to know or possibly discovered a weakness? "I can call my sword to me. I have dragon teeth and..." He looked at his hands as he recalled his experience when Ellonia insisted that he get cleaned up. "Claws. I can also levitate to great heights."

"Without wings?"

"Aye."

Cirvel gave an impressed nod. "Anything else?"

"I sometimes get feelings about things that are about to happen, premonitions, so to speak."

"That is the Humline of the world as well as the Onesong speaking through you. Anything else?"

Rivic felt certain that he was lacking an ability that Cirvel was waiting for him to reveal. He finally just shook his head.

Cirvel returned a disappointed look, but before he could say anything further, a knock came to the door. "Very well. We will carry on tomorrow with information about saperes.

For the remainder of the day, be reading this book. 'Twill fill in some details for you." He summoned a book, floating it from a nearby stand, and handed it to Rivic. Cirvel smiled, but it lacked a genuine feel, and he looked toward the door. "Come in," he said in a louder, hurried tone.

A Necroatheling entered with a girl held slightly before him. Her white acolyte dress stretched over her hugely pregnant belly, which she held onto as if it would fall off. Sweat tangled her brown hair and her eyes were wide with fear as she took in the whole room with one sweep. She seemed scared to see Rivic with Lord Cirvel and her feet came to a stop beneath her. The Necroatheling stepped into her, then shoved her forward. Blood dripped off her bare legs onto the floor.

"I will see you tomorrow, Dominus Rivic," Cirvel said, dismissing him a little stronger this second time.

Rivic jumped up from his chair. "Of course, my lord." He hurried from the room, but he glanced back before drawing the door shut. The Necroatheling nudged the girl closer to Cirvel.

Cirvel reached for her, pausing for a brief moment as his eyes raised to meet Rivic's. Then Cirvel put his hand on the girl's back and drew her closer to him. With gazes still locked, Cirvel leaned in and whispered something to the girl.

A shiver went through Rivic's shoulders as he closed the door and hurried down the hallway, not daring to look back.

CHAPTER 22

For the remaining morning and into the afternoon, Rivic pondered about the girl he'd seen in Cirvel's antechamber. He wanted to tell Alityka about it, but she'd be in the middle of her daily training. Besides, he wasn't certain he had anything to report.

After pacing about his room and throwing furtive glances at the book he had dropped onto the desk, he decided that he should probably pass the time better by starting the reading Cirvel requested of him. Rivic hadn't even looked at the title yet.

Grabbing the book, he stretched over the quilt on his bed and flipped the book open. He quickly found that it wasn't a book, but rather a hand-written journal. More than that, it belonged to Cirvel. Had the Lord of Gohaldinest intended to hand this to him?

A part of him excited over being privy to Cirvel's innermost thoughts, then he realized it wasn't a diary, but rather observations about the planet, the circling moons, and their patterns within the universe. It didn't take long for Rivic to realize how studious and dedicated Cirvel had been in making these records, and how the puzzling questions Cirvel had gave way to proven theories.

It certainly gave insights into how Cirvel plotted and planned. The thoroughness of it gave Rivic a brief flash of depression about there being no way he and Alityka could certainly overcome this type of mind. Yet, it obviously took Cirvel a while to decipher what was actually happening around him and sometimes he overlooked the simple details while his thoughts dwelled on the complex.

Rivic lay reading when a knock came to his door and broke his concentration. Not sure if he'd really heard the sound, he swung his legs off the raised mattress before realizing that he wasn't expecting anyone. It gave him pause until the second knock when he finished rising.

"Vochey, Honor," he said. The sword came to his hand. A thought that he was being a little ridiculous floated through his mind. He reached out, feeling the power on the other side of the door. It had to be a Necroatheling.

Holding the sword loosely by the hilt, he leaned it partially against the wall as he opened the door. "Aye?" he said, swinging open the door.

The Necroatheling flipped back his hood revealing a stout face topped with reddish-brown hair cut close to the scalp. "Lord Cirvel tells us that you are soon to join our little elite society. We thought we'd invite you to join us."

We? Rivic thought seeing no one else out in the hallway. He couldn't believe he'd called his sword to him for this. "Not tonight," he began to say, but something inside him thrummed. "In The Playground?" he asked.

"Aye," the Necroatheling answered, his eyebrows rising above his smiling brown eyes.

"Sure," Rivic said. He took a half step backwards and reached his hand out for his domini sword. The weapon, belt, and scabbard rose into the air and snapped from where they had been to his hand. He knew the Necroatheling watched. "Vochey, armor," he said, smiling to himself as his armor wrapped around him. The Necroatheling's eyes widened. Then Rivic picked up the sword that rested by the wall and slid it under his belt, letting the hilt catch on the leather so it hung loose.

"That's a nice sword," the Necroatheling said.

"Aye, 'tis that indeed," he replied, wondering if the Necroatheling would try to take it from him tonight. With the mood he was in, he almost wished the man would try.

"My name is Undar," the Necroatheling said, holding out his hand.

Rivic stared at the man's white palm. "I'm Rivic," he said, though he presumed the Necroatheling already knew that. He returned Undar's grasp and squeezed hard. The last thing he wanted was a Necroatheling believing that he would submit to them, or, even worse, that they were friends.

After Undar broke away from Rivic's grip, he began walking down the hall. As Rivic closed the door to his room and began to follow the Necroatheling, Rivic reminded himself that the man in front of him no longer had a soul contained within his body. Somewhere, a cahaster had that stored away.

Undar glanced back. "You know, you can go down to The Playground anytime you want, right?"

Rivic hadn't known that. He gave a non-committal grunt, followed by, "That right?"

"Aye. Lots of us like to go there every day to practice."

It explained why he never saw any Necroathelings train-ing. "I've noticed, generally taking down a promising acolyte or after fetching one of the domini." Rivic felt the scathing sarcasm on his words and wondering what Undar would think about it.

The Necroatheling smiled. "'Tis not always like that," he

said, but they both knew the truth. Rivic wondered what poor, unsuspecting person awaited them tonight. He secretly hoped it wasn't Alityka.

Undar used the lion-head knocker, then said, "Helst velipya."

Rivic expected a bright light, but instead the door clicked as it unlocked. Undar opened the doorway to The Playground.

Following Undar, Rivic found that they came out into an area leading into a hallway. This opened up into several staircases that went up into the seating area around the arena, very similar to the amphitheater in Gohaldinest. He let Undar pick the stairs and they emerged several rows up in the seating area. There were already several Necroathelings sitting here.

Undar seemed to be looking for someone specific, but how he could tell which Necroatheling was which in the sea of purple hoods, Rivic wasn't sure.

More than that, Rivic couldn't believe there were so many Necroathelings.

He hadn't noticed it before when he'd been down in the arena, but maybe he should have. There were several hundred Necroathelings, maybe even pushing over a thousand.

Undar started down an aisle, then he knocked the shoulder of a man with the back of his hand. The Necroatheling glanced up at Undar, who then pointed back toward Rivic. The seated Necroatheling shot to his feet. "Dominus Rivic," the man said boisterously. "Come, sit with us. Everyone, move down."

The shuffling began as Necroathelings began to scoot down a seat to make room for Rivic.

"That wasn't really necessary," Rivic said, a little embarrassed by the scene they were all causing.

"Nonsense. We've been waiting for you to come up and join us," the man said.

Undar stepped over the seat backs to join the others that had just finished moving over. Rivic did the same, and the only seat that remained was by the man that had greeted him so eagerly.

"My name is Rthstead. I'm Lord Cirvel's first lieutenant," the Necroatheling said.

"A pleasure to meet you, Rthstead-na," Rivic lied. The last thing he wanted to do was get to know any of these Necroathelings, and certainly not by name. Still, it wouldn't do to disrespect them either. Somehow, he doubted that Rthstead was as glad to meet Rivic as he seemed either. With all this pretense surrounding a careful dance, Rivic began to understand why Kalt had wanted to keep Alityka from it; as a Dominari, she wouldn't be able to lie, and the powers given to her from the unicorns would make it hard for others to tell her dishonesties. He suspected that wouldn't gain her any favors and might actually make her more of a target. Had the Guardian suspected this as well?

Rivic couldn't help another glance around. "There sure are a lot of Necroathelings. I didn't know Lord Cirvel had trained so many."

"He's had a lot of cycles. Let's just say that not all of them are corporeal either."

"How do you mean?"

Rthstead grinned. "Lord Cirvel doesn't need you alive. In fact, you're more useful to him if you're not."

"But I thought Necroathelings were hard to kill," Rivic said, trying to withhold the stammer from his voice.

"We are, even more so when we're dead," the Necroatheling on the other side of Rthstead said, leaning forward to speak around the lieutenant.

Rivic forced a smile and a hesitant chuckle.

Undar slapped him on the back. "See, I told you you'd like it here."

Rivic nodded as he grinned at the other Necroathelings around him. He wished he'd gone with his first instinct to stay and read Cirvel's journal, but he couldn't back out now.

Below, two combatants appeared in the arena below them.

"All right! Let's go!" Rthstead shouted, standing up and throwing a fist into the air.

But as everyone else's attention dropped to the fight going on below, Rivic noticed a cage hanging just slightly above the arena partially hidden in the shadows. While the sides had iron bars, the bottom of the cage was glass. The whole thing swung from a single chain from the ceiling. Worse, there was a person trapped within the bars.

Lihn sat inside. A chair had been provided for her, but she chose to sit on the glass floor. She had blankets wrapped up all around her legs.

Undar followed Rivic's gaze. "Aye, Cirvel must be very displeased with her now to send her here. Usually he keeps her in a glass prison within the castle. This is no fit place for her. She'll be crying before too long. She does every night."

Rivic stood up.

"What are you doing?" Rthstead asked.

"Sit down," Undar warned. "That one's trouble, her and her cahaster. Leave them alone."

Rivic held his arms out to his sides and felt the power ripple through him as his feet left the ground.

Both Undar and Rthstead jumped to their feet and moved away from Rivic as he levitated to the height of Lihn's cage. "Talcor dun," he said, hoping he wouldn't lose his altitude during the spell. The last thing he wanted was to come crashing down into the fighting. As the world reappeared, he shot his hands out and grabbed onto the cold metal bars. As soon as he did, he felt the enchantments which would refuse to allow him entrance to retrieve her.

Lihn, at seeing him, gasped. "Rivic, what are you doing here?"

"I was about to ask you the same thing, though I suspect I know the answer." Rivic gave her a sad smile. "This can't be very good for you or the baby."

She shifted to kneel beside the bars. Rivic steadied the cage from swinging as she moved. "I'll manage. Have you been through the Necroatheling ceremony yet?"

"Nay."

She gave a tiny laugh. "You can tell Dragzel that now would be a good time to make the bargain we talked about." Rivic knew that she meant the bargain with Cirvel to be the cahaster to hold Rivic's soul; it was her subtle way of saying that she was done being here.

"We're working on it."

The crowd roared beneath them. Rivic wondered if Undar and Rthstead were even paying attention to him anymore.

Lihn began to move stiffly as if she were not controlling herself. She raised her head, her face scrunched up painfully, as she looked at him with pleading eyes. "Don't watch this," she begged, speaking through her open mouth but unable to move her lips. "Don't be mad at them. They are just following orders. Remember who gives those orders."

"Lihn?"

She said nothing further as she crawled to the center of the glass bottom cage and was held to watch what was going on below. The blankets all zoomed up into the air and shook out right in front of Rivic, blocking his view, but that didn't prevent him from hearing her initial sob.

The crowd roared with excitement, making Rivic wonder what was going on. He couldn't teleport himself back to the seat where he'd been while grasping the bars. He turned, still holding on while wishing he knew how to take Lihn with him so she wouldn't be crying. Taking one last look at the empty spot by Undar, he released the bars and fell forward. "Talcor dun."

He wasn't sure who was more stunned by his reappearance: himself or the Necroathelings around him.

Undar turned to him. "Are you done? You're best off if you leave them alone. And certainly don't bring Cirvel's wrath down upon us by trying to help her escape."

Even though it went against every fiber of his being, Rivic nodded and said, "I won't."

"Good. Now enjoy tonight's entertainment."

Rivic glanced toward the arena where he saw a Necroatheling suspended partially in the air. The hood of his cloak concealed his face. Then, almost with the same mechanical movements Rivic had just witnessed with Lihn, the Necroatheling removed his purple cloak. Rivic recognized Kalt.

The deep purple cloth dropped to the floor, leaving Kalt in a white shirt and black pants. His vacant, reddened eyes stared forward to a spot on the dirt floor near the base of the wall as he began to unlace his shirt and pull it over his head. It dropped to the ground beside the Necroatheling's cloak. Rivic noticed Kalt was barefoot, and it looked like blood and dirt blackened his feet.

Lihn's cage lowered into the light of the arena, revealing her kneeling on the glass floor.

Kalt began to make a slow turn in the air. The same coiling red marks that had been on his face also ran down his muscular chest and back, though some of the spirals were larger than others.

"Dek'tae," someone shouted.

"Dek'tae," replied another from the crowd.

"Dek'tae," responded a third as it slowly grew to a chant. "Dek'tae, Dek'tae, Dek'tae!"

While still rotating in the center of the arena, Kalt raised his head. Rivic saw him look up toward Lihn, though he didn't tip his head back that far.

Undar knocked his shoulder into Rivic as he began to clap with the rest of the crowd. "Dek'tae, Dek'tae," Undar said, a smile sliding onto his face as he encouraged Rivic.

"What is Dek'tae?" Rivic asked, having to lean toward Undar and shout in order to be heard.

Undar pointed toward the arena.

Kalt tried to flex his arms. His legs uselessly pedaled beneath him as if he were trying to stop his spin.

But it was below Kalt that drew Rivic's attention now. The red clay of the floor undulated and sparks of blue lightning ran through it. As the swirl grew, the iron-colored earth gave way to a smoky blue mist.

A dark shadow moved beneath the surface.

Kalt tried to draw his legs up.

A black loop sprang from the mist, trying for Kalt's foot, but it only snagged his toe.

A snap rent the air. Kalt yelled. He tried to draw back his leg, but being levitated as he was didn't afford him any way to maneuver. His toe hung at an awkward angle. Kalt's scream elevated until it faded into silence, leaving only the echoing Dek'tae chant.

Kalt reached up as if he could crawl his way to Lihn's cage.

Blood began to spew and Rivic realized that Kalt's toe was being peeled away from his body. The crowd grew quiet, seeming to lean forward in anticipation.

Rivic thought he might puke just as he did the day Kalt had raped Nyree.

He was about to look away when a dark tentacle

emerged. For a moment, it waved around in the spurting blood as if enjoying it, then it wrapped around Kalt's leg.

Another tentacle rose from the depths and stuck onto Kalt's chest in a coil. Flesh began to burn beneath the monster. Now, Rivic understood where the marks had come from.

Kalt screamed again. The pain seemed to be pulling him out of his trancelike state. His cheeks huffed as he puffed out large breaths of air. Half grimace, half growling holler, Kalt reached down to his leg that the tentacle had a hold of. "Vodicous!"

His leg fell away and disappeared into the mist.

The Necroathelings watching went wild. Undar and Rthstead both jumped to their feet, reeling with cheers.

Rivic couldn't look away.

The chants resumed. "Dek'tae. Dek'tae. Dek'tae."

Kalt grabbed his chest. "Vodicous," he said again. His chest ripped open and Kalt grabbed his own ribcage and cracked it apart. He reached inside, digging, to pull out his own heart.

Rivic gasped as Kalt broke his heart away from everything holding it inside him. The muscle still pulsed in the Necroatheling's hand as he held it out in the air.

As Kalt went limp, the bleeding heart rolled from his fingers and disappeared into the churning swell beneath. Kalt's dead body continued to rotate.

Rivic looked up to the glass cage. Lihn, curled up in a fetal position, sobbed on the floor.

Kalt's body dropped into the maelstrom.

"Dek'tae," the crowd continued to shout.

Undar reached down and punched Rivic's shoulder. "Come on. Why aren't you cheering with us? You're the reason he's here after what he did to your sister."

Rivic's back and chest felt stiff while his arms and legs felt numb. He wanted to magic himself from this place, but he couldn't manage it. He was positive that the images of this night would stay in his dreams for some time.

"Dek'tae!"

"What is that thing?" Rivic asked.

Undar sat down. "Dek'tae? You seriously don't know what Dek'tae is?"

Rivic shook his head, but he caught an amused glance that went between Undar and Rthstead. He wondered what the Necroathelings were plotting. Were they figuring out how to make him next to hang for the Dek'tae?

Though Lihn remained on the floor of the glass cage, it rose back into the semi-darkness, then higher until Rivic couldn't see it any longer.

The mist filling the arena dissipated and left a man lying whole on the ground of the arena. Rivic caught it in his peripheral vision first, then turned to look more fully. There was a deep red gash on Kalt's chest, but there was no blood. He began to stir.

"What?" Rivic asked.

Kalt climbed to his feet and wobbled. He lifted his head only enough to see where he was, then began to walk as fast as he could shuffle along out of the arena.

"How can that be?" Rivic looked at Undar, then at Rthstead as the lieutenant sat back down.

"Are you ready to rip yourself apart for your lord's amusement?" Rthstead asked.

Rivic shifted forward and tried to stand. He didn't quite have the strength. "I'm sorry. I think I'm in the wrong place." He attempted to rise again.

Undar's hand landed on Rivic's shoulder. "Riv, keep it together. Come on, I thought you'd be tougher than this, especially after what Kalt did to your sister."

"Give it up, Undar-na," Rthstead said. "He has too much heart himself."

Undar reached around Rivic to push on Rthstead's arm. "Oh, come on now. 'Tis not like that. 'Tis just too soon. He still has—" Undar couldn't find the words to finish the sentence.

"His soul?" Rthstead said for Undar. "That he does. Let's hope he can get rid of his heart before the cahaster takes his soul."

"He will," Undar stated.

"We will see, won't we?" Rthstead fixed Undar with a hard look, then rose to his feet. "Let the boy go home." The lieutenant cast one final pitying glance at Rivic, then he turned and walked away. Most of the Necroathelings along the line stood up, crossed their arms up by their chest, and banged their wrists together. Those that dared to remain seated turned their head as if not acknowledging Rthstead. Rivic hadn't realized that there were factions between the Necroathelings. How much more did he not understand about them?

A lot apparently, since he hadn't thought that they could rip themselves apart and still walk away.

Rivic turned to Undar. "Why are you doing this? Why did you bring me here?"

Undar gave a lugging shrug. "I have this feeling about you. When you become a Necroatheling, you're going to do something amazing."

Rivic wanted to laugh and tell Undar how wrong he was. In this whole stadium of Necroathelings, he was one small man against a tide. If he turned his back to it, he'd be swept out into the ocean.

"'Tis the monster of knowing," Undar began.

"What?" Rivic asked.

"The Dek'tae, 'tis your little subconscious speaking to

you. It knows what you have done wrong. And every night that the Necroathelings call it upon Kalt, he rips out his heart."

Rivic wasn't quite sure what to make of that. "He rips out his own heart? Why?"

"Because he has either given his heart to someone other than Cirvel, or he feels that his own heart has been ripped out."

After what had been done to his sister, it was hard to see Kalt as just a man. He knew he shouldn't feel pity or sorrow for Kalt, but he had often suspected that Kalt hadn't been in control of his body on that day any more than he had been at the start of tonight's presentation. "I think I'd like to go back to the castle now."

"But the Necroathelings have had their first blood. This is about to get good. The night has just begun."

Down below in the arena, a Necroatheling came out and stood, waiting. From the opposite side, another Necroatheling appeared, red bands running along the shoulders of his cloak.

Undar pointed. "He's one of the undead Necroatheling's. He has given his blood in honor of Lord Cirvel."

"And the other guy is alive?"

"Possibly not for much longer."

CHAPTER 23

*R*ivic woke, still feeling just as numb as he had when he left The Playground and wandered the hallways trying to make some sense of everything that had happened. Somehow, he'd found his way back here and collapsed into a disturbed sleep. He felt like he traveled a gauntlet that kept whipping him, making him spin around and reel with each hit. He wondered how much more he'd have to endure.

He woke early, as Cirvel had wished, but he wasn't ready to rise and make his way to his lesson with Lord Cirvel.

Rivic sat with his head in his hands. What had he gotten himself into? He was certain that Alityka didn't know how unprepared they were. A novihomidrak, a Dominari, a unicorn, and a watcher of worlds; four very powerful beings and so overwhelmed by the forces against them.

Would two thousand cycles even matter in this battle or would the time only strengthen Cirvel's plans?

After Undar had convinced him to stay, Rivic had seen the Necroathelings' magic at its fullest. When they weren't afraid of dying, if knowing that ripping themselves to pieces wasn't a permanent condition, when cold and dark magicks swirled around them, then they had no reason to hold back. A Necroatheling in battle seemed like nothing compared to the undead Necroathelings, who took fighting each other to higher levels.

And Cirvel had nearly a hundred cycles of letting these undead Necroathelings try to destroy each other.

What was more time going to accomplish other than letting those forces grow even more immortal?

He didn't want to sit here and contemplate how many ways his doom would come.

A knock came to his door. "Lord Cirvel wishes to know if you are attending him today," a male voice said from the other side.

"I will be there presently," Rivic called back, then he returned his face to his hands. What was he going to do?

He stood, squared his shoulders as he took a deep breath, and walked toward the door.

The hallway was empty when he stepped out. He hadn't expected the messenger to wait. Then, with steady steps, he headed toward Cirvel's antechamber, where he knocked on the door and waited. The door glided open without anyone having touched it.

Cirvel looked up from his book, then beckoned him further into the room and motioned for him to take a seat. He had a plate of cheese, grapes, and strawberries before him, as well as a steaming mug. "Hungry?"

Rivic shook his head. His legs felt stiff as he moved and sat down more out of habit than from making the conscious decision to do so.

Cirvel slowly closed his book, then rubbed his chin. "Bored, are we?"

"Nay," Rivic answered with another shake. "Just tired, and lost in thought."

"Then maybe a session today is not a good idea."

Both panic and relief washed over Rivic in waves. He couldn't believe Cirvel would make such a suggestion.

"I am driven to achieve," he said when he seemed to notice Rivic wondering. "I was not always this way, and I forget that sometimes. I think today would be a lovely day for a break, don't you?"

Rivic nodded. He started to speak, opening his mouth to do so and drawing in air, but then he thought against it and snapped his mouth closed. It made his breath seem more like a sigh.

"What do you wish to say?" Cirvel encouraged while watching him with those dark eyes for longer than Rivic would have wished. "Take a day. Visit Madame Orcee's little tea shop. Perhaps she can give you a little something to relax. Walk a bit and think. You may find that you need more than a day."

"Really, my lord?"

"Aye. Go." He gave a dismissive wave of his hand and reopened his book.

Rivic dashed from the room. He didn't stop running until he was out of the castle. He went all the way down to the main gates.

Not surprisingly, he found them closed and Necroathelings standing guard. He couldn't help but to note that none of them had red bands on the shoulders. Had he ever seen any with those red stripes? He couldn't recall. Where were the undead Necroathelings if they weren't here? Did they just stay at The Playground fighting and tearing each other to pieces all day?

He began to wander through the city. Nyree had loved it and said that she and Kalt had gone for many strolls through the streets. Rivic wished Kalt hadn't entered into his thoughts, for as soon as it did, Rivic saw the man tearing out his own heart. No one deserved that.

Soon, he found himself standing in front of the window decorated with Madame Orcee's Tea Shop in bold letters. A few people were inside, enjoying the day and delicacies provided by Orcee.

Cirvel had recommended Rivic go, and he doubted that Cirvel ever did so lightly.

Rivic went to the door and pushed it open. A little bell above the door announced him coming in.

"Be right there," a female called out from in back.

It felt warm in here with a small fire burning toward near where the voice had come from. All sorts of jars and cups lined the wall.

Rivic moved among the small channels between tables as he moved up toward a counter filled with pastries. He realized that he still hadn't eaten anything yet today.

A woman a few cycles older than Rivic came out of the back. She had long brown hair. "Blessed morning, Dominus," she said to him.

Rivic had to look down, surprised that she knew his title until he saw that he really had put on his armor earlier. He nodded his acknowledgement, not sure of what else to say, as he took a seat on one of the stools.

"Can I get you something?" she continued when he said nothing.

"I'm told that you can put something in some tea to help me relax a bit."

She turned slightly away. "I see." She slid her dark brown gaze to him. "Who would be telling you this?"

"Lord Cirvel."

"Well now, that changes things just a little." She made her way around behind her counter and picked up a spoon which she used to ladle some water off the kettle hanging over the fire. She began pulling a variety of jars from their slots on the wall. It seemed like she didn't even have to look at what she reached for. "Relax you say?"

"Aye."

"A strong Dominus like yourself doesn't look like you should worry about much."

"Looks are often deceiving," he muttered.

"Wow. 'Tis a lot of tension running through you." She reached back for one more jar. "Would you seek more than just a drink to work off that tight energy?"

Rivic had to stop himself from reeling backwards. Was that why Cirvel had sent him here? "I don't seek companion-ship," he said firmly. "Just a warm cup to lose myself in."

The brunette smiled. "While some tea houses here may specialize in providing companionship to lonely hearts, I seek to give a little more peace of mind that goes beyond the immediate moment. I am more than certain that would be why Lord Cirvel has sent you to me."

"How would you do that?" Rivic asked, wondering if he would have to tell her that his heart belonged to someone else.

"There are always ways, if one listens to more than just the words being said. I'm not certain that anything I'd do would be what you need. You are too guarded."

Rivic let her turn away and begin to attend some other task before he said, "I'm certain Lord Cirvel will be disap-pointed when I tell him that I didn't find any relaxation here."

She looked at him through narrowed eyes. "You don't play very fair, do you?"

"Wrong, Madame Orcee. I don't play games. I leave that to others. I don't have time for it."

"Oh, strong words. Let's try this another way, shall we?" The image of her wavered and she transformed into an old woman with gray hair of tight curls. Her eyes were as the patches of sky he saw between the buildings while on the way over here. It reminded him a lot of Nyree.

She nodded her head, amused. "Aye, a more motherly type might be to your pleasing. Cirvel is training you well. You are slowly becoming just as sharp and cunning as he is. Perhaps that is the shadows that gather around you."

"I don't need a fortune teller for that." He shoved himself off the stool.

"Perhaps not, but maybe you do need to know that if you continue this game with Cirvel, you will need to protect your heart as well as your mind and body. Do not mistake me to think that the heart I speak of is the one that lies in your chest."

"Then what is your meaning?"

"Your soul is boundless, but 'tis the heart backing it that gives it intent. You, Dominus, seem to have a heart of courage, but most Necroathelings have only the blackest of hearts, if you get my meaning."

"I do get your meaning, but I think you're wrong if you believe I am pure hearted. I have done terrible things and I am in a horrible position."

"Perhaps you merely need some clarity to define your roles and the events which have played in your life."

He placed his hand on the counter and leaned against it. He turned his head so that he could just barely see the edge of where she stood in his peripheral vision. "Are you as shrewd and calculating as he is? Did you tell him that you would do his bidding?"

"Whatever conversation Lord Cirvel and I may or may not have had becomes nothing in the face of what the leaves show me. His Lordship knows that."

"Does he?" Rivic turned back to face her, but he dropped his hands to his sides, ready to exit in a moment.

"Aye."

He stared at her for a moment. Once he felt himself able to speak without being crass or sarcastic, he said, "So what does it tell you?" He pointed toward the last splattering on the white wall.

She sighed while her mouth pulled downward. Her entire stance was one of being displeased. "That one would be no good for you. Let's start over, shall we?" She slid his untouched cup back over to him. "Drink."

Rivic sat back down on the stool.

She placed the cup in his fingers, her wrinkled fingers a stark contrast to the smoothness of the cup. "Make a wish," she said.

"A wish?"

"Sure. Direct your thoughts." She smiled. "You do know how to control your own thoughts, don't you, boy? Or do I need to give you guidance with that as well?"

He shook his head. If he had a wish, it would be to have Lihn released and Ellonia freed from the lamp. Did that count as two wishes? Rivic contemplated the cup sitting before him.

"Drink your tea, boy, and let us have a look."

He raised the cup and began to sip.

"Orcee ockree." Orcee's fingers touch the bottom of the cup, then she lashed her fingers toward the wall.

Rivic heard the magic hit the white wall and a new splatter overtook the previous. His fingers trembled as he set the cup down without looking to the side.

"Let's see what your peace of mind has in store," she said, winking at him. "Oh, there is a lot. He will bend you and break you in every way until you submit. You will be ravaged until you surrender the girl to his desires. He will get what he wants."

Which girl did Orcee mean? Alityka, a Dominari whose

broken bond could make her into an effective killer? Lihn, a transformed unicorn who currently carried Lord Cirvel's baby? Or Ellonia, whose captivity assured that Rivic would go through with the ceremony to become a Necroatheling. Or perhaps Nyree, who Cirvel had placed in a threatening position even while putting her to work for his own purposes.

Madame Orcee waved her hand. As if the Guardian was coming through the wall, the leaves took shape as a dragon, reaching off the wall toward them, and roared. Then it collapsed back onto the white stone as if it were a burned impression of the dragon.

"The leaves scream that you need to visit the dark beast in the belly of Gohaldinest. She waits for you."

"Why do you want to send me to see the dragon?" Rivic asked.

"'Tis not I. 'Tis in your fate."

"She called me flawed the last time we saw each other."

Madame Orcee stared at the spread of enlarged leaves on the wall and did not seem to have heard him.

"Madame Orcee?" he asked as she continued to stand still.

"Only ghosts survive."

"What?" he asked, not sure he'd heard her correctly.

She faced him. "When people leave our lives, 'tis not like we forget them. Their ghosts remain with us and walk through our hearts and souls."

He began to wonder when his peace of mind would come along. Nothing she'd said to him since he came into her shop had made him relax in the slightest. She'd warned about blackness surrounding him and now spoke of ghosts around him. The question Alityka had asked him, when he would get over having caused the death of so many, loomed in his mind. Nyree married away in a country he could not visit. Ellonia trapped within a lamp and enduring whatever tortures Cirvel felt like. Knowing that he needed to become a Necroatheling to have a chance against Cirvel and wishing he didn't have to dance with those powers. Those lingering thoughts, ghosts, chased him.

"Does it feel cold?" she asked.

"Huh? Does what feel cold?"

"Your thoughts, the place where they go?" Her eyes still had a faraway look to them and it made him wonder what she was seeing.

"Nay," he replied, glad that Alityka wasn't here. He didn't want to know if his answer was a lie or not because he so badly wanted it to be the truth.

"Now you see that ghosts can be merely words too. See how what I have already said darkens your thoughts and fills you with doubts. I have done nothing but speak to you. But words always tell two tales: the one that is real and the one you feel." She blinked and her gaze focused on him. "Do you understand?"

He thought he did, but he still wasn't sure. "The dragon told Cirvel I was flawed, but was that for his benefit or mine?"

"Now your eyes begin to open."

If Rivic's overwhelm hadn't pressed hard on him before, it did now.

CHAPTER 24

*R*ivic wasn't certain which way to go to get to the Guardian. Every time he came to an intersecting hallway, he stopped and let his magic reach out to feel for his novimather. When he had a sense of her energy, he moved in that direction. It led him a few times into dead ends. The walls had been transformed purposely to make this place an utter maze so that no one would haphazardly stumble upon the Guardian in her lair.

"Lair?" Rivic scoffed. "More like prison."

The ancient magicks that seeped through this area were faint. He doubted that any of the older enchantments could withstand anything he could throw at it. If Gohaldinest had a weakness, it would be in this strange magic.

He paused, hesitating in his step as that realization fully came to him. Destroying Cirvel meant destroying Cirvel's access to power.

With that, he continued to search for the Guardian.

"So, you are beginning to realize what must be done?" His dragon mother's voice came out of the darkness. "All noviho-midraks receive their powers from their novimather."

Rivic stepped into the dark cavern where the Guardian lay curled, her head upon the stone floor. "But I also received my power from you, as well as Cirvel. Do you seek to destroy me as well?"

The Guardian raised her head. "You have only half discovered what must be done." Her yellow eyes now glowed in the darkness, but Rivic realized that may have been his own eyes beginning to adjust to the blackness. "He has me trapped here like a possession. He called me, knowing that I would come, knowing that if I were closer to him he could withdraw more of my power. He is the one that has me trapped. But if you were to change that situation, if you were the one to imprison me, then the source of his power could be cut. Were he not completely situated in this dimension, he could be made nearly powerless. A genie is always servant to the lamp. I knew this when I created him. He was an experiment, and a dangerous one at that."

Rivic created a couple magical floating orbs for light so he could see his novimather better. "Cirvel is a genie?" Rivic felt something deep inside of him, like a note struck and sustained.

"Half genie," she corrected him. "He couldn't have become a novi without at least some human blood. Cirvel was a half-breed misfit not wanted by either side when the saperes came to me with an idea."

Rivic didn't know how, but he completely understood that the Onesong had urged her to create the hybrid novi-homidrak.

Still, she continued her story, "I swallowed his genie lamp and incubated him. The saperes prepared him for the transition. What we were doing might have been seen by some as unnatural, but I saw it as an extreme necessity to save a world which needed an extraordinary champion. Genie magic exists outside of space and time. It comes from the dark matter of the universe, which lets it exist close to chaos."

"Are you saying the genie lamp is a different dimension?"

"The inside of a lamp is."

"So, since the interior of a genie lamp is a dimension of its own, does that mean that if we put Cirvel into his lamp, he will not be a threat any longer?"

"Cirvel will never willingly return. He has found a way to cut his ties to his own genie lamp. But that doesn't mean that another prison could not be constructed. It just has to be dimensional." She blinked and set her head back down on the floor as if she were tired. "All novihomidraks have their flaws."

Her words emboldened him. "Did you have Sontre' give most of my thread to Nyree for a reason, or was it just to lame my abilities?"

The Guardian looked weary. "My reason was twofold. I had to make sure you had a fear of the Necroathelings and that you were cautious of them. Sensing their powers would have drawn you in too fast. But I also had to make sure that some fracture existed in your power."

"Why?"

"If you and your sister had emerged whole, Cirvel would have known instantly that you were novihomidraks. By severing a thread from you and giving it to your sister, 'twas enough to confuse the energies, especially since your twin should have been powerless. I risked damaging you and your sister with such a move, but I had to take the chance. I couldn't have Cirvel instantly identifying what you were. I had to make you a mystery, draw him to you, rather than risking him realizing what you were."

Rivic stepped closer. "If we had a painting that acted like a genie lamp and could lure him into it, could we trap him?"

The Guardian hunched her shoulder, but with her lying

on the floor, Rivic wasn't certain if she was shrugging or just getting comfortable. "Possibly," she said. "But that would only be temporary."

"What will it take to really defeat him? What would you like to see happen to him?"

The dragon lifted her head once more, but she didn't raise it all the way. Rather, it was only a few feet off the ground, yet it still put her nose level with his head. "His mission was to save this world, but the depravity ran far deeper than anyone could have known. He became an even worse corruption. He succeeded in his purpose while assuring that this world couldn't return to the Onesong while he remained. He is the toxin poisoning the very realm he tries to rule. Yet he also keeps back the deeper evils."

"But you brought me into this world to destroy him. Now you tell me that if I kill him, the reason he was sent here to stop comes back. I don't get what I'm supposed to do then."

"You were needed for two purposes: only a novihomidrak can injure another, and only a novihomidrak can defeat what ails this world. I only hope that your connections to this world keep you stronger than Cirvel was."

"What was his initial enemy?"

"The Shniktaur."

"What is that?"

"Pray you never have to find out. Cirvel may very well have destroyed it for good, but I still believe 'tis too early to know for certain." She tilted her head. "I know that you have been told that 'twill take you two thousand cycles to defeat Cirvel. I beg you to consider the source of those words. Besides, I don't know if this is even enough time to assure the Shniktaur won't return, but when you reach the end of this span, you might be glad to have access to him. His help might be needed."

"Would that be trading one evil for another?"

"Or perhaps picking the lesser of two. If you can trap him in a painting until then and beyond, I would take that opportunity. As separated as this world has become from the Wells, the Onesong still tries to save it, much as you would fight to save a severed limb."

"The Shniktaur... is that why he gathers Necroathelings and why he is building an army of undead?"

"Such an army would be two-fold for him. First, he can control the humans of this world from an uprising with them. Secondly, aye, he could weaken the Shniktaur with them."

Weaken? Rivic let his thoughts linger on the word she had said. An army of undead would only weaken the Shniktaur, not destroy or even hurt it. Only weaken.

"Face one dilemma at a time," the Guardian said. "Cirvel is the one who destroys this world presently. He must not be allowed to continue. As valiant as his underlying motives may be, he must not succeed. Beyond that, should the Shniktaur return, this world is already spun off from the Onesong and is meant to die. The Shniktaur will bring chaos even faster and no one will suffer for long."

"I'd rather not see anyone suffer at all," Rivic said.

"'Tis another way to ensure the safety of all living in this world should my two novihomidraks fall to the Shniktaur."

"What would that be?"

"Forge a sword, a true novihomidrak weapon. I know you tried before. I felt it. But that weapon does not hold the power you need. Create another and bring it to me. Then, you must put this blade into the hands of someone with strength, courage, and true valor. If you fall, the weapon will remain."

Rivic contemplated who he could entrust with such a sword, or how he would safeguard it until he found this person. "Do you think the Shniktaur will return soon, if it does at all?"

"Nay, it could potentially be beyond your lifetime even," the Guardian said. "Everyone you know will long since have passed. You need not worry."

"Is there any way to know for certain if this creature is dead?"

The dragon turned her head slightly, glancing at Rivic through her right eye. "Only Cirvel knows for certain. Were you brave enough, you could ask him. What he revealed to you might be enlightening." She set her head down and closed her eyes. "Or you could leave through the door over there and see if you find any enlightenment there."

He leaned to look around the dragon to the direction the Guardian's gaze travelled. "What's behind that door?"

"An easier route to bring yourself here, plus a special place not often seen in the Onesong."

"I don't suppose you'd tell me why it's special?"

The dragon grinned. That takes all the fun out of it. If you want the truth, 'tis best you don't know more than that on your first venture."

"You said it was an easier route. I take it that it's through tunnels back to the castle."

"Aye."

Figuring his novimather had no reason to lie to him, Rivic bowed to the Guardian, then started to walk toward the indicated door. He couldn't say that her parting words made him feel any better.

The tunnels beyond looked exactly like the prior ones. With a sigh, he began his way back to the castle. The hallways ran with several turns, but there were no optional paths here for him to follow. In that sense, the trip was easier.

Until he ran into total darkness.

Rivic stopped, the blackness pouring in around him along

with a sensation that he couldn't breathe. He tried to turn but realized that the way behind him was swallowed up and he wasn't certain where exactly he stood. Even the air down here was too still to indicate by a breeze on his skin which way the tunnel ran.

Stretching out his hands before him and shuffling his feet out along the floor he could no longer see, Rivic moved forward. Sooner or later, he'd either be out of this darkness or he'd hit a wall which he could follow.

A spark lit in front of him. Then another. Soon, intense, bright flashing white lights went off everywhere around him, leaving painful, stinging throbs in his head.

He closed his eyes against the harshness and waited for a moment. When he opened his eyes again, the flashes remained but not nearly as intense as they had been a moment before.

A white mist in the shape of Nyree stepped forward. Even though he was pretty sure she wasn't really there, as he sensed her as an element of magic, her eyes were black with the glowing yellow torches. "You must stay strong, my brother. You have always been told this. You are the only one who can put this to an end. Why do you doubt?"

Rivic was about to answer the image of Nyree when she swept away before his eyes, the white mist curling into nothingness. He turned, sensing more magic beside him and wondering if she was about to reform somewhere else. Instead, a new ghost stood before him. This one looked like Alityka. "Which side are you on?"

More magic, this time behind him. He whirled around. Lihn turned to face him. "Winning is all that matters. We must each do whatever it takes to return this world to the Onesong."

Lihn whisked away and when Rivic looked back to see if Alityka was still there, she was also gone.

Rivic saw a man form from the flashes before him. He didn't know this stranger, yet he seemed vaguely familiar. "A dominus can show no weakness. Those who bear the mark of Rivic shall always pay the greatest price."

"Who are you?" Rivic asked.

The man smiled. The ghost held up his hand, and on the right palm it bore a torch-shaped mark, black against his ghostly white. "Someone who is here to help, but who has not yet discovered who he is. We all must play our part in this." The ghost dropped his gaze to the ground for a moment as he lowered his hand. When he looked back up at Rivic, he said almost bashfully, "I thank you for bringing her to me."

"Who?" Rivic asked.

"The one who made me realize who I am. I couldn't have done it without her."

"Alityka? Are you referring to Ali--?"

But like all the others, the ghost had vanished and Rivic had no answers.

Rivic continued walking.

Four more ghosts rose before him. Two he barely recognized and the other two were an even more distant memory: his aunt and uncle, and his parents.

"The magic rises in him," his mother said. "The healer says 'tis too soon for him to be magic spun, but what else can it be?"

His uncle reached out and touched Rivic's father's arm. The men moved off together, then they seemed to freeze in place.

"Please, Ren, certainly one of the healers or talesman of your tribe knows what we should do."

"I shall ask when we return," his aunt said.

Rivic moved over to where the men stood. They came to life as he got close to them. "My sense of the boy is that he is dangerous," his uncle, Lyre, told his father. "Tragic accidents do happen to toddlers, especially ones that walk too close to cliffs."

"Are you saying that I should murder my son?"

"I fear him killing you first."

Rivic felt his body tighten at the memory of first coming to live with Master Lyre and Mistress Ren after the involuntary destruction of his village. His uncle had terrified him and Rivic made sure to never wander off with Lyre. He saw now that the instinct may have saved his life.

Or would have the Guardian intervene and taken him sooner, perhaps without Nyree?

"If you can't do it, find someone who will," Lyre continued. "I could take the boy, tell Ren that I'm taking him to see a talesman in the mountains that I know. The boy awakens one morning before me..."

"Nay! I will hear no more of this. If 'tis true that he grows in magic, we will find a way to deal with it."

"I only hope 'tis not too late." Lyre looked disappointed. "Maybe you should take him to the Lord of Gohaldinest, certainly before the child brings down the gargaxes upon your village."

"He might sacrifice Rivic to assure that my child never becomes a threat to him. I couldn't bear to watch my child being fed to Cirvel's beast."

"Or he might take the boy to be raised as a Necroatheling, but at least he'd be out of your hands."

His father nodded. "Do you think such a bargain could be arranged?"

"I think that might be the only option you have." Rivic's uncle turned and walked back to Ren as the ghosts faded.

Rivic forged ahead through the near blackness and recalled that Mistress Orcee had mentioned ghosts walking through his thoughts. Had she had a premonition of this? Or had all of this been orchestrated by Cirvel, from sending Rivic to see Orcee and what she instructed him to do? It galled Rivic that he'd walked the path they set before him. He wished he could see one of the walls so he could slam a fist against it.

Magic behind him made him turn. He came face-to-face with a ghost of himself.

"You know that Cirvel and his magicks will devastate your body and mind. He will try to make you as twisted as he is. You know you have to let him do it. The best advice you've had is to protect your heart. 'Tis the only way to keep you from being completely broken."

"How do I do that?" he asked himself.

"Energy seems like a stream, but it flows and ebbs around itself through everything, sometimes high, sometimes low. Just as trees know when to lose their leaves and when to grow them again, like the plants sink back down to their roots and rise once again to flower, you must choose your return. When will you rise from the seeming dead and reincarnate into yourself?"

Rivic swallowed a lump in his throat, his mind spinning over what the ghost of himself was trying to say.

The spectral image gave him a hard look. "How do you make yourself timeless?"

Then, like a Shant'olin blowing into the wind, the duplicate visage pulled away, casting little white wisps to trail behind the lingering afterimage.

With new ideas racing through him, Rivic practically ran from the under depths of Gohaldinest.

CHAPTER 25

*R*ivic never felt so happy to see a Necroatheling in his life. "Undar-na," he called out, glad that he'd recognized the man as they passed in the hallway.

Undar turned and lowered his hood as Rivic chased and caught up to him. It chilled Rivic a little when the Necroatheling smiled at him, but he tried to shake it off and return a friendly face.

"Ready to go back to The Playground?" Undar asked.

"Nay, I do have questions for you though, about being a Necroatheling, if you have a moment."

"Questions, aye, smart to ask about what you're jumping into." Undar continued walking. "Ask away."

"I guess my first question is: if a Necroatheling already has no soul, how can one die and become one of the undead Necroathelings?"

"Start with the hard question first, why don't you?"

"Well, there must be something because the undead have the red band and I haven't seen very many of them in the castle. Something makes them different and I'm trying to understand what that is?"

"Dismemberment during battle. Usually someone loses their head. Let's face it, there's no coming back after that."

Rivic knew his face had to be going white. He had once beheaded a Necroatheling, when they had come to kidnap Nyree. He'd watched the Necroatheling heal and come back to life then. What exactly did Undar mean? "Coming back?"

"When the time comes and their souls are returned, they will die and it'll probably be painful. They have no chance at life. Being a Necroatheling will be their last act."

"You think you are going to get your soul back someday?"

"We all will."

"When?"

Undar looked confused. "Have you been living under a rock? I thought you were studying directly with Cirvel to prepare you to become a Necroatheling?"

He knew that trying to explain about his lessons with Cirvel to Undar would be complicated, so Rivic merely answered with, "He hasn't gotten there yet. I still have much to learn. Please, tell me."

Undar looked uncertain and for a moment Rivic thought Undar might tell him that Cirvel would want to explain himself. "We will be freed when Cirvel no longer needs us."

"What circumstances have to be met for that to happen? Surely he can say that he always has need of Necroathelings. Are you certain you are not holding onto false hope?"

"Nay. We are part of a plan to force this world to create a Winctonicht. Without it, all magic is doomed."

"What's a Winctonicht?"

"Cirvel really hasn't told you any of this?"

"Nay. Now what's a Winctonicht?" Rivic wished he had Alityka's ability to compel someone to answer him. Since he didn't, he hoped he'd put enough force into his voice to get Undar to answer.

"What reason do you have for becoming a powerful but soulless maege?"

It took a moment for Rivic to realize that Undar actually seemed afraid. "I don't know. That's why I want to know why you all have done it?"

Undar sighed and seemed relieved by Rivic's answer. "You haven't been here long, I guess. I suppose I shouldn't be surprised that you haven't been told. A Winctonicht is a fabled creature of ultimate magic. When the time is right, Cirvel will call forth this energy into himself and lead us into a great battle. We will act as a channel for Cirvel as we share the power of the Winctonicht. Afterwards, when we have been successful, we shall all get our souls back and dance in victory."

"Except the undead Necroathelings just get to die."

"They may die then, but they have served their lord and country, and they have extended their lives beyond their first death. 'Tis not blood spent in vain."

Rivic wasn't certain he was convinced. "Who are we going into battle against? Cirvel already has all the power in the land. Who could stand against him?"

Undar looked uncomfortable once more. It took a long moment before he answered, "There are many things that exist in this world that we cannot see. Things far older than this castle. If you want to know about them, look at Azote. Cirvel holds a treaty with the gaxlors, but there are creatures far older and magical who sleep through the centuries. One day they will wake. That is when Cirvel wants to be ready. If humans want to survive, we need people brave enough to become Necroathelings."

"You're not afraid Cirvel will betray you?" Rivic asked, remembering the overwhelming notion that Cirvel wanted to cut humanity from the bloodwave.

"He needs us and he has yet to break his word on any

agreement he has ever made, even those that have left him at a disadvantage."

"Nay, but he's not above coercion either."

"True, but a smart man knows how to move his pieces effectively. I know I'm a pawn in his higher scheme. I'd rather be fully aware than manipulated unknowingly."

Rivic found himself nodding in agreement. He'd never known what the dragon had in store for him, but Cirvel had always been forthright with his intentions. "Thank you, Undar-na. I think I understand now."

He bid a quick farewell to Undar and went off to find Alityka. He located her in a hallway speaking with some acolytes in hurried, hushed tones. While she acknowledged Rivic's presence, the acolytes seemed nervous about his being there and they rushed away as soon as the conversation was ended.

She crossed the room toward him, her face taking on a look of deep concern with every step.

He had promised himself he wouldn't tell her, but even before she asked the question he knew was coming, he felt the Dominari magic working over him.

"You've discovered something," she stated. "What is it?"

"I found Lihn," he said. But when Alityka asked where Lihn was, Rivic could only shake his head. "'Tis not good. Cirvel is furious, and to not make it even worse for Lihn, we need to tread extremely carefully."

"What's going on?"

"Ali, he's keeping her caged and is torturing her. I really can't talk anymore about it."

"He's not hurting her, is he? In her condition—"

"She's fine, physically. What he's making her endure is emotional and mental. It still can't be good for the baby, but she assures me she is fine."

"You spoke with her?"

Rivic nodded.

"Take me to her."

He felt his magic retaliate against her command, breaking him free of the hold she had over him. "Nay. As I said, we don't want to jeopardize her or ourselves. Testing Cirvel's fury would not be wise."

She placed her hand on his arm. "Rivic, you're pale. 'Tis really that bad, isn't it?"

"Aye. Satisfy yourself with knowing that she is alive. Cirvel doesn't hold anyone indefinitely. We will get her back." He couldn't even meet her gaze.

"But you didn't come to tell me that?"

"Nay. I've learned several other things today which we should discuss. Let's go find somewhere we can talk."

They headed out of the castle into the courtyard. From there, Alityka directed him to the tower where she headed up to the top of the staircase to check for Lihn's room. Finding disappointment, she sat down on the stairs and Rivic joined her.

"What have you found out?" she asked.

Rivic heard her trying to push the vain hope from her voice and how badly she failed as she teetered on the verge of tears. "Cirvel can work genie magic." Rivic explained. "He's only half human. His other half is genie. Remember how Lihn said that there was a magic she couldn't identify? That was it."

Despair showed through Alityka's shoulders as they drooped with defeat. "A genie and a novihomidrak. How are we ever supposed to dominate someone with that much magic?"

"We're not trying to defeat him, remember? We just have to hold onto him for two thousand cycles. All we have to worry about is how to contain him, how to trap him."

"Aye, that's all!"

The image of the hundreds of Necroathelings he'd seen in The Playground flashed through his mind. Rivic rubbed his hand over his face. "Look, Ali, I've had a long couple of days where I have seen horrible things. But I've also received hope. Cirvel has flaws. He's not perfect. I just need more time to figure it all out."

She tilted her head. "What flaws, Rivic. What do you think is going to help us?"

"'Tis not just flaws. 'Tis things I've heard and seen too. There's a monster, I think 'tis a dimensional beast, called a Dek'tae. It forces people to show what's in their heart, their real motives. Plus, there are old beasts, very powerful, who are sleeping and waiting. If Cirvel can get the gaxlors to his side, who's to say we can't negotiate with these other beings?"

"We won't be able to. That's what he meant." Her look became as distant and unknowing as her words. "If one evil is defeated, there is always another waiting to rise. We have no hope."

"W-what?"

Alityka faced him. "Since Galault wouldn't tell me how we defeat Cirvel, I had to go to the other person who knows."

"You went on your own to visit Galault's father?"

"I was always alone." She lifted her head as her voice filled with resolve, but she stared out into the darkness of the tower. "I don't think we win."

"Ali, what are you talking about?"

"We don't defeat Cirvel. I'm not certain we can trust Galault."

"Why? What happened? What did he tell you?"

"Nothing. Galault told me nothing, only that I wouldn't be happy with how things were going to turn out, that I wasn't far enough along the path to understand the circumstances that would happen. I didn't listen to his warning and

I did the spell again. You, Steigan, and Cirvel were all working together. This is all my fault."

Rivic saw tears rolling down her cheeks. "Ali, you were jumping in on a scene, so maybe it was out of context. If you overheard many of my conversations with Cirvel, you might think that I was working with him too. You know that fine line we have to tread. You taught me how to walk that path."

"As I have stated. This is my fault."

"Gods, Ali, nay! There is more. Cirvel is trying to defeat something called a Shniktaur and he's amassing the army of Necroathelings in order to create a Winctonicht. Don't you see that we might be fighting for a common cause, all of us trying to save this world?"

"There's more. I saw myself wake up from a spell, one I performed while battling Azote. I'd been turned to stone, and apparently so had Azote. If I woke up alive, then I have to assume that Azote did too. Which means he's out there too."

"We'll deal with it. All of it."

"I'm sorry, Rivic. I'm good with waiting two thousand cycles. At that time, I won't care about anyone who is around. Everyone I know will have been dead for a long time. Then I can do whatever needs to be done. I'm guessing that Galault didn't want to tell me because he knew about the betrayal and how I'd feel."

"Nay, Galault said we were there with his father. He knew you. He practically dropped to your feet in worship. Ali, we can't worry about the future. We have to figure out how to deal with Cirvel now. You've said this yourself."

Alityka looked to Rivic and the expression on her face told him that he wouldn't like what she was thinking. "The book Galault's father first gave me was a combination journal and spellbook. 'Tis actually something I started shortly before I met you. But this one I was given was complete. I know the path I must follow."

Rivic tried to decipher the words Alityka had just told him when she stood.

"Let me see your hand," she requested.

He raised his palm to her. As she held it, she put her finger in the middle of his palm. "Your first brand in The Playground was a torch, right?"

"Aye."

A searing pain filled his hand. He tried to draw back, but she grasped onto his wrist. In the midst of the torment, she whispered three words he couldn't make out. Agony flashed like the wildfire that accompanied the blue webbing he'd experienced while being magic spun as a child, then dissipated. She released him and he drew his hand back against his chest, staring at the silver brand of a torch now etched on the skin.

"I'm sorry that I can't let you in on my plans right now, but there is more I must do," she said. "If the old gods and demons of this planet still sleep, let them remain that way."

Rivic watched as Alityka descended the stairs and exited the door. He understood now why Dek'tae made Kalt rip out his own heart.

CHAPTER 26

The eerie feeling in his gut wouldn't leave and the urge told him that Alityka was in trouble. It drove him from his bed and hurried him down before daybreak to the forge. While he normally met Master Glayth there, today the building was empty. Yet, shortly after Rivic resumed his work, the weapons master came in and merely nodded to Rivic.

"Your blades are getting better," Glayth stated as Rivic set aside his tools after noticing a Dominus appear in the arena outside, signaling that it neared time for training to begin. That meant Cirvel would be waiting for Rivic to attend his lesson.

Stripping down, Rivic dunked his upper body into a tank of cold water to wash the sweat of his work from him. His long black hair felt like a curtain over his back as he pushed it away from his face, striding shirtless out into the sunlight falling on the practice area. Rivers of water ran off him as he paced around, the cool mountain breeze on his skin, yet soon he was dry enough to tug a new tunic over himself.

Realizing that the Domini had begun their practice, Rivic

realized how late it had become. Running, he gathered his things and dashed up to Cirvel's room. He knocked on the door and waited. The door glided open without anyone having touched it.

Cirvel beckoned him further into the room and motioned for him to take a seat.

Rivic bowed before sitting. "My apologies for the lateness. I was down with Weapons Master Glayth."

"I have had other business to attend to this morning, so I am presently settling in myself," Cirvel responded. "I figured you had seen Alityka on her way down."

"Alityka was here?"

"Aye. My business this morning." Cirvel waved his hand and breakfast food and tea appeared on the table before them. "I had hoped that you would convince her to stay, as we have previously discussed."

"She's leaving?"

"I will be most disappointed to see the Dominari depart. I believe 'tis only temporary, but I would certainly like to have your reassurance that she does plan on returning."

"I didn't even know she was planning on leaving."

"Once again, I am sensing you will be too distracted to focus on lessons. Go now, and see her out of the gates of Gohaldinest. But once she and the other acolytes have departed, I expect you to return with your mind set to resume your studies."

Rivic nodded so hard he nearly stumbled as he stood up from his chair. "Aye, sir." His body trembled as he walked from Cirvel's chamber. How much patience would Cirvel have with him? Rivic felt that invisible line growing short.

Once out in the halls, Rivic started to run down the staircase to the domini basement.

"'Tis true then. You are leaving," he said when he saw Alityka packing. "You know 'tis not safe."

"I have a pass."

"A pass?"

"Aye, to get by Azote. Cirvel has granted me my pass to go visit my tribe. I'm going home."

"You don't think that Cirvel knows that your father is Ellonia's as well? This could be some sort of trap. I don't think you should go."

She seized the book and placed it into her bag. "I have to, and you know that as well. If Ellonia is here, I must go visit my father to let him know that she's all right so he won't do anything foolish, like attacking Gohaldinest. I want it to look like I'm just going back for a visit. Cirvel can't know anything otherwise."

"Which is why you're not even going to tell me what you're doing, though I can sense that it is something drastically more."

"Aye, that's right. And I'm not going to tell you." She shoved something down hard into her pack, then straightened and put her hands on her hips. "Can I trust you? Will you keep my sister safe?"

Rivic felt the Dominari magic enforcing him to tell the truth. His jaw clenched tightly. "I'm not upset that Ellonia's here. Honestly, I feel much better knowing that she's close enough for me to protect. Cirvel has shown me that this world was a terrible mess before he came. He has made it better."

"Better? You think all of us fleeing for our lives, wondering if we're to be destroyed by the gargaxes is better?"

"I didn't say it was perfect, I said better. Lihn once told me that it didn't matter how we defeated Cirvel as long as we did. Defeating doesn't necessarily mean we have to kill him. We just have to convince him that there is another way to save this world. If I can do that as his lineage brother, I will do that. I won't regret the good things he's brought to my life, including your sister."

"Oh, so you feel tender toward him because he's become a benefactor to you, thrown you a bone as if you were a starving dog? Is that why he's worthy of loyalty?"

"I'm just saying that things might not be as black and white, good versus evil, as you want them to be!" Rivic found himself shouting back at her.

Alityka stood there staring blankly back at him, her mouth hanging open. It took a long moment, one where Rivic knew a hundred times over that he ought to apologize, before she composed herself and said, "Well, that's that." She yanked the ties on her bag and swung it over her back.

"Ali, I… I don't know…" He didn't know where he was going with his statement as she walked right by him.

He watched her tread the stairs until her boots were out of sight, then he continued to listen until the footsteps had completely faded.

He couldn't believe he'd just betrayed her.

The only one who remained in his life was Cirvel. And that thought terrified him.

Rivic ran up the stairs and out of the castle. He sensed Alityka's magic in the air; she'd teleported herself forward to escape from him faster. "Talcor dun," he said, taking her lead to follow her. Anything to catch her.

Azote stood on one of the tall pillars of the archway holding the heavy wooden gates. Ahead on the road, Alityka walked toward the gaxlor but didn't seem to take notice. Three acolytes hurried along before her. Rivic proceeded at a run. "She has Cirvel's permission to return to her tribe," he shouted.

"I'm not stopping her from leaving," Azote sneered. "I come to prevent those such as yourself who secretly harbor escape in your heart."

Rivic glared at Azote but didn't deny the gaxlor's claim. "Ali, wait!"

"We have nothing more to say."

Before Alityka reached the gate, Azote flapped down to the road and stood before her. "I do not scare you, do I?"

Alityka raised her head, daring to look the gaxlor in the eyes. Rivic wished she'd back away.

"My mere presence makes most tremble in fear," Azote boasted. "You are different."

"Nay, I do not fear you. I do not know why others do, but I will not cower," she responded.

"Let her go, Azote," Rivic shouted again.

Alityka slid a step forward, bringing herself nearly against the gaxlor.

Azote lowered his muzzle, drawing back the lips on one side as if to demonstrate the length of his teeth as he spoke so very close to Alityka's cheek. "I wait for the day he runs. I have patience. You scurry from Gohaldinest, but you'll be back. Your welcome may not be warm though. At that moment, I will be there."

Alityka held up her hand as she stepped around Azote. "On that day, I will make you dust."

Azote roared and, for a moment, Rivic feared Azote might attack her from behind, but the gaxlor flapped his wings and took off into the sky. When Rivic looked back to Alityka, he found her slipping through the separation of the gates which the guards had allowed her. Then she too was gone.

CHAPTER 27

"'Tis a fine blade," Master Glayth said, taking the sword Rivic had finished into his hand and turning it. The blade glinted in the light from the forge. "Nicely balanced. Do you have plans for it?"

Rivic accepted the weapon handed back to him. "Aye, I do. 'Twill be a gift." He lowered his head, afraid that Glayth would see the plans written in Rivic's mind. The sword that he'd given to Krithstand when he left the tribe to come here had been crude and unfinished. Now, he knew what had been missing from that blade and he meant to correct it.

"The recipient be a lucky person indeed. Anyone I know, someone I might be able to buy it from?" Glayth said with a smile.

"Nay, no one you would know." Starting for the door, Rivic added, "'Tis time I turn in for the evening. Cirvel does enjoy his early mornings."

Glayth nodded and went back to finishing the tasks he'd been about before stopping to admire Rivic's sword. Rivic used the moment to hurry toward the castle. But his steps didn't take him to his room as he'd told Glayth, but rather toward the entryway to the tunnels which ran beneath Gohaldinest. In a short time, he'd traveled this path so many times he now knew his way quite well.

"Guardian, 'tis I," he said as he approached the door to his novimather's cavern.

"Come, Rivic. The weapon, have you finished it?"

Rivic entered and held the sword on his palms before him. "'Tis done."

Salvarae's eyes widened. "Very good. 'Tis the first step."

"Aye." He nodded, feeling the energy of her correctness, but still not knowing what plan she had built.

"Remove your clothes," Salvarae told him. "You will need to stand with the weapon in my dragon breath. Since you have no breath of your own to seal the enchantments of the weapon, we must use mine. The material will not survive."

He lay the sword on the stone floor and tugged the boots from his feet. "Tell me about the Shniktaur," he said. Each time he came, he asked for more information. The Shniktaur was one subject he had yet to broach. "I know it was the enemy Cirvel came to defeat, but I don't understand what it is or why it might not be defeated."

"The Shniktaur was energy of chaos manifest. When a world is in enough turmoil, chaos slips in and begins to collect. Once coalesced, it becomes its own being, a monster, and 'tis given a name. The Shniktaur did not originate on this world, but on one further down the branch of the Onesong. Had Cirvel not stopped it here, it would have gained access to the rest of the Onesong."

Rivic pulled the tunic over his head and began to loosen the laces on his pants while mentally reviewing the lessons he'd had with Cirvel. "That means this is a seedling world created by a dragon. Did you create this world? I thought Cirvel brought you here."

"He did. 'Tis not my world. Only imagination dragons can create worlds."

"What happened to that dragon? Did it escape?" Now standing naked before the Guardian, Rivic picked up the sword and held it up before him. Knowing the blast would be coming, Rivic let the metal rest against his bare chest.

"You only have partial protection from the pearl," Salvarae commented. "I suggest that if this becomes too much for you to bear, you teleport out. Hopefully 'twill be enough."

Rivic nodded, but he couldn't bring himself to look at the dragon. Ever since he'd asked his novimather what it would take to create a novihomidrak forged weapon as she had suggested, he'd ruminated this moment with worry. However, after Cirvel telling him about the creation of saperes, he knew that dragons could control their breath. Rivic had to trust his novimather. That didn't mean he wanted to see it coming.

Salvarae began to breathe on Rivic.

Particles striking him forced him to close his eyes. The initial shock and pain of it made Rivic inhale and choke. He stood strong though, determined to endure this. Begrudging his hands to move when all he wanted to do was remain perfectly still, he began to slowly rotate the sword around.

Then Salvarae's breath stopped and Rivic sagged with relief that he'd outlasted the final firing of the weapon. The sensation ended when Salvarae whispered, "Quick, hide!"

Where was one to hide in a huge empty cavern with only a dragon and its chains. Rivic made the decision to circle around behind his novimather.

"Clothes," the dragon reminded him.

Rivic dashed back, seizing his clothes off the floor, and clutched them as he raced back to the shadows he'd been heading toward. He felt Cirvel's magic drawing close.

Salvarae swung her head around toward Rivic. "Pull in your magic as much as you can. He must not find you here, lest he thinks that you are creating the sword to be used against him."

What other purpose did a novihomidrak have in creating such a weapon? Salvarae was correct, but surely the dragon wasn't that naïve either. Rivic did intend for the sword to be used against Cirvel, only not now.

As Rivic knelt behind Salvarae's thick tail, he set the sword on the ground but kept his clothes close against him. He did as his novimather suggested and tried to suppress his magic as much as he could, hating the way that it disobeyed and sought out Cirvel's anyway. Shutting his eyes, he tried to focus on drawing into himself even as he heard and felt the door open and Cirvel's energy entering the cavern.

"Guardian, I have brought woman and child before you. Bestow blessing upon us and deem to make the babe into a sapere." While Rivic felt that these were words of a ceremonial request, the snide anger of Cirvel's tone made it more of a command.

Rivic peeked around the dragon, seeing the young acolyte that had entered Cirvel's chamber several weeks ago in the middle of their lesson, her birthing disrupting what Cirvel had been teaching. The girl in her white dress clutched the naked baby to her and looked purely terrified. Three Necroathelings stood behind them.

"Bring the child forth," Salvarae said.

With trepidation in her movements, the acolyte stepped forward and started to raise the baby before her. She shook so much that Rivic feared she might drop the child. Obviously Cirvel thought the same thing as he moved up beside her, spoke, then tenderly removed the baby from her hands. He turned the child with such care that it shocked Rivic. The girl stepped backward aware that the Necroathelings were there, but not wanting to stand near the dragon either. She put quivering hands to her mouth.

Cirvel held the child up, raised flat in his palms, so the Guardian could smell the baby. Salvarae took her time.

"A sapere the child could be," the dragon announced. She swung her head toward the girl. "Do you relinquish the baby?"

The acolyte looked first at her child, then to Cirvel before taking her hands away from her mouth to speak. Tears ran down her cheeks. "Aye."

"What have you called the child?" the Guardian demanded.

"Mettazin."

"Place the child on the floor and return when I call," Salvarae said to Cirvel.

As Cirvel bowed to his novimather, he spoke magic which made a bassinet appear on the floor with black and silver blankets opened to receive the child. He set the baby inside and folded the blankets over. Then he leaned in and kissed the baby's forehead. "I gratefully offer you to the dragon. Thank you."

The acolyte cried out and started to rush forward, but the Necroatheling seized her and drew her back. Cirvel jerked his head and the Necroathelings started to remove her from the cavern.

"This may not work," Salvarae said.

"I've done as you've asked." Cirvel knelt down on the ground beside the bassinet and took a supplicant position before his novimather. "You know how much I need this, what dangers we will be facing. I need you to do this. 'Tis the only way we will have a sapere ready and trained for what is to come."

Salvarae remained quiet for the span of several breaths while Cirvel stayed with his head to the floor. "It still doesn't mean the child will survive. Many are offered, but few can endure."

"I understand. Please do your best." Cirvel paused, letting humility keep him in place for a little longer before he rose and started to back away from the dragon. "I accept what is to come and I await your calling."

Cirvel turned, went through the door, and closed it behind him.

Salvarae turned her head back toward Rivic and whispered, "Dress quickly."

Rivic was already pulling on his clothes.

"You must take the child away from here."

"Why won't you create a sapere for him? What dangers are coming that makes a sapere so vital?"

"There is no time. You must find a way to hide the child."

Rivic suddenly understood Cirvel's frustration. "Both he and I need a sapere. Are you denying me as well?" Picking up the sword, he went over to the bassinet. How was he to carry both?

"Nay. Your sapere you will have when the time is right. 'Tis not the correct moment. Dispel your weapon and take only the babe; leave the basket."

"Vochey," Rivic said and the sword vanished. Then he took the child out of the bassinet. "What am I to do with it?"

"'Tis a problem you must solve. Go now. Leave out the back and when you are far enough away to not easily be sensed, teleport back to the castle."

Knowing he had to trust his novimather's advice, Rivic headed for the door in the darkness. He recalled the last time he'd gone through and remembered the room with the ghosts who spoke to him. Would he be able to transport himself back to the castle from there? Was it far enough or would Cirvel sense the spent magic?

The cavern brightened as Salvarae blew dragon breath at the bassinet, turning it to ashes.

"Hurry!"

Rivic realized he'd paused to watch the cinders darken and that he needed to remove the child from here now. Fleeing out the back door, he dared to cast a little light to see by. As he entered the area where the ghosts lived, darkness consumed the glowing orb.

A wisp circled around him, looking down at the babe, then it took the form of Galault. "Stabbed by my eldest brother… the blade slid beneath my father's breastplate."

Rivic waved out a hand, wiping the ghost away. He moved forward, certain that he knew where he needed to go now. Another image took form, this time of Ellonia. "I knew you would be the one to save us."

He felt Cirvel's magic lash out with hot anger. The room once filled with shadows around Rivic lit up, black turning to white. A dark image of Cirvel roared before him. ""This won't hold me, boy!" Rivic flinched, expecting Cirvel to emerge right out of the smoke and demand the child from his arms, yet it evaporated as the others had.

Rivic ran to the other side of the room as it darkened once more. Recreating the orb of light, Rivic waited, panting, while gripping the baby tightly to him.

When his panic subsided enough for him to feel the urgency return, Rivic began to rush back through the tunnels toward the castle. He knew he had to get back there in a flash and teleported twice to get to Lihn's library where the painting holding Galault hung.

He placed his hand on the frame. "Galault? Galault, I need you."

The paint rippled and Galault stepped out. "I am here. I have been watching."

"Then you know I need to hide this child. His name is Mettazin."

"Aye. I will take him where he will be safe."

Rivic handed the child to Galault, who then stepped back into the painting. "I wish I could return him to his mother," Rivic said. "Maybe now is not the time or place for her to be raising him. Maybe you will see another opportunity."

Galault turned, a sad look on his face. A tear dripped down his cheek and splashed onto the baby's forehead. "I'm afraid that isn't possible. The child must remain dead in this time. He has another purpose to serve, I'm afraid."

"Where are you going to take him?"

Galault merely tried to smile behind his sadness.

"Galault, what is the name of your eldest brother, the one who killed your father?"

Already, the paint began to stabilize and Galault started to freeze within it. "Mettazin." Then the watcher of worlds disappeared.

CHAPTER 28

*R*ivic sat in a corner of the library trying to understand what he was reading. It had been an interesting book about the creation of genlaes, a sort of demon which possibly sounded worse than the gaxlors. But he couldn't focus on the words. He swore he'd read the same passage three times now and none of the words made sense to him.

He'd come here, hoping to find a reference to the Shnik-taur and found nothing. In finding the written tales of the genlaes, he wondered if he'd found the most arcane monsters listed in the library here. Only Cirvel's own collections might hold darker and far more ancient fiends.

He had no desire to search deeper.

He worried about Alityka. He'd thought that she'd be back by now. Had she decided not to resume her training? At least he sensed her magic in the world today. Too often lately, she seemed to have completely disappeared. The first time, he'd wondered if she was dead. Then she had returned. Every time she vanished, he longed to go out and find out what she was doing and why this kept happening, but as long as Cirvel had Ellonia trapped in the lamp, Rivic wouldn't be leaving Gohaldinest.

A dark shadow fell over him and Rivic knew only by the power that he sensed that a Necroatheling had come to fetch him. Had Cirvel discovered that Rivic had taken and hidden the baby away? The Lord of Gohaldinest's mood had been foul for days, yet no one seemed to know why, except Rivic who was glad that lessons had been kept short.

"He says it's time," Kalt said beside him.

Rivic almost asked what it was time for, but his mind gave him the answer before he voiced the question. It had nothing to do with the child, but rather the oath Cirvel wanted Rivic to make. "Let's go." Rivic rose from the chair and turned to face Kalt. "I'm sorry for what happens to you in The Playground."

A flicker swept through Kalt's eyes. He seemed about to shake his head. Instead, Kalt put a hand on Rivic's shoulder. "Talcor dun."

Standing in an empty hallway of the castle, Kalt turned to face Rivic. "I have been reincarnated and my body ensorcelled. Cirvel has made me whole. I am a man once more and no longer under his control."

"Why are you telling me this?" Kalt still wore the robes of a Necroatheling, so Rivic was disinclined to believe him.

"You need to know. Talcor dun."

They reached the doorway to The Playground. "You must see if it will admit you," Kalt told him, briefly pointing at it.

Rivic stepped up to the door with a lion-head knocker on it. His fingers trembled as he picked up the ring held in the lion's mouth and hit the nub behind it against the thick metal plate three times. The lion opened its eyes. "Seelihest vadica," Rivic said, his voice barely more than a whispered choke.

He glanced to Kalt as nothing happened. Was he allowed to try again? Would Kalt laugh? Or would Kalt kill him where he stood? Rivic couldn't help his gaze dropping to the opening of Kalt's cloak where it didn't hang quite right due to covering a weapon at his side.

Then a white light came down upon them.

As the world came into dark focus around Rivic, Kalt grabbed the back of Rivic's cloak. "Do not ever speak with fear again," Kalt warned. "Not to the door, or Cirvel, or the Necroathelings. They all sense it. 'Tis always been your weakness."

Rivic thought Kalt might release him now, but the Necroatheling held tightly onto the material. Rivic looked back at him.

"I will not close my eyes," Kalt said before he moistened his lips to continue. "Nyree told me what is going to happen, though I must not show fear to Cirvel. I accept the judgement upon me. You have no choice. I merely ask for you to be quick and merciless. Let your rage fuel it as he wants. But know that I will not look away."

"I don't understand."

"You will when the time comes." Kalt let go of him and it felt as if Rivic dropped a few inches, though he knew he didn't. He wanted to ask Kalt what he meant by that, but Kalt shoved him forward. "Just do it," Kalt muttered harshly.

Rivic expected to head out into the arena, but the magic surrounding him felt strange and bright. Almost celebratory rather than prepared for battle.

Before Rivic even had a chance to wonder about it, he found himself at the end of a hallway with tall rising walls interspersed with arches and plants growing through the openings. A large arch stood at the other end and beyond seemed to be a courtyard. Though there was no ceiling and Rivic could see the rising seats of the stadium beyond the walls and the roof even higher than that, artificial lighting brightened the area as much as if he were out in the sunlight.

Pots of fully bloomed pink flowers sat at the base of every column between the archway openings.

"What's happening?" Rivic asked, not ready for the sight of so much beauty when he thought he was going for another of the brutal training sessions.

"I was told to bring you, not to explain." Kalt's flat reply hid unspoken words and Rivic knew it. Kalt knew very well what was going on. "Walk on."

Rivic moved forward, but it felt more like he was being dragged. Magic flowed over him as he passed through the archway at the end of the hall and stumbled out onto the courtyard. He found his armor stripped away from him and his robes changed to black.

A quick glance around confirmed that he was indeed in The Playground with several Necroathelings watching from the stadium around them.

Cirvel stepped forward from where he'd been standing off to the side in a cluster of shadows. A smile played at the corner of his lips. His black and silver robes swept over the paving stones as he moved toward Rivic as if he were sunlight rippling across water. A thick silver collar lay heavy on his chest, a juxtaposing piece compared to the thin silver circlet around his head, yet the rings on his fingers seemed to be the intermediary bringing all his jewelry together. The one piece that didn't seem to fit was a bracelet with a purple stone which fit tightly to Cirvel's wrist. Only as Rivic saw Dragzel in Cirvel's arms did Rivic realize that he was here to become a Necroatheling.

Cirvel stopped beside a tall, stone column.

Two Necroathelings rushed forward. At first, Rivic thought he was under attack, but they seized Kalt instead. Thick iron cuffs were wrapped around Kalt's wrists. They dragged him to the stone column, latched his cuffs to a chain, and hoisted Kalt off the ground.

In the commotion, Rivic was pushed aside and he seemed to flow toward Cirvel the way that a leaf gets carried in a stream, buffeted and spun around by rocks along the shallow riverbank as it goes.

"He is a bit young and small," Cirvel said as he pet Dragzel. The cahaster's face seemed expressionless as Dragzel watched Rivic with its blue-green eyes. "But I think he will do nicely. It seems only fitting that he volunteered to house your soul since he is the one that brought you to me. Do you accept Dragzel as your vessel cahaster?"

As Rivic looked once more at Dragzel, the cahaster raised the ridge right above its eye almost as if he were cocking an eyebrow and telling Rivic to do it. "Aye," Rivic answered.

"Lovely." Cirvel set the cahaster down on a nearby pedestal.

Rivic fully expected Dragzel to jump down and run away, but rather the cahaster looked above them while staying where he was. Rivic knew why: Lihn watched from her hanging cage.

"Vochey," Cirvel said, calling his novihomidrak dagger to hand.

Sensing the novihomidrak weapon in the room, Rivic felt his entire body tightened for battle and he had a hard time not flinching. As much as he wanted to draw away and hiss, he held himself still.

Cirvel approached Rivic. "Holi'arc tron, versad. Kasida tarden al'laleaha." A bright orange glow lit up the etched marks of the blade. Cirvel glanced up over Rivic's head. Rivic saw it too. A thin but wavy red line rippled like a stream in the air above them. A fine white mist surrounded the line, making it appear as if it were floating among clouds.

Without lowering his eyes, Cirvel reached out and picked up Rivic's hand. He deftly sliced the tip of Rivic's index finger and smeared the emerging blood along the etchings of the dagger. "Blocadiou tor'na vakan primidious tooka."

Rivic watched as the blood vaporized off the dagger and undulated to the wavy line above. As the two connected, he noticed Cirvel's white smoke within the purple stone on his bracelet turn red.

Cirvel's gaze moved back and forth over the line above them. "You are so wrapped in the bloodwave of this world. It sheaths you. Do you know how important you are?" Cirvel seemed pleased by the results, and he brought his dark eyes down to stare at Rivic. His delighted smile brightened. "Do you accept me as your Lord and Master, and as your Necronosti?"

Rivic's mouth felt so dry that he couldn't speak. All he could do was nod.

"Then I cast you from the bloodwave. Sha'tauk cril khowhest un irriago lamay para-evita soona'anamay. Sadavita."

Rivic felt a pinch run straight through the centerline of his body. It made him stand up just a little bit straighter. A moment later, the pain dissipated and a new sensation ran through him. It had a power wrapped in a bit of darkness, yet held an unfathomable depth as if this ancient power understood the entire expanse of the universe. Timeless. Strong. Ruthless.

He looked up into Cirvel's pleased eyes. Rivic knew beyond a doubt he'd touched Cirvel's world. Every secret, every arcane magick, and every flow of movement would never be hidden from him again.

"Welcome, brother," Cirvel said.

A swirl of images tingled through Rivic. He couldn't see more than a blur, but he understood anyway, as if he were receiving all of Cirvel's memories. So this is what it meant to be a novihomidrak.

Cirvel pushed his hand out as if he were moving a door and a wall of weapons materialized hanging in midair. Daggers and swords hung alongside maces and hammers. Cirvel gestured with a flourish of his wrist and said, "Choose how Kalt dies."

Rivic looked back at Kalt. "I don't understand."

"You are getting a very rare treat," Cirvel said. "The final step in becoming a Necroatheling is killing someone dear to you. But since I have the only two people you love and I very much need the people you have aligned yourself with, I thought revenge might be a better benefactor in your case. It will make the task easier. I have softened your heart toward him just enough to make this work."

Even knowing he'd been played, Rivic couldn't help the rage with him at the similarities. To see Kalt dangling helplessly in the air as Rivic had once been, remembering his sister's cries, the familiarity made his hands curl into fists at his side. Rivic nodded, then looked to all the magical weapons. He pointed toward a long, thin dagger on the wall. "That one."

"Very well." Cirvel retrieved the blade off the wall, then returned with it held flat across his palms. He stood before Kalt as if to taunt the Necroatheling with his impending demise.

Cirvel raised the dagger over his head. "Sha'tauk cril knowhest un irriago lamay para-evita soona'anamay. Sadavita." His long fingers wrapped around the hilt, and then he made a slashing cut with the dagger.

Rivic jerked as he felt the slice break over him.

"Take the dagger and kill Kalt, take his life and complete your oath to me," Cirvel commanded. He extended the weapon hilt first toward Rivic.

The dagger felt cold in his sweaty palm. Rivic tightened his grip and exhaled a long breath as he turned toward Kalt.

It wasn't as though he wanted Kalt dead, but he did want the man to suffer for what he'd done to Nyree. Not like he experienced in The Playground, even that seemed too extreme for anyone to endure day after day. Bringing death to Kalt would be a mercy to stop that torment. Could Rivic be that hand which brought pity and released him?

Cirvel moved. It wasn't quite a shuffle, nor was it a full step, but some slight adjustment which startled Rivic. He could suddenly sense the Necroathelings sitting high above, leaning forward with anticipation. They all had taken someone's life.

Rivic thought he might be ill.

Cast your heart away, Rivic remembered Mistress Orcee telling him in the tea shop as she read his future in the leaves.

A golden magical lamp slid seemingly out of nowhere at Rivic's feet. He realized that it had to be hidden from Cirvel's sight by the lengths of Rivic's robes. An urge to create smoke rose within Rivic and he opened his mouth to exhale as hard as he could.

Smoke billowed from him. Pain scorched his throat as the dark cloud churned in the air.

"Holicathida," Rivic heard Alityka whisper.

He felt something drop in front of him and realized Kalt had disappeared.

His prey was getting away. Rivic slashed out with the dagger. It slid through the air, yet struck nothing.

Angry now, Rivic turned his smoke to fire. The deep hiss raged against his throat as flames spewed from him. He doused the stone and ground in flames.

And the fire deflected back at him.

A hand grabbed onto his smoldering robes and jerked him backwards. The force of the throw made Rivic close his mouth. The dragon fire stopped.

Rivic blinked as he staggered to keep his balance. He

wasn't sure what had happened, only that Cirvel now stood near him, hissing, his face morphed, and lips drawn back to show sharp teeth extended.

Above them, the Necroathelings hoped for a fight.

Rivic dropped to his knees. He caught sight of Dragzel hiding a little distance away. The cahaster's eyes held uncertainty. Rivic bowed his head. "I submit, my lord Cirvel, my Necronosti." He didn't close his eyes but kept his gaze on the ground, though he so urgently wanted to lift his head.

It took a moment, but Cirvel said, "Incineration, very interesting." He stepped closer to Rivic. "Rise."

Rivic got to his feet. The smell of smoke still lingered in the air though only a few small sooty clouds remained. He looked for the lamp and found it gone. He didn't see Alityka either, but he was certain she had been there.

The stone where Kalt had been hanging had blackened.

Dragzel rushed forward and slid against Rivic's leg. It got Cirvel's attention too.

"Aye. We should continue. Cahaster, prepare yourself," Cirvel said. He took the dagger carefully from Rivic and slid it into the belt at Rivic's side. Then he rolled his hand in the air and a clear orb appeared in his fingers. "Hold this."

Rivic took the globe from Cirvel and held it out in front of him with both hands.

Dragzel came to sit at Cirvel's feet. He looked up at Rivic, who wondered what silent communication the cahaster was sending him as Dragzel blinked his blue-green eyes slowly. Rivic relaxed under Dragzel's trusting gaze and he gave the cahaster a nod.

"Cha'li nok tae krontek valisp su," Cirvel began.

Rivic's head began to swirl and he wobbled on his feet. His mind grew cloudy as he felt the world twist around him. The sensation that started at his head moved down over his shoulders, then to his waist. It felt almost like a blanket being dragged off of him.

Dragzel opened his mouth and began to inhale. Rivic saw a white energy, his soul, seep out of his chest, focus through the orb, then syphon down to Dragzel.

"Pa'rek mey forlee sharnbah. Nok'tae shan."

The sensation reached Rivic's ankles as Cirvel finished. Then the flow stopped. Dragzel moaned, then fell over.

"Dragzel," Rivic said, reaching down for him.

"Talcor resht'to," Cirvel said and the cahaster disappeared before Rivic could reach Dragzel.

"What have you done to him?" Rivic asked, afraid that Cirvel might have sent the cahaster somewhere that would put him, nay both of them, in danger, like off the edge of the cliffs.

"Relax," Cirvel said. "I sent him back to Lihn. She will care well for him until he awakens."

It did ease Rivic's mind a little. As he stood back up, he searched through himself to see if he felt any differently. He didn't, not really. He wasn't certain how it would feel to be without his soul, but he couldn't say he felt strange as he figured he would. His thoughts still seemed to be his own too.

Cirvel turned Rivic to face the Necroathelings seated above them. "I present to you Rivic-na!" he shouted as he forced Rivic, like a puppet on a string, to raise his arm to the shouts and hollers of the Necroathelings.

They only had one more problem to take care of.

Rivic's gaze lifted to where Lihn sat in her hanging cage. She held Dragzel in her lap, but as she caught Rivic's look, she shuddered.

As she should.

Festivities with the other Necroathelings ran late, but eventually Cirvel beckoned Rivic to his side. "Let us leave here and be getting back to the castle. You have someone else who is waiting to congratulate you."

Rivic wished he could say that Cirvel's words brought him comfort, but they didn't. What other torment could Cirvel have for him?

The air twisted around them and then they were back in the castle.

Cirvel opened the door to Rivic's quarters. Rather than being dark as it normally was when Rivic came in at night, the room was bright with candlelight. Cirvel stepped inside. "I believe there is someone here to see you."

At first, Rivic felt Cirvel was talking to him, but then Cirvel moved aside and Rivic saw Ellonia. His breath caught in his throat. Cirvel moved back, allowing Rivic to dart through. Rivic ran over to Ellonia and embraced her. "Are you all right? Has anybody hurt you?"

"I'm fine," she whispered back. "Glad to be out of that lamp."

He raised her hand, pressing it between his, her warmth reassuring him. Sliding closer to her, close enough that he could smell the earthy scent of her and realize how much he'd missed the fragrance of freshly picked herbs, he brought her wrist up to his lips.

Rivic heard the door closed behind him and he whirled around, casting one arm out protectively to keep Ellonia behind him, and the dagger coming to his other hand. Rivic found himself alone in the room with Ellonia. He reached out with his senses and found Cirvel walking away through the hallways.

He turned back to Ellonia. "He's gone. We're alone now."

She nodded softly.

Then she took a step back, but her fingers trailed over the opening hem of his purple robes. "This is how you had to comply, in order to help me." It wasn't a question; she knew the truth.

Rivic cupped his hands over hers. "A small negotiation."

"But you are a Necroatheling now. Why do I feel that he has you completely under his thumb? I know he's manipulated you every step of the way. My dreams have never left you."

Rivic wondered just how deeply her dreams went, how much she knew about what had been going on with him while he been here. Her words were enough.

She continued, "I knew he was coming. I was able to warn my father so he wouldn't panic."

"Did it do any good?"

"Nay, he began negotiations with other tribes to form an army even before I was taken. When he's ready, he'll be marching to Gohaldinest for me and Alityka."

"Alityka has left. Maybe she will be able to persuade him that attacking wouldn't be wise."

"Alityka... not take on a fight? Do you even know my sister?"

When she smiled at him, his heart warmed with all the emotions of missing her that he'd felt for so long.

She reached out, pulled back his hood, and touched the back of her fingers against his face. Her eyes grew in sadness. "I think we didn't have enough time then. I don't want to waste another moment now."

He bent down slightly, closing the distance between them. She stretched up, coming to meet him halfway. Her lips pressed against his. "Let us waste no more time."

CHAPTER 29

*R*ivic sat up suddenly, surprised that daylight filled the room.

He turned and saw Ellonia still sleeping. Trying not to disturb her, he slid from beneath the down quilt and began to gather his things. In the growing light of day, he wondered just how late he was. Now that he was a Necroatheling, how would he spend his days? What did the Necroathelings do when they weren't going around torturing people or battling in The Playground? Did they have a routine? Was he to continue his lessons with Cirvel? What exactly was he supposed to do? For that matter, was Ellonia allowed to stay with him? Should he report to Cirvel now to find out what she was supposed to be doing? It seemed like he had more questions than he had ever had in his life before.

The heavy lengths of his purple cloak tossed in the breeze as he swung it around his shoulders. Ellonia stirred.

He put his boots on while standing, not wanting to sit down anywhere and further disturb Ellonia.

As he neared the door, he heard Ellonia say behind him, "Are you leaving me?"

He didn't want to take his hand off the handle, afraid that if he went back to her, he wouldn't leave. He didn't even want to look back at her. "I'm certain I need to report to Lord Cirvel. He deals very harshly with those who do not follow his rules. And right now, I don't know what those rules are. I need to keep you safe. Stay here. I will be back to see you just as soon as I can. I know you will be brought food and anything else you need. Just don't leave and wander. I can only promise that you will be safe inside this room."

He shut the door behind him, then turned and created two spells over the trim, one to keep Ellonia inside the room, and the other to keep anyone else out.

The door to Cirvel's antechamber opened as Rivic approached. A Necroatheling came hastily out with Cirvel calling after him, "Send Azote and the gargaxes. Let this be dealt with quickly and decisively."

The Necroatheling left the door open for Rivic and hurried by with his gaze down. Rivic stopped in the doorway. "Problems?" he asked.

Cirvel sat back in his chair at the end of the table, one leg crossed over the other. He didn't bother to look away from the book he was reading. Rather, he turned the page as he said, "Rivic-na, come in. Take a seat."

Rivic slid into a chair and scooted closer to the table. "Sending Azote and the gargaxes out. What trouble could justify such actions?"

"Retaliation," Cirvel said flatly as he turned another page.

Rivic waited.

Finally, Cirvel snapped the book closed and flipped it down onto the table so that it spun around a couple of times before coming to a stop. "'Twould seem that your woman's father is intent on coming here to fetch his daughters. 'Twould seem he has a novihomidrak forged weapon as well."

Realizing that Cirvel had to be speaking about the sword he'd given to Krithstand after Nyree had been taken, Rivic answered, "A young, smitten novihomidrak most certainly made inept work of a hunk of metal. I would doubt it would cause you much trouble."

"Indeed," Cirvel answered, a humored smile coming to him. "Unfortunately, 'twould seem to be giving my Necroathelings some difficulties."

By difficulties, did Cirvel mean that the sword had sliced through the protections of the Necroathelings and killed them? With luck, the new sword he intended on giving to Krithstand would work even more effectively. "Let me speak to Krithstand-chief. He will listen to me, especially when I tell him that his daughter is safe."

Irritation flashed through the cold, dark depths of Cirvel's eyes. "We both know his Dominari daughter has incited all of this. Compared to Alityka, your lover is inconsequential."

"I told you, my lord; Ellonia is the healer for the tribe. She is important and most certainly needed there."

"Is that why you left her behind when you came to Gohaldinest?"

"Nay, I left her with the tribe because she was safer there than traveling with me. Your Necroathelings already had Nyree. I wasn't about to risk Ellonia as well."

Cirvel thought on this for a moment, and then his lips tightened. "Would you return her now to her father rather than keeping her here for yourself?"

"Nay."

"As I have stated, the woman holding your heart is not worth going to war over. Keep her here if you must, but you must find a way to turn his armies away for home when he would lead his men to their deaths. Do you believe words alone have such a power, especially coming from you, Rivic-na?"

Rivic knew Cirvel had placed special emphasis on the newly gained title. "Krithstand is not a dull man. His intellect remains sharper than the weapon I provided to him for the protection of his daughter, that I assure you. I believe my words can have much influence over his decision."

"'Twould be best if you would let go of your holds to this world. They bind you too much. I have much to teach you," Cirvel said, "and the truth is that your beloved Ellonia, and your children with her as well as their children, will long be dead and dust before you know all you can learn about being a novihomidrak. But you cannot travel down those trails if you don't release your ties."

"Tell me of the Shniktaur."

Cirvel's breath caught in his throat and his eyes widened slightly. He flicked his hand. "Go. Leave now and go quickly before Azote and the gargaxes get to Krithstand's army. Try your best to get him to turn away. We shall see what he says. Don't be surprised if his motives have nothing to do with getting Ellonia back." He reached over, picked up his book, and reopened it as Rivic got to his feet.

His questions regarding Cirvel's odd reaction deepened, but he didn't want to lose this opportunity. "Thank you, Lord Cirvel." He bowed, then disappeared out to visit with Krithstand.

Rivic appeared outside the gates of Gohaldinest, amazed at how far he could travel now that he derived power from Cirvel. The afternoon sun stung his eyes and made short the shadows coming from the forest. Only where the trees grew thickly together was it dark.

He glanced back over his shoulder to see the reddish-brown stone of Gohaldinest rising behind him. In no way would Krithstand be able to penetrate those walls.

He started walking down the deeply rutted trail.

"Are you serious? He sends you?" came Alityka's voice from the forest. "I'm not sure I like that look on you."

Rivic stopped, turned toward the shadows where he'd heard Alityka speak, then looked down at his dark purple cloak. He felt resolved as he lifted his head and spoke. "He sends more than me. Azote will be following, along with several gargaxes. If I do not speak to your father, he, his men, and anyone standing against Cirvel will lose their lives."

She stepped from the darkness of the trees. She wore her golden armor over the white dress of the acolytes. "Good. I am waiting for Azote. I have my plans set to trap him and turn him to stone. When Azote arrives, I shall lead him away."

"Ali..."

"Rivic, don't. I know how I get through two thousand cycles. I've seen the other side. Let us not argue about this. I know I am victorious on this path against Azote. Do not fear for me," she told him, her eyes sharp between the nosepiece of her helm. "As for my father, he will not retreat. He and I have worked too long, too hard, to let you mess this up now."

Rivic felt taken aback. "You've been planning this attack? How long?" He had to know if they'd been planning on it since before Ellonia was taken or not.

She seemed to expect the question, and knew exactly why he'd ask, for she answered, "Ellonia dreamed of being in Gohaldinest. She knows if you don't get her out of there, she will die."

"Why don't you just take her out the same way you got Kalt out of The Playground?"

Now it was her turn to look confused. She tried to recover from the misstep by continuing, "Ellonia had her dream before I left for Gohaldinest. 'Twas what made me leave to become an acolyte. I had to be the other part of the plan."

"What plan?"

"You had to be the one to get close to Cirvel. You would be the distraction. I, meanwhile, would be talking to acolytes and domini, getting them to relay information back to their tribes for a unified uprising. Right now, we have people all over preparing to channel power to us. Cirvel's magic is great, but ancient. I doubt many of the enchantments can withstand a cohesive attack."

"That's why Kalt was helping you. He was sidetracking Cirvel from noticing your power and promoting you. You wanted to remain an acolyte."

She nodded.

"Once he was gone, you couldn't hide anymore."

Her lips pursed. "I had to follow in your footsteps. Lihn's life depended on me advancing at that point. The three of us all had to be in position for this moment."

"Ali, Cirvel doesn't only have an army of Necroathelings, but three times the number in undead Necroathelings who take pleasure in ripping each other to pieces. Even with additional magic, if you send your father's army into Gohaldinest, they will die. All of them." He reached out and put his hands on her upper arms. "Cirvel will squash this rebellion and if he finds out about the other tribes, the vengeance will be swift and terrible."

"Which is why you have to trap him in the painting while his attention is diverted." She stepped back to break his hold. "He is powerful, but he is not all-knowing. We confirmed this when he came after me thinking that I was your lover. We can be assured that he knows we are plotting together, but he doesn't know what our plans are."

Everything inside him screamed that she was correct. They had one chance to get this right.

"I must speak with Krithstand-chief. Will you take me to him?"

"Aye," she replied, but she didn't look pleased.

"Where else have you been?" he asked as he followed her forest. "Your magic has been scattered, and sometimes non-existent."

"You were following my magic then?"

"Aye."

"I suspect that is as close to an apology as I'm going to get from you." She glanced over her shoulder at him. "I went to Plenelia."

"Plenelia? Are you insane?"

"I had questions and I had to seek answers. Aye, I know I risked my life, but there was someone there I really needed to talk to. Plus, I got to test the absorption stones."

Absorption stones?"

"Aye, that's what I'm calling them. I took down a gargax on my way to Plenelia. I hacked a piece off of it before I killed the beast. When I got close to Plenelia, I began to actually carry it with me. It seemed as if all my magic disappeared."

"I don't understand."

She looked at him as if he were the one not making sense. "A gargax… when you cut limbs off of it, they turn to stone."

"Right."

"Normally, these all roll back together and the gargax becomes whole again." When he nodded at her, she continued, "If you hack pieces off of it and then impale the monster to the earth or burn it, those pieces stay as rocks. But because the nature of the gargax is to eat magic, you can use these pieces to pull in magic."

"How do you know this?" Rivic asked. Of course, if Cirvel knew about this weakness with his creatures, he certainly wouldn't want it advertised.

"You're not the only person who has ever killed a gargax. Ellonia has a bunch of these stones hanging inside her lodging to attract stray magic from escaping while she is helping to heal someone. We've never known if it could actually be used to temporarily remove magic from someone, or if the effects would last. I finally got to find out the answers."

Rivic shook his head. "Ali, that was still dangerous."

"I know, but I really needed to talk to one of their healers there. Plenelia is not completely self-sufficient. They do still need to trade, and that creates talk."

"Don't they generally trade with centaurs?"

"Aye, so I started there. That got me into other places. Don't look at me like that. I had to find out what was truth and what was rumor."

"Which was?"

"While the Plenelians aren't doing magic per se, they have been doing blood work. I needed to speak with them in order to find out what they know."

"What did you find out?"

"Well, I found out a few things. First, Cirvel has been to Plenelia for the same reasons I was there. They weren't surprised I was from Gohaldinest. Apparently, Cirvel wanted to send some acolytes there to learn what the Plenelians were doing, but, aside from allowing Nyree, a magicless twin in, they refused him. They were afraid that Cirvel had misunderstood them and I was there to train. I had to convince them I wasn't. Second, I confirmed that Cirvel has been working with separating the different types of magic."

"Separating the magic from the bloodwave?"

"Nay, he can already do that by looking for markers. He wants to pull whole magical strands from the bloodwave, not just the markers. This would be like separating your human magic from your novihomidrak magic."

"But if he knows the location of every acolyte who has

ever come to Gohaldinest, not to mention your markers and mine, why does he not yet understand enough to do this?"

"Because it is constantly flowing. You cannot take a drop of water from a river, put it back in, and catch the same drop again."

"So how can he think he will ever be successful?"

"Because he hopes to divert the stream and channel off what he needs. He needs a successive chain with the right markers."

"How can Lihn's baby do this for him?"

"Because," she said excitedly, holding up her index finger, "he has come to realize only recently that markers of a family are generally close together on the bloodwave. He cannot predict where they will be yet. He has only been at this a couple generations. He hopes that with Lihn's child, since he himself is not on the bloodwave, will yield him some interesting answers."

"But he won't find them."

"Exactly." Alityka's face lit up again. "Lihn's child cannot give Cirvel the answer that he needs. That is what I learned from the Plenelians. Since her child doesn't exist on this human bloodwave, he won't be able to find the missing piece."

"She'll be relieved to know that."

"We're not going to tell her."

"What? Why not? I think she needs to know. 'Twill ease some of her anxiety."

"Aye, that might bring her peace of mind, but we have to use her as a diversion for a little while longer."

"A diversion," Rivic said, the word flat and distasteful in his mouth. "How does he not know that she is a transformed unicorn? He knew about you and about me, so why doesn't he know about her? Certainly he already knows that her child won't give him the answer." He almost told Alityka where he'd found Lihn, and certainly if Cirvel could put her there, he already knew that she and her child were worthless to him or else he wouldn't risk harming the baby. "I still think Lihn needs to know."

"She needs to remain the diversion for a bit longer. You were the only other possible link he had, but his own plans worked against him."

"Me? I don't understand."

"You were on the human bloodwave of this world and you are a novihomidrak. All he had to do was sort out the novihomidrak magic, which he could compare to his own. You are his family whether you like it or not. If he had realized this, he would have the piece that he needed."

"When he made me a Necroatheling, he took my markers off the human bloodwave, destroying his chance at getting the answer."

"Aye, but now you see why Lihn has to remain the distraction. He must not see how close he was."

It disturbed Rivic to think how close Cirvel had been. Little wonder that the Guardian had thought through the removal of his connection to the Humline and why she had once called him flawed. The dragon knew Cirvel would puzzle it out if he suspected Rivic was dragon born. Needing to change the subject, Rivic held out his hand. "I want to see your absorption stone."

Alityka nodded as she lifted the flap on a pouch at her side. From it, she pulled out a small wooden box. "I found that if you keep the stone in cloth or leather, it still will take your magic. But wood seems to negate its powers."

The box didn't have hinges, but rather the lid slid through grooves on the side. Rivic pushed the lid with his thumb and retrieved the stone from inside. He held it in his hand and waited, but he didn't feel any different. After a moment, he shook his head. "Nothing is happening."

"You still feel your magic?"

"Aye."

Alityka shook her head. "Try casting a spell, something small."

"All right." He held up his other hand. "Lazator." A small ball of light began floating next to him.

"Nay," Alityka said in disbelief. She reached forward and plucked the stone from Rivic's palm. "Lazator," she said. Nothing happened. She held out her hands and closed her eyes as she shouted, "Lazatorian dydactica highmulktien!"

"Woah," Rivic hollered, throwing his arm over his face. As he realized that there hadn't been any explosion around him, he slowly relaxed his arm and looked at Alityka standing there staring at the stone.

"Why doesn't it work on you?" she asked. "Could it be because you are a novihomidrak?"

"I don't know," he answered. "But if it doesn't work on me, then it won't work on Cirvel either."

"Unless it doesn't work because of your markers on this world's bloodwave. Maybe being a novihomidrak specifically from this world makes you immune to it."

"Ali, I know that you want to believe that's possible, but I just don't know if human magic can be separated from novi-homidrak magic. I think it's a stretch."

She placed the stone back in the box, seeming a bit more relieved after she closed the lid. "I know that you're not going to like this, but I bargained for a dagger."

"Why wouldn't I like it?"

"I got it from the Plenelians. 'Tis what they've been using to test their own people for magic, or to remove it." She spat out the last part of the sentence so fast that Rivic realized that she had more to say but was abbreviating what she was going to tell him.

"Remove it?" he asked, letting his thoughts stretch out to

follow her words. He sensed it come back to him. "You mean to remove someone's markers from the bloodwave so that they no longer possess magic."

"Aye. Or to put them onto another," she answered slowly. Alityka rolled her eyes when he still looked at her with questions. "Markers just don't disappear. They have to go somewhere. New lines can be started."

"So what you're telling me is that if Cirvel can cut humanity from the bloodwave, the markers would all just make a new line, like a self-healing thread? Does that mean that he can't do it?"

"He needs this knife to fulfill his plans. He can't do it without this."

"What makes the dagger so special?"

"It detects markers and can remove the energy of the whole thread. It was created by energy workers."

"What makes me think that the Plenelians didn't just give this dagger to you?"

She smiled. "I did say that I had to bargain for it."

"What kind of bargain?"

"The kind where they don't know that I took the dagger, and you don't have to sweep in bringing novihomidrak vengeance upon them in order to get it."

Rivic gave a moment to see if Alityka would say anything further. When she didn't, he spoke, "I have spent long enough here. How much further until we reach him? Should we teleport to him? If I don't get him to stand down before Azote gets here, there will be bloodshed."

"I have people waiting for me too. We have enough power there to get the attention of Azote and the gargaxes. Those remaining with my father will be safe."

"You are so certain these plans will work?"

She nodded. "Gohaldinest falls. 'Tis another city built

over the top of Gohaldinest in two thousand cycles. We succeed."

"At what cost, Ali? Do acolytes lose their lives when your father attacks. Does Cirvel raze the city himself because he can?" He could tell that none of this had entered her thoughts. "I have to talk to your father now. So many will die if he tries to take on Gohaldinest."

She grabbed his wrist. "Rivic, there is something else you should know."

He glanced down at where she gripped his arm. "What?"

"Your sister wasn't in Plenelia. Cirvel entered alone. She never went there with him and he didn't negotiate a marriage or position for anyone while he was there. He bargained for the dagger and that was all."

"Which means Cirvel has her?"

Alityka released him. "Aye."

"Thank you." He knew she probably hadn't wanted to confess this fact to him, but he was glad that she had. Alityka had seen he needed that additional push to keep him from going to Cirvel's side, and she knew the betrayal would affect Rivic deeply. He stepped over and embraced her. "I appreciate you letting me know. Please take care against Azote."

"Take care of my sister," she said once they broke off their hug.

Rivic stopped her before she turned away. "I have something for you. I was going to give it to your father, but I think 'twould be better in your hands. Vochey." The newly forged sword came to him.

She gasped as she took a good look at it. "Rivic, 'tis beautiful."

"'Twill look better when you impale that demon on it."

She grinned, taking the sword from his hands. "I will do my best. Until then, I'll see you on the other side of time."

He watched as she slid the sword on at her side.

"One more thing, Rivic." Worry pressed over her face. "When you feel it coming, put a magic shield around you and Ellonia if you can. I think that might be the only thing that can negate it. And don't go to sleep."

"Negate what?" Rivic asked.

Alityka shook her head, indicating that she didn't want to tell him. "A very powerful spell." Her blue eyes fixed on him. "Please, Rivic?"

"Fine." He nodded, releasing all the questions he wanted to ask to the wind. He had to trust her. "But regardless of all you have said, I will still speak to Krithstand. I want him to be aware of what he is walking into and what is coming for him."

She looked about to speak, but then she merely nodded her head instead. She waved a hand toward the heavy path where horses, wagons, and men had moved through now evident on the forest floor.

As he turned away, she rushed forward a step and touched his arm. "Please be fast. Trap him quickly, then get yourself, Lihn, and Ellonia out of there. Please?"

He realized that she was begging him. He placed his hand over hers to hold her there. "Blessings of bright fortune upon you."

"Bright blessings," she whispered, drawing her hand slowly out from beneath his.

He stood, watching her, while she walked away from him. In her next few steps, she vanished.

He had a terrible feeling it would be a long time before he saw her again.

CHAPTER 30

"Talcor dun," Rivic said. The teleportation spell took him to near enough that he could see the long caravan of wagons stopped along the forest trail. They were waiting, preparing. As he went to step forward, he felt a shift as if something in the surroundings had changed. He glanced down.

A line of gray rocks, absorption stones, were set on the path before him. He noticed several more tied in the trees. They were hiding their numbers and their power while Alityka had people to take on Azote and the gargaxes. This had been what Alityka meant when she said she would divert the demons' attention.

This wouldn't stop him though. "Talcor dun."

He appeared in Chief Krithstand's wagon. It rocked beneath his weight. He threw back his hood so the others with Krithstand would see that it was him. Rivic hoped the guards would still recognize him. They didn't lower their tense stance right away, but Rivic moved toward Krithstand anyway. "Krithstand-chief, I should like a word with you."

Besides Krithstand's guards, there were others in the

room as well. A large centaur stood between Rivic and Krithstand. For a moment, Rivic had to wonder how the centaur had gotten in the wagon, but he'd probably used magic. Would the gargaxes have sensed that, even with the absorption stones placed around the camp's perimeter? Rivic noticed a fairy, with a tall feather sticking up from her hair, sitting up in the rafters, but that there were no stones hanging up there with her.

"Can we," Krithstand began, "count on your help, Rivicna? Have you come to aid us"

"If I were to, I would put Ellonia in danger. While she is within the Lord of Gohaldinest's grasp, I don't dare play games against him."

Knowing that Krithstand was about to plead for help, Rivic rushed forward and grabbed the thick, coarse sleeve of Krithstand's brown traveling cloak. He turned Krithstand around so they had their backs to the group, allowing them to speak in semi-privacy. "My chief, if there was any way I thought I could persuade you to go back down the mountain and leave this battle behind for the sake of the larger war, I would do so. I would even plead in the names of your daughters if I thought 'twould help." Rivic paused, wishing his words would have the full effect he desired from them. "But somehow, I suspect you will not flee from the gargaxes."

"What kind of father would I be if I showed up to save my daughter, then turned and ran away at the first sign of danger?"

"One who would not be throwing his life away senselessly!" Rivic snapped back. "Don't you think that your daughters wish for you to remain alive? You cannot win. Cirvel doesn't even have to get close to you in order to bring defeat. You will never get to look him in the eyes. He has given me the opportunity to attempt to turn you from your course, a generosity not often extended. But if you continue, I must be one of the ones that keeps you from getting to him."

Krithstand nodded. "Then, you call me your chief, but your allegiance has completely changed."

"If it had, I wouldn't have even come to warn you. I would merely let you march to your death."

"I cannot turn. Alityka has been planning this for far too long. My daughters have faith in you."

"I know."

"Stop Alityka from going after Azote," he asked.

"I cannot. I gave her--"

Krithstand moved away from Rivic. "Then we are at an impasse. I suggest you leave now."

The centaur barged over. "If you have something to offer other than words, do so now. We all have men out there helping Dominus Alityka. I should not like to see them sacrificed if there is something that can prevent it."

"I gave her a sword powerful enough to defeat Azote."

"Then why not wield this sword yourself?" Krithstand said. "Do you leave her to fight the demon while you cower?"

This conversation was definitely not going the way he'd planned it. "I must return to Cirvel with your word that you aren't going to attack Gohaldinest."

"Then you would do better to stand with our men and Krithstand's brave daughter," the centaur noted. "Your breath is wasted here, Necroatheling."

"Please, Krithstand, listen to me," Rivic said, turning back to the chief. "My advice to you has never been faulty before."

Krithstand sighed. "Very well. Tell the Lord of Gohaldinest that peace has been negotiated."

"Krithstand," the centaur started in protest.

But Krithstand held up his hand.

Rivic bowed to Krithstand. "Then let me aid you where I can." He stepped outside the wagon while the others followed closely behind. Feeling several curious gazes turn to look at him, people evaluated his purple robes and moved out of his way. He watched hands go to weapons, but none were raised against him.

While the army wasn't happy to have a Necroatheling walking out among them, they were glad to have Rivic there once more. He took their shy smiles as more of a thank-you than he deserved.

"Now let's see what we can do about your caravan," Rivic said. He glanced to the sky and saw that it neared evening. "Chief Krithstand, the protection will last as long as it is not used. You and your men will have a safe night and travel in peace back to your homes."

Krithstand nodded, but there was something in his eyes that told Rivic the attack would come tonight. If only Rivic could sense a lie like Alityka could. If only he could trust Krithstand's words about negotiated peace were true.

He knew he must follow the path he'd already started, which was to help Krithstand. Rivic raised his hands over his head. "Miex'balish palikiem a't porta'mentay balishmel achta sumet."

Some of the people around him gasped at the magicks rising around the caravan, but only had terror held in their eyes. They understood the strength of the spell he'd just cast, what dark and ancient magicks backed it. If they hadn't thought him a demon before, their thoughts pushed in that direction now.

A roar overhead drew his attention toward the sky where Azote currently flew with several gargaxes behind him. Azote gestured to the gray demons, then changed his course from the others.

Azote was going after Alityka.

"The gargaxes arrive," Krithstand stated. Certainly he felt

their moments were numbered now. But the gargaxes turned and took to the rocks and trees of the mountain.

"Cirvel promised me that I would have time to persuade you to retreat," Rivic said, though he wasn't sure he could promise the Lord of Gohaldinest would be faithful to his word, a gesture he hoped for in kind. "However, 'tis time for me to return. I have done for you what I can."

Rivic moved aside, but Krithstand followed. "Keep Ellonia safe," the chief said. Rivic noticed that Alityka hadn't been in his wishes. That made a chill sweep along Rivic.

"I will," Rivic responded. He tucked his head down and waited until the leathery flap of wings above him subsided, wanting to be sure that the gargaxes were settled. "Talcor dun," he said when all was quiet.

CHAPTER 31

*I*t felt almost as if Rivic's spell was pulled, for he reappeared in Cirvel's reading room as if he'd been summoned. Cirvel wasn't in his chair anymore and his book lay open but discarded on the table. Rivic couldn't help but to glance at it as he walked by as if it were there for him to see. The spells referenced were for reanimating the dead from between dimensions.

Rivic saw Cirvel in the secret room off to the left. He smiled at Rivic as he went by the sliding panel. "Were you successful?" Cirvel asked.

"I'm not certain. I feel as if I live in false hope. I wish I could say Krithstand will heed my warning, but I suspect he still intends to march against Gohaldinest."

"'Tis time we give them a demonstration of power then," he said thoughtfully.

"Taking out Krithstand's army?"

"Out of your lips."

"I won't. I refuse to hurt Ellonia's father or the men following him. They are people I know, my friends."

"There's a curious thing about power," Cirvel said. He flourished his hand and a glass appeared on the table. After picking it up and taking a sip of the dark reddish-purple liquid inside, he continued to hold it by the stem. He swirled it slightly, making the drink slosh against the sides. "When you are a leader, even for something as simple as being in charge of a mission, you have the ability to decimate or show mercy to, not only your own people, but your opponents as well."

Rivic refused to weaken his position. "Kristhstand will come and you will lose Necroathelings."

Cirvel grinned and shook his head as if entertaining the notions of a small, naïve child. "I should need one Necroatheling to stand out there against his army. I believe I shall place you there."

"Then I will let him and his army by."

Cirvel laughed. "Then you still do not understand the nature of the Necroatheling. You will decimate this tribal chief's invasion force and you will love every drop of blood you spill." He raised his hand and gave a waggle of his fingers. "But I assume you fortified them as best as you could while you were there to give them a fighting chance?"

Again, a chill breezed against Rivic's skin. Did Cirvel know this as a fact, or merely a guess? "I did." He raised his gaze to Cirvel's to inspect for irritation.

Rather, the Lord of Gohaldinest seemed amused. "Good, good."

Rivic stood in the doorway, the same fear he'd had upon arriving in Gohaldinest clenching in his stomach now. Cirvel knew that Rivic had helped Krithstand and that had been part of the plan all along. Yet Rivic couldn't help the feeling that he'd betrayed both Krithstand and Cirvel. He was playing both sides and that would not end well for him. Alityka swore that Cirvel wasn't all-knowing, but Rivic wasn't certain. Cirvel always remained one step ahead of them.

Always.

"How is it that you heard of the Shniktaur?" Cirvel asked.

"The Guardian told me."

"Of course she would."

"She seems to believe it will return and the two of us will have to combat it together." As Rivic stepped closer to Cirvel, he felt bravery growing deep within his chest. It surprised him how thick his voice sounded when he spoke next. "If that is a possibility, then I would like to know what we are up against."

"Well, we are not up against the Shniktaur right now. Krithstand and his armies are facing us presently. When we get through this, we shall discuss the Shniktaur."

Rivic saw the bait set before him, like magic set before a gargax. But if the Lord of Gohaldinest thought Rivic had nothing further to ask, then Cirvel was wrong. "Where is Nyree?"

The initial emotion which flashed unidentifiably across Cirvel's face faded into a suave smile. "You are well aware that she is in Plenelia, married and happy."

"I don't believe she is there. I believe you have her."

Cirvel made a slow turn to face Rivic. "I'm uncertain how you came to this information or if 'tis merely a good guess, but I wish you hadn't brought me to a confession quite so soon. Aye, I have Nyree."

Rivic wished he hadn't heard the words. Why couldn't Cirvel had denied it? "Why?"

"Did you not just fortify Krithstand's army in their attack of Gohaldinest? Were you not to send them on their way back to their village instead of encouraging their march to our city?"

Knees weakened, Rivic thought he might collapse to the

floor. "You have her because you know you can't trust me. Like Ellonia, you want to make sure you have something to make me do as you wish."

"Come now. Even I am not as callous to use our sister as insurance to assure your loyalty now that I know who she is. Follow. If we are soon to be in battle, then this step must be done soon anyway to secure our safety." Cirvel's fluttering robes changed to black and silver as he strode from the room. "I will explain along the way."

Smelling the lingering scent of magic in the air, Rivic noticed that Cirvel had called one of the golden lamps to his hand. The handle looped around Cirvel's index finger while the spout pointed toward the floor, rocking with each stride Cirvel took. Considering how Cirvel usually carried the lamps before him as if each one were precious, this indicated his disappointment. Hopefully Nyree wasn't getting banged around inside.

"Once upon a time," Cirvel began as he walked through the castle, "I felt a great power rise in the forest. I sent gargaxes out to investigate and they returned to tell me that a whole tribe had been destroyed by one surge of magic. Necroathelings were sent to investigate further. Imagine my surprise when I found out that two toddlers had survived."

Never had it crossed Rivic's mind that Cirvel would have felt the destruction he'd once caused.

"A toddler who was still far too young to have experienced magic sickness," Cirvel continued. "But then, I discovered this child had a twin. I knew that if a mere babe could handle such magicks, the magicless twin would surely be capable of handling dragon magic, especially after having also survived the blast. 'Twas possible I could make that unlucky, disadvantaged being into a fantastic sapere."

"Nyree... you were after her?"

"Aye. I never figured that anyone in a tribe would let you live after what you had done. I thought you'd be left in the forest for the gargaxes if nothing else. Who dared to be brave enough to take you in?"

"My aunt and uncle." His stomach compressed, pushing the words from his mouth though the words were barely even audible to him.

"Family." It could have been a question, but it wasn't. Cirvel sneered the word as if it left a distaste in his mouth. "They probably thought they could help you control it, that 'twas a one time fluke. Didn't help them, now did it?"

"Nay."

They had reached the tunnels, a path Rivic now knew too well. To his surprise, they took a different turn than they would have to visit the Guardian and went down another flight of earthen stairs.

Cirvel created a light overhead for Rivic to see by. Cirvel, with his dragon vision, wouldn't have needed it. Flawed, Rivic thought.

"I sent Necroathelings to fetch Nyree in the middle of the night. You sensed them coming."

Nausea rolled through Rivic.

Cirvel chuckled. "That's right. You destroyed them along with everyone else in your aunt and uncle's village. I was with Salvarae and we both felt it. She convinced me to unchain her and let her go out to track you. She was supposed to bring the magicless one to me. I never thought she'd be reckless enough to swallow you, let alone both of you. She returned and told me that everyone had perished in the explosion. Since I never felt the strong magic again and there were no more recurrences, I took her at her word."

They continued for several paces along the tunnel before Cirvel glanced back at Rivic. "I hope you realize how she has lied to both of us. Since finding out that she took you to be a novihomidrak and asking me to train you, I have expanded all my efforts to include you as my brother. This world I build now, I do for both of us. I need you to understand that."

"I never asked for power."

"Nevertheless, 'twas given to you. While I understand your need to see the people around you to be safe, I know that they will all cast off this world and you will be left with me and the dragons."

"Dragons?"

"Salvarae and I have long been the guardians of something very precious. She made you to be my companion on this quest. But she still denies me what I need, and in doing so, now spurns you." He now held up the lamp, indicating it to Rivic. "I hope you understand that I am left without a choice but to attempt this. Nyree may be the only hope either one of us has."

"You still plan to make her a sapere?"

Cirvel didn't answer. He waved his hand before him and an enormous door appeared. The iron bars which would make up a cell door were long, round tubes of crystals that seemed to have melted and merged together, sealed within what looked like the glass windows of the castle but thicker to contain the cylinders. Ancient magicks protected the door and set firmly into the wall for extra protections.

"Pay your utmost respects, lad, and mind your manners, for what lies beyond this door is one of the most spectacular creatures which ever lived."

This was it, Rivic knew. The thing that Cirvel kept secret and hidden so that no one knew what he was doing. Rivic had told Alityka and Lihn that Cirvel had a greater plan. It had to be a dragon. Considering the size and density of the door, the beast behind it would have to be massive.

Cirvel set to speaking a chain of magic with practiced

ease as if it were a lullaby. The door swung open with his barest touch.

The first thing Rivic noticed as he followed Cirvel inside a gigantic cavern were all the little twinkles of light within the walls. "Magic," he whispered, watching as an exceptionally bright one expanded, then winked out of existence.

"Magic," Cirvel confirmed.

"Cirvel, is that you?" a voice called out from in a deeper, darker section of the cavern.

"'Tis I, and the one I have told you about, my novi-brother, Rivic."

"Ah."

Rivic felt he should be seeing something, but there seemed to be nothing in the cavern. Cirvel waved his hand and all the little sparkles of light intensified. Rivic noticed them blinking out faster, and being replaced by fresh curls of magic.

"I also have brought a possibility for a new sapere," Cirvel said.

"N-nay," the voice gave an elongated growl. "Given enough magic out already. Not a drop more."

"Leschemal, we've talked about this."

The darkness rippled and suddenly Rivic saw the shiny outline of scales moving over one another. It resembled the silver colors on Cirvel's robes, flashing as they moved. Then there were luminous eyes which seemed to shine with the same ancient magicks Rivic often sensed in the castle. The spells which crawled over the stone walls had originated and still lived with this beast.

"Come closer, novi-brother of Cirvel."

As Rivic moved forward to obey, he looked over the dragon. "'Tis barely bigger than Dragzel," Rivic said. Upon catching a stern look from Cirvel, Rivic remembered he was supposed to be on his best behavior here. Of course, the dragon was also bigger than Dragzel, yet he did wonder if it would match Azote's size. While the gaxlor made a better comparison, compared to Salvarae, this dragon before Rivic was more comparable to a cahaster.

"Leschemal has been sick for a long time," Cirvel explained patiently. "Only recently has he started to regain his size now that his strength has returned. Strong enough to create a sapere, I hope."

"I will not give in to your foul request. This world and everything on it should die," Leschemal responded.

Cirvel reached over and grabbed Rivic's dark plum cloak, yanking him closer to the dragon. "Look at him, Leschemal. He is from your world. Look at how powerful he is."

Leschemal, with effort, pushed himself up onto his front feet. In this sitting position, the dragon matched him in height. The dragon's face came closer to him and Rivic noticed that Leschemal's scales sparkled with their own light. The dragon's nostrils widened as he breathed deeply of Rivic's magical scent. "Oh!"

"That is your world, what 'tis becoming." Cirvel shook Rivic as if for good measure. "I am almost there. I need more time. For that, I need a sapere. The one I brought is aged and rots with magic. I have prolonged his life enough. But with another, I can continue to bring magic into this world."

Leschemal sank back down to the dirt floor. "Very well. Show me this one who wishes to become my sapere."

"Actually," Cirvel said, stepping back and raising the lamp before him, "there are two." He rubbed the side of the lamp with his long fingers.

Smoke rolled out of the end and a moment later Nyree stood before Cirvel as well as another woman.

"Ellonia," Rivic gasped.

She rushed over to Rivic, but instead of accepting her embrace, he pushed her behind him.

"Brother, you look as I have seen you in many visions," Nyree said. Her eyes were black with the golden torches as she turned her gaze from Rivic to the dragon and bowed. "Leschemal, 'tis an honor to finally meet you."

"She must have gotten the manners in your division of novihomidrak powers," Cirvel muttered to Rivic as he came over and grabbed Ellonia's wrist.

Rivic seized her other hand. "Nay. She is not yours to offer."

Cirvel released Ellonia, but they exchanged a look and Cirvel gave her an acknowledging nod. She turned, prying her arm from Rivic's grasp, though she took his hand and held onto him. "I made this choice by myself to be here. Cirvel explained to me the importance of what you, and he, need. We knew we'd only have one shot at this. One of us needs to make the appeal to Leschemal."

"Not you. Please?" Rivic remembered seeing the dead arm of the last sapere Cirvel had tried to make. He suddenly wished he'd left the baby when it had been offered up to Salvarae, but now that child was destined to kill the man who would help him and Alityka in the future. The weight of his actions settled in like a plague.

"Please, Rivic. You need this. Someone has to do this."

He dropped Ellonia's hand. Though still unwilling, he nodded.

"You are the twin of Rivic and novi-sister to Cirvel," Leschemal was saying as he looked Nyree over. She'd walked closer, unafraid, to the dragon.

"'Tis correct."

"You are a novihomidrak. This cannot work. You are unable to become a sapere."

"Then I will do it," Ellonia called out behind Rivic. She practically pushed him aside as she went to face Leschemal. "I submit myself."

"You both are too old to be trained properly."

"I know all the dragon magic already," Nyree protested, "but I do not have the magic behind it. You can give me that ability. Rivic and I split the novihomidrak powers, leaving us both incomplete. Those who have no powers when branded by a dragon into a sapere do gain the abilities to wield the magic." She took a step closer. "If you give me your blessing, I will have magic. Is that not what you want for your planet, a place where no one is without magic? If I am unable to handle it, then you have destroyed a powerless being which you are trying to eradicate anyway. I am your best choice."

Leschemal raised his head and spoke to Cirvel. "She is smart and speaks with sense. I will take her."

Fearing what might happen to Ellonia, Rivic reached out for her. His fingers closed around smoke as Cirvel drew her back into the lamp. Cirvel then said to Rivic, "We need to go. A novihomidrak should never see the making of a sapere."

Compelled to follow, Rivic started behind Cirvel toward the door. Trepidation filled in his stomach with every step. This was his sister. He couldn't leave her.

"Come," Cirvel commanded again.

Rivic's feet shuffled on the floor. Being a partial novihomidrak, would she survive the transformation? Did she still have enough humanness in her to accept the dragon's blessing?

You clung to him, Rivic remembered Salvarae saying to Nyree. She hadn't left his side. It felt wrong to leave her now.

"I can't. She's my twin," Rivic said. He turned to see Leschemal already starting to breathe over Nyree, who knelt on the floor before the dragon.

"You can't watch this."

"I'm not going to watch. I'm going to cling to her. Talcor dun."

As the world returned to Rivic, he felt himself inside the intense heat of the dragon's breath.

"I won't leave you, Nyree. No matter what happens, I won't leave you." He threw his arms around Nyree as she started to scream. His own shout followed hers. It felt like sand blasting against the skin. She wrapped Rivic in a tight embrace. Clinging to her was the last thing he remembered.

CHAPTER 32

*A*s soon as Rivic woke, he realized something was terribly wrong. He opened his eyes to bright sunlight and found everything sharp and cast with a yellow glow. He blinked, trying to clear his vision. It didn't help. Moaning and freeing himself from the blankets around him, he raised his hand intending to rub his eyes, but Cirvel caught his arms and held them away.

Cirvel peered down from above. "Well, 'tis an interesting development."

Rivic tried to look away, finding Cirvel too harsh to look at so close up. Rivic noticed Nyree approach.

"Dragon lids," she whispered as she sat down on the bed beside him and leaned in. "'Tis like he has been forged into a full novihomidrak."

"He is marked as a sapere too though," Cirvel muttered.

"Could it be possible that he is both now, since we split the novihomidrak powers before?" Nyree glanced up toward Cirvel.

"Unprecedented, definitely."

Rivic found his voice. "What's going on? Why is everything yellow?"

"Blink slowly and imagine your eyelids pulling in and grasping your eye," Cirvel instructed.

Rivic tried, but the world still held a yellow cast.

"Once more."

Again, Rivic blinked, and when his eyes opened the world had returned to normal. Almost at once, he missed the clarity with which he had been seeing, even though a moment ago it had seemed so harsh.

Cirvel helped Rivic to sit up. "'Twould seem that being in the dragon's breath fired more than a blessing of sapere magic.

"A new novihomidrak ability?" Rivic asked. He glanced around, taking in the furniture of his room though he didn't remember being brought back here. Cirvel must have brought them.

"At least one. Potentially more."

"Nyree?"

She shook her head. "I have nothing new. I was never meant to possess any of the novihomidrak abilities. I am glad for my visions, always have been, but now I do have the sapere magic." Nyree extended her arm toward Rivic and he saw a webwork of designs on her skin that sparkled like the dragon's scales had.

Rivic reached up, a tingle of something still not being right running through him, and he took Nyree's hand. She came closer.

As if in a vortex, Rivic saw a vision of Cirvel holding a dagger over Nyree while chanting magic.

"Watch as our world falls away," Rivic muttered.

Her black eyes stared back at him and he seemed pulled toward the yellow torches as the swirling, out-of-focus image swallowed him.

"Aye, brother." Nyree's voice sounded distant.

In the vision, Cirvel cut something from Nyree. Her eyes returned to their normal color and he felt a loss so deep it edged on indescribable. Cirvel took the red thread and stuck it in a jar. Blue webbing bled from the markings Rivic had just seen on her arms. She reached for Rivic. He knew what was happening. She was never meant to have magic.

Then the false world exploded and Rivic practically jumped from the bed where he lay. Nyree drew away and stood up slowly, her gaze refusing to come to him even though he tried so hard to mentally will it. He wanted to see her eyes.

Rivic caught Cirvel watching him. "Ellonia?"

"Aye." Cirvel called the lamp to hand. "Do not be angry with her. 'Tis I who went to her and asked for her submission. You have seen Sapere Berrik and know firsthand how dire our situation had become."

"Your situation," Rivic corrected. "I have always been able to heal on my own with time's natural course."

"True, though that may not be the case now."

Rivic hated how Cirvel so easily countered his statement. It felt like they were already sparring with words. How soon until weapons crossed as well?

"Besides," Cirvel began, irked energy falling off him as he stepped forward, "we should test to see what your boundaries are and if you can heal yourself with sapere magic." He took his ordinary dagger from his belt and reached a hand toward Rivic.

"Let me take the lamp for you, my lord," Nyree offered. As if remembering an irritation, Cirvel passed the lamp to her. Nyree turned to set it on a nearby table.

Rivic submitted to Cirvel, who pressed the dagger against the flesh of his forearm. The blade didn't break the skin. "Last time it cut," Rivic said as if Cirvel needed reminding.

"Vochey Submit," Nyree called. She offered her dagger to Cirvel. "Try this."

As if she were a clever girl, Cirvel gave her a pleased smile as he took her dagger. When he dragged it over Rivic's arm, the blade sliced into the flesh easily. "Let us see if you can heal yourself now with the sapere magic."

The words of a spell instantly jumped into his mind, but the darker shade of a tingle ran up his spine in warning. It seemed as if two sides of himself battled to win. His novihomidrak-self listening to the Onesong won. "I'm sorry. I know the spell, but I can't speak the magic."

This news didn't seem to please Cirvel. He stopped Nyree as she started forward to heal the wound. "Try again. Try as if your sister depends upon it."

Rivic's gaze went to Nyree's dagger which Cirvel now held toward his twin's stomach. Was this what he'd seen in the vision they'd shared? Or had Cirvel turned the dagger on her because Rivic had healed himself? Looking to the Onesong gave him no answers.

Yet as he decided to speak the words, the same creepy sensation returned, sending his stomach into a horrid churn. Maybe this was more than a warning, but a flat denial of letting a novihomidrak have the powers of a sapere, even by a fluke in the universe. "I can't."

Cirvel sighed, but he spun the dagger in his hand to present the hilt back to Nyree. "'Tis unfortunate." Then his mind seemed to wander off as he muttered, "I shall have to make a note of this... even a novihomidrak that gets sapere powers is unable to use them."

Nyree moved closer to Rivic. "May I heal him now, my lord?"

Cirvel looked up sharply, and it took another moment before his countenance soften as he realized he'd been talking to himself. "Sorry. There are just so few discoveries that have been made between novihomidraks and saperes that each one is important, especially when you're on a world that has been spun off from the Onesong. Aye, heal your brother."

Nyree leaned over and whispered dragon magic over the cut. Rivic watched the skin mend and the scar vanish. He mouthed his thanks to Nyree, but he didn't say the words aloud. She gave him an acknowledging blink, letting him see that her eyes were their normal color.

A huge crash vibrated through the castle, sharpening Rivic's senses. He noticed Cirvel turn, fighting with his own instincts to keep his mouth from filling with dragon teeth. Cirvel's eyes were even darker when he looked at Rivic. "Krithstand attacks."

Another volley of whatever had struck the castle again sounded against the walls.

Rivic spun toward the door, sensing footsteps in the hallway before the knock came. Cirvel opened it magically and a Necroatheling entered.

"My lord, the enemy has reached the gates," the man reported as he bowed.

"It sounds as if they are in the city already. Send out Azote."

"He has not returned."

The sound of Cirvel's heartbeat quickening startled Rivic. He'd known that his senses were better than a normal human's already, but now his prior existence seem muted.

Had Azote already caught up to Alityka?

Awareness of her galloping through the forest on a unicorn came to Rivic. Centaurs and unicorns followed while fairies did all they could to obscure Azote's vision and hold him back by gripping to his leathery wings.

Did Cirvel know this too?

"Ready the Necroathelings."

"Aye, my lord." The Necroatheling bowed once more then exited the room.

It wasn't but a moment later that another appeared. "The southwest wall has fallen. The city is in chaos," Undar-na reported.

Cirvel seemed genuinely shocked by this. "How?"

Rivic noticed Nyree pick up the lamp which still held Ellonia in it.

Undar-na's eyes shifted as he looked everywhere around the room but at Cirvel. "Maeges from Hallon have joined with Krithstand's forces."

Cirvel glared back at Rivic. With this news, Cirvel was unable to keep his emotions in check and his face morphed. "Did you know about this?" he snapped between his dragon teeth.

"Nay, my lord," Rivic responded, glad for it to be the truth, though he did wish the Onesong would feed him some information about why this upset Cirvel.

"Have the inner city fortified," Cirvel commanded. "I shall deal with those in the outer city and anyone still coming up the mountain for their potshots."

"Aye." Undar-na left as quickly as he'd come in.

"Our time grows increasingly short and I have two pressing spells which must be done presently. Come."

The hallways shook as they went from Rivic's room to Cirvel's antechamber. As they crossed through the room, Rivic felt Nyree nudge him as she went to set the lamp on the table. As much as he wanted Ellonia out of the trappings, at least knowing where she was, he could keep her safe. Out of Cirvel's sight also meant out of his mind, Rivic hoped.

Cirvel slid open the wall revealing the magical room behind. The sharp smell of rich spices and the humidity indicated something brewing inside. At the sights of the Alkelker slowly boiling on the counter, Rivic wondered why Cirvel hadn't sent the gargaxes out. He felt it had a deeper meaning, but Rivic couldn't fathom it. Not since Cirvel was known for keeping magical control by sending gargaxes out to attack maeges. Why not now?

Cirvel turned from stirring the additional mixture he had on the counter, his smile soft. "Come. I am about to finish. When I am done, we will take to the tower and watch the results."

An acidic smell burned in Rivic's nose as he got closer, being sure to keep Nyree behind him and nearer to the door.

"Meanwhile, another lesson, shall we?" Cirvel asked.

Cirvel's sudden calm and desire to instruct after having just been in an impatient hurry unnerved Rivic. Or had that all been for show with the Necroathelings?

"Everything takes energy," Cirvel began to explain. "Magic is no exception. You can have just a little extra if you add something else in and change its energy."

Rivic took a sliding step closer as Cirvel beckoned him forward.

Cirvel picked up the bowl and slung the contents out over the counter. Wisps of purple steam rose from the mass. "Il'li wrok ghass mekx vanatornae."

The dragon magic whipping from Cirvel slammed into Rivic like a wave. Cirvel, nearly falling, grasped onto the counter as he issued an overwhelmed breath. Such explosive magic had taken a toll, even momentarily.

A two-headed creature looked up from where the mixture had been spilled, the mess gone and only the serpent-like beast remaining.

"Vochey, Impact." A black leather guard appeared around Cirvel's wrist. He twisted and a spear sprung from a hidden slot. Lashing out, Cirvel impaled the creature through the throat. The poor beast let out a weak mewl as it collapsed, blood surging from it.

"I give life to take life," Cirvel said upon noticing Rivic's horror. "From the essence I created, it returns."

As it died, another purple curl rose from the body. Cirvel reached out and wrapped his fingers around it, allowing it to collect in his palm.

"Gontac forsath."

The purple wisp vanished.

"Let this be a lesson to you," Cirvel said, his eyes now dark and cold. "Your novimather gave you life and she feeds you magic to strengthen you, but 'tis to the slaughter she intends to lead you. That is the truth for all novihomidraks."

Rivic felt his heart pounding, especially as he continued to sense Cirvel's novihomidrak weapon so very close to him. Quick, short breaths moved through him.

Cirvel raised his other hand and motioned Rivic's sister to come into the room. "Nyree, please come have a seat."

"Aye, my lord," she said flatly as she followed the order.

"What are you doing?" Rivic dared to ask. Considering he'd just watched Cirvel, without hesitation, slaughter a beast he'd created only moments before, he wanted to know exactly what Cirvel planned for his twin.

"Our sister still has a flaw," Cirvel said. Nyree confirmed his words with a little nod that she understood what Cirvel was talking about. "You see, she was born non-magical in a world which strives to be full of enchantments. Now that she has been blessed by Leschemal and gained the magic of a sapere, she can remove the part of her which remains impure."

"The non-magical part of her? But they don't have markers on the bloodwave. Only magical beings do."

"Ah, so you and Alityka have been trying to figure out what I'm doing. I figured as much. Lihn too, I suppose?" He held up a hand where he already had his fingers curled in a coil of yellow magic. "Of course, without Alityka's help, I couldn't have gotten this. Ferram sang'in mutari'tae pok'lis a undan sada'miet. Raishen poc'toi malen ferram sang'in mutari'tae."

The blood dagger Alityka had stolen from Plenelia appeared in his hand where the magic had once been.

"Tis not like she or the Plenelians would have given it to me willingly." Cirvel smiled, looking fully amused. "Ah, lad, your anger is not needed. When has it ever served you? You have always been right about me having a larger plan, and you told them so repeatedly. 'Tis their own fault that they wouldn't listen to you. I could have stepped in at any time and squashed your rebellion, but rather I participated."

He walked around behind Nyree, his fingers lingering on the back of her chair. "Our sister even told you to submit. 'Walk the path,' she told you over and over. She never said to fight or resist it. It always was her way of telling you to accept it."

Rivic felt so betrayed. From the moment they'd been born from the pearl, she'd been pushing him toward Gohaldinest, toward Cirvel. Everything felt shattered and destroyed. Slowly he nodded his resignation. He still had one last question to cling to. "What is the Shniktaur?"

Cirvel looked so angry that Rivic thought he might throw the dagger. But then with two breaths, Cirvel regained his composure and moved his head so that his long black hair swayed over his back. "'Tis the doom of this world. Leschemal is an imagination dragon and created this world to cultivate the highest magicks possible. But his own creations turned against him and opened the door for the chaos to enter. This world entered a crisis so quickly that Leschemal lost faith, and the moment he decided to destroy his creation, the Shniktaur was born. I sealed away the Shniktaur for a time, but if I don't serve Leschemal and create the world he wanted, 'tis all doomed."

"That's what you meant when you made Leschemal look at how powerful I was. And you aren't sending the gargaxes out to defeat the maeges attacking the city because you don't want them devouring that much magic."

"I have to keep a balance in this world until Leschemal is strong enough to see reason and to let go of his vengeance. 'Tis the only way we make it back to the Onesong. To keep him from destroying his creation, this world must have magic."

"So, 'tis not magic that you want to remove from the bloodwave, but everything without magic, like the Plenelians."

Cirvel looked disappointed. "There is still so much you don't understand."

"Nay, I think I do. 'Tis why you want to *purify* Nyree. She was a magicless novihomidrak and that drove you crazy. I can't let you experiment on Nyree." He pulled her from the chair and pushed her toward the door.

"So even after all I have done for you, all I have tried to make you understand so that you can help me shoulder this journey, 'tis betrayal that you choose." Cirvel looked to the floor and seemed to take a moment to steady his emotions before he glanced up again. "I knew you would have two choices to your path. I am sorry that your choice means I have to destroy you. Vochey, Luminous."

Rivic saw the spiked ball on the end of a short chain appear in Cirvel's hand. He didn't have time to react before Cirvel jerked the weapon up and the ball slammed into Rivic's face.

White diamonds flashed in Rivic's visions as he felt himself stagger backwards from the strike. "Vochey, Honor," Rivic said, calling his sword to him. His other hand reached for the dagger tucked into a sheath on his belt. He raised the dagger. With a flick of his wrist, he tossed it at Cirvel. It wouldn't do any damage, but Cirvel might still flinch away and give Rivic a moment to dash for the door. This room didn't offer space enough for battle with inflexible weapons and gave Cirvel's mace and retractable dagger a much bigger advantage.

Then Cirvel disappeared in a wisp of smoke. Rivic bolted for the door. Cirvel, having made the same calculations, reappeared before the door, crouched while flipping the ball around in small circles.

Rivic pounced, slicing downward with his sword.

The ball struck Rivic shoulder, knocking him sideways while the spikes dug into his muscles. They tore out, shredding his flesh like claws. Rivic crashed to the floor, sliding across the stone. He involuntarily reached for his arm, his fingers warming in the blood.

As he got up, Rivic felt the metal spike affixed to Cirvel's wrist impale him through his shoulder. A punch impacted with his face and Rivic fell away from the spear. The spiked ball, swinging freely, grated against Rivic's face. As he landed on the floor for the second time, he felt his blood crawling all over him.

Cirvel knelt beside Rivic and placed a heavy hand on Rivic's chest. "Such a shame you can't heal yourself. Let's go see if the ships are arriving yet."

The world spun around Rivic. A moment later, he found himself still flat on his back and alone with Cirvel in the high tower. Beyond the one open window he could see out of, puffy white clouds floated in the blue sky as if nothing were very wrong with the world below.

Cirvel stood and kicked Rivic's shoulder, making Rivic hiss with pain and he tried to curl away from a second attack.

Cirvel started walking away from him, but now stopped and pivoted back around. "I require power. The chaos that lies deep within this world is more formidable than one or two novihomidraks. When I arrived, this world was sick with wars, famine, disease, and every misery that one man could place upon another. It deserved to be cut off from the Wells of the Onesong." Cirvel shook his weapons. "With Luminous and Impact, I brought light and hope to this world while restoring Leschemal to health."

Rivic raised his head. "Then you wanted power and tried to lord over the people you sought to save."

"They needed me!" Cirvel roared. "They are little better than animals without me."

"You take those with magical abilities and demand that they become a Necroatheling or be destroyed." Rivic pushed himself up so he was sitting on his hip and elbow. "You call that 'needing you'?"

"I channeled their natural need for fighting and destruction. Aye, I am using them for my own ultimate purposes, but those I use now will be remembered for their sacrifices in the end. You, however," Cirvel said, raising his hand toward Rivic, "will be marked as a traitor to this great city."

The magic slid around Rivic and he felt himself no longer in control of his body. He rose and walked to the window, then climbed up in the sill. A plummet from this height, having already taken wounds from a novihomidrak weapon, would certainly bring him to the edge of death. Especially if he couldn't speak any magic to stop the fall. He tried, but no words came from his lips.

"I am still your Necronosti and you do as I command," Cirvel threatened through grit teeth.

From here, the window looked out at the bay. Further below them would be the town of Montikovert.

"Look there," Cirvel said, pointing.

Rivic saw a single dark mass floating out on the ocean, a silhouette against the sunset. It broke into two, then three.

Rivic blinked down his dragon lids to see them better. They were ships.

"My army of undead Necroathelings," Cirvel said. "All they have to do is reach land, then they will sweep through Montikovert and up the trail right behind Krithstand and his men. While they worry about getting into the castle, they will never see their true means of defeat coming from behind. Did you prepare them for that?"

With his back bent, Rivic turned back to face Cirvel. Then he knelt on the sill, sitting on his heels as his hands gripped the stone to keep him from falling. It seemed to be the only control he had.

"Nay," he admitted. He knew that Krithstand and his men would face Necroathelings, including the undead, as soon as they reached the city. Had Krithstand even planned for a strike of Necroathelings from outside of Gohaldinest?

"'Tis hard to not care about the people in your life, isn't it? I fervently wish I didn't have to do this, but you know I have to." Cirvel held his hand up toward Rivic's chest. "Shi'baten to'a helcord."

Rivic felt himself blown backwards out of the window.

CHAPTER 33

*R*ivic felt himself falling backwards from the tower window. His arms pinwheeled. Cirvel had released control of Rivic's body, but not of the ability to say spells. As Rivic started to plummet toward the city below, he had a flash of all the times he'd soared easily up above the treetops to fight the gargaxes. Cirvel could hold the words of enchantment at bay, but he couldn't restrain the primal instincts within Rivic.

The descent slowed. Rivic closed his eyes as he started to rise. Placing a hand on his shoulder, he gave into the compulsion to speak the dragon language held in his head. His wounds healed, not from sapere magic, but rather from the power of deeper impulses. He knew that Cirvel was far too vain to be watching Rivic now and regretted that Cirvel missed seeing Rivic's victory.

Though surely Cirvel didn't expect Rivic to die from the fall.

Had Cirvel teleported to the ground below where he could lord over Rivic's broken body until he decided to bring the finishing blow with one of his novihomidrak weapons?

Or did Cirvel want him to wait, broken and battered, listening as the sounds of battle raged in the city until it was over? Then what? Would Cirvel bring death or haul Rivic back to the castle and mend him? Maybe he'd thought to leave Rivic maimed and twisted so that he could break Rivic's mind much slower than his body.

Was the sense of all this from the Onesong, or from Cirvel?

He wasn't yet use to his full novihomidrak powers or his new sapere powers. He reminded himself that soon he'd have the time to learn what all he could do. Now he needed to focus on Cirvel.

Rivic strode forward, walking on air toward the window. Of all the things he'd imagined, none turned out to be real. Cirvel had stayed to watch his ships reach harbor and now stood in the window, his eyes wide. His lip twitched as he sneered, "Levitation."

"Aye. You still seem surprised by it as you were in our lesson. I take it this is something novihomidraks usually don't do."

"Nor do they heal themselves. Shakalal."

Air lashed out at Rivic from multiple direction. He threw up his arms, but not nearly quick enough. The spell disrupted his concentration and Rivic plunged once more.

As he dropped, Rivic found his magic return. "Talcor dun," he shouted, not questioning why he had the ability to cast enchantments once more, certainly not if it allowed him to get back inside the castle.

Rivic rolled over the gray stone of a hallway, slamming to a halt as he hit a wall. Pain ripped through him, but it didn't feel like any bones had broken. His shoulder wrenched against the fresh healing, but Rivic thought it might hold. Another blessing he didn't want to examine too closely.

Cirvel would be tracking Rivic's magic now. Picking

himself up off the floor, Rivic began running, knowing it was only a matter of time before Cirvel took control of him again.

The Lord of Gohaldinest had returned to his chambers.

Why?

Cirvel had gone to fetch the lamp which held Ellonia.

Rivic prayed that Nyree had it and had gotten herself somewhere safe.

What if Nyree was really on Cirvel's side?

Rivic couldn't think about it. He had to run and get through the castle.

Taking a corner sharply, Rivic saw several of Krithstand's men charging down the hall. Somehow, amazingly, they had breached the castle. Only when they raised their weapons against him did Rivic realize that his purple robes weren't serving him very well. "Talcor dun," he hollered, evaporating right before a sword struck him.

He raced through the hallway where he landed. If he teleported again, he'd be there in a flash. Time after time he cast the spell until he finally appeared in Lihn's library.

"Galault," he called out breathlessly. "Galault, I need you."

Rivic leaned over with his hands on his knees while he panted, waiting, hoping.

"Galault!"

The painting didn't shift.

If Cirvel knew about what Rivic, Alityka, and Lihn had been up to, was it possible he knew about Galault too? Had he somehow captured the watcher of worlds as well?

Rivic hauled the painting off the wall and shook it a couple of times while shouting Galault's name as if that would awaken the watcher. It didn't move.

He couldn't stay here. Remaining in one place made it far too easy for Cirvel to catch up to him and Rivic preferred for it to be the other way around. Galault's help would have been preferred. That wasn't an option now.

Tucking the painting beneath his arm, Rivic left Lihn's library and ran upstairs for Cirvel's antechamber. Arriving at the hallway with the black and white tile floor, he found the passageway blocked by stone and wooden rafters from the crumbled ceiling. The door opened only slightly, then budged no further. "Talcor dun," he said. Once on the other side, he saw boulders smashed down on the bodies of Domini trying to make their escape. Blood splattered against the lattice windows.

Rivic darted for Cirvel's antechamber. The door was knocked askew and Rivic had to press his full weight against it to get it open.

Part of the ceiling had collapsed in here too. The table where he and Cirvel had often sat for lessons was smashed and the wood broken into four sections by a boulder which struck it in the middle. Lamps lay scattered all over the floor, their tables overturned.

Another tremor went through the castle. He felt the floor beneath him buckle. Somewhere, not far from where he stood, stone collapsed.

Rivic crawled over to the lamps. He had no idea which one, if any, belonged to Ellonia. She might not even be in one of these. He wished he'd been able to watch Nyree a little closer, to know if she got away with the lamp.

Yet, Cirvel may have swept her into the lamp again just as easily. Rivic just didn't know what had happened to his sister.

How could he not know? The question rocked right through him. How many times had he been in here and he'd never once felt his sister's presence within a lamp, just as he couldn't sense Ellonia? He couldn't believe that, with as close as he and Nyree had been, he hadn't known about her imprisonment. He'd been so willing to accept Cirvel's story that she was married in Plenelia. He hadn't even questioned the blank letter!

Frustrated, he growled as he got up, then he seized one of the fallen chairs and slammed it against the floor. It didn't do any good and it didn't make him feel any better.

Rivic rushed around the room and gathered every lamp into one spot on the floor not yet covered too much in debris. Once he'd gathered them all, he stood over studying them. He certainly couldn't carry all of them. "Ellonia," he muttered as if she would answer him. There had to be a way to tell if she were in any of these.

Each lamp looked identical to the ones next to it.

He tried to sense the magic within, reaching out for something familiar. How could he tell?

He found a part of him that missed Cirvel's guidance already.

Rivic knew he'd always been meant to stand against Cirvel, to defeat the Lord of Gohaldinest which kept the outside civilizations from growing.

Yet he'd lost a mentor, a brother.

A blur of silver caught his eye as Dragzel came running through the door from Cirvel's chamber.

"She's gone!" the cahaster cried out.

"Who's gone?"

"Lihn. He took her. Where did he take her?"

"Who?"

The building shook again and Rivic rocked on his feet. "Look, we have other things to worry about right now, Dragzel." He nearly fell to his knees as he reached forward to grab the painting then he held out his other arm for Dragzel. "Jump," he called to the cahaster.

Behind them, the walls shook once more followed by the sound of falling stone. Rivic felt mountain air breeze by him and as he turned to look, he saw the balcony outside Cirvel's chambers crumbling away along with the wall. The floor beneath his feet began to split apart.

Then Dragzel was on his arm and leaping for his shoulder. Rivic threw up his hand to steady the cahaster.

"Hurry!" Dragzel yelled, but too late.

The crack zipping over the stone made it to the doorway before Rivic even started to move. The archway collapsed, rocks tumbling before him.

"Talcor dun."

Dragzel clung tightly to Rivic's purple robes, the fabric clenching around his curled claws. "Why is the castle falling apart?"

"Because Krithstand is attacking the castle," Rivic replied as if the cahaster had gone daft.

"Nay, that's obvious, but why?"

"Cirvel has Ellonia."

"Again, not the right answer. You're not seeing the bigger picture here."

"Which would be?" Rivic asked as he ducked around another barrage of falling stone.

"This place has multiple layers of enchantments...the Guardian, Cirvel.... It shouldn't just be falling apart. Not unless..." The cahaster heaved a large sigh. "Let me guess; Leschemal is awake."

"Aye."

Dragzel loosened one paw from the fabric and slapped Rivic in the back of the head.

"Why did you do that?" Rivic snapped.

"Because I couldn't do that to Cirvel. You realize that dragon wants to destroy the world, don't you?"

"I've heard."

"Well, he's clearly going to start with this castle!"

"Then we should be," Rivic said as he ran through a disintegrating doorway, "getting out of here." The words trailed off as Rivic realized that this side of the doorway wasn't where he expected to be. He'd come out in the middle of the amphitheater. He felt Cirvel nearby.

"Oh," the cahaster quivered. "I think I hear my mother calling me."

"You're leaving me now," Rivic said as Dragzel scuttled from his shoulder.

"I hold your soul, remember? I don't think you want me here either."

As much as he hated to admit it, Dragzel was right. "Squirrel," he shouted anyway to the fleeing cahaster.

Rivic lay the painting on the floor, wishing that Galault would appear and beckon him to safety on the other side. It wasn't happening. Then he straightened and looked around at all the empty seats above him, but he couldn't see the Lord of Gohaldinest. He dropped down his dragon lids, but still saw nothing. "Leschemal is destroying your castle and everything you've worked for," Rivic called out.

"Seems like a common theme these days, but the dragon will return to sleep soon enough."

"Will it be before Gohaldinest is in ruins?" Rivic turned in a circle, trying to listen for where Cirvel was.

"Anything built can be rebuilt. Destruction is but a temporary condition, a transmutation of energy from one thing into another."

Rivic thought he heard a footstep and he turned. But then a shuffled stride made him spin around again.

Cirvel punched him.

As Rivic staggered backwards holding his nose while tears stung in his eyes, Cirvel vanished. Rivic blinked, trying to clear his vision.

"Kind of like your aunt and uncle's village? There one moment and dust the next," Cirvel taunted. "What would be left of you if the dragon hadn't swallowed you for your magic? Would you have killed more people?"

Rivic suddenly realized why Cirvel had brought him here; Cirvel meant to break his control and knew that it would be weakest here where Rivic still felt guilt over Melodin's death.

Deciding he didn't like playing on Cirvel's terms, Rivic fetched the painting and whispered, "Talcor dun." He didn't really care where he landed in the castle as long as it was away from the amphitheater, and he hoped that Cirvel followed.

He knew he risked a lot if Cirvel didn't track him down. It depended on what exactly Cirvel was planning for an end game, not this intermediary cat-and-mouse they were currently playing. But Rivic knew he had more control of the moves if he was the one making them.

Rivic teleported twice more before realizing he had an important task, keeping Cirvel from escaping Gohaldinest, and he then went to the courtyard. Sounds of battle raged around him, but the grassy area locked so far inside the castle seemed untouched thus far and peaceful.

Rivic raced across the grass and walkways toward Lihn's tower with one thought in mind. He had to keep Cirvel from leaving Gohaldinest. Standing at the base of the tower, he looked up at the massive structure. He loathed destroying it, but he couldn't leave it here either.

Setting the painting down and placing his hands against the cool, stone walls, he wondered briefly where he should send it if he were to hide it. He thought of the lake where he'd first discovered his novihomidrak abilities. He'd put it as close to there as he could. It wasn't as if he could actually see what he was doing and where he was putting it. For all he knew, it would end up in the lake regardless of anything he did. "Vochey."

He pushed, both physically and with his magic. A

moment later, with the stone wall before him gone, Rivic stumbled forward. He practically laughed as he stared up toward the sky, the tower no longer blocking his view. He'd done it, but where it had gone, he had no clue. He only hoped he'd gotten it close to the lake.

He bent to fetch the painting, but as he rose, he felt a hand on his shoulder. "Talcor dun matahass'n," he heard spoken. Rivic felt the tug of extra magic pulling him and his body tightened against it instinctively, even while knowing it would do no good.

When light came through the darkness, Rivic realized the painting was no longer with him. He was in the room with Cirvel. At least he didn't have to worry about Galault being here too. What would happen if Cirvel destroyed Galault or even the frame holding the portal?

"Pada raysa kadalon."

At Cirvel's spell, Rivic felt all his magic drain from him. Then Rivic lifted into the air with his arms and legs no longer moving of their own accord. He drifted backwards until he came against a wall. The fingers Cirvel held before him twitched as if making subtle manipulations to the position of Rivic's body. Cirvel extended his left hand out to his side and whispered a quick spell which brought forth a long trough, which Cirvel magically slid against the wall beneath Rivic.

"Vochey Submit," Cirvel called out and Nyree's dagger appeared in his hand while he smiled back at what must have been the stunned expression on Rivic's face. Stepping closer, Cirvel held the dagger up toward Rivic's throat. "Don't worry, my novi-brother, your death will serve a good purpose. I have a debt for dragon's blood for which you will do nicely." Cirvel's gaze dipped toward the trough at Rivic's feet.

"Pay your own debt," Rivic spat.

"That has always been the plan. Just 'twon't be with my own blood; again, which has always been the plan."

A ripple went through Rivic and he found himself suddenly tired. He fought to not fall asleep right there. Blinking away the exhaustion, he noticed the magic over him fall away. Cirvel also looked as if he were about to stretch out on the floor and doze.

A crash below them made the whole tower rock, jerking Cirvel from his stupor. He staggered to the window, his face twisting in rage. "Nay," he called out.

Rivic slid down, his feet landing inside the trough. His magic returned, but it felt different as if someone had muted it.

Cirvel whipped away from the window. A flashing blaze of lightning crackled behind him, hiding the anger on his face in a silhouette. He approached, raising Nyree's dagger before him.

Rivic shoved forward on legs that weren't fully beneath him and he tackled Cirvel. Somehow, his fingers managed to wrap around Cirvel's wrist. "Vochey, Submit."

"Nay!" Cirvel raged as the weapon disappeared. He pushed Rivic.

Why wasn't he using his magic, Rivic thought, knowing it would be more effective for Cirvel to magically control Rivic. Something had happened.

Alityka.

He knew that she'd confronted Azote and that strangeness he felt around his magic had to do with her victory. Somehow, it had left Cirvel powerless too.

They scrambled on their feet, locked together in hand-to-hand combat. Cirvel's robes tangled around his legs, the mass of material seeming to hold him back.

A strange sight appeared on the wall; a frame holding a blank canvas seemed to slide out of nowhere and hang itself upon a nail embedded in the mortar between the stones.

Rivic rammed Cirvel back against the wall, then clenching the black robes in a locked fist, dragged Cirvel toward it. "Prachium impetitin." His other hand he used to reach up and smack the painting placed on the wall.

Cirvel disappeared from the room and appeared in the painting. The canvas bulged as Cirvel pressed against it. He hissed, his dragon teeth extending as if he could shred the material. "This won't hold me, boy," he shrieked as if a dire promise.

"Not forever," Rivic agreed. "But long enough."

Rivic seized the hem of his cloak, extended a white claw from his fingertip, and tore the fabric. Once he could get a good hold, he rent the cloth in two. "Palixa jotal."

A length of chain appeared in his hands. Rivic took it in one hand while reopening the wound at his shoulder. With fingers now drenched in his blood, Rivic smeared the airy chain with it. The chain lengthened and turned to gold. "I seal you with an essence of your enemy's blood." He looped the chain around the painting. It seemed to lengthen even more as he wrapped it several times around the painting. "So'de ta fasae sancti'aro diadecita sa'ta expectimous ro'sandae." The power exited Rivic and for a moment the chain glowed yellow-white before settling back to gold. Beneath the surface, Cirvel froze until he looked like nothing more than an elaborately painted portrait.

Lightning outside the window lit the room, which Rivic realized only now had darkened so much he'd instinctively blinked down his dragon lids in order to see better. He reached up and took the painting from the wall, then ran down the circular tower staircase.

All he felt were the old enchantments of the castle crumbling around him without Cirvel's reinforcing magic backing them. The once ancient and tempting pulls he felt on him were now decaying rapidly.

Rivic forced himself to think about the painting and his missing sister. Where could she be?

"Get down!" a voice yelled at him.

Rivic turned as a Necroatheling tackled him to the ground. The painting flew from his hands and skittered across the floor as a barrage of arrows flew overhead. They struck the wall and rained to the floor.

As the Necroatheling looked around, Rivic realized it was Kalt as he spoke, "So much of the roof and walls are gone. They are taking blind shots now." Kalt stood and offered his hand to Rivic, who saw a lamp in Kalt's other hand and reached for it. Thinking Rivic was accepting the offer of help up, Kalt grabbed Rivic's wrist and drew him to his feet.

"What are you doing here?" Rivic shouted.

Once Rivic's balance had settled, Kalt thrust the lamp toward Rivic. "Letting you know that Ellonia is safely outside the gates with her father."

"And Nyree?"

Kalt indicated the lamp. "Inside."

"Why? We need to get her out."

Kalt stopped Rivic from rubbing the lamp. "Nay, she has commanded me to tell you that she needs to stay in there." Kalt paused. "You will put me in there as well. I will guard her."

"Nay!" Rivic shoved Kalt aside. "Where's the painting that holds Cirvel?"

Another flight of loosened arrows whizzed overhead, bringing pause to both Rivic and Kalt.

Magic hit the castle next and the hallway they stood in broke in half. Rivic grabbed Kalt's robes and hauled him against the wall. The painting of Cirvel tipped, sliding toward the chasm. Rivic stretched out his arms to see if he could grab it.

"Behind us. Leave it." Kalt started to scuttle along the ridge created by fallen stone, careful to keep his head down as he went. "At the rate Gohaldinest is being razed, it won't last long. We can always hope he'll be forever buried."

"I can't do that." Rivic started back toward the painting, hoping that Kalt wouldn't fire a spell at his back.

The painting hung precariously by the wire where the stone wall had crumbled away. The canvas bobbed in the evening breeze, coming loose from the jagged rock which held it just as Rivic grabbed the frame. He looked over the abyss below.

Turning, he knew he had to get out of the castle now. Kalt tottered precariously as the edge of the ridge crumbled away. His fingers dug into the stone wall, knuckles whitening.

Rivic thought about letting the Necroatheling fall away and crash down onto the rocky debris below. "Teleport," he called out instead.

"I can't. My magic is weak. I don't have enough power," Kalt said.

Rivic cursed himself for not letting the Necroatheling fall. Instead, he flattened himself against the wall and scooted along the ledge, one hand reaching for Kalt and the other gripping the lamp and the painting of Cirvel. The moment his fingers felt the fabric of Kalt's robes, he said, "Talcor dun."

Rivic crashed to the cobblestone street as they reappeared out in the city. The painting issued a hard crack as the frame hit the stone. Kalt fell in another direction. Rivic finished his tumble with a roll, landing him on his back. Somehow, Rivic still held onto the lamp.

"Let me help you up," a voice said. Rivic saw a hand reaching toward him.

"Galault," Rivic replied as he took the offered assistance.

As his vision refocused, Rivic looked around and saw the main castle of Gohaldinest disintegrating into a large cloud of dust. Catapults stationed on the streets continued to sling boulders. Rivic could hear men heaving battering rams. Magic drenched the air.

"Let me take the painting," Galault said. "Soon, when victory has been had here, you can give this painting as an offering of peace, but for now 'tis too dangerous for you to carry."

Kalt moved up beside them, but his gaze moved over their surroundings as he watched for danger.

Rivic agreed with Galault and handed the painting over. "You slid the blank canvas to me, didn't you? It had suddenly appeared in the room where Cirvel and I were fighting."

"Aye, as well as helping to slide the tower to its new location. Good magic, just needed a small push. I must go now. Vocha chia cada'dada." A blue light appeared. Galault stepped into it and vanished.

Rivic glanced around to see if he could figure out where Chief Krithstand would be. Gray smoke from the city drew his attention and he saw the thatched roofs of several houses burning. He could make out people scrambling around. The looting had begun as the citizens of Gohaldinest realized that Cirvel had not stopped the raid on the castle. "Come on, Kalt. We need to find Krithstand."

"Nay. 'Tis my wish to go in the lamp with Nyree. 'Tis hers as well. She told me to tell you that this next part of the journey you must walk alone, but that she must walk the path with me. She said you would understand."

Rivic looked at the remains of the castle, a tattered shell of what it had once been. "So much rebuilding to be done?"

Kalt appeared confused.

"You once told me that you loved my sister. I hope for your sake that is true. She will see your true nature and she can harm you more than you will ever be able to hurt her." Rivic waved his hand as he'd often seen Cirvel do and spoke the words of enchantment which swept Kalt inside the lamp. He fastened it to his belt. Now, he wanted to make sure Ellonia was safe.

The lamp clacked against his thigh as he took off running.

What he didn't see were Necroathelings in the streets. He didn't feel them either. He wondered if they had fled to other dimensions. Or had they become powerless with Cirvel's disappearance and been killed? At least they were gone.

Smoke poured through the narrow streets as wood and possessions gave way to fire. The cobblestone streets looked golden in the light of the flames.

A large crash sounded behind him. He stopped and turned to look back at the castle. The building gave one final shudder, then sank. A cloud of dust raised in its wake, along with shouts of victory.

Rivic raised his gaze toward the three moons beginning to dominate the sky. Each had a shining halo from the rising dust and smoke. Silence would come with the night. Tomorrow, in the new day, rebuilding would begin.

Peace had come to the land.

Rivic walked away from Gohaldinest.

CHAPTER 34

1 0 cycles later...
Rivic swung the torch around as he walked deeper into the mountain cavern. Cold air surrounded him, whistling from crevasses between rocks somewhere further back. The ground had grown slick here, covered with a thin layer of ice. The sound of water dripping, nearly as far off as the ghostly wind, made him edgy. Already he missed the warmth of the valley and he wanted to be home. Instead, he expected to be face-to-face with a demon at any moment.

"Rivic?" Ellonia asked from the mouth of the cave. "Did you find her?"

"I'm looking," he called back. Frustrated at the sheer darkness, he blinked down his dragon lids and let his sight get flooded with the visions of various shades of heat and depth. There, cornered in the far back, he may have found what he sought. He needed to get closer still.

Sadness echoed through him as he confirmed the sight. He shouted back to Ellonia, "There are centaurs here. Humans too."

He now had to step over the skeletal remains of those

which had fallen. But worse were the stone bodies standing frozen in battle against foes which no longer existed in front of them. He knew Ellonia would want to come in here and see for herself.

Resigned, he headed back toward the mouth of the cave where he'd left her. "'Tis here. Her final stand."

Even though she had known this was coming, her dreams and trances all told her, the tears came quickly to her eyes. She blinked them back, furiously trying to restrain them, and yet failing. She wiped them away. "I want to see."

Rivic nodded, much as he had suspected. He put his arm around her and began to guide her through the petrified battle. He kept the torchlight away from sights he didn't want her to remember. The final one would be enough. She'd already seen that in her visions.

"Are we there yet?" she asked, her voice quivering with trust.

"Almost," he responded with as much force as he could manage. Her body felt so warm against him. She'd said nothing about how he had changed, if he seemed alive to her or not, but he sensed she knew he was different. He often wondered if she only loved him now because she'd never known how to do anything else.

"Rivic?" she asked.

"Aye?"

"Do you think it hurt?" Her gaze fixated on a stone body as they passed.

He thought that pain was left for the living. "Nay," he said, hoping it stretched far beyond a lie. Could anything have been worse than what had happened in the aftermath of Gohaldinest's fall?

They arrived at the back of the cavern and the spot where Alityka now stood frozen in time. He raised the torch for

Ellonia. "See? She looks calm. There was not any pain, only strength."

But it wasn't Alityka that Ellonia stared at, but rather Azote's looming form as the demon shoved through the defenses Alityka had put around her while she completed the spell to seal higher magicks from the world. Azote's hand reached out, claws nearly at her throat.

"We can't leave her here, Rivic," she whispered as if fearing a louder voice would awaken the monster.

She was right.

Rivic nodded. "We shall take her home. She belongs with us." He glanced around, hoping to see the sword he'd forged hanging from Alityka's waist. It wasn't there or anywhere else around the cave that he could see. What had happened to it?

Rivic's words made Ellonia smile, probably the first one he'd seen since they'd started this search. She wrapped her arms around him, knowing what would come next.

He held onto her and placed his hand on the cold, stone shoulder of Alityka. "Swalon sudinada kali Lilinar binpada."

The cave's darkness vanished and the light of the great hall swirled around them. Ellonia stepped away from Rivic as they arrived so that she could better look over her sister. "She looks like a beautiful statue," Ellonia commented. "She's like a goddess."

He murmured an acknowledgement while curiously wondering how Alityka had gotten the enchantment to cling to her in the same way Cirvel's ancient magicks had pressed against the walls of Gohaldinest.

"I will make sure she remains safe," he told Ellonia. In secret, he had already prepared the chamber where the statue would stay until Alityka was needed again. "I should go see how the tunnels are coming."

"I will go with you," Ellonia said, reaching her hand out for his.

He took it, letting his fingers once again enjoy her warmth. "Talcor dun."

They arrived on a balcony overlooking a stretch of land made barren for all Rivic needed done. Ellonia's hair stirred in the breeze as he watched her survey the massive expanse of tunnels being dug through the earth toward the lake. From this vantage point, he often recalled when he had once bathed and discovered some of his novihomidrak attributes while she gathered herbs. Did she still reflect on those times as well?

He glanced to the tower from Gohaldinest sitting off to the west corner of the city, a shadow beginning to silhouette it in the sunset.

"Is there anything you see which still needs done," he asked.

"Nay." When her lips tightened, he knew she had something further to say. At last, she spoke, "My father wishes for me to return for the naming of the new city."

"You should go. I will take you to just outside the city gates." Rivic had watched as her family and tribe had begun rebuilding the city on top of the ruins. He'd never found himself able to return. Maybe his memories were just too strong.

"I wish you would reconcile," she said softly.

Rivic shook his head. "You know I can't do that. Lilinar is our home now, but I will not keep you from your family."

She leaned against him.

He held her for a long moment, enjoying the feel of her against him.

"So what happens now that we are free of Cirvel's tyranny?" she asked. "What are we going to do?"

Rivic had never had the heart to tell her that they hadn't

truly won yet, merely postponed the inevitable. He'd had a glimpse of Cirvel's plans and knew he now carried the mantle of protecting this world. Two thousand cycles seemed like a long time. Rivic glanced down at the mark on his palm. He gave Ellonia the answer which the Onesong prompted him to say. "We live and we rebuild."

Ellonia wrapped her fingers into his and smiled. "Together?"

He kissed her hand, then put his arm around her back and clung to her. "Always. Let's look to the future with confidence."

The courage to become legendary:

discover the magic in the epic fantasy adventure of
Sacred Knight

The Missing Thread (book 5) coming soon!

READY FOR ANOTHER QUEST?

*S*ign up for Dawn Blair's newsletter to learn about new releases, get access to fun and free stuff, hear about events, and more!

It's easy.

*G*o to **www.dawnblair.com/newsletter** to join the adventure and get a free PDF of the reading order to Dawn's books.

About the Author

Dawn Blair grew up on a ranch in a rural Nevada town. The old buildings provided inspiration for her imagination as she thrived on stories of unicorns, princesses, heroic knights, and hidden doors to other dimensions.

For as long as she can remember, Dawn has had a passion for storytelling. Though she started out writing, her creative life expanded into painting and illustration.

She loves creating worlds and spinning tales for people to enjoy. The best ones are the stories that surprise her as she's writing. She loves her characters doing the unexpected. She'll gladly tell you that the most exciting part about being a writer is being the first one on the journey.

Thank you for taking the time to join her on these adventures.

Find more about Dawn and her work at:
www.dawnblair.com

facebook.com/dawnblairbooks
twitter.com/dawnblair
instagram.com/dawn.blair